Praise for *I Thought I Knew You*

'A standout novel that blends irresistible characters with an engaging plot'   *Woman & Home*

'A truly compelling story that exactly captures the complexity of friendship and motherhood and how everything we think we know can be challenged in one heartbreaking instant ... Wonderful'   Jenny Quintana, author of *The Missing Girl*

'Thought-provoking ... The characters' dilemma really does leave you on a knife-edge'
    Michelle Frances, author of *The Girlfriend* and *The Temp*

'This emotive and thought-provoking book will keep you guessing to the end'   *Woman's Weekly*

'Guaranteed to send chills down every mother's spine, cutting to the heart of what it means to be a parent. It's also an incredibly clever, nuanced analysis of female friendship and its limits ... Beautiful, highly atmospheric prose and superb plotting'   Kate Rhodes, author of *Hell Bay* and *Burnt Island*

'You'll probably want your friends to read it so you can compare notes – were you Team Holly or Team Jules (or both, alternately)? And when you've finished discussing the book, you'll make extra sure you part on good terms'
    Women's Institute Life

'This is a great example of "grip-lit", where the narrative pull is strong'   *Literary Review*

I Thought I Knew You

Penny Hancock is the author of *Tideline*, a Richard and Judy Book Club pick, *The Darkening Hour* and *A Trick of the Mind*. She works at Anglia Ruskin University, supporting students with their writing, and lives in Cambridge. She is married with three children.

PENNY HANCOCK

I Thought I Knew You

PAN BOOKS

First published 2019 by Mantle

First published in paperback 2019 by Mantle

This edition first published 2019 by Pan Books
an imprint of Pan Macmillan
20 New Wharf Road, London N1 9RR
Associated companies throughout the world
www.panmacmillan.com

ISBN 978-1-5098-6787-5

1 3 5 7 9 8 6 4 2

A CIP catalogue record for this book is available from the British Library.

Printed and bound by CPI Group (UK) Ltd, Croydon, CR0 4YY

Visit www.panmacmillan.com to read more about all our books
and to buy them. You will also find features, author interviews and
news of any author events, and you can sign up for e-newsletters
so that you're always first to hear about our new releases.

For Anna D'Andrea

1

HOLLY

He's alone again. Head bowed. Cumbersome bag hanging from bony shoulders. Trousers flapping around clownish shoes at the end of lanky legs. He's at that age where nothing's in proportion. Elongated but not filled out. A curtain of straight dark hair swings across his face, hiding the angry smattering of acne on his cheeks.

Saul finds himself a space on the green and stares at a patch of ground where the grass has been trodden bald by decades of school shoes. A girl approaches from the far side. One of Saffie's friends, but more bookish-looking. Less confident. *Go to him. Talk to him*, I urge her. *Please. He's nice. He's gentle and sweet.* She gives my son a wide berth and makes a direct line to the popular crowd.

I wish he didn't have to go to school. I wish he didn't have to mix in the world. Nothing about him fits.

More gaggles of girls appear, laughing, skirts short, shiny hair bouncing, hands clutching their mobiles. Then a group of handsome almost-men. Glowing skin, sharp haircuts, perky quiffs. They gleam with good health. These groups of children have been passing my front window for the last half-hour, gathering for the bus that will carry them off to secondary school before the village falls silent again.

'You're too attached,' Pete says, coming up behind me, surprising me. 'You have separation anxiety.' Pete's a psychotherapist. Attaching labels to feelings is what he does.

'I have not got separation anxiety,' I say, my breath misting the window. 'I'm simply a mother worrying for her son. Who still doesn't have friends.'

'Come here.'

Pete's arms slip round my waist. He lifts my hair, kisses me on the neck. I lean back into him.

'Saul's fine, Holly. He's sixteen. Searching for an identity. You need to let him be. Believe me, I see enough kids with problems. Saul's quiet, and sensitive, and he lost his father six years ago. But he's not displaying behaviour I'd consider a reason for concern. It's you who needs to back off a little, if I may say so.'

I rub a circle of condensation from the glass. Saul remains alone on the green.

'It's hard. After everything he's been through.' I turn and kiss Pete on the cheek. 'I need to go.'

Money, mobile, make-up. The mantra Jules and I use to check we don't forget anything in the morning. All ready in my bag. The pizza dough's in the fridge, waiting to bake when I get home.

'Wish I was in tonight,' Pete says. 'I'll get back as soon as I can tomorrow. D'you want a lift to the station?'

'I'll walk,' I say. 'Thanks, Pete. It's the wrong direction for you.'

'See you tomorrow, then,' he says, and his lips on mine send a fizz through my whole body. An unexpected bonus of my two-year-old relationship: Pete and I married soon after we met. A brisk ceremony at Cambridge Registry Office. That's how certain we were about each other.

Once I'm at work, I won't think about Saul. Not until tonight when we begin the argument about homework. The nagging that masks my worry about how unhappy he seems since I moved him from his London school for a fresh start in the Fens.

My mobile vibrates as I set off along the side of the green, head bowed against fine rain. The school bus draws up and swallows the teenagers.

'Where are you?' Jules asks.

'On my way to the station. I haven't got any tutorials until eleven, so I'm getting the eight thirty-five. It's horrible out here. Peeing down. Pete's taken the car.'

'You should have said.'

'It's fine. Good exercise.'

'You haven't forgotten about tonight? Tess's birthday drinks at that new gastropub in Fen Ditton. Girls' night out.'

'Oh, of course. Yes. That's something to look forward to.'

'Come round to mine first? Rowan's away. We can have pre-drinks, then get a cab together.'

'Sounds good. You OK?'

'Apart from dealing with the mood swings of a thirteen-year-old,' she says, 'fine. You?'

'Better for hearing you. We'll talk later.'

When she's gone, I tuck my mobile into the pocket of my parka and pull up the hood. It will be good to get out after a day dealing with students and their stresses and their heartbreaks. I haven't had a chance to get to know the local women, never made those school-gate friendships you form when you have primary-age kids. Saul was already fourteen when we moved here two years ago. I envisage sharing my concerns about him tonight; there's always another mother worrying about her own child who'll help put things in perspective.

The fields either side of me as I leave the village are striated with puddles of water shimmering to a black fuzz of trees on the horizon. Brown, muddy fens and high, colourless clouds. It's hard to say which seems longer, this narrow road leading beyond the level crossing to a vanishing point where the land meets the sky or the ribbons of ditch water fading to nothing where they merge with clouds. Squeeze your eyes half shut and everything blots into a watery murk.

Soon after we moved here, I thought I'd made a terrible mistake. The land seemed a place with the life – along with the floodwaters – drained out of it. Not a tree or a flower or an animal to draw the eye. Industrial storage units built from concrete breezeblocks and corrugated iron the only features on the vast flat fields. The sky so huge you could turn in a circle and only see one continuous line of horizon. I didn't belong here. It wasn't my home. I knew no one but Jules, and found it hard to make inroads into the tight-knit community. I'd had to do something, though, despite the fact it meant leaving the place where Saul was born and where Archie had died. Saul was miserable at his London secondary school. And the mortgage repayments on our Hackney house were crippling us.

'Move up here,' Jules had suggested. She'd moved out of London herself four years earlier, when Saffie was going into Key Stage Two. It was Rowan's home village. 'There's a really supportive community. And all this space. You'll love it.'

She swiped through property sites on her iPad. 'Look at this. Two-bed terraced house with garden. In this village. For half of what you'll get for your Hackney house. You could probably buy it outright.'

'I'd feel I was betraying Archie,' I said. 'If we moved.'

'Holly, it's been four years. You have to let him go. And so does Saul.'

Jules was right. In the four years since Archie died, Saul had grown from a ten-year-old primary-school child to a

towering teenager. We both needed a fresh start. I
ing on to an old plan, an old dream.

'What about work?' I'd asked Jules. 'I'll never h
other creative writing lectureship. They're in high den...

'Commute, like everyone else.'

'You think?'

'It's only an hour to King's Cross. It could take you as
long on a bus from Hackney. Look, no one can afford to
live in London anymore. This village is deserted by day, but
in the evenings, barbecue smoke fills the air and everyone's
popping corks and levering tops off beer bottles.'

'Very poetic!'

'Every night's a party night. And there's loads for kids to
do. Rowing, tennis, riding. Much more wholesome than
London. Saul will love it.'

In the end, I put an offer on the little house Jules had
spotted, got it for just under the asking price. Unheard of in
the South-East. Perhaps it said something about the village.
Perhaps I should have taken it as a warning.

Saul wasn't keen on the idea. But what teenager wants to
be shifted sixty miles from his birth home to a village where
he knows virtually no one? I persuaded him he'd grow to
like it. The school would be an easy bus ride, unlike the
two long Tube journeys he took to his London one, where,
anyway, he wasn't happy. And so two years ago, when he
was fourteen, we moved into our small terraced house, just
off the green. Two years. And even though I have Pete, I still
feel an outsider here.

*

The train this morning is full of kids travelling to the private
schools and colleges in Cambridge. They fill the space by the
doors, laughing, showing each other their phones, talking

about their latest Instagram posts and WhatsApp groups. I try to spot whether there are other loners, like Saul, but fail. The high-spirited youngsters get off at Cambridge Station and I manage to find a seat. The train passes between flat ploughed fields, flooded in places, glassy water throwing back reflections of trees turning red at the tips. Then the land begins to roll, green slopes dotted with redbrick villages, station signs – Hitchin, Stevenage, Welwyn Garden City. Within an hour we're among the first trailing suburbs of North London. My mobile pings as we pass the Emirates Stadium. I hesitate, then check it anyway. As I feared, it's a tweet from 'the Stag'.

@Hollyseymore says yes, but who'd fuck her anyway? #sex #consent #feminazi

A troll, responding to the freshers' workshops at my university on sexual consent. The students' union set them up to tackle the increasing problem of 'lad culture' in the university. As one of the longer-standing members of staff, I'd been asked to help advise on the issues they wanted to address. The students had also discovered (thanks to Google) that I had volunteered for Rape Crisis many years ago as an ardent young student myself. In those days, I'd been unable to resist a cause or a protest, an opportunity to 'reclaim the night', or to argue for a 'woman's right to choose'.

The workshops, however, had raised heated debate. Some students questioned whether a half-hour discussion was the best way to teach young men that the absence of a 'no' does not equal consent. The students who most needed to think about it, the 'lads', probably wouldn't attend the discussions anyway. Others were furious we considered workshops like this necessary. They found it patronizing. I wrote a piece for one of the broadsheets suggesting better sex education at school, particularly for boys, might be more effective than non-statutory meetings for students, but that given the status quo, consent workshops were the only way of tackling sexual harassment and the escalating problem of campus rape. I had been trolled on and off ever since.

The tweet leaves me shaken. The hatred in it. *It's just words*, I tell myself. *Ignore it*. Which is ironic when words are my stock-in-trade.

*

When I emerge at King's Cross, the rain's stopped and London's shining, wet pavements, glistening windows. I'm in good time, so I walk to the university, taking the streets of early Victorian terraces leading south from Euston Road, then right through an alley and past a block of 1950s council flats. This area of the city is quiet, just an old Bangladeshi man sweeping the pavement in front of his general store and a few people drinking coffee behind the steamed-up windows of one of those small independent Italian cafes that still exist away from the busier thoroughfares.

On the other side of Woburn Place, in Gordon Square, trees cast shifting shadows on the gravel paths that wind between the now ragged flowerbeds. The shrubs are laden with bright berries, the tall grasses are turning gold.

The surrounding townhouses have a proliferation of literary blue plaques. Christina Rossetti, Virginia Woolf, Vanessa Bell all lived here. Emmeline Pankhurst lived on the site of the Principal Hotel. I feel as if the square contains the spirits of those writers and feminist trailblazers. Archie used to tease, 'You believe you'll imbibe their talent by osmosis!' He didn't understand – how could he? – that it wasn't as simple as that. I felt, still do, a connection with those women who loved the city the way I do.

Our plan back then was that he and I would take it in turns – Archie would earn the money as a lawyer so I could write in the gaps when Saul was at school. ('One day, there'll be a blue plaque outside your office,' he joked. 'Holly Seymore got the idea for *A Stitch in Time* as she drank her latte in this very building!') Then, when I'd finished my PhD, which consisted partly of the novel I was working on, I would return to work as a course leader, on a better salary, so he could write *his* book.

Instead, abruptly widowed, I'd had to take a basic lecturer's job, teaching undergraduates creative writing. It wasn't quite the literary career I'd had in mind. But I still love working here, within sight of the British Museum and among the Georgian terraces, with their white stucco facades and black railings. And Archie was right: part of me did – still does – feel only good can come of working in the geographical slipstream of so much feminist thought and literary talent.

I cross Montague Street to the forecourt of the university, unlock my office. On my laptop, I click on the file marked, 'Novel – A Stitch in Time.' I had some idea, and it seemed so bright and alive at the time, of writing about two women, one in this area of London – Bloomsbury – in the interwar period, one now, linked by a single object – an inkwell – the contemporary one finds in her attic. After Archie died, however, the idea deflated like a balloon. I could no longer believe in it. I've barely looked at it since. Fifty thousand words gone to waste. Once I was bereaved, I lost the plot. Literally. I ought to bin it.

*

'How do I get it published?'

Jerome, my first student of the morning, has written an

experimental novel that omits the letter 'e'. He is a blue-eyed hipster with a red beard and a flesh hole in his ear. His face is full of naive optimism. I hand the work I've marked back to him, and we talk about whether these kinds of constraints – lipograms, made popular by the Oulipo group – paradoxically give writers more freedom to be creative. I suppress the urge to tell him to write something a little more mainstream if he wants to sell his work. He has impressive self-confidence, arguing his case when I suggest that constraints like these shouldn't be at the expense of story. He leaves full of the self-belief that will propel him through life even if his writing doesn't.

Mei Lui's a quiet, wan-looking second year whose skin I've always thought belies a poor diet or too many late nights. She's written 60,000 words of a novel in which she describes a Vietnamese girl's experiences working as an escort to pay for her degree in England. We discuss point of view and agree that the confessional tone lends itself to rewriting in the first person. As she leaves, she turns.

'It is . . . semi-autobiographical,' she says.

'Ah. D'you want to talk about it?'

She shakes her head, embarrassed, and hurries away down the corridor. I'm about to call her back when Luma, our head of department, appears.

'Holly. Hanya says she'll chair the consent workshop scheduled for next Friday but she'd like you to check what she's prepared.'

'That's fine. She could pop in at lunchtime.'

'You been getting any more tweets?'

'One or two,' I say. 'I'm ignoring them. It's just some guy with a chip on his shoulder.'

'Nasty, though. And I'm sorry they've targeted you.'

'Better me than one of the students.'

9

'You think so?'

'There's something particularly unpleasant about the anonymity of a Twitter troll. I'd hate to see students become victims. But I've a duty to help publicise their workshops. I'm not letting the Stag have his way!'

Luma steps into my office and closes the door behind her.

'I've just had Giovanna in. She's that first year – the talented one. Italian? Long dark hair? She spent the tutorial in tears. Turns out her boyfriend's threatened to dump her if she won't sleep with him. I suggested she attend one of Hanya's sessions. She's afraid he's going to leave her. Which would be a blessing IMHO. She says she loves him. That he's a genius. He's writing something based on an idea of the Oulipo group, but he's made her feel her writing's rubbish.'

'Not called Jerome, is he?'

'How did you know?'

'One of mine. Rather too confident if you ask me.' We exchange a smile. 'It's he who should attend the session, not just Giovanna, but I can guarantee that won't happen.'

'I still wonder what makes these kids take writing degrees,' she sighs. 'What comment by some English teacher set them down a track that probably won't go anywhere. So many of them are too young to take the knocks on the way.'

'Dreams?' I suggest. 'The desire to make sense of a world that makes very little sense otherwise?'

The trouble with having lectured for so long in the same institution is we've seen it all before. The ones who are too young to cope, the mature men who believe they're imbued with comedic genius, the experimental ones like Jerome who might or might not have the commitment to see it through. More often, sadly, not. Our students come with their writing but also a litany of other concerns. Almost all suffer from anxiety. Several have money worries. A few are struggling with gender identity. At times I feel treacherous that I'm earning a salary on the back of the belief that our students can and will make a living from writing, when I know how much they're up against. And when I've failed to do so myself.

*

After a chat with Hanya about her screening for the next consent workshop, and delivering an afternoon lecture on Pillman's 'Lean and Mean' theory ('Pare your writing back until you can pare no further,' I tell my earnest sea of young faces, wondering if I'm helping or hindering their creative flow), I walk back to King's Cross. There's the smell of crisp leaves, a sweeter tinge of smoking chestnuts, and the shops are filling with pumpkins. Autumn's arrived. I pass the Friend at Hand, a pub Archie and I frequented, opposite the Horse Hospital. (Once used to stable sick horses, it's now an arts venue.) The pub's filling with post-work crowds; a glimpse through the doorway reveals pints on tables, candles guttering. I have a fleeting nostalgia for the days when I would have stepped inside, sat at one of those scrubbed wooden tables, drinking and chatting until late. As it is, however, I pick up balls of fresh mozzarella for Saul's pizza and a jar of artichoke hearts from Carlo's Italian deli, tucked away in a corner behind Marchmont Street, and walk on towards King's Cross.

*

I'm back in the village just after seven.

'D'you wanna cup of tea?' Saul asks, leaping down the stairs as I get in the door.

'You're a sweetheart. That's exactly what I want. How did you know?'

He shrugs and I want to hug him, tell him how he lifts my heart. How I love him more than words can say.

'How was your day?' I ask instead, pulling off my boots.

'Shit.'

My mood dips.

He switches the kettle on, puts a teabag in a mug for me.

'Not getting better?'

'It was school. So what d'you expect? I don't really want to talk about it now, Mum. What's for supper?'

'You OK with pizza? I'm off out tonight. With Jules.'

'Sure. Pizza's cool.'

'The dough should be ready. Oh, and I got you some of that nice mozzarella from Carlo's.'

'You could've just got a bought one,' Saul says, and I grin at him. He knows how I frown on shortcuts when it comes to food. When I've assembled Saul's pizza and put it in the oven, I take my cup of tea upstairs. I've had a shower, changed into clean clothes, sprayed a bit of Coco Mademoiselle behind my ears and am putting my earrings in when Saul appears in my bedroom doorway.

'I can't get on the internet,' he says. 'Broadband's down. That's going to screw up my evening.'

'Shouldn't you spend it doing homework?' I say to his reflection in the mirror.

'It's done.'

'Saul, you can't have done it in an hour.'

'I'll show you the essay I've written on *An Inspector Calls* if you like, but it'll bore you to tears.'

I have to restrain myself from launching into a lecture about the nuances of the play, its subtle shift of blame for a woman's suicide from one character to another to another until we realize everyone's implicated.

'It's dumb we can't get broadband,' Saul growls.

'Saul, we do have broadband. It's just—'

'It's just it doesn't work. What's the point in living here? What's the point in a fucking house with no broadband?'

It's true our connection is erratic, and that neither Pete nor I have had time to sort it out.

'You want me to do my homework, but half of it they put on the fucking website, and if I can't go on it, how am I supposed to do it?'

Saul raises his iPad, knocking my bottle of perfume flying as he does so, narrowly missing my ear, and for a second looks as if he's going to hurl it at the mirror.

'Saul, watch it.' He stops at the last minute, but not before my bedside lamp has tumbled sideways, smashing onto the floor. He's only got to lift an arm these days and things go flying. He doesn't realize how long his limbs have become.

'I'm so bored! There's nothing to do in this arsehole of a village.'

I take a deep breath. Saul's mood swings are new. I know rationally they're due to the massive hormonal changes he's undergoing. Changes that mean he can't cope the minute he's overtired, bored or hungry. But when he's in this state, my sweet boy seems possessed by someone else entirely.

'Your pizza will be ready. Go and get it out of the oven.'

*

He's playing some game on his phone, thumbing the screen, eating pizza with the other hand when I go down to him fifteen minutes later.

'I was starving,' he says without looking up.

'Can't you use your phone,' I say, nodding at it, 'if you must go online?'

'Used up my data allowance.'

'How about I ask Jules if you can use her internet round there? Then you could come over with me.'

He doesn't reply.

'Saul?'

'I guess.'

*

'Of course,' Jules says. 'Saul's welcome. He can keep an eye on Saff at the same time. Rowan's away and she's objecting that she has to do her homework. Saul can be my security guard.'

I laugh, go back to Saul. 'All sorted. Rowan's away and Jules was worried about leaving Saffie so she's thrilled to have you there.'

He glances up. 'Why's Jules worried about leaving Saffie?'

'She's been acting out lately. Finding her teenage feet. You can keep an eye on her. Make sure she doesn't spend the whole evening on *her* computer.'

'So Jules wants me to be, like, her minder?'

'All you have to do is be there. She says Saff's got home-work to do. You can watch their home cinema. And they have everything – Netflix, Sky, the lot.'

*

It's a twenty-minute walk to Jules's house, across the green and down what Fenlanders call 'the drove'.

'They ain't from round 'ere,' Saul mimics as we pass the pub. 'Them's townies. Don't trust 'em.'

'You'll find a lot of the pub clientele are commuters,' I

say. 'Like me.' He knows this, of course, but I'm trying to distract him from what I know is coming next.

'Why did we have to move out of London?'

I glance at his bowed head. He kicks a stone along in front of him. I sigh. We've had this conversation so many times. 'You weren't that happy in London, if you remember, Saul. You hated your school.' He doesn't reply, and I don't blame him: he's not exactly happy here either. He was subjected to a lot of bullying at school when we first arrived, and even went through a stage of refusing to go at all. I try another tack. 'You love the photography course at this school. They didn't even offer that in London.'

'It's still all revision and exams for another whole year. It's shit.'

'And some of the kids on the green look . . . well . . . nice. Can't you make friends with some of them? I don't like to think of you being lonely. Being alone.'

'"No man is an island,"' Saul quotes, '"entire of itself."'

I stop. Laugh.

'Since when did you read Donne?'

'Since . . . I dunno. Since I found the poetry book in the loo.'

'That's not technically a poem, you know.' I'm delighted to discover Saul actually reads the books I leave on the bathroom shelf. 'It's what he called a "meditation". He wrote it when he thought he was dying. He became obsessed with sin, and what might happen to him in the afterlife . . .'

'Anyway' – Saul senses another imminent lecture and diverts me – 'I don't want new friends.'

Having watched Saul on the green morning after morning, I know this isn't true. I know he's hoping someone will notice him standing there alone and invite him to join their group. But one of the edicts of good therapy, and therefore good parenting, Pete says, is to reflect back what your kid tells you. Not block it or deny it. I should echo Saul: *So you don't want new friends?* Instead, the words burst out before I can stop them: 'You need new friends. It's not good for you to spend so much time on your own.'

'You spend time on your own.'

'That's a choice.'

'It's a choice for me too.'

And now I do know I should stop.

*

We walk on in silence for a bit. Then Saul says, 'At least the countryside here's sick.'

Is he trying to placate me? It would be just like him. But he's gazing up at the sky, which is crystal clear now the clouds of earlier have blown away.

'You can see the Plough – look.' He stops and points upward. 'And that's the Milky Way.'

I draw alongside him and look up. The air is sharp, the stars bright as pins in the dark sky. On cue, an owl hoots as if it's conspiring to connect us to the countryside and we both laugh.

'It's another world here. I mean, I'd never seen swans' nests or muntjacs before we moved. I'd never heard the word "drove" for a road, or "roddon".'

'Roddon?'

'It's a dried-up silt bank,' he says. 'Don't you know? That's the kind of shit they teach us at school here.'

'Never heard of it.'

'It's mental. We could be in another country. Oh, stop looking so worried, Mother.'

'Do I look worried?'

He mutters his reply and I have to ask him to repeat it.

'I said, you look worried all the time.'

'I'm fine,' I tell him, hooking my arm through his. I'm surprised that he lets me, but then it *is* pitch-dark and there is no one else for miles around. 'I'm fine if you are.'

'I'm fine if *you* are,' he says.

*

Jules's house is the other side of the railway line, and overlooks the open countryside and the river. From her large picture window, you can just see the lock, and the bridge that crosses it, and miles of straight horizon. As Saul remarks, you could fit our house into theirs five times.

'Rowan loves his extensions,' Jules told me soon after they moved in. 'He's got a builder friend to construct a deck for us and he's going to install a hot tub.' They extended the kitchen too and had a Corian ('It's the new thing') work surface put in, in Glacier White. Everything else they painted a fashionable pale grey.

In the summer, Jules and Rowan's parties are legendary. They invite everyone, all the villagers, Jules's staff from her shop and various franchises – she has a very successful business selling high-end children's clothes – and Rowan's golf club mates. They fill plastic buckets with ice and bottles of wine, and everyone lies on black rattan deckchairs under patio heaters and talks or dances until late. I imagine Saul will enjoy sitting in their big house, lounging on their enormous comfortable corner sofa, watching films on Netflix, once he's finished whatever he wants to do on his iPad. Secretly I'm pleased, too, that he has agreed to come. I don't like to think of him in his room on his own, evening after evening.

'Saffie's upstairs doing her homework. She might not come down at all,' Jules tells Saul. 'So you can hog the screen and help yourself to whatever you want from the fridge. Put your head round the door about ten and make sure she's gone to bed, will you?'

Jules is wearing her black lace dress, and high suede heels. I wonder if I'm too casual in my jersey tunic over leggings and flat boots.

'Holl, I poured you a G and T. And there's beer in the fridge if you want it, Saul.'

'Thanks, darling.' I get the drinks from the side in the kitchen. Saul takes the beer I wave at him and levers off the top.

'You're looking very handsome, Saul,' Jules says, standing at the mirror in the hall putting on her mascara. 'You're going to be a great asset in the shop once you start. How does the Saturday after next sound? That way, my present Saturday assistant, Hetty, can train you up before going off.'

Saul gives an awkward shrug and lets the hair flop over his face to cover his blush.

Saul's very tall for his age. He had a premature growth spurt at twelve and it was like being catapulted into the body of an adult while he was still into doing magic tricks and coming into my bedroom at night when he had nightmares. He hates his height. I've told him one day he will appreciate being six foot, but he continues to see it as a terrible affliction where he's exposed, where it's impossible to hide. As a result, he's crippled at times with shyness. He freezes like this every time he's in a social situation. I want to tell him to relax, and other people that this gormless, gangly thing isn't the real Saul. That the real Saul is affectionate, funny and considerate. I love Jules for offering him a job in her shop to 'get him out there', but I worry sometimes that he isn't going to be up to it, that his poor social skills will let her down.

'That's great, Jules,' I say when it becomes clear that Saul isn't going to reply. 'Let's put the TV on,' I chirp, and he follows me across Jules's vast sitting room and slumps down on the sofa. He does look nice this evening, I notice, sipping my drink. He's in a grey lambswool jumper I got him last Christmas, dark jeans and trainers that make his feet look huge. He's getting a look of Archie about him. He'll be just as good-looking once he emerges from the chrysalis of adolescence.

'What time will you be back?' he asks.

'Not too late. Eleven? Eleven thirty? Jules?'

'I guess.'

'What's the Wi-Fi password?' he says.

'You'll have to ask Saff. *Saffie!*' Jules shouts up the stairs. 'We're off. Can you come down? Saul needs the password for the Wi-Fi.'

My 'odd daughter' appears at the top of the stairs. When Jules and I became mothers – just three years apart – we bestowed upon one another the greatest honour of all: I asked her to be Saul's honorary godmother and she asked the same of me for Saffie. Since neither of us was sure about our religious beliefs, we adopted the title 'odd mother'.

Now, the change in Saffie almost knocks the breath from me. She's become, overnight, it seems, a young woman. She's in her school uniform, tie loosely knotted, her short skirt and tight black V-neck jumper hugging her newly curvaceous figure. She looks like Jules's mini-me. She thumps down the stairs. She's been trying on some smoky eye makeup and overdone it, and there's a waft of sweet fruity perfume as she comes over to me for a hug. I feel a pang for her, remembering how excruciating it feels when you want to keep up with your peers who all seem to know how to dress, and how to be. When your body starts to gallop ahead of your mental age.

Saffie's not so different to Saul in that regard, of course – it's just that they have responded differently: Saffie's accentuating her changes, whereas Saul is plain uncomfortable with his.

'I've told you, Saffie, you're not to wear all that make-up. You don't need it,' Jules says into the mirror.

'I'm not,' Saffie says, barely audibly.

'But you are!' Jules turns to me with a 'what on earth do I do?' gesture.

'Leave her be,' I mouth.

'I'm not compared to what most of the girls wear at school,' Saffie snaps. 'I've toned it down like you said. But you just don't notice. You just don't notice anything.'

Saffie's blushing under her veil of foundation. She doesn't need lecturing in front of Saul and me.

'You look gorgeous,' I tell her. 'You're becoming a stunner, just like your mum.' Saffie glances up at me, and the little girl she was last time I saw her emerges as she flashes a wide-eyed, grateful smile at me.

'Flattery will get you everywhere,' Jules says, winking at me.

I put my arm round Saffie and kiss the top of her head.

'I thought you might like to come to the ballet with Freya and Thea and me again this Christmas, Saff.' Freya and Thea are Pete's girls – my stepdaughters. Freya and Saff are good friends. '*The Nutcracker Suite*. Shall I get you a ticket?'

'Oh my God! I love the ballet!' Saffie leans her head against my shoulder and I catch another blast of sickly perfume.

'Saul won't come, will you, Saul?' I say. Saul goes a little pink and shakes his head, his hair swinging over his face.

'It'll be girls only, then, won't it, Saff?'

She smiles up at me.

'Right, we're off, Saffie.' Jules reaches out to kiss her daughter, but Saffie ducks away from her. She stomps into the sitting room and curls up a few chairs away from Saul. He barely lifts his eyebrows in greeting and I'm tempted to tell him to say hello, as if he were six years old. Saffie recites a password, letter by letter. Saul punches it wordlessly into his iPad. You would never know they virtually grew up together back in London, in the days before Jules moved. Saffie flicks on the TV and Saul fixes his eyes on his own personal screen.

'No more than half an hour of that, Saffie,' Jules says as we leave. 'Then you're to go and finish your homework.'

We leave them in silence and I follow Jules into the cold night air, where the taxi's waiting.

*

'You see?' Jules says as we set off. 'That's what Saff's like with me these days. Stroppy, rude and dressed like she's going on twenty-one.'

'She's fine, Jules. Poor girl. Don't you remember how it felt? Thirteen years old! She'll be on an emotional roller-coaster.'

'Try living with her,' Jules says. 'It's more like the dodgems.'

I laugh.

The road ahead of us is slick with the rain that fell earlier, the headlights picking out the raised banks of ditches that separate us from the land beyond. Through the passenger window there's an uninterrupted stretch of night sky and, far away on the flat horizon, a thin strip of orange lights. The only sign there is any human habitation out there at all.

'Good day?' Jules asks.

21

'Apart from this blasted trolling. Which is getting worse.'

'What are they saying now?'

'That I'm a feminazi for helping with the consent workshops. That I say yes but no one would fuck me anyway.'

'Nasty. D'you have any idea who it is?'

'Impossible to know. I'm maintaining a dignified silence for the time being. I can't abandon the workshops – they're important. I can't believe boys – men – think it's OK to have sex with girls for a laugh. Or for kudos. And that girls need reminding that only "yes" means "yes". You'd have thought the women's movement never happened. All that marching to reclaim the night we did! All that shaving of heads and burning of bras our mothers did.'

I think about Saffie in her make-up and short skirt. 'How *is* Saff? She's grown up so much recently.'

'Ha! You honestly wouldn't believe the grief she's been giving me this week. Throwing hissy fits about the slightest thing – usually to do with the way she's dressing. Or wanting to stay and hang out with friends after school. And that's not the half of it. Her moods! Slamming doors. Shouting. And it smells like a bloody fin de siècle bordello in her room! Plus she's slapping on that make-up for school. She says all her friends do it. It's such a fine line, letting her fit in and, on the other hand, attempting to preserve what's left of her childhood.'

All of a sudden, my worries about Saul fade into insignificance. Dealing with a girl must be so much harder. The pressure they're under from social media to look a certain way, versus giving them the confidence to believe they're fine just the way they are.

Jules continues, 'Meanwhile Rowan's fixated on that show – what is it, *Child Genius* or something? Saff's not got that kind of IQ. It's unfair on her.'

'He's not the only dad to have aspirations for his kid.'

'He's got this crazy idea she's Oxbridge material. He wants her to go to every extra lesson on offer. But the more he lays down the law, the stroppier she becomes. I tell him it causes her unnecessary stress, but he won't listen.'

'It's tough, Jules, I can see that. Achieving the right balance. But you should be glad Saffie at least has a social life. I'd love it if Saul joined a crowd. Had a bit of fun. I worry he's developing some kind of social phobia. That I shouldn't have moved him out of London.'

'That's nuts, if I may say so,' Jules says, as we draw into the pub car park.

'Is it? He hasn't any friends. It was understandable at first, when he was the "outsider" here, but it's been two years and you'd have thought he'd have made at least one mate. I'm afraid there's something else going on with him. That it could get worse. It's such a worry having a child who's a misfit . . .'

'Saul's not a misfit!' Jules laughs. 'That's a ridiculous exaggeration. The way he is has nothing to do with moving here either. You mustn't blame yourself. Saul lost his dad when he was ten. He's getting used to your new relationship. He's a sixteen-year-old struggling to find an identity, *completely* normal. He'll be fine. I forbid you to worry about Saul anymore.'

'Then you mustn't worry about Saff.'

She puts her arm round me and kisses my cheek. 'Try not to overthink. Saul's lovely. He's handsome and sweet and generous-hearted, as he always was. But he's an adolescent, and we all know how tough that is, even for kids who haven't been through what he has.'

It's an unspoken rule that Jules and I stand up for the

other's child. Especially when we're at our wits' end with our own.

'You matter too, you know,' she adds, after we've paid the cab driver and are making our way across the pub car park to the entrance. 'You need a night off.'

Jules waves, spotting Tess and five other women on the far side of the pub in an alcove. I recognize some of them from Jules's parties or from around the village.

'Sixteen, in the playground after the end-of-term disco,' Donna Browne is saying. Jules and I drop into a space on the soft leather sofa. Donna's the village GP. I've been to her for antibiotics, and she saw Saul about his school refusal when we first moved here, and when he was bullied.

'I hope you won't be vetting our units?' I smile as she pours me a glass of Prosecco.

'Ha! You're all to behave yourselves while there's a doctor in the house,' she laughs. 'I was just saying ... my first time was with Paul Mayhew. I was sixteen.'

'Paul Mayhew? Get you! The school heart-throb?' Tess says.

'Yes, but it was awkward and unpleasant. For both of us probably. We never spoke again. I often wonder if anyone had a good first shag.'

'My first love was a boy called Jozef back in Poland,' Jules says. 'I was fifteen but totally and completely in love. We didn't really know what we were doing, but we did it somehow. It was messy, let's say. Then he buggered off with my best friend and there followed a series of disastrous one-night stands. Until I met Ro.'

'I married my first love, of course,' another woman says. Samantha. I remember meeting and liking her at one of Jules and Rowan's parties. She'd asked me about applying for an

English degree and I'd promised to email her the details, then completely forgotten.

'We used to like the fact Harry was exactly twice my age,' Samantha's saying. 'We were crazy about each other. Still are. And he's nowhere near twice my age anymore. So numbers are arbitrary in the end.'

'All the school mums fancy Harry Bell,' says Tess. 'We were green with envy when we found out you were together.'

'Mr Bell? Oh! Your husband's Saul's form teacher?' It all clicks into place.

Samantha grins, and flushes. 'That's the one.'

I'm only just fully appreciating what a very small world it is here.

'So, come on, Fiona. How old were you?'

'It was on my eighteenth birthday with my boyfriend. Bobby. Remember him? We were engaged. In my box room while my parents were out. I wasn't ready. It hurt. We split up after that. My real sexual awakening came later. When I finally came out.'

'Ooh, tell all.'

'Another tale for another time,' says Fiona, smiling and squeezing the hand of the woman next to her, whom I don't recognize.

'What about you, Holly?' they all chorus. I knew this was coming. I could try to wriggle out of it, but the women are all looking at me expectantly, and so I say, 'I'm afraid my story's a bit tame. My first time was very lovely. And then I stayed with him.'

'That's good, though,' Donna says.

'What I want to know is, are you still together?' Jenny asks me.

Jules fills in for me. 'Holly's widowed.'

There's an awkward silence.

'It's OK,' I say. 'Please. Archie died six years ago. I've met someone else now. And yes' – I look around at the stunned faces – 'the sex is also good. Don't hate me!'

There's a pause, and then a hesitant ripple of laughter.

'Shall I get another bottle?' I pick up the fizz that's left, refill everyone's glass and go to the bar for another. By the time I've returned, they've moved on and are discussing fundraising for a multi-sensory room that's being built at the secondary school, planning an Auction of Promises in the Baptist Chapel Hall. Death, I've learned since I lost Archie, is always a far more awkward subject than sex.

*

'I enjoyed that.'

We've called a taxi back to Jules's house, later than we meant to. It's nearly one by the time we stumble through Jules's door. Jules says she'll make me a camomile tea and disappears into the kitchen. Saul appears at the top of the stairs and comes down, clothes crumpled, hair dishevelled.

'I thought I might as well go to bed,' he snaps. 'I didn't realize you'd be all night.'

'I'm sorry. I know we said elevenish. I thought you might have given up on me and gone home. We'd better go – you look shattered.'

'I see you got through a couple of beers, Saul,' Jules says, coming out of the kitchen with a mug in each hand.

He hangs his head.

'Don't look so worried. You know I like you to feel at home here. I made you a tea, Holl. You can't go till you've drunk it.' She kicks off her shoes and sways over to the sofa.

'Saul's exhausted. We should've got back earlier.'

'Stay. Have a little nightcap – don't be such a bore.' She collapses onto her voluminous corner sofa, curling her feet in their glossy tights under her. An echo of her daughter earlier. 'Did Saffie behave herself, Saul? I hope she wasn't too late to bed. She tries it on, my daughter. Especially when her dad's away. You have to be firm with her.'

I wonder if I imagine that Saul's gone pink again.

'I didn't see her,' he says, looking down so his hair falls over his face. 'I left her to it.'

'You're a good boy,' Jules says. 'I've always loved you like my own son. You know that, don't you, Saulie? Do you know, I was the first person ever to hold you? Before your own mother even?' Jules's words are slurring into one another. 'Such a cute newborn, you were.'

Saul doesn't know where to look at this. I sense his embarrassment, but Jules is too far gone to notice.

'Come on, Saul,' I say. 'Let's get back. We're all in need of some sleep.'

*

'How was it, then?' I ask as we retrace our steps of earlier up the dark fen road.

'What?'

'Your evening?'

'OK.'

'Get on the internet OK?'

'Yup.'

'Eat anything?'

'Nope. A few crisps.'

'Talk to Saff?'

'Why would I talk to Saffie?'

'No reason. Just wondered if you two had anything in common these days.'

'She's *thirteen*,' he says, as if this explains everything.

He won't be drawn. I feel the familiar crushing in my

27

chest. The anxiety that even after our chatty walk earlier, he's still fundamentally unhappy – depressed even – and that there's nothing I can do about it.

'Saul,' I say, when we're home, and before he disappears into his room. But he's gone, shutting his bedroom door behind him, shutting me out. 'Night-night,' I say, to the air.

*

It's two weeks before I see Jules again and the weather's turned warm and mellow. The train's delayed so I'm running late for work. I take the Tube at King's Cross and emerge into the bright sunshine of a golden autumn day in the midst of London with its bustle and life. I hurry past Russell Square Station's garnet-coloured walls, and across the gardens. Everything's gleaming. Silver water jets from the fountain, ebony railings, ivory terraces beyond. New shiny red Route-masters trundle past; amber sycamore leaves are strewn over the grass. Jewel colours. There's a spring in my step. Pete's course in Bristol finishes today, and it's one of the weekends we have the girls.

Jerome comes back to me with his reworked story. He's decided to use 'e's after all but to replace every noun with the seventh one after it in the dictionary. 'Another constraint devised by the Oulipo group,' he explains. I remember Luma telling me about his girlfriend, Giovanna, and as he leaves, I hand him a leaflet about the consent workshop scheduled for the afternoon. I watch him screw it up and toss it into a bin as he walks down the corridor.

Eleanora, who is seventy-three and taking her first degree, comes to me with her sci-fi novel. In it, people fire embryos to a planet that's been identified as suitable for human habitation when ours is done for. Robots accompany them, programmed to nurture the babies to adulthood.

Existing Loans

Tooting Library

Id :: 01611****
Name:: Mrs Nasima Jama

Total Number of on loan Items 0
26/06/2021 12:14

Manage your account online at
capitadiscovery.co.uk/wandsworth

Call **01527 852 385** for 24 hour

renewal charged at national rates

Thank you for using self service

'I'm trying to apply Pillman's theory,' she says. 'It's proving very difficult to achieve his economy.'

We discuss whether she can shorten her sentences, lose adverbs and still achieve what she wants to say. I love Eleanora's writing, and tell her so. I don't say that even she is going to find it hard to publish. After all, there's always one who will surprise you.

At lunchtime, I grab a sandwich and a coffee from Kate's Taxi Kiosk, eat it sitting on a bench in Russell Square. A man with a leaf blower is attempting to tidy golden leaves into heaps, which swirl into the air the minute he turns his back, somersaulting in the wind before freckling the grass again. I watch him repeat his task, blowing, gathering, turning to see his work undone. He doesn't look frustrated. Perhaps the pleasure is in the task after all, rather than in the end result. Perhaps I shouldn't worry so much about my students; perhaps the pleasure for them, too, is in the task of writing rather than the end result.

As I walk back along the English department corridor, I'm surprised to see someone outside my study. I have no more tutorials today, have been looking forward to some quiet time catching up on marking. I get nearer and see that it's not one of my students at all but Jules. She's huddled into her black coat on the chair I keep in the corridor for students waiting to see me.

'What a nice surprise. You didn't say you were in London today.' I unlock my door.

She doesn't return my smile. Her face is pasty, unusual for Jules, normally a picture of vitality. Her hair's scraped hastily back, her eyes puffy, and she's not wearing her usual make-up. A small shiver passes over me, barely perceptible, which I would later recall.

'I had a couple of things to do in town,' she says. 'Thought I'd combine it with talking to you.'

'Is there something wrong?'

She follows me into my room.

'Let's sit down and I'll tell you.'

'Would you prefer to go out somewhere? I've got a free couple of hours, and my office is a complete mess.' I tuck Jerome's assignment into my filing tray, drop my coffee cup into the recycling bin. 'If you like, we could get a proper drink at Pied Bull Yard. I've designated the cafe there a UDP.'

Jules and I have our own code for places we rate: 'Unique Drinking Points.' We have particular requirements – they can't be chains, have to be tucked away (so not many people know about them), must sell decent coffee if it's daytime, wine if it's night, and be quiet enough to hold a conversation. It helps, too, if they have an interesting history or location. So I expect Jules to relax, smile and agree. Instead, she says, 'I'd prefer to talk in your study.' She looks around. 'It's ages since I've been here.'

'One of the perks of having worked here so long is they've finally given me a decent room. With a view of Senate House.' I wave a hand at the grey facade of the tall art deco building that looms over ours. 'I can't decide whether I like it or not, though. Evelyn Waugh described it as "the vast bulk of London University insulting the autumnal sky".'

'It was the inspiration for the Ministry of Truth in *1984*,' Jules mutters, pipping me at my literary post – as usual. 'Orwell's wife worked there.'

'Ha! There's always a woman behind a genius idea.' Again, I wait in vain for Jules to smile. When it becomes apparent she's not going to, I sit down on my swivel chair and examine her crumpled face.

'What is it, Jules?' I ask at last.

She rests her elbows on her knees and bows her head. 'This is difficult for me,' she says. 'I don't know where to begin.'

For a second, I wonder if she's come to tell me she and Rowan are splitting up. I lean forward, lift her hand, give it a squeeze.

'I couldn't bear to tell you over the phone,' she says.

I reach for a box of tissues and pass it to her. I'm thinking, if Rowan *has* finally pushed her to her limits, it might be a good thing in the long run.

'I'm here for you, Jules, whatever the problem – you know that.'

'It's not . . .' she begins, then stops.

'It's not what?'

'It's not my problem. Not really.' There's a quake in her voice. 'More, both of ours.'

'You have to give me a clue here.'

'I don't know how to tell you. It's to do with that night,' she says. 'When we left Saul with Saffie . . .'

'When we went to the pub? Tess's birthday night?'

'I realize now it wasn't appropriate to let Saul come. I should have listened to Rowan. And Saff, in fact.'

Something slams down inside me. *Listened to Rowan.* What's Rowan been saying about Saul now? He once made some reference to Londoners bringing drugs into the idyllic enclave of his Fenland village. Which is nonsense – everyone knows drugs are as rife in small rural communities as urban ones. Anyway, Saul has shown no interest in drugs. If Saffie's got hold of anything, it'll be through some other channel. Not through Saul.

'Saffie didn't want me to tell you. But I decided you had to know. So we can deal with this together. You're going to find it hard, Holly, but . . .' She purses her lips, adjusts her position. London seems suddenly to have fallen silent, as if the city, too, is waiting for her to speak. 'OK.' She takes a breath. 'There's only one way I can say this.' She looks up at me. 'He raped her, Holly.'

'What do you mean, "He raped her"? Who raped who?'

'Saul raped Saffie.'

The ridiculousness of this almost makes me smile. It's a cruel joke but one I guess might be interesting for Jules. Seeing how I'd respond after expressing my despair that male students, still, in the twenty-first century, believe it's OK to sleep with unconsenting partners. After being trolled for speaking up for better sex education to protect young people.

'Who told you this?'

'Saffie, of course.'

'Why?'

'*Why?*'

'Yes, I mean, why would she say such a thing?'

'She hasn't made it up, Holly. She gave me all the details.'

'She said Saul *raped* her?'

Jules looks down at her fingers, weaved through each other on her lap. 'She didn't call it rape. But the things she described . . .'

'What on earth *did* she describe?' There's something wrong here. It makes no sense.

Jules shifts in her chair. 'She wasn't going to say anything. But I insisted when I saw how distressed she was, this morning. It was so clear something was preying on her mind and she didn't want to tell me. Didn't want Saul in trouble. But apparently, he went up to her room when she was getting ready for bed. For which I blame myself. I told him to put his head round the door and check she'd gone to bed, didn't I?'

I don't know how to reply to this. Yes, Jules had asked him to check on Saffie, and presumably he had. But that doesn't mean he would have gone into her room, or tried to touch her, or . . .

'She was getting undressed. She'd left her door ajar and she thinks he'd been watching her. Then he came right into her room, and when she asked him to leave, he grabbed her. Said she was asking for it.'

'Jules, those words aren't Saul's.' My voice is calm. I'm in tutor mode and I'm dealing with this as I would with one of my students. Waiting for the emotion to settle so we can reach firm ground upon which to untangle the details of this ludicrous allegation. 'He might have checked up on her, but Saul would never say a girl was "asking for it". He lives with me, for goodness' sake.'

'It's what he said.'

'When did she tell you this?'

'This morning.'

'Just this morning? Why not that night? Why would she wait two weeks to tell you? If it's true.'

Jules looks at me incredulously. 'Holly, you know the reasons girls don't cry rape better than anyone. She was afraid. Afraid of snitching on Saul. Or that I wouldn't believe her. Or that I'd blame her. She's been traumatized all this time and trying to carry on as normal. I feel awful that I didn't bloody notice there was anything up. She's been refusing her tea, which is very out of character. And looking exhausted. I put it down to those teenage mood swings, or PMT . . .'

I stare at my friend, letting her words sink in. She's right, of course. I know the reasons women – girls – keep silent better than anyone. So I should believe what Jules is telling me. That's the theory, though. Reality is different. Reality is always more slippery, more fuzzy-edged.

'I'm at a complete loss, Holly. I don't know what to do. Saff doesn't want me to report it . . .'

'*Report it?*' I'm only slowly taking in what a serious allegation Saffie has made. How difficult it will be to disprove if she sticks to it. Though also, of course, as I know all too well from my Rape Crisis days, how difficult to prove. If Saul denies it. Which he will. Because he cannot have done this.

'She begged me not to tell anyone. She didn't want me to tell you. She wasn't going to tell me, even. Poor child.' Jules stops, takes a breath. 'But she realized she had to, because an experience like that, an assault, it doesn't just go away. As you know.'

'Is she hurt?' I ask quietly. 'Is she bruised? Is there any evidence that she's been assaulted?'

'I didn't want to say . . . but her period's late.'

'She's not pregnant, is she?'

'We don't know yet.'

'How late is it?'

'Only a few days. But she's terrified, of course. Distraught, in fact.'

'Oh my God.'

'Is that enough evidence for you?'

Yes, I should say. Yes, of course. *If* she's pregnant. But even then we don't know Saul's responsible. It could be anyone.

I open my mouth to speak. Then stop. I can't imagine the gauche Saffie I observed the other evening in a relationship. She's still such a child, for goodness' sake.

Jules goes on, 'I've decided the best thing, the only thing, is to deal with this together. Without telling anyone else, as Saffie requested. So we have to talk to Saul. See what he has to say for himself.'

A ray of sun has highlighted, as if deliberately, the photo of Archie and Saul I keep on my desk, the one where Archie's carrying Saul, aged about two, in a backpack up a hill in Scotland, both of them squinting with identical expressions into the camera.

'We can't do that. Saul's not in any state at the moment to have things like this levelled at him,' I say.

'Holly! You talk to boys about this kind of behaviour all the time. Surely you aren't afraid of asking your own son what he did to my daughter that night?'

'Please don't say "my daughter" and "your son" as if we barely know each other!'

A thick silence settles between us. The ray of sunlight on the photo flickers and fades, leaving us sitting in the dark shadow of Senate House. There's the rumble of traffic outside. The chatter of students passing on the street below. From above, the plaintive, out-of-place squall of a seagull.

'I'm not telling Saul Saffie's accused him of the vilest act imaginable when he's got so much on his plate right now. It'll ruin his life at school and in the village forever. Knowing she's saying things like that about him . . . he'll go under.'

'You're saying you're going to ignore it?'

'I'm saying you should question whether Saffie's telling the whole story. Saul's an easy target. Everyone at that school's got it in for him. The kids bullied him mercilessly in year nine . . . don't you remember? He refused to go to school at all because of it; Donna said he'd developed school phobia as a result.'

'That has nothing to do with this.'

'But this is Saffie and Saul we're talking about. You don't

believe Saul would risk something like that, even if he had it in him? In your house, while you and I were out together and could have come in at any time? You know him. Think about it.'

'Guys in that state don't do a risk assessment.'

'*In that state*? Who exactly do you think Saul is?'

Out of the blue the image comes to me, Saul wielding his iPad when I was getting ready to go out that evening. The fleeting fear that he'd turned into someone else entirely in a matter of seconds. It's happened a few times lately. But only when he's been tired after school, or hungry, and the moods recede as quickly as they come. It doesn't make him violent. It doesn't make him capable of rape.

'Have you forgotten the poster on your wall when we were students?' Jules asks. '*Every man is a potential rapist.*'

I can't believe how clipped my voice sounds, even to me, when I reply, 'Except my son.'

Now Jules's face darkens. 'You have to believe this, Holly. You might not like to think Saul has it in him, but you yourself called him a misfit. Well, you were right. He's been in dire need of serious help for some time now, and you've done nothing to sort him out.' These words explode from my friend's, Saul's odd mother's, mouth as if they aren't new thoughts but ones she's been waiting to vent for months.

I begin to tremble. For a few moments I can't speak. Only the other night, when I expressed my concerns about Saul, she was telling me not to worry about him. That he was a normal, healthy adolescent boy. Only the other night she was telling him to his face how much she loved him. As I stare at Jules, her hands in her lap, her blonde hair pinned up, her face with its high cheekbones, her narrow, knowing eyes, I see Saffie curled on the sofa in front of Saul with her make-up and too-tight jumper.

If we're going to start casting aspersions about our parenting, I can play at that game. Only a few weeks ago, Jules had discovered a cache of expensive cosmetics in Saffie's room, but found it impossible to prise the truth out of her daughter. In the end, she'd called me in to talk to Saffie, and we learned she'd been shoplifting with one of her friends for weeks.

I *try* to stop the next words coming out of my mouth. Jules is the person who has accompanied me through life since university, through the birth of my son and the death of my husband. I love her – and Saffie – more than any other friends in the world, and if I say the words that are on the tip of my tongue, I risk losing them both. But what she's just said about Saul has punched the breath from me.

'I think you need to take a closer look at what's going on with Saffie,' I say. 'Who she's mixing with. Because she's turning into a devious little troublemaker.'

*

Jules and I got to know each other back to front. It was one of the things we both joked about way back when we were students: I first met her as she emerged from her bedroom in our tiny university flat in her pyjamas, before I'd ever seen her dressed. I'd made her a herbal tea to ease her through a chronic hangover.

'Don't you break the shells first?' she asked, coming into the kitchen, where I was boiling us eggs.

'That's poached. You don't know how to boil an egg?'

She'd never learned to cook, had lived mainly off microwave meals since she was a child. She thought you added pesto to spaghetti water, so I showed her how to make pasta and pesto too. In turn Jules taught me how to blow-dry my hair, and how to apply eyeliner so it flicked up at the edges. I held her fringe away from her face as she threw up into the sink after another night of too much cheap Chardonnay, before I knew her Polish parents had split up and that she'd come to live with her mum and an older brother in England at sixteen. We learned each other's domestic habits (she chucked tins into the bin without washing them, while I rinsed them out for the recycling; she stocked up on essentials, while I liked to live hand to mouth) before we knew the courses we'd picked.

Jules was upbeat, positive and open, always telling me what was going through her mind, while she said I was empathetic, that she could tell me anything. At times, she drove me mad. She was vainer than me and fussed about her clothes and which shoes to wear. Her love life was of eternal interest to her whether I wanted to hear it or not. She was pernickety about money, never spending a penny over whatever she owed for our kitty, while I would happily assume it would all even out in the end. And yet, despite our differences, we were hardly ever apart. Living together from the start meant that there were no demons to uncover. And so we flat-shared throughout our university years.

People commented that we were opposites: blonde, pretty Jules who liked heels and full make-up when she went out, and shy me, with the floppy brown hair that refused to be coerced into anything other than a straight bob even after Jules's blow-drying lessons, uncomfortable in anything other than black jeans, black T-shirt and DMs. Even our degrees were miles apart. She took business studies, while I took English literature.

All the boys loved Jules. Often, my hopes would rise as a boy I had my eye on made his way across the room towards me, only to be dashed when he asked, 'Who's your friend?' But we bonded firmly in those first weeks and became inseparable.

'Our friendship is the intersection in a Venn diagram,' Jules said once. 'On one side, there is my love of fitness and partying and dance, and on the other, your love of literature and cooking and feminism, but in the intersection are our emotional lives. And that's where we're a perfect fit, where we understand one another absolutely.'

Someone else said that Jules was the cover, while I was the book. It wasn't quite as simple as that, of course. The reality was Jules was complex: vivacious one moment, anxious the next. She worried about her mother, who suffered poor health and whom she felt she didn't see often enough. She was unusually perceptive, too. And although I was the English student, she tackled harder books than I did, had raced through the whole of *War and Peace* and *Anna Karenina* in English, her second language, neither of which I had read back then. At times it was me who had to drag her out, encourage her to have a drink and to go out dancing. So we weren't quite as easy to pigeonhole as it might have appeared. But the main thing is, we loved each other.

Our friendship continued when we were both living and working in London.

We lived in the same postcode and were in and out of each other's houses the whole time. In addition to becoming Saffie's odd mother, I was a listening ear after each of Jules's miscarriages. She confided in me the time she was unfaithful to Rowan and, at her request, I had never spoken about it again. She stood by me during the dark months after Archie's death when I was so wrapped up in my own grief I took no interest in anything else. And we shared the care of each other's children before she introduced me to Pete

2

JULES

Holly's words left Jules speechless, as if winded. Eventually, she managed, 'I didn't come in here to have my daughter insulted. I came to seek your help. I thought we could sort this out together, but I was wrong.'

She rose from her chair and left Holly's office, her eyes pricking, her throat aching. Once in the corridor, she turned back. Put her head round the door. 'I shan't be employing Saul on Saturdays. It goes without saying I don't want him coming anywhere near my family anymore. Or my shop.'

'Jules, wait!' Holly called after her, but Jules didn't look back.

She hurried down the silent walkways, beneath the portraits of alumni she'd never heard of. Outside, along the side of Russell Square, tourists moved in shoals towards the British Museum, selfie-sticks held aloft. Jules kept moving against the tide, afraid if she stood still, she would start to cry and wouldn't be able to stop. She took the path that cut a diagonal line across Russell Square, passing the central fountain, where children in wellingtons and bright scarves jumped in and out of the spray. It occurred to Jules that it was only a few years since Saffie would have been one of them, leaping through jets of water, not caring about getting her clothes soaked. She had always been an extrovert, guileless child. A vision of her that morning came to Jules. Saffie's eyes were wide with panic, her face full of anguish as she told Jules what had happened to her. Would her daughter ever be happy in her own skin again? Rape took away a person's sense of self, their security and their identity. Everyone knew that. Jules should never have left her daughter alone in the house with Saul. Saffie had been assaulted in the place she should feel her safest, by someone she trusted. Which made Jules feel doubly awful. And yet how could she have guessed that the boy Saffie had known since babyhood had become so disturbed he was capable of doing that to her?

As she reached the Underground station, Jules's throat constricted. She found the city oppressive. The air closed in on her. She couldn't face a crowded Tube and decided to walk back to King's Cross. She took the surprisingly quiet backstreets and was almost at the station when she stumbled upon a pharmacy tucked away in a little row of shops and went in.

The petite Asian woman behind the counter was discreet and informative. She said what Jules already knew in her heart of hearts – that it was too late for Saffie to take the morning-after pill. Jules felt a further stab of remorse that her own actions had resulted in Saffie facing a possible pregnancy. This could all have been avoided if she hadn't drunk so much, and if Saffie had told her that same evening. No, she corrected herself, it would have been avoided if she had listened to Saffie and never let Saul come to their house in the first place.

Saffie had stood in the kitchen in her school uniform on the night of Tess's birthday drinks, a peanut-butter cookie in one hand, her big blue eyes made wider by lashings of mascara and smoky eye shadow, and literally stamped her foot when Jules had told her Saul was coming to use the internet.

'I don't get why you object so strongly,' Jules had said. 'You and he are practically siblings.'

'Were. When I was five.'

'You used to call Saul your odd brother. He's your oldest friend.'

'No, Mum. Holly's *your* oldest friend. That doesn't make Saul mine. My friends think he's a creep.'

'What? Even Freya?' Freya, Pete's daughter, spent whole weekends with Saul during her stays at Holly's. Holly had never mentioned Freya disliking her new stepbrother.

'No, *not* Freya.' Saffie had rolled her eyes, as if her mother were slow on the uptake. 'But everyone knows she *has* to be nice about him. Because he's her stepbrother. No one else is. Everyone else avoids him.'

'I think that's very unkind. I hope you don't exclude him because he looks a little different to the rest of you?'

Jules hadn't been able to understand her daughter's reluctance about having Saul over. After all, her friends wouldn't be there, so no one need know he'd been. In the end, it had only been by insisting that Saffie could spend the evening in her room if she wanted and didn't have to speak to Saul that Saffie had agreed to have him in the house at all.

Jules knew how devastated Holly would be to hear what the kids had already been saying about Saul at school, so she had omitted this part of the story in Holly's office. Why did I spare her feelings? Jules wondered now, as she scanned the pharmacy shelves for a pregnancy test. Holly needed to know how Saffie's friends viewed Saul – then she would realize that this allegation wasn't so very far-fetched after all.

Jules's breath caught in her throat. Holly hadn't spared *her* feelings. Having your child insulted was worse, far worse than being criticized yourself. It was like having your very core attacked. And it was deeply unfair. If Jules could have shown Holly the terror in Saffie's eyes, Holly wouldn't have accused her of being a troublemaker. But Holly should have believed Saffie anyway. As her godmother. As a woman who had argued for years – even before the furore over recent high-profile cases – that all rape claims should be taken at face value.

The pharmacist didn't look at Jules as she folded the paper bag over the pregnancy test and handed it to her, for which Jules was grateful. The box deep in the pocket of her coat, Jules continued to the station.

She wasn't sure she was doing the right thing, buying the test. She'd already agreed to take Saff to their GP and family friend, Donna Browne, rather than to a well-woman clinic. And if – God forbid – her little girl *was* pregnant, it was perhaps best they found out with their doctor present so they could get advice about how to deal with it as quickly and with as little fuss as possible. But she had to do something, and this felt like the only thing she could do.

On the train home, without having registered the rest of the walk back to King's Cross, Jules turned her face to the window and allowed the tears to cascade down her cheeks. She had never expected Holly to find this easy, but she had not anticipated a point-blank denial. Or for Holly to turn on Saffie. Holly had always stood up for her 'odd daughter', even when Jules and Rowan were at their wits' end with her. Saffie was ebullient, always had been, and excitable at times, but she had never been devious; it was not a word you could apply to her. If anything, she was the opposite. Naive, and gullible. And although she'd got herself caught up recently in that shoplifting incident, which Jules suspected was driven by one of her less savoury friends, she had never been prone to lying. Saffie had no front. What you saw was what you got. Having her daughter described like that was deeply unfair. As the train passed Alexandra Palace, and they rattled through the first green spaces of the Hertfordshire countryside, Jules wondered whether she could have handled the meeting with Holly better. She replayed in her mind Saffie's revelation earlier that morning, ending with her seeking Holly's support. Pointlessly, as it turned out.

When Jules had got in from her morning run at eight, she had found Saffie up but curled on the sofa, her face puffy and streaked grey with mascara. She was in her school uniform but had made no effort to put on her shoes or to do her hair.

'What on earth's the matter?' Jules had asked, sitting down next to her. 'Aren't you feeling well?'

Saffie had shadows round her eyes as if she hadn't slept. Her lips were sealed into a tight line, and drawn down at the edges.

'Saffie. What is it?' Jules's heart had begun to thump. She hadn't seen such a look of misery – or was it fear? – on her daughter's face since, as a small child, she'd woken with a fever in the midst of a nightmare.

'Please, darling, you need to tell me what's wrong.'

'I can't say,' Saffie whispered at last. She looked up at Jules. 'It's something really terrible, Mum.'

'So terrible you're prepared to miss the bus?' Jules smiled. 'It's about to go, you know.'

Saffie never usually missed the chance to meet up with her friends at the bus stop, to discuss the latest blogger craze or YouTube star.

'I can't go to school.' Saffie's breath came fast. Her hand when she grasped Jules's was clammy. 'I'm in terrible trouble.'

'Come on, Saff.' Jules pulled her daughter's head to her. Kissed her hair.

'Remember how much better you felt the time you stole that make-up after you admitted it to me and Holly? There's nothing you can do or say that will shock me.'

'There is. There is this time.'

'Well, I'm not forcing it out of you. Speak if and when you're ready. I'm here to help. To listen.'

After a long silence, Saffie drew in a breath and said, 'OK. It's ... Mum ... my period's late.' Her voice broke as she uttered the words and she began to cry quietly.

'Ah. Well,' Jules had said, releasing her head, taking her face between her palms so she could speak into it, 'you know periods can be very irregular at your age, don't you?'

'But this one's later than it's been before.'

'All kinds of things can cause that.' Stress, for example, Jules thought. Rowan pushing the poor child to go to extra classes after school. That could have caused her to miss a period. She felt a flicker of annoyance at the pressure her husband put their daughter under.

'I'm afraid I might be pregnant.'

There was a pause as Jules took this in.

'What makes you think you might be pregnant?' Jules asked softly. As far as she knew, Saffie hadn't kissed a boy, let alone had a proper relationship. And Jules had always prided herself on the fact Saffie told her everything, always had done. Until the shoplifting incident.

'You do know it's not possible to get pregnant without having full sexual intercourse, don't you?' she soothed.

'I know that, Mum. What do you think I am? An idiot?'

Jules took a sharp breath. It was a relief, in some ways, to hear Saffie hadn't lost her newfound capacity to snap, but what lay beneath the retort made Jules's heart trip.

'Ah. So who ... ?'

'I can't say.'

'Saffie, it would be better if you did.'

'I don't want to get him into trouble.'

A chill ran from Jules's head to her feet. She shut her eyes. There was a 'him' involved after all. The thought of her little girl sleeping with anyone was abhorrent. She thought back to her own teenage crush on Jozef, and the fumbled sex they'd had. She'd been a couple of years older than Saffie, which seemed far too young to her now. But they all grew up even sooner these days. She had the sense of her daughter's childhood tumbling away on a rapid, out of arm's reach.

'OK,' she said. 'We're going to sit down in the kitchen, and I'll make you your favourite cappuccino, and you're going to tell me exactly what's going on for you. If you've been having some kind of a . . . relationship, and you're out of your depth, you have to tell me. And then we'll talk about whether or not you could possibly be pregnant.'

In the kitchen, Jules threw a teabag into a mug for herself, poured boiling water onto it, filled the machine with coffee and pressed the button that made the espresso come out. She steamed the milk and spooned froth on the way Saffie liked it. All this gave her time to think things through. She was determined not to show how this revelation had thrown her. Knocked her assumptions about having done a good job bringing up the daughter she thought she knew better than anyone. The daughter who was outgoing, sunny, warm and very close to her mother. And open. Saffie must not be allowed to see how rattled – no, *scared* – Jules was about having, out of the blue, to deal with something for which she wasn't in the slightest bit prepared. Saffie had had *sex* with someone?

Jules placed the cappuccino in front of her daughter, sat on a bar stool and took her hands.

'Saffie, have you got a boyfriend you don't want to tell me and Dad about?'

Saffie took the cup from her mother but didn't drink from it.

'It's worse than that.'

'Worse than having a boyfriend at your age who might have made you pregnant? How can it be worse?'

'Because I . . . He isn't a boyfriend. And I didn't want it to happen.'

Jules shut her eyes.

'Are you telling me someone forced you? Are you saying . . . ? Oh my God. You have to tell me what happened to you.' Jules knew she was losing her poise, and that this could make Saff clam up, but she couldn't stop herself. 'Tell me, Saff. Tell me who did this to you.'

'He told me not to tell anyone.'

'I bet he did!'

Saffie just looked at her, tears in her eyes, her mouth turned down. She was trying her best not to cry.

'You *have* to tell me.' Jules fought back the urge to shout that she'd go and find the culprit and take him to task for it right now. She forced herself to steady her voice. 'So I can help you.' *So I can go and throttle the person who touched you.*

'I'm afraid he'll be angry if I tell you . . . He might do something.'

'Saffie! No one will do anything to you. Not if I'm here. They wouldn't dare.' Jules was startled by the ferociousness in her own voice.

'I tried to carry on as normal,' Saffie was saying. 'I *was* carrying on as normal, until I realized . . . it's four days late, Mum. I'm so scared.'

'Was this someone we know?'

48

'I'm not saying.'

'If you won't tell me, then we'll have to tell the police.'

'*No!*'

'We'll have to. If someone assaulted you—'

'OK!' Saffie shouted. 'I'll tell you, but only if you swear not to tell anyone else.'

Jules took a deep breath.

'I swear I'll do all I have to do to take care of you. I'm your mother. We're in this together.'

'OK, then . . .'

Saffie's words came out so fast Jules didn't catch them.

'*What* did you say, Saffie?'

'I said . . . it was Saul.'

'Saul? Holly's Saul?'

'I didn't want to tell you,' Saffie said. 'He'll be mad at me. He'll do something to me . . .'

'When did this happen?'

Saffie looked at Jules imploringly. 'Do we have to talk about it?'

'I have to know, Saffie. When was it?'

'When do you think?'

'I don't know . . . Was it at school?'

'Don't be stupid.'

'But when, then?'

'Of course it wasn't at school. It was . . .'

Saffie paused and Jules found herself rifling back over the past couple of weeks, trying to envisage an occasion when Saul might have had an opportunity to lay his hands on Saffie.

When Saffie next spoke, it all fell into place.

'It was that night he came round here.'

'When Dad was away? The night I went out with Holly? When Saul came over to use our broadband . . .'

Saffie shrugged, then nodded reluctantly.

The irony! Jules had been in the pub with all those women, laughingly discussing the first awkward times they'd had sex, while her daughter was having her virginity snatched from her in a truly vile way.

'You're telling me . . . you and Saul are having some kind of a relationship?'

'*No*, Mum. Gross. You asked him to come over. *Not* my idea. If you remember.'

Saffie looked up at her mother through her childish blue eyes, her lashes sticky with tears. Something about her had changed. Jules could see it now. Didn't some women say they could *see* when their daughters lost their virginity? It was in their eyes, in their facial expressions. A kind of hardening. Or knowingness. No, that was it. A loss of innocence. All of a sudden, Jules knew for certain what it was about her daughter that had altered recently. She kicked herself that she hadn't identified it sooner.

'Tell me exactly what happened.'

'I don't want to. I don't want to remember it.'

'I know, my love, but you need to tell me.'

There was a pause and then Saffie said, 'I thought he was downstairs on the internet, but he . . .'

'He what?'

'He came upstairs. When I was getting ready for bed.'

Goosebumps prickled all the way up Jules's legs in the Lycra leggings she hadn't had time to change out of yet. *She* had asked Saul to check Saff had gone to bed that evening. Was this *her* fault?

She put her arm round her daughter. She stroked back the fine blonde hair from her forehead. Saffie smelled strongly of sweet perfume, as if she had been planning on a night out rather than preparing for a day at school. They all wore perfume, and hair and skin products these days, even the boys, or so Saffie argued. Some of Saffie's friends had 'been out' with each other in year four, five or six. They didn't really know what it meant, of course. But they still behaved as if they did, worrying about who liked whom. Fussing over their hair and their clothes and their nails the minute they were out of babyhood. Emulating the celebrities who posted all over Instagram. Jules didn't like it – what mother would? She yearned for the days when Saffie would have preferred to spend a day practising her ballet positions in front of the mirror to painting her nails and straightening her hair.

'He came upstairs,' Saffie said again. 'I didn't know he was there. I was getting undressed and he must've been looking in my door.'

Jules remembered Saffie saying the school kids called Saul a creep. Is this what they'd meant?

'Then he came right in and he . . .' She stopped again.

'Oh, Saff!'

'He came in and . . . he pushed me onto the bed and held me down. I thought he was joking, at first. I said, "Get off, Saul," but then he . . . he said didn't I realize I was asking for it. Letting him see me undressing like that. I couldn't stop him and so I thought, well, no one has to know. It will stop and no one will ever know.

'It was horrible and rough and I didn't want it. But now there's . . . My period's late.' Saffie's mouth turned down at the corners and her lower lip trembled. 'And so I had to tell you.'

Jules tried to take in what her daughter had said. Her long-held image of Saul as a sweet, shy, if rather awkward boy had been turned on its head in a few seconds. Things

Rowan, and Saffie, and her school friends had said about him hovered at the periphery of her mind.

'You're telling me,' she'd said after a pause, 'you're telling me Saul raped you?'

Saffie crumpled then and she began to cry quietly, a soft keening sound as she bent over and held her stomach as if in pain.

'Are you hurt? Did he hurt you? Why didn't you tell me, Saff? Why didn't you tell me straight away?'

'I don't know ... I was scared. And I ... I didn't know if you'd listen. Holly was there. You'd been out drinking. I didn't want to spoil your evening.'

Jules closed her eyes. 'You could have told me anyway,' she said. 'Or you could have told me the next day. Any day between then and now.'

'I thought you wouldn't believe me.'

'Of course I would have believed you. You wouldn't lie to me, would you? Not about something so serious?' Jules examined her. It was obvious Saffie had felt trapped. Terrified of what would happen if she told, terrified of what would happen if she didn't. 'You're my daughter,' Jules went on. 'I love you. I trust you. I feel awful that you didn't feel you could tell me straight away.'

Saffie sat up suddenly and wiped her eyes.

'But you have such a thing about Saul.'

'What do you mean?'

'You think he's so, like, perfect. You wouldn't listen. I told you I didn't want him here.'

Jules took a deep breath. Guilt stirred deep in her gut. It was true. She had ignored her daughter's reservations about Saul, let him come round while they were out. Then she'd had too much Prosecco with her friends and Saffie hadn't been able to tell her on the evening it had happened. What kind of a mother did that make her? This was another thing Jules hadn't told Holly. The guilt she felt. That she'd drunk so much Saffie hadn't thought she could tell her that night.

'Have you told anyone else?' Jules asked at last, trying to think straight. 'A teacher? A friend?'

'I don't want anyone to know. It's horrible and embarrassing and I'd decided to forget it happened. My friends will think I'm desperate that I went with him. If my period wasn't late, I wouldn't have said anything to you. I've only told you because of this.' She placed her hand on her abdomen.

Jules looked at her little girl. Saffie had been trembling all this time, holding her other hand to her mouth, biting the back of it. She was crying again and dribble was running from her nose into her hand. What she'd gone through, what Saul had put her through made Jules shudder.

'I'll sort this out,' Jules said at last. 'What Saul did to you is not only violent, it's a criminal offence. He has to be made aware of that. The school will have to take measures to—'

'Mum, please don't tell anyone.'

'But he *raped* you, Saffie. My goodness, wait until Holly knows.'

'It wasn't . . . I don't want him to get into trouble. I mean, I didn't think it was rape. It probably *was* partly my fault.'

'How on earth was it partly your fault?'

'I should've shut my door, so he couldn't spot me getting undressed.'

'That's absolute nonsense, Saffie. It's outrageous that he barged into your room. And you must know it's rape unless you tell a boy you actively want it, out loud, and mean it, and are in the right state to say you want it!' She stopped. She was echoing Holly. The lectures she'd practised on Jules for the consent workshops. Had she never had this conversation with Saff? She softened her tone. 'And you won't understand how that feels until you're much, much older. Saul has done a terrible thing. He has to know that. And he has to suffer the consequences.'

Jules looked at Saffie, at the desperation writ large across her face. Of course it was all too much for her to take on board at once. The rape, the fear she was pregnant. The idea of having to explain it all to strangers. Jules wasn't a hundred per cent sure whether she should inform the school. She had no idea, she realized, who she should tell.

'I don't want Saul to get into trouble,' Saffie repeated. 'Really, Mum. I'll just keep away from him from now on.'

Jules decided not to pursue this, since it was only adding to Saffie's distress.

'We'll need to make sure you're not pregnant,' she said softly, instead. 'I'll get a test and we'll check you're OK as soon as possible.'

'What will we do? If I am?'

'We'll sort it,' Jules said. 'It's early days. We'll go to a well-woman clinic and they'll take care of you . . .'

'Mum, please. I don't want to go to some horrible clinic. Everyone will know. Couldn't we just go to Dr Browne?'

'You'd rather go to Donna?'

'I think so. At least I know her. She won't tell anyone, will she?'

'She's a doctor. She isn't allowed to. But listen. I don't want you to worry about that. I want you to leave it all to me. The main thing is we look after you. You're to stay at home today. You've been through an ordeal and you need time to recover.'

'You won't tell anyone?' Saffie begged again, plucking at Jules's sleeve. 'I don't want anyone to know.'

'Not even Dad?' Jules asked.

Saffie's face froze, her eyes wide.

'*Especially* not Dad,' she said.

*

Jules suggested Saffie watch one of the films she'd loved as a child, *The Parent Trap*, to take her mind off things. Once she was settled under a blanket on the sofa, Jules went back to the kitchen. She cleared up the mugs, opened the dishwasher to stash them inside, wanting to restore some sense of normality to the morning. Outside, a pale autumn mist closed in on the skylights of the extension, bathing the kitchen in a soft yellow light. Sometimes this house felt almost afloat in the fens, only a thin veneer of glass and breezeblock protecting them from the weather outside. She had tried not to overreact in front of Saffie, but inside her thoughts were bubbling away, tripping over themselves, coming to the boil.

Jules understood why Saffie didn't want Rowan to know, given his temper. His daughter hadn't seen the worst of it – he'd once put a man in hospital – but she had recently witnessed his reaction to some random guy in the street who had made a lewd comment about her burgeoning figure. Jules had barely been able to prevent him from going over and punching the man. If Rowan knew she'd been assaulted – no, *raped* – what kind of a rage would he fly into? But Jules had to talk to someone.

As she absently wiped surfaces, she rifled through a mental list of her friends. Tess had a daughter who was the same age as Saffie. But their conversations often became competitive, each trying to trump the other's child's achievements. Tess was not someone to whom you could confess self-doubt or failures. She was the last person you would tell that your daughter had been caught shoplifting, or smoking, or staying out later than she should. The last person in the world to ask for advice about your child being raped by a friend's son. As for the others – Samantha, Jenny, Fiona – Jules didn't feel, lovely as they were, that she knew them quite well enough to have such an intimate conversation. There was Donna, of course, but the GP had often complained about people using her out of work hours as a sounding board for their problems.

That just left the group of local mums she went to boot camp with. She could not trust any of them with this kind of confidence. Gossip flew around this village. People often knew what you were about to do before you knew it yourself. And you couldn't second-guess opinions. Some of them, the most sympathetic-seeming, could be very judgemental in unexpected ways.

Of course, the first person Jules would have phoned for guidance in any other circumstance was Holly. Not just because Holly was Jules's oldest, closest friend, her go-to person for emotional or moral advice, but also because Holly often said she thought of Saff as the daughter she never had. Plus, of course, Holly's discussions at her university about rape and consensual sex put her in the ideal position to deal with this. Holly would be just as concerned as Jules about what Saul had done. Might do again. Holly would *want* to know. She would be furious if she discovered Jules hadn't told her. She would want to get the truth out of Saul before he got into deeper trouble. Which was what would happen if Jules overrode Saffie's panicked plea and did what her instinct told her to do and reported him to the school, or to the police even. It would be better all round if she and Holly could deal with it quietly by themselves.

And so Jules had made the decision, that morning, to go and see Holly. Away from either of their homes, where they could both be detached. Holly would know exactly how to approach this. They would talk to their children without involving anyone else, as Saffie had requested. A boy who could assault a girl in her own home had something more than chronic shyness up with him. Holly would have to deal with Saul, seeking professional help for him if necessary. And Jules would get Saffie seen by Donna and ask for some counselling. And then they would all move on. They would sort it out without drawing anyone else in. Not the school. Not the police. Not the men. As Saffie had asked.

Woman to woman.

Mother to mother.

Odd mother to odd mother.

*

Saffie reluctantly agreed, when Jules explained her reasoning, that Jules would have to talk to Holly. And that in this way, they could deal with it without telling anyone else.

'You're to leave everything to me. And you're not to worry anymore. Promise me?'

What inadequate words! How could Saffie not worry . . . and yet Jules knew that the only way to keep her daughter from breaking down was to remain calm herself. Jules phoned Hetty, her shop assistant, and asked her to hold the fort for the day. When Rowan came in, she told him Saffie was off school with a stomach upset, needed quiet and was lying in bed watching a DVD. Rowan said he'd keep an eye on her, and Jules, telling Rowan she had a buyer to meet, had taken the next train to London.

As she neared the university buildings that lunchtime, however, Jules wondered if she'd be able to trust herself to speak to Holly in the measured way she planned to. Calmly, without bias.

Once, soon after Holly and Saul had moved to the Fens,

Jules had tentatively suggested that a shorter hairstyle might help Saul fit in – she was actually quoting Rowan and regretted it immediately – and Holly had snapped at her: how did she know what was best for her son? Jules had realized it was fine for Holly to express concerns about Saul, not fine for Jules to agree; that Holly did not accept any criticism of Saul that didn't come from Holly herself. And until now, apart from that one slip-up, Jules had respected this. The two women had always reassured each other when they were concerned about their children. They did not want or need affirmation of their anxieties from each other. It was a tacit understanding they had always abided by. Now Jules was about to break it, by telling Holly what her son had done to her daughter and that he was therefore more troubled even than Holly feared.

Jules arrived at Holly's university in the early afternoon. The receptionist gave her a visitor's badge and directed her up to the English department, where the corridors smelled of books and dusty paper. It struck Jules that Holly's work world and hers couldn't be much further apart. Hers was all about profits and losses and money, and involved frantic sorting of orders and dealing with deliveries, accounts and invoices and stock checks, while Holly's involved intelligent conversation with quiet students, books and quotes and deep thoughts. Jules trusted that Holly's ability to think objectively, as she had to when constructing a lecture, or when running her consent discussions, would make all this manageable.

She arrived at Holly's office, but the door was locked. Jules could have texted her and warned her she was coming, but she couldn't think how to explain her visit and in the end decided it was best to catch her in an unguarded state.

She sat on a chair outside the office and waited for her friend. Opposite her on the wall was a poster.

Ask First. Consent is Hot. Assault is Not.

Underneath, it gave a date and a time for the next discussion on sexual consent. Consent. Holly's favourite subject, Jules thought sourly. But she had not to let such thoughts intrude. Poor Holly had no idea that the very words she had pinned up outside her door were about to smack her full in the face.

At last Jules could see Holly's tall, slim figure coming towards her down the corridor, past the closed mahogany doors of studies. Holly was deep in thought, a takeaway coffee in a cardboard sleeve in her hand, her slightly knock-kneed walk so familiar, her intelligent, thoughtful face, her pale, freckled skin, a strand of flyaway chestnut-brown hair caught over what Jules had once joked was an aristocratic nose. Straight and narrow and elegant. Like the rest of her frame. They used to say, as students, that she looked like her muse, Virginia Woolf. Her clothes were always effortlessly stylish, loose grey linen jacket, simple blue A-line jersey dress, flat soft leather boots. A small, unconscious smile played on Holly's lips. She was happier these days, since she'd moved out of London. Since meeting Pete. How beautiful she is, Jules thought, and felt like weeping.

In the event, however, Holly's reaction was worse even than Jules had feared. But it was when she declared that Saffie had become 'a devious little troublemaker' that Jules knew the conversation had nowhere else to go. Reporting a crime dispassionately was one thing, but the bottom line was that mothers did not insult each other's children. And so, as much to protect Holly from her fury as to nurse her own feelings, Jules had left.

Now, on the train home, as she neared the village, and

the land flattened out, and Jules felt the relief she always experienced when she reached the countryside after being in the capital, as if she could breathe again, she fingered the cellophane wrapping of the pregnancy test in her pocket. The little tube of plastic within was the only thing that could make Holly retract what she'd said. It would provide solid proof that Saffie was neither devious nor out to make trouble. If it was positive. Which of course Jules prayed that it wasn't.

*

'Is Dad in?'

'He popped into the village for beer. Said he'd be back by six.'

Saffie was in her room, sitting on her bed with her iPhone. Two red dots on her cheeks betrayed the fact she'd been crying again. Jules sat down on the duvet next to her.

'How are you feeling?' Jules asked.

'OK. What did Holly say?'

'She's going to talk to Saul.'

Saffie took in a breath, paled. 'He's never going to admit to it.'

'It depends how we approach it,' Jules said, her words ineffectual, even to her own ears. 'Holly and I will make sure we are very sensitive about it. Holly's used to dealing with this kind of thing. She does it all the time at work. Now, can I get you anything?'

Saffie shook her head.

'I got us a test,' Jules said.

'Oh, Mum. I'm scared.' Saffie's face crumpled again. 'I'm afraid it's going to be positive . . . What will we do if it is? What will I tell people?'

'You don't have to tell anyone. We'll deal with it straight

away, with as little fuss as possible.' *You shouldn't be having to go through this.*

'Can we wait? I think I'll die if it's true. Like you said, periods can be late for lots of reasons – it might come soon. It might come tonight. Let's wait at least another day. Please, Mum . . . *please.*'

Jules took Saffie's hand. She could feel her daughter's fear, and could understand her not wanting to know the result if it was positive. But if it was negative, that would remove a huge burden of worry from both of them.

'We'll give it another day,' she said at last. 'If that is what you want. And meanwhile I'll phone Donna, book an appointment, just in case.'

*

'Dr Browne's on annual leave until Friday,' the receptionist said, when Jules dialled the surgery, and she felt her heart drop. 'If it can't wait, I can put you in with Dr Alwin.'

Jules didn't want to take Saffie to Dr Alwin, the only male GP at the surgery. He had a reputation in the village for being tactless and impatient. The thought of her little girl explaining the rape to a doctor at all was ghastly enough. She made an appointment with Donna for Friday.

'If you change your mind,' the receptionist said, obviously curious now as to what the problem was, 'you can phone for an emergency appointment with one of the locums in the morning.'

Saffie seemed relieved when Jules told her they couldn't see Donna for a week, and Jules allowed this to reassure her for the time being.

When Rowan came in, it was difficult not to blurt out everything to him. Rowan had walked from the village and was in high spirits, his face pink with fresh air. He tore his fleece off at the front door.

'How are my beautiful girls?' he asked, spreading wide his arms, enveloping Jules and planting a kiss on her cheek. 'I've done my exercise for the day and I've earned me a beer and some crisps. D'you want a wine, honey?'

'I'm fine,' Jules said. 'I'll wait till we eat.'

'Saff,' Rowan yelled up the stairs, 'are you better, baby? Come and give your dad a hug.'

Rowan went into the sitting room, slumped on the sofa, opened his beer.

Saffie came down from her room when she heard her father but shook her head at the offer of crisps. Rowan caught hold of her and dragged her onto his lap. Saffie looked far too big for this, Jules thought, swamping Rowan like a baby bird whose ruffled feathers make it appear bigger than the parent. Rowan put his arm round her anyway, and squeezed his daughter close.

'Is your tummy better, gorgeous?' he asked.

'I'm OK,' Saffie said.

Jules watched her, admiring her plucky attempt to behave as normal.

Then Rowan lifted a lock of her silky blonde hair and kissed her on the neck. The two had always been close, but Jules flinched as she witnessed the physicality between father and daughter given everything Saffie had been through recently.

'If you've finished your homework,' he said, 'we could catch up on an episode of *Sherlock*?'

'I don't really feel like it, Dad.'

'I'll even suffer *Call the Midwife* if you prefer.'

Bloody hell, thought Jules, this couldn't get more ironic. Rowan usually point-blank refused to watch the series about

1950s nurses coping with pregnancies, including unwanted teenage ones. She almost opened her mouth to say, 'Not *Call the Midwife*, Rowan,' but stopped herself in time.

'What's for dinner, Jules?' Rowan asked. His hand, Jules couldn't help noticing, had found a resting place on Saffie's hip.

Jules hadn't thought about food. It would have to be something quick and easy.

'Pasta and pesto,' she said, going to the cupboard to get out a packet of penne. It was Holly who'd taught her to make that when they were students together, she remembered, miserably. Pulling the seal apart with her teeth. Trying to look normal. Wondering how normal looked. It wasn't something you thought about when you weren't trying to hide anything.

'Mum, I don't think I'll have pasta.' Saffie had climbed off Rowan's lap and come into the kitchen. She tugged at Jules's sleeve. 'My tummy's still upset.'

Jules looked at Saffie. Her heart tilted at the sight of her frightened face.

'It's OK, darling.' Jules kissed Saffie on the hair. 'You don't have to eat.'

'I think I'll go back to my room.'

'That's fine. I'll pop up and see you in a minute.'

'You're not going to tell Dad?' Saffie whispered, her face contorted with anxiety.

'Not if you don't want me to.'

'Promise?'

'Promise.'

*

Jules knew if she kept busy, cooking, clearing up, getting things ready for the morning, she could distract herself from blurting out to Rowan, once they were alone, the real reason Saffie hadn't felt up to going to school. As she grated the Parmesan to sprinkle over Rowan's pasta, she reminded herself that Rowan's attitude towards Saul would make telling him about the rape, and expecting a measured response, impossible.

'Saul looks like a bloody stoner,' Rowan had once said to Jules after an evening at Holly's house in which Saul had barely said hello. 'He's obviously got access to drugs from his London contacts. I don't want him mixing with Saffie. Giving her a bad name. Influencing her and her friends.'

Jules argued that Saul was not a stoner and shouldn't be judged by his image alone. And even if he did smoke a bit of weed, it didn't mean he was going to foist his habits onto the youth population of the Fens.

'You have a selective memory,' she'd teased her husband. 'Remember what we took in the good old days, before Saffie? When we were both working in the City?'

'We weren't sixteen, Jules. We were in our twenties; we knew what we were buying, what we were taking.'

'Anyway, I don't think Saul's antisocial behaviour has anything to do with drugs. He's had a very tough time, as you know,' Jules said. 'Since his dad died. It's been a struggle for Holly getting him through it alone. And he's suffered. He had anxiety and school phobia when he first moved here.'

'School phobia?' Rowan had snorted. 'Who coined that phrase? Slacker, more like. Holly overindulges him. Always has. She's so anxious about fucking him up him she pussy-foots around him. He needs a firm hand. A haircut and a decent diet and some regular exercise. And until then I'd rather Saffie didn't mix with him.'

'You can't say that, Rowan. He's my godson. And since

I'm the main reason they're living in the village, it's only fair to welcome them with open arms.'

Jules was determined to be loyal to Holly and Saul in the face of the hostility they aroused in her husband. That was why she had agreed to employ Saul as a Saturday assistant in her shop; she'd wanted to help get Saul out there into the real world. To give him some work experience that he could put on his CV. And it was why she had agreed that he could come over and use their internet connection the night she and Holly went out for Tess's birthday drinks. Now she wondered if she should have listened to Rowan after all and refused point-blank to have Saul in the house. Ever.

3

HOLLY

I sit for some time after Jules leaves my study, grappling to make some kind of sense of what she's told me. I need time alone to process it all, but Luma appears and reminds me I'm due to attend the consent workshop at three. I open my mouth to say I can't face it. Before I can speak, however, she reminds me that Hanya's now received some unpleasant tweets too, accusing her of being a feminazi. Hanya is only nineteen. Luma is right that she needs back-up.

I climb the stairs to the lecture theatre where Hanya is screening her film. The workshop has attracted a collection of mostly young women, a couple of those who don't like to have their gender defined and just three boys. Jerome hasn't shown up, as I might have guessed. Neither has Mei Lui, who I managed to give a leaflet to the week before. I sit at the back of the room while Hanya introduces the drama.

'We hope everyone will join in the discussion about what you think is really going on,' she finishes, then clicks the mouse and the film comes up on the screen. A girl dressed in short skirt, high heels and bomber jacket stumbles drunkenly into a studenty-looking bedroom: single bed, clothes strewn about the floor, takeaway carton on a bedside table. A boy holds the girl steady. She collapses on the bed and all but passes out. The boy lies down next to her. The camera pans back; you don't see what he actually does, but the implication is that he has sex with the girl while she's barely conscious. The girl is shown making some half-hearted attempts to shove him off.

Jules's distraught face telling me Saul raped Saffie comes back to me. I try to imagine Saul behaving like the actor in the film but cannot. The voiceover tells us the boy is an ex of the girl. That she'd asked him to walk her home. But that there was no invitation for him to get into bed with her. 'Do you think the boy was within his rights to assume she was consenting?' Hanya asks, as the credits come up.

The discussion takes off immediately.

'The girl let him come into her room. She was consenting.'

'But if she was too wasted to say no, then she wasn't able to give consent. I'd say he raped her.'

'They obviously already knew each other, had been out drinking together, so that's not rape.'

'That's so offensive! The girl didn't give consent, so it's rape. You can't assume someone wants sex just because they've had a drink with you and you know them.'

'Oh, come on. I mean, the way she was dressed, he would have assumed she was up for it, especially as they had been boy- and girlfriend.' It's one of the boys making this comment, of course. 'She should have thought about that before she asked him up to her room.'

'That's slut-shaming.'

'What would be in it anyway,' someone asks, 'for the guy? If she was genuinely out of it?'

'That's not the point. He was taking advantage and that's assault. Boys have to learn they can't just fuck who they want when they want.'

The boys at the back snigger.

'The girl obviously wanted it too,' one of them says. 'She was just too wasted to tell him.'

The rest of the discussion revolves around whether the girl had capacity to say yes. If she didn't, was it OK for the boy to assume he could sleep with her, based on their history together? The workshop has been a success, in so far as it's got the students thinking and questioning and talking.

I make no attempt to direct the discussion as I sometimes do. Because to my horror, thoughts I've never had before worm their way into my mind as I listen to the students argue, and I'm shocked to find myself half sympathizing with the boys at the back. Wasn't it understandable that the boy assumed it was a come-on when the girl let him walk her home? How else was he to know she wanted sex, other than the fact she let him into her room in her skimpy outfit? How are boys supposed to know? Girls can be so convoluted, so devious. The nuances of the drama suddenly seem murky, far less clear-cut than usual. I apologize to Hanya and hurry away, my own doubts goading me as I walk back to the station. *Girls are so hard to read! It's so easy to shout, 'Rape!' Such a slick way of targeting a boy all your friends have got it in for.*

The intrusive thoughts won't be silenced. They whisper relentlessly in my ear, unsettling me, driving me mad.

However, I'm regretting insulting Saffie by the time I get off the train that evening. It's dark as I walk from the station through the village. The only lights come from the blue flicker of televisions behind windows that face straight onto the narrow pavement. I hadn't predicted when we moved here how long the winter nights would be. I curse the black Fenlands. This is when I miss the city most, when the village has closed down for the day by five. I miss pubs and restaurants, the illuminated statues and bridges along the river, the lights on the boats. People sitting outdoors – even in winter, by candlelight – amid London's jumble of walls and squares, courtyards and buildings. While here everyone is hidden, boxed away within their houses. (I choose to forget London's traffic jams and crowded Tubes. The polluted air. The constant ear-splitting sound of police sirens and traffic.) London is my home. Not these dark, silent fens. Or maybe I'm just angry with Jules for dumping this story about Saul on me. I'm taking my fury out on the village she encouraged me to move to.

I reach my front door. The house, too, is in darkness, though I know Saul should be home. I wish Pete were here. I need another adult perspective on what Jules told me. But Pete's not back from Bristol till later. And anyway, Saul's my son, not Pete's. I'm the one who should deal with it.

'Saul?'

I don't know what I'm going to say, but I need to look at him. See whether I still know the son I've borne and raised more or less single-handedly since he hit puberty. Or whether I've missed something. Some detail that suggests he's capable of raping my best friend's daughter while we were out enjoying Prosecco at a gastropub.

Saul doesn't answer, so I dump my bag of files on the floor, peel off my coat, sit down at the kitchen table, my chin in my hands. I try to picture Saffie through Saul's eyes. To imagine what would have gone through his head when he popped his head round her room. Caught her half naked, from what Jules implied. Saffie's pretty well developed for her age, anyone can see that. How might it feel to be a teenage boy with his hormones raging who finds himself alone in a house with a girl he has known since he was tiny, who is now beginning to resemble, in body shape, women he's probably seen on the internet? Does Saul watch porn? I think of him alone in his room. Any kid with a smartphone has access to it, I know that. And whatever my objections to the way the industry presents women, airbrushed, silicone-enhanced, waxed to the nth degree (views I've made Saul aware of in discussions over dinner), Saul has to live in the modern world. I have to give him space, as Pete is always reminding me.

Is it possible that Saul, aroused, asked Saffie if he could kiss her and she'd agreed to it, curious herself? And then, perhaps, he pleaded, 'I want to know what it's like. We've known each other since we were children. Come on, let's try it.' In which case, Saffie may have gone along with it, only afterwards regretting it. Afraid of what her bitchy peer group would say if they knew. And so decided to call it rape.

But Jules said Saul went uninvited into her room. He'd even accused her of 'asking for it' when she told him to leave. What if Saffie is telling the truth? I quickly dismiss the idea because it doesn't bear thinking about.

When I volunteered for Rape Crisis as a student, all the things you hear about rape were confirmed for me. We heard of rapes at home or on public transport, in dark alleyways or brightly lit hotel rooms, at night or in broad daylight. Women and sometimes men came to us. Some had been raped at knifepoint by strangers, others in their own beds by their husbands, or by boyfriends or by exes. Some had been gang-raped. Some involved members of the victim's own family. All were terrified to report what they'd gone through. For fear of not being believed, or of retribution, or because they blamed themselves. Some came many years after the rape, when the full trauma of what they'd experienced continued to limit what they were able to do, or had come back to haunt them. I learned how hard it was to get men who raped convicted, how biased the criminal justice system was. Still is, judging by recent media cases.

So I am going against everything I know and believe by assuming Saffie is lying. I do my best. I try to envisage every possible scenario in which Saul might have assaulted Saffie. But I cannot believe her. Saul might be six foot, but he's little more than a child himself. A year ago, he was still coming to the cinema and for Wagamama noodles with me. Asking me to drive him back to see his friend Zak in London at the weekends so things could be like they used to be, eating pizza with him in front of *Gavin & Stacey*. He's a child himself, for goodness' sake.

I stand up, go to the cooker and stare at the couscous and almonds I put out this morning, ready to accompany the autumn casserole I've made to welcome everyone home for the weekend. Five minutes later, I'm still there.

I make a decision. I'll ask Saul to account for every minute of that night. Then I'll prove to Jules he couldn't have raped Saffie and persuade her to discover why she said he did. What motivated her to target my son in this way? Because this is what I believe Saffie has done. Although ostensibly the bullying may have stopped, I've seen how they all avoid Saul on the green. He's the victim of some kind of vindictive campaign. And somehow, Saffie, in her naivety, has got caught up in it. I've just reached this conclusion when there's a voice behind me and I look up, startled.

'What?' I ask.

Saul has come into the kitchen and yanked open the fridge door. A carton of milk falls onto the floor as he rummages through the shelves. He picks it up, leaving milk pooling under the cupboards, then stares into the fridge. He's become so clumsy recently, as if he doesn't know where his limbs begin and end. His trousers, which can't keep up with the rate he's growing upwards, hang off his skinny frame. A small exposed area of flesh reveals his bony spine, vertebrae like marbles under his skin. I try to imagine him coordinating the gangly body that he can barely control even in the kitchen in order to have sex with an unwilling partner. Knocking things over and bumping into things because he's growing faster than his brain can register. I can't picture it, because it's beyond imagination.

'I said, there's nothing to eat.'

'I haven't cooked yet. There will be.' I fetch the mop, wipe away the spilt milk.

'There's never anything to eat when I get in from school. Jules's cupboards are full of food you can snack on. Ours are bare. I'm fucking starving.'

I'm absurdly affronted that he's comparing me with Jules when I've been silently defending him against her. 'There's bread. You can make yourself a piece of toast. Don't think that's beyond even you. I'm making a casserole and cous-cous for later.'

'What time?'

'About seven thirty.'

When I next look, he's holding up his phone, and grinning.

'What is it?'

'What does that say to you, Mum?'

The photo on his screen shows a lollipop man in a high-vis jacket holding up his yellow 'Children Crossing' sign. Behind the man is a rainbow, arching from one side of the fen to the other. The fluorescent jacket and sign against the perfect rainbow create a tableau like an archetypal children's drawing.

I laugh. 'That's brilliant.'

'I caught it at the exact moment that he stepped out to

stop the traffic. When the rainbow was at its brightest. Just as the sun and the rain were at the right angle to one another. It's only because the land's so flat here I could catch the whole arc of the rainbow. But what does it say to you?'

'It says happiness. It says innocence. It says synchronicity.'

'Exactly.'

'It's a great photo, Saul.'

'I know. And I've heard about this arts college where you don't have to do A levels – you can do photography B Tech. Mr Bell says this could win a prize. He says to put it in my portfolio and he's pretty sure I'll get in.'

It's the first time I've seen Saul enthused about anything in months. Enthused by a photo that speaks to him of childhood, of innocence. Of nostalgia for simpler times. Because he's still a child at heart. *I rest my case*, I whisper, inwardly.

I refrain from telling him he's capable of doing A levels, that he could do English literature – look at the way he's taken to John Donne. Saul hates school and anything that excites him must be encouraged. I wipe my hands on a tea towel, hug him, marvelling again that I have to widen my arms to get them round him, noticing the breadth of him, the fine bones, the way he is so thin even while he's got so tall, so broad. And he hugs me back. It's something that has surprised me about having a teenage son, that he can still be demonstrative with me. He still shows affection when he's at ease, when he's happy.

'All I've got to do is apply. I can start my life at last.'

'I'm thrilled for you, Saul.'

I look up at him, at the little boy's grin under the curtain of hair over his spotty face.

'Saul . . .' I rinse the mop. Return it to the cupboard.

I have to get this business out of the way, so that he can

indeed start his life, as he puts it. I fold my arms, lean against the work surface. 'Jules came to see me today.'

I wait for a response.

'Oh?'

'I just want to ask you. What did you do the night you came with me to Jules's? The night she and I went out?'

'What d'you mean?'

He's taken two slices of bread and is piling a selection of fillings onto them. Peanut butter, cheese, avocado, grapes. He takes a jar of chilli flakes and sprinkles them on too.

'Did you talk to Saffie at all?'

'You already asked me that. I didn't see her. She went up to her room after you left.' He puts the second slice of bread on the top and pushes it down. Picks the whole thing up and takes a bite. He turns his back to me.

'So what did you do all evening?'

I sound sharper than I mean to because I'm angry that I'm forced into the position of questioning my own son.

'What is this?' He turns and scowls. 'I was on the internet.'

'You were upstairs when we came in . . .'

'Yeah. When you weren't back by midnight, I began to think I'd be there all night. So I lay down in one of Jules's fuck-off spare rooms. Because you were drinking and I know what you're like when you get wasted.' He gives a kind of half-grin.

'Please,' I say. 'That's a bit harsh.'

'It's true. You get talking; you get drunk and forget the time. So I figured I might as well go to bed. But then you came in.' He takes another mouthful of sandwich.

'You didn't check Saffie had gone to bed as Jules asked you to?'

'Oh yeah, like she'd love it if I checked up on her,' he

says, spraying crumbs. 'She'd really thank me for treating her like a kid. Her light was off around eleven so I left her to it.'

'How do you know? If you didn't check up on her?'

My heart's racing. I'm afraid of catching him out.

'Derr. There was no light shining under her door. What time did you say dinner was ready?'

'As soon as Pete and the girls get in.'

'Cool.'

Saul turns and I hear his feet thump up the stairs.

And I am left none the wiser.

My phone pings the minute Saul's gone. The tweet from the Stag reads, @Hollyseymore hopeyougetraped #feminazi #consentworkshops

I switch off my phone and bang it face down on the counter.

To distract myself until Pete and the girls arrive, I put Leonard Cohen on and pour a glass of chilled white wine. I try to lose myself in his gentle lyrics, remembering how, as students, Jules used to hate his gloom-laden melodies as much as I loved them. I brown meat in the pan, and the aroma of coriander and cumin rise into the kitchen. Should I have pressed Saul further? I wonder. Asked him directly if he'd tried to sleep with Saffie? But he'd have been devastated that I could even entertain such a thing. At last, when I've finished the couscous with a sprinkling of flaked almonds, put a lid on the pan to keep it warm and dumped five forks and plates on the kitchen table, I hear a key in the lock, the familiar thump as the front door bangs back. A blast of cool damp air rushes in, there's the sound of girls' voices, and then the smell of wet coats and the bustle of bodies coming into the kitchen and my heart lifts, warms. I love having the girls over. When Pete and I got married, we converted the attic so they had somewhere to stay; I want them to think of this place as their second home.

Thea, only ten, puts her arms round me and I kiss the top of her head, her cool, silky black hair catching in my mouth as I do so. Freya, thirteen, lets me give her parka-clad figure a hug, blotting my pale grey cardigan with raindrops. She takes off her coat and flings it on the back of a chair. Pete comes over to me, kisses me on the cheek, his lips lingering a little longer than necessary while his hand rests for a moment on the small of my back and moves downwards. A shock of desire bolts through me. I've missed him. A lot.

'Just what I like to see,' he teases. 'A good woman at the stove. Getting the tea on the table.'

I smile.

He squeezes me to him. 'It's been a hell of a week. I would've cooked, of course, if I could've got back earlier.'

'Your turn tomorrow, honey!' I say, my stomach churning. How am I going to tell him what Jules has dumped on me? He gives a brief look that says he's in the mood for sex later. I wish I could return it as I usually would, that we could share that delicious complicity that makes our relationship work so well.

'Fucking hell. It's mingin' in here!' Saul's come down again at the sound of voices. 'Smells like a brothel.'

'Saul!'

'It does. It's contaminating the dinner. Who're you trying to pull, Freya?' He looms over his stepsister and cuffs her on the head. Freya blushes and backs away from him. Thea tugs at Saul's long hair and he grabs her, making her cry out, squealing with delight at the same time.

'You smell delicious,' I reassure Freya. 'What is it?'

'It's Juicy Couture,' she says, blushing again. 'Mum bought it for me.' Freya's come over to the cooker and is lifting lids, peering into the pans. She's the same age as Saffie, but nowhere near as developed, her frame still boyish beneath her short T-shirt and high-waisted jeans. She's got tall lately, and has started to wear mascara, but she's still more child than adolescent, gawky and awkward. The thought of a child her age having sex – even willingly – is abhorrent. I shudder inwardly and put my arm round her.

'It's lovely,' I say, though the tropical-fruit notes are overpowering.

'Have you told Pete about your course?' I ask Saul, who is slumped at the table.

'What's that?' Pete asks.

'It's a B Tech arts course I'm applying for. You can do photography.'

'Sounds good. I'd like to hear more about it. Meanwhile, guess what, mate?' Pete prises the lid off a bottle of beer. He nods at it. 'Have some.'

'Cheers, Pete.'

'I got us tickets to go and see Slaves at the Forum in March.'

Saul's face lights up. 'Sick!'

'Thought you'd be made up.'

Pete grins and his rosy cheeks fill out and his eyes crinkle. His delight in pleasing Saul is one of the first things that made me love him. Right now, it makes me love him all the more. We'll sort this thing between us. I know we will.

'I should have thirty quid by tomorrow night so I can pay for the tickets.' Saul sloshes some of Pete's beer into his glass as he sits down at the table.

'How come?' Freya says. 'You never have any money.'

''Cos I've got a job. At Jules's shop. Starting tomorrow.'

I put a hand on the kitchen counter to steady myself, while Saul, blithely unaware, continues. 'Why do you think

I'm getting up at eight on a Saturday morning? Which reminds me. I need a lift into town in the morning. I've got to be there by nine.'

'Saul.' I wipe my hands on the tea towel. 'I forgot to say. Jules is sorry but she made a staffing error. She can't take you on after all. I'm so sorry.'

'Really? Shit.'

'I know. But you'll find something else . . .'

'Not so loaded after all,' Freya quips, and Saul pulls a face at her.

'At least I won't have to get up early on a Saturday,' he says.

'You don't mind?' I ask, anxious.

'Only about the money.'

'You don't mind forgoing invaluable experience selling booties and Babygros?' Pete says. Saul flushes and grins at Pete. 'You don't have to pay for the ticket anyway. It's my treat.'

'You would never have been up in time,' Thea says to Saul. 'You're a lazy slob.'

Saul gets up and chases her, screaming, out of the room, and Freya follows.

I pour Pete a glass of wine. He sits at the kitchen table and flicks through his mail.

I catch another waft of Freya's perfume and realize that its effect on me isn't because it's so powerful, it's that I've smelled it before. It has uncomfortable associations. The last time I smelled it was at Jules's house when Saffie came downstairs. She was wearing it the night she says my son raped her. Saffie and Freya are friends. It's understandable they would want the same perfume at their age. But now I wonder what they talk about to each other. I wonder what Freya says to Saffie about Saul. Or, more pertinently, what

Saffie says to Freya. I wonder if Saffie's rape allegation might become the stuff of school gossip.

'Are you OK?' Pete asks, looking up. 'You look upset.'

'I'll tell you later,' I say.

*

After supper, when the children have dispersed to their rooms, there's a ping on my phone. I find it lying beside the cooker where I slammed it down earlier. It's a tweet.

@Hollyseymore bitchwhodeservesraping #feminazi

'Oh,' I say out loud.

'What's up?'

'Nothing.' I put my hand over the screen.

'What is it?' Pete frowns. 'Are they still trolling you? Holly? You have to tell me. Let me see.'

I hand him the phone.

'Bloody hell,' he says.

The phone pings again. This time, the tweet reads, @Hollyseymore likesitrough #feminazi

Pete reads it, then drops my phone onto the table.

'This is going too far,' he says. 'Who is it?'

Freya comes into the kitchen then, asking where her headphones are, followed by Thea complaining that Freya won't play with her. She's shut herself in their room to listen to music. So Pete and I are in our bedroom before we find a moment alone.

I sit on the edge of the bed. He reaches out to me and I get the little electric pulse his touch always arouses in me. But I lift his hand, place it back on the duvet. 'I've been trying to deal with this on my own. But I can't.'

Foolishly I find I'm close to tears again. What's wrong with me? I'm not usually prone to crying. But since Jules's visit, and her allegation, the tears have been poised, ready to fall. I try to get the words out.

'Come here,' Pete says, his hand on my shoulder now, pulling me down towards him.

I swing my legs under the covers and snuggle into him.

'I don't blame you for feeling upset,' he says. 'It's really nasty, this trolling stuff. Perhaps you should stop attending those consent discussions?'

'I can't,' I say. 'They're important. The students can't run them on their own. But anyway, Pete, that's not why I'm upset. It's something else. Worse.' I shut my eyes. 'I wanted to sort this out with Jules, but it seems as if Jules has got it in for Saul. That's what's upsetting me more than anything. That she can believe such things about him.'

'Hey, hey. Slow down. I'm confused here. One thing at a time.'

I take a deep breath and turn onto my side so I'm facing Pete.

'Two weeks ago while Jules and I were out, Saul went round to use her internet. And Saffie says . . . I want you to know I don't believe her, before I go on . . .'

'What does she say?' Pete asks.

I look into Pete's soft grey-green eyes, trying to gauge his possible reaction. He's the best listener. It's what I was so attracted to when I first met him at Jules and Rowan's. When I found I could talk and talk to him and he would never look bored. Even when I regaled him with my concerns about Saul, my mixed feelings about leaving London, he would just nod and go on listening. He doesn't judge. He doesn't react. And so I can tell him.

'Saffie says Saul raped her.'

Pete flings the duvet back. Sits up. 'She *what*? Whoa . . . hang on a minute,' he says. 'That's a very serious allegation.'

'I know. You know. Jules knows. I just don't think Saffie understands how serious it is.'

Pete asks me to tell him all the details. I dredge up everything Jules told me again, including Saul, allegedly, saying she was 'asking for it'.

At last, Pete sighs and says, 'And you think it's a lie?'

'Pete! How can you even ask that? Of course it's a lie. I just can't work out *why* she's lying. Saffie's known Saul all her life. I'm her godmother. Why would she say a thing like that about Saul when they used to play together as kids, for goodness' sake? They were like brother and sister. I don't understand why she would turn on him like this.'

'You've asked Saul? Whether something happened between them?'

I swallow and look at Pete. 'I tried. I probed.'

'You probed?' Pete straightens up. 'You have to ask him outright, Holly. You have to check every last detail against what Saffie's said.'

'I can't tell him she's accused him of rape. It will devastate him.'

'You're overprotecting him again, Holl. You have to be upfront with him.'

'No, I don't. Not with him as he is at the moment. When the bullying only stopped a while ago. He's still so alone here. He'll be gutted to know something so heinous has been said about him. Especially since it's Saffie who's said it. It will destroy him.'

'If he's got nothing to hide, he can tell us, and we can get to the bottom of it.'

I put my face in my hands.

'Saffie gave Jules intimate details,' I say through my fingers. 'She's made it sound very plausible. She's not going to retract it now.'

'Fuck.'

'But it isn't true. Saul was on the internet all that evening. Besides, he's never had a sexual relationship with anyone. And when he does, he'll respect them. He lives with me, for goodness' sake. Saul knows better than anyone about sex, love, mutual affection. He just would not do this.'

I pause. Have I ever had the 'sex' talk other mums refer to? Or have I skirted round it, assuming that my son would have picked up all he needs to know by virtue of living with me? Because I've discussed my consent sessions with Pete over dinner?

'Why would Saffie tell such a blatant lie?' Pete asks.

I shrug. 'She's been acting out lately. Who knows?'

Pete and I both fall silent for a while. Then Pete says, 'Bloody hell. This is crap.'

'I know.'

I look across at him, sitting up in bed, his face impossible to read.

'Pete, I need to know you don't believe Saffie, do you?'

His expression shifts, from perplexity to helplessness.

'I can't imagine Saul has it in him, no,' he says at last. 'Of course I can't. But it's such an outrageous accusation. What on earth has triggered it?'

The sense I get when I look at Pete is of a vast sinkhole opening up under the ground, which I had only recently begun to believe could feel solid and safe again.

*

I lie awake, only falling into sleep towards dawn. When I open my eyes, it's eight. There's a smell of coffee drifting up from the kitchen and of batter frying. I push back the duvet, grab a dressing gown and go downstairs.

Pete's girls are dressed, eating pancakes at the kitchen table.

'Isn't it a little early for you to be up on a Saturday morning?' I ask, filling the kettle. 'You haven't got ballet this morning, have you, Thea? And you've finished your exams, Freya. You could both have had a lie-in.'

The windows are steamed up with condensation from the warm kitchen. It's cold outside. I rub a clear patch in the misted window. Frost glistens on the grass and on the rose bushes and branches of the apple tree in our small, tattered garden. Yellow windfalls lie all over the grass. I've forgotten to collect them and they're beginning to rot.

'We're going to Mum's,' Freya says.

I stop and turn and look at them. 'But it's your weekend here,' I say. 'What do you mean you're going to Deepa's?'

'Dad's idea,' Freya shrugs.

Pete comes into the kitchen from outside. He's fully dressed in jeans and his outdoor jacket.

'What's happening, Pete?' I ask. 'It's the girls' weekend here.'

'Ah. Just been scraping the car. There's a frost. Deepa's asked if they could go over there. Her dad's made a surprise visit from Delhi. He arrived late last night, and she texted early this morning saying she wants them to see their grandpa. You don't mind, do you? You didn't have any plans for them?'

I shake my head. Though I have. Of course I have. I always make plans the weekends they're here. 'Nothing special. It's just . . . I was looking forward to spending time with you girls. Thought we could have had a pizza and a film tonight.'

My stomach's churning. The conversation Pete and I had the night before haunts me.

'Aww. That would have been so nice,' Thea's saying. 'Do we have to see Grandpa, Dad?'

'Thea, shush,' says Freya. 'Mum wants us to go. You'll hurt her feelings if we don't.'

'But we're hurting Holly's feelings by *going*,' Thea says.

'It's fine.' I run the back of a finger down her cheek. 'I'm not hurt, darling, just surprised. I didn't realize he was coming this weekend.'

'It was unexpected,' Pete replies. 'Deepa sends her apologies. For the short notice. Come on, girls, eat up. Grandpa's only there for a short time and he wants to make the most of it.'

Before I know it, it seems, they are up off their chairs, pulling coats on, grabbing their weekend bags and Pete is hustling them out of the door.

Pete turns to me as they get into the car. 'We'll talk later.'

'Are you spending the day with Deepa's father as well?'

I don't mean to sound upset. We have, so far, managed to remain civil about our blended family. I tolerate Pete spending family holidays with Deepa and the girls, and Deepa tolerates us having the girls every other weekend at our house. She let them spend last Christmas with us, only the second since Pete and I got together. And I accept that there are times when they prefer to stay at hers, that it should be the girls' choice, especially when there's a family occasion like this one. But Pete has agreed to talk with me about Saul once he's had a chance to process what I've told him. It now looks as though I'm going to be tormenting myself all day alone.

'I'll stay for a bit. Then I thought I'd pop to the library in town and catch up on my assignment, but I'll be back this evening,' Pete says. He grabs my collar, pulls me to him and kisses me quickly on the lips. 'Love you,' he says. Then he turns and walks out to his car, and I watch him pull out into the road and drive away, the girls in the back.

I clear up the suddenly vacant kitchen, the plates, a mug of coffee half drunk, the pancake pan still smouldering.

'Where is everyone?' Saul comes in, grabs the cafetière and pours himself a mug of coffee.

'Pete's taken the girls over to see their grandfather. He's made a surprise visit. D'you want a pancake? There's plenty of mixture left over.'

I make the pancakes and he scoffs two with bacon and maple syrup in quick succession, then stands up and says he's going to cycle down the river and take some photos.

'Really?'

'I want to capture the landscape in this frost. And anyway, I need to get some exercise. I spend too much time sitting around.'

'That's true,' I tease. 'It just seems a bit out of character. You could've had a longer lie-in since you're not working after all.'

'I need to get out.'

'Well, wrap up warm,' I say pointlessly as I watch him set off.

It's a mixed blessing having a house that overlooks the green where I can see Saul's comings and goings. I can't stop myself going to the front window in the sitting room, observing his lanky stance as he bends over his bike to pump up the tyres. The solitary figure he makes as he pedals away, in his trackie bottoms and with his beanie pulled down over his brow. I wonder if this sudden display of energy is a sign of enthusiasm for the future, now he's found his photography course. Or whether he has something on his conscience.

I stay and stare out of the window when he's gone. The

grass on the green glistens with frost, and the trunks of the trees are more like pieces of industrial scaffolding than anything natural, shiny grey, their leaves frozen and etched in white. The windows in the yellowish Cambridgeshire brick houses opposite are dark. On the other side, where the new estate begins, cars, their windows made opaque by the ice, are a sign that the commuting contingent of the village has returned for the weekend. At last I turn from the window and have to stop myself from ringing Jules. Saturday is when she persuades me – the reluctant jogger – to do the park run with her. I miss her morning call, her insistence I will feel better after it, the coffees we would have had in the cafe to reward ourselves. I wonder if she's missing me too.

Jules and I have barely ever gone more than two days without speaking to one another. On holiday with Archie and Saul once, in Scotland, where there was no mobile signal, we wrote to each other. Long, handwritten letters, sent in envelopes with proper stamps. Jules has been my sounding board for almost every thought I've had over the last twenty years, and, as far as I know, I am hers. Yet the things that were said yesterday in London, in my office, have driven a wedge between us and it feels unbearable.

*

Before I know it, I'm upstairs, pushing open Saul's bedroom door. My compulsion to search for clues comes from the same source I imagine a wife might feel when she's been told by a 'well-wisher' that her husband is having an affair. She might not believe it, she might not *want* to find evidence that will prove her worst fears, but she is driven to search his wallet, his pockets, to scrutinize receipts, bank statements, texts, emails. It's more a search for disproof than proof. I'm searching Saul's room to find evidence that Saffie lied. Or perhaps what I'm really looking for is clues as to who my son *is* these days. He's moving away from me as he reaches his mid-teens, which is absolutely, as Pete says, as it should be. But he's still my son. He is still, deep down inside, the boy I gave birth to, nurtured, treasured and brought up on my own since he was ten. I need to know who this person is becoming. The person for whom I would lay down my life.

The surfaces in Saul's room are thick with a silvery layer of dust you can write your name in. I haven't cleaned it in weeks. But Saul's tidy for a teenage boy. I've heard other people describe their sons' bedrooms as pits or dumps or festering holes. Saul's room is organized, his schoolbooks lined up on his desk, his vinyl and CDs neatly stacked on shelf units, his clothes put away in drawers. There are posters on his walls, pictures of Kurt Cobain, with whom he has developed a fascination, and of contemporary bands, tickets from concerts he went to in London before we moved. There's a pile of photography magazines next to the bed. And a book of John Donne's writings. The collection I left in the loo.

Saul's computer is an old one Pete gave him when he replaced his. I try to log on, punching in the password Pete always used: Arsenal 2014. Nothing happens. I try a few other ideas but get the same response: 'The password you have used has not been recognized.'

It doesn't surprise me. Any self-respecting teenager would change their password. I give up on the computer and look at his fitted cupboard, with its drawers and compartments. These days, I usually toss dry washing onto his bed for him to put away himself and never go near his cupboard. I find it touching that he's this organized when I've never taught him to be so. And am not like that myself. His boxers have been folded up and stashed in lines, and his socks are balled and kept in a separate drawer. He has a bigger drawer beneath this where he has folded his T-shirts and hoodies. I lift them and put them to my nose to smell the washing powder I've used on them since he was a little boy.

The scent conjures days we spent together in our London house after Archie died, Saul curled up next to me, grounding me when everything felt as if it was disintegrating, when nothing felt safe anymore. He used to smooth the two lines he said I had on my brow. He was always checking in those days whether I was all right. Always ensuring I was smiling or laughing. Have I been too dependent on Saul? Did I lean too heavily on him? Is he finally trying to make a break from me?

Then I pull out the biggest, bottom drawer and stop, shocked. There's a tub of protein powder and a pair of dumb-bells. Saul's never been the kind of boy who worries about his body shape. Of course, though, it isn't just girls who are under pressure to look a certain way these days. Boys are bombarded by images of men with six-packs and biceps and waxed, bronzed torsos. If Saul has been worrying about what he looks like, I had no idea! Is this behind his sudden interest in cycling? Is he trying harder to fit in than I realized? Should I have been more aware, got him a gym membership, encouraged him to join the sports events all the local boys participate in?

I never realized my son had this side. But why did he feel he had to hide it from me? I rifle through the smaller drawers. Halfway through his carefully folded pile of T-shirts, I stop. There's a tiny plastic bag containing what looks like weed. I open it and recognize the distinctive smell that sends me rocketing back to my student days. Rich and vegetal and heady. A wave of heat washes over me. My heart races, thumping against my chest. My son does have a life I know nothing about.

I tuck the packet back between the T-shirts. Then, my heart galloping, I continue to look about his room. I've given him his own laundry basket, and rummaging through it now, I spot the grey lambswool jumper he was wearing the night he came with me to Jules's. I remember the little flicker of pride I'd had that he was, beneath his hunched and uncoordinated self, going to be handsome just like Archie. I put the jumper instinctively to my nose and breathe in. It's there. The unmistakable sugary fragrance that Saffie was wearing the night we left them together. Juicy Couture. I close my eyes, feeling my pulse quicken.

I rummage faster through his drawers. I shouldn't be surprised that my teenage son has pornographic images ripped out of men's mags enclosed between the pages of one of his school textbooks. Jules would have said, before all this, that I should have been surprised if he hadn't. Jules is, and always was, by far the more open-minded of the two of us when it comes to anything to do with sex. It's nothing too hardcore. But it's porn none the less. And I *am* surprised. I'm disturbed and angry with myself for opening a Pandora's box and coming face to face with things I have refused to see about my own son. Then I look at his iPad. The screen reveals he's been playing things on iTunes, and when I click on the icon, the song that comes up and hits me in the face is a Nirvana song and it's called 'Rape Me'.

4

JULES

Lying sleepless next to her husband's hefty form the night after Saffie's revelation, Jules could not stop turning over in her mind what her daughter must have gone through.

She found it was like pulling up weeds, thinking you'd got the lot and then realizing they'd thrown out another network of taproots that needed pulling up too. There was Saffie's obvious distress. She hadn't been physically hurt, she said, thank goodness, but the psychological damage could be irreparable. Then there was the possible pregnancy. And who could say whether Saul had already been sleeping around? They all assumed he was a loner and there was no way he had a girlfriend, or a boyfriend, but who knew? Rowan thought Saul took drugs. Saul might have been out there, stoned and shagging at festivals. He might carry all manner of STDs and have no idea – many of them had no symptoms.

Jules was out of touch with the world of sexual risk-taking. It threw into relief how very monogamous and sensible her relationship with Rowan had been for the last twenty years. Apart from one minor dalliance she'd worked hard to forget. Now she was going to have to inform herself, and fast. Should she take Saffie to a clinic for tests?

Jules turned onto her side and tried to sleep. But sleep wouldn't come. She sat up and looked at Rowan, who continued to snooze, blissfully oblivious. She got up and went to the kitchen. Made herself a camomile tea. She sat at the counter, drinking it, hoping it would induce drowsiness, but it had no effect. She went back upstairs, opened Saffie's bedroom door to check on her. She was asleep. Jules got back into bed and lay on her back, staring at the ceiling. They should have done the pregnancy test straight away, and got help if it was positive, even if Saffie was, understandably, terrified of the result. It was too bad it was now the weekend and that Donna Browne was away until next Friday.

Then she thought of Holly and what this must feel like for her. Something was going horribly wrong with Saul to make him think he could assault Saffie and get away with it, although presumably he didn't think of it as rape. Holly had mentioned her concerns that he didn't fit in that night on the way to the pub. But it was clear his problems ran way deeper than that. Holly had always been very close to Saul. Closeness between a mother and son could be a good thing in theory, but with Holly it was different. There had been an almost Oedipal feeling at times. Had it been at the expense of allowing Saul to develop a natural and healthy interest in girls? To read the signals they were actually giving him? Had he suppressed all his instinctive sexuality to please Holly, so that now it was popping out in this perverse and predatory way? These thoughts raced through Jules's mind until at last, when she could see the first blue light splitting the dark clouds over the fens across the river, and her eyes felt dry from lack of rest, her clock told her it was half past seven.

Unable to lie still, Jules got up, pulled on her pink body warmer, Lycra leggings and trainers, and tucked her phone into her iPod sleeve.

Rowan stirred, looking at her fondly from their king-sized bed as she prepared herself.

'Where are you off to?'

'Thought I'd do the park run. I'll nip to the supermarket first, get some stuff for breakfast.'

'Rather you than me this morning,' he said. 'Looks freezing out there.'

'You're a pathetic fair-weather runner,' Jules said. 'It's best when it's cold. It's invigorating and it makes you run faster. Tea or coffee before I go?'

'Shame you can't persuade Saff to come with you,' Rowan said. 'She could do with losing a little weight.'

'Please. Don't let her hear you say that.' Jules tucked her hair into her sweatband. 'I don't want her developing body dysmorphia. Her weight's not a problem, Rowan. She's just growing up.'

'You taking Holly?'

She could see Rowan in the mirror. He'd sat up now and was flicking through the catalogue for pool accessories he kept by the bed. They would have a fully constructed self-cleaning swimming pool by next summer. He'd been made redundant a few months ago and Jules had worried about going ahead with it, but Rowan insisted there was no way he was changing his lifestyle just because he'd been given the heave-ho by his company. That he didn't intend to be out of work for long. There was no hint that he was concerned about his daughter apart from the comment on her weight, which Jules believed was an inability to accept that Saffie had developed hips and breasts and was becoming a woman. Which he couldn't fail to have noticed each time he sat her on his lap in front of the TV.

'Holly's not coming this week.'

'Given up, has she?'

'Don't know. She's probably had a stressful week at work.'

'She still got that Twitter troll?'

'I . . . Not sure.'

'She brought that upon herself, if you ask me,' Rowan said. 'She should keep her views to herself instead of ranting all over the internet.'

'If her troll had bothered to read her article, he would have seen her concerns are as much to protect men as women.' Despite everything, Jules's instinct was to stick up for Holly.

'My point is, she gets men's backs up with all her feminist clap-crap.'

'Rowan, that's unfair.'

Jules felt her stomach churn. He had no idea. She wanted to tell him that she and Holly had fallen out, but was afraid to. Even without knowing the details, he would say, 'I told you so. You and she are polar opposites.'

Rowan and Holly were civil to one another, but Rowan had never understood Jules's friendship with her. He always said Holly was too earnest by half, and that Jules put her on a pedestal just because she worked in a university and had been published in the papers. He mocked Holly when she got on her high horse about women's rights, joking with Jules behind her back that it was men who needed rights when Holly was around. Rowan didn't have much time for Pete either, despite the fact that it was because of him that he and Holly had met in the first place: Saffie was close friends with Freya, and after Pete and Deepa had split up, Rowan had introduced Pete to Holly at one of their summer parties.

'Poor old Holly,' Rowan had quipped when he heard they'd become an item, 'to have lost Archie and found Pete!'

Archie, too, had been quite different from Rowan, but he at least had the kudos – in Rowan's eyes – of being a dashing

London lawyer from a North London intellectual background. He and Rowan had got on in a man-to-man mutual-respect kind of way, able to pass the time talking about cricket even if they had different outlooks on politics, the economy, the world. Pete, in stark contrast to Archie, was overweight and sedentary. A couch potato compared to Rowan and the other menfolk around here, who were all into cycling, golf, cricket and football. Holly had smiled when Jules asked what sport Pete did and admitted she didn't think he moved many muscles apart from his facial ones. 'Even those he keeps still half the time!' she had laughed. 'It's a requirement in his work.'

Pete had no drive, no ambition, according to Rowan. And in addition to that, he was the worst sort of woolly liberal. Pete wasn't the kind of guy Jules would have put Holly with either. Archie had been tall, handsome and cultured, while Pete was short, rounded and unsophisticated. He had a kind face, but he wasn't what you could call good-looking by any stretch of the imagination. Rowan was right, Jules had thought – Pete wasn't a substitute for Archie. However, he was gentle-natured and unassuming, which would, Jules supposed, be good for Holly, especially as she had been so raw, so thin-skinned ever since she'd been widowed. And at least Holly wasn't lonely anymore. She had been distraught with loneliness in the years after Archie died. Besides, Holly clearly adored Pete, as he did her.

*

Jules did the supermarket shop in a daze, piling things into the trolley without much attention. It was a quarter to nine by the time she got back into her shiny new Fiat, bought since she had franchised her children's clothing brand, and set off towards the country park.

Now Jules wondered if she should have told Rowan straight away about the rape. Having a daughter who was growing up meant she was entering uncharted territory where her loyalties were bound to be divided at times. But was it fair to keep from Rowan something he would argue he had the right to know? Keeping secrets from him felt counterintuitive. Jules and he shared everything (well, almost everything. He would never know, *must* never know, about her affair with Rob) and always had done since they met at a ball at uni all those years ago. But Saffie had begged Jules not to tell her dad, and she had to respect her daughter's wish. Didn't she? What if he were to find out anyway? He would never forgive Jules for remaining silent. As a devoted father (and he was almost overly devoted to Saffie, if such a thing were possible, Jules thought), he had a right to know his daughter had undergone an assault. Saffie, with her distressed pleas, had placed Jules in an impossible position.

At the park, Jules left her car and walked across the mud to the starter line. She usually loved the convivial atmosphere here. Everyone was out with their families or dogs, chatting and in a good mood. Jules had a pang of nostalgia for the days when Saffie had come with her, before she started secondary school.

It was cold this morning. There was frost in some places, a fragile layer of ice over some of the puddles. A wind had got up, which shook the smaller leaves from the trees. Jules was positioning herself near the thirty-minute marker (though her aim was to get her time down to under twenty-five) when she spotted Saul on his bike. He was impossible to miss over the heads of the families. He had his ear buds in and wore a beanie, and his skinny frame was exaggerated by the trackie bottoms he wore as he pedalled past the runners gathering at the edge of the track. It gave her a sick feeling in her stomach to see him. Cycling past so nonchalantly after what he had done to her daughter and all he had left her to sort out. Jules felt a mixture of emotions bubble through her. Rage and upset and indignation and . . . bewilderment. She hadn't doubted Saffie for a minute. And yet for a second, as she watched him, her old affection rose to the surface and for the first time she wondered, Could he really have *raped* Saffie? Was it possible, rather, that they were seeing one another? That they'd taken the opportunity to use the empty house to have sex, and that Saffie had panicked when her period was late, not wanting her friends to know . . . but then Jules remembered Saffie's violent objection when she told her Saul was coming round to use their internet, calling him a creep. Hardly the response of a girl in love. Doubts flooded her again.

Jules realized she had no idea really what kind of person Saul had become these days. She had the urge to approach him, to question him herself since she guessed Holly hadn't done so, judging by his nonchalant demeanour.

'Jules?' She turned. Tess was coming across the park towards her, flanked by her two daughters.

'How are you?' Tess said, drawing alongside her.

'Good, thanks,' Jules lied.

'I'm going for a personal best,' Tess said. 'How about you?'

'Just wanted to get out, to be honest,' Jules said. 'I'm going to take it easy.'

The starter whistle blew. Jules looked around. Saul had vanished.

'See you at the end,' Tess said.

Jules was trembling with pent-up feeling as she began her run. She put on her playlist, told herself the exercise would help. A flock of ducks took off from the lake as Jules

rounded the corner and set off down the track past industrial storage units. The problem was, she'd known Saul since
he first slithered into the world.

She relived the day she had gone with Holly to the mater-
nity unit to help her friend give birth to him. Archie, unlike
most men around that time, had expressed a desire not to
be at the birth. Holly had been upset. Jules had convinced
Holly she ought to forgive Archie; after all, it was only in
the last generation it had become the norm for men to
attend the births of their children.

'Better that he recognizes his limitations than forces himself through some spurious sense of what it is to be a "new
man", to attend something he won't be able to cope with,'
Jules had said to Holly.

'So it means I'll be all alone,' Holly had said. 'I'm frightened, Jules. I don't want to give birth alone.'

'I could be there,' Jules had said, and Holly had looked
at her with gratitude and said, 'Oh, Jules. I hoped you'd say
that. I didn't want to ask, in case you felt obliged. If you
really want to, I'd so appreciate it.'

They'd prepared the birth plan together, the three of
them, Jules, Holly and Archie. Jules had read up about natural childbirth techniques and how to support a mother in
labour. They joked that she had become more excited than
the actual parents about the whole event. And Jules had
been unprepared for how moving she would find it. How
much love she would feel for her friend's newborn baby. The
midwife had wrapped his hot, vernix-streaked body in a
towel and put him straight into Jules's arms while she dealt
with the umbilical cord and then the placenta, and Jules
remembered the amazement she had felt as his bluish skin
turned pink, at how *alive* he had felt, how warm and wet
and light. And squirming. And real. He had eyes that peered

quizzically into hers. He had a little red mouth that was moist when he opened it. He smelled of newly risen bread. She had fallen for Saul before his own mother held him. It was Saul who had convinced her to have a child of her own. She had really felt love for that newborn baby.

But babies change. And it was hard for anyone to accept that one's beautiful newborn would turn out differently from what you had in mind when they were a blank slate, an unformed piece of human Play-Doh for you to shape. Which, anyway, was a misconception. You couldn't mould your child. Did what you fed and read and said make any fundamental difference in the end? Coercing and rewarding Saffie for going to extra lessons would never make her *Child Genius* material, however much Rowan would like it. Nurture, Jules now believed, was just one small part of the process of creating a human being, and even that was a random stab in the dark. The secret was to accept your child, to encourage their strengths, not to force them into a shape they weren't ever going to fit.

They had their own personalities from the word go. You had to let them be who they were. You could steer them, or try to. You could guide them and rein them in and do your best to set an example. But if what you got was a long way from what you hoped, if, on the way, something you unconsciously said or did, or some quirk of genetic material hidden way back in the ancestral DNA meant you produced a psychopath, or a terrorist, or a rapist, well, wasn't your role then to deal with it? Not to put your head in the sand and deny it? As Holly was doing with Saul?

Saul *had* been a gentle, quiet young soul, easily humoured and unusually thoughtful for a little kid. She and Holly had always managed to distract him when he headed for a two-year-old tantrum simply by getting down to his eye level and pulling funny faces. Once, when Jules had gone to see Holly in tears about another failed pregnancy, Saul had brought the baby doll he had been playing with (Holly had always insisted he should have dolls) and placed it in her lap, as if he knew. He couldn't have been more than two then, but he had a kind of intuition. He was by nature very sensitive, very thoughtful. And had continued to be so throughout his boyhood. Always the quiet one, always happy to play alone. But with moments of uncanny perception, in which he revealed an awareness that was beyond his years. Could he have changed so dramatically now he was a teenager?

Jules's playlist finished and she flicked her music onto shuffle. James Taylor began to sing 'You've Got a Friend' – one of Holly's favourite's. The irony, Jules thought. Holly was the most sympathetic friend Jules had ever had, but there was a side of her Jules had not experienced first-hand yet. And that was the side that closed off completely when she was affronted. Holly was estranged from her older sister, Suzie. They had fallen out years ago over something Suzie had said about Archie after he died. Holly had never forgiven Suzie. Her sister and their mother now lived in close proximity in Glasgow, and Holly visited them rarely. So Jules knew Holly had it in her to cut people off when she felt she had been wronged.

And yet . . . Holly grounded Jules whenever things with Rowan got rocky. Without Holly, Jules would be alone next time Rowan had one of his outbursts. Holly was the only person Jules could turn to when Rowan got angry. She didn't want the rest of the village to know the darker side of her affable husband whom everybody loved. Only Holly knew about it. Holly understood that it was a tender part of Rowan that occasionally got inflamed. It was not his core. Holly had always reminded Jules of this, whenever she'd been on the verge of giving up on him. Jules had some-times wondered over the years who she needed more, her husband or her friend. Now, though, she knew the things that were said in Holly's office meant she was at risk of losing her forever.

Jules had been so busy turning these thoughts over in her mind, she finished her run almost without noticing it, and looked around. She had her barcode scanned, dropped her finish tab in the bucket and went to grab a bottle of water from the cafe. Tess was there with her daughters, Gemma and Daniela. Rowan's words about Saffie rang in her ears: *She could do with losing a little weight.* How was it some people found parenting so effortless? Gemma and Daniela were happy to continue to do the park run with their mum even now they were thirteen and fifteen. They were the stars in every school concert or play; they got A grades in every exam; they were both naturally beautiful.

'Hi, Jules,' Gemma cried out now. 'How did you do?'

And they were nice with it.

Jules thought of Saffie spending all those hours practising in the mirror with her make-up and hair straighteners. Her daughter had no confidence in her own natural beauty. She felt tears rise again, anguish at what Saffie was going through as she became a woman. *Had* her daughter been courting the attention of boys? In which case could Saul be blamed for believing she was flirting with him? Of course it didn't excuse what he'd done. But did she need to give Saffie a talking-to about messages she might inadvertently be giving out? It was all so difficult. Was it her and Rowan's fault, after all, that Saffie thought it OK to dress as she did? With those short skirts she'd taken to wearing to school and her shirt buttons undone? Saffie did dress sexily, but it was hard in a way *not* to with her figure. Jules had been the same. Rowan had always admired Jules's buxom, hourglass figure. And as a young girl, Jules had enjoyed the attention it seemed to afford her. She'd liked wearing tight-fitting T-shirts and skimpy dresses and getting appreciative looks from men. She still did. It was a woman's right to dress as she pleased. But it would be so much easier to have daughters like Tess's who were happy in their own skin, who didn't bother with make-up or balcony bras. Who were more interested in their personal bests and their piano exams than in how they looked.

Jules felt fury sear through her at what Saul had done to her daughter, but also to *her*, to her confidence in her parenting skills. She wished she'd gone over when she'd spotted him earlier on his bike. She imagined taking him by the shoulders and shaking him. Telling him he was lucky Saffie didn't want anyone to know. Shouting into his vacant, glazed face. She wanted him to know that *she* knew what he had done, even if no one else did, and that she had the power to take it further. And yet, Jules thought, watching Tess, who was so carefree, while she was having to grapple alone with Saffie's rape claim, Holly and Saul, who had caused all this, had so far suffered no repercussions.

She paid for her bottle of water at the counter and sat down with Tess.

'You look exhausted,' Tess said. 'Are you OK, Jules?'

'Things on my mind,' Jules said. 'Thought the run might perk me up a bit.'

'Before I forget – I was wondering if you're still OK to donate some children's clothes to the Auction of Promises?'

'Sure,' Jules said. 'Yes. I was going to donate some stock from the shop.'

'Where's Saffie?' Gemma asked, arriving at their table. 'She wasn't at school yesterday.'

'She's had a bug. A gastric thing. She's having a lie-in.'

'Shame. It was a good morning for a run.'

'You do look a bit pale, Jules. I hope you're not sickening for it. Do you need something sweet after your run?' Tess asked. 'I've got some Nākd bars in my bag.'

'I'm fine. A little preoccupied but fine.'

Jules was going to tell Rowan, she decided. Not about the possible pregnancy – that would be one piece of information too far – but about the rape. Because Rowan would know how to deal with it. He would express what Jules really felt. He would do what she really wanted to do. Which was to question Saul about what had gone on and make him and Holly suffer at least some of the anguish she and Saffie were experiencing. The run *had* clarified things for her. Rowan needed to know, whether Saffie liked it or not, because Rowan wouldn't just let it wash over him. He would channel all the confusion and hurt and indignation Jules felt, and he would take action.

*

Rowan was up and dressed in black sweatpants, a navy polo shirt and white trainers when Jules got in.

'Jules,' he said, taking mugs from the shelf, 'I was thinking, we should have a big bonfire party in November. We could invite everyone, kids included, get some mega fireworks in, do a few vats of soup, light a brazier. What do you think? If we start planning now, we could have a really big bash. Ask the whole village.'

'Sounds like an idea,' Jules said, her heart thumping.

'Saffie would love it. Get some sparklers, stick some gazebos out there. Ask all her friends. Invite all ours.'

Rowan whistled as he ground coffee in the enormous espresso machine he'd invested in once they'd done the kitchen. Jules was loath to spoil his good mood, but she couldn't carry the turmoil around alone any longer.

'Rowan, is Saff still asleep?'

'Yup. Out for the count when I looked in a while ago.'

'There's something I need to tell you.' Jules found herself speaking before she could stop herself. 'Saffie asked me not to, but I did some thinking while I was running and I've decided you have to know. I've given it careful thought. We have a joint responsibility to deal with this.' She sat down on a bar stool.

Rowan turned round and handed her a coffee.

'Not yet,' she said, pushing it away. 'I'll shower first, thanks. Ro, you have to hear me out.'

'Fire away,' he said, banging the tin jug on the counter so he could pour froth on his cappuccino.

'Don't fly off the handle, though. We need to deal with this calmly and reasonably if we're to get to the bottom of it and take appropriate measures. A couple of weeks ago, while you were away and I was out with my friends, Saul came round. He wanted to use the internet, so I left him here with Saffie.'

'Bloody Nora!'

She glanced at him, but he was joking. He thought that was it. That Jules felt bad just for letting Saul come round to their house. He had no idea what she was about to land on him.

'No, Rowan, that's not it. That's not all.'

'Really?' His expression changed, creases deepening across his forehead. 'Don't tell me,' he said. His cheerful look vanished. 'Don't tell me he offered Saffie some weed?'

'No, Rowan. It's . . . Well, it's worse than that.'

Jules was in too deep to retreat now. She could feel the heat off her husband, could sense his anger brewing. She should have thought about this more carefully. Waited until her response to seeing Saul on his bike just now, followed by Tess's perfect, untroubled daughters, had subsided. Yes, they needed to take some action, but just how far would Rowan want to go? He hadn't had one of his outbursts for quite some time now. He had calmed down a lot since he hit his fortieth birthday. But this was different; this would not elicit a rational response.

'Get it out, then,' Rowan said.

'He ...' She shut her eyes. 'Saff didn't want me to tell you. They had sex. Well, *she* didn't have sex. He did. He ...' She couldn't turn back. 'He ... Well, she says ... Saffie says he raped her.'

Jules didn't know why she put it this way. Why she didn't say, 'Saul raped her,' instead of sounding as if there was some question about it. But telling Rowan now felt so precarious. Something about Saul infuriated him at the best of times. She was afraid she was unleashing something more damaging even than what had already happened, and so she injected an element of doubt into the story.

Rowan put his coffee down on the counter. He turned to face Jules. He balled his hands. His neck began to turn red, and the colour rose slowly, slowly up to his face. Jules drew back. She shouldn't have told him. Saffie hadn't wanted her to. She should have predicted this reaction. As Saffie had done.

'Tell me this isn't true.' Rowan's irises were like pale stones, the pupils retracted to dots.

'Saffie says it is. But we need to be adult about it, Rowan ...'

'Saffie didn't want you to tell me? Why the hell not?'

'I think because she's ashamed. She thinks . . . Well, girls in these cases often think it's – partly – their fault.'

'Jesus Christ.' He began to walk around the kitchen tugging at his hair. 'I am going to get that clueless fucker Saul and beat the shit out of him. I'll cut his balls off. He's going to suffer for this. Oh my Lord, this can't be true.'

'Hang on, Rowan.' Jules's heart was racing. 'I am as upset as you are, and I agree we have to make Saul face the consequences, but we need to approach it carefully. We don't know for sure what happened.'

'We have to tell the police.'

'Saffie doesn't want to involve them.'

'*What?*'

'Rowan, she's really frightened. She thinks they'll quiz her, examine her even – and I think we've got to get her through this one step at a time. She's overwhelmed at the moment.' Jules didn't mention the late period. 'And we shouldn't add to that by pressing her to do something she really doesn't want. It's traumatic enough as it is, and humiliating. She particularly asked me not to report it, and I do think we should respect her wish. For now.'

'Have you told the school? The school should know one of their pupils is a sexual predator.'

'I'm not sure it's a good idea, Rowan. Really, I think it's best we sort this out between ourselves.' Jules was still thinking of Saffie, her plea that Jules told no one. Again she wondered if she was doing the right thing in agreeing not to report it.

Rowan finished circling the kitchen island and came to rest on one of the tall stools, his legs wide apart, his face hidden in his hands. Jules spoke gently to him: 'Saffie doesn't want *anyone* to know. I'm wondering whether it might be better to approach an independent support centre. Rape Crisis or something. Seek some advice from them.'

Rowan took his hands away from his face. 'Rape fucking Crisis? Holly's hobby-horse organization?'

'It isn't. Not anymore. Holly only volunteered for them years ago when she was a student.'

'Fuck that. I'm not having a load of hairy feminazis poking their nose into my daughter's business. How is she?' he asked. 'Did he hurt her? Is she bruised? Is she bleeding? Oh, my poor baby!' He sat down and put his head back in his hands. Was he crying?

Jules moved over to him and put her hand gently on his neck. It felt clammy.

'She's OK,' Jules said. 'She isn't too bad. She's upset, of course, but she's carrying on as normal.'

'And what has Holly said to Saul?' Rowan asked.

'I don't know if she's talked to Saul yet, but—'

'Hang on a minute.' Rowan took his hands away from his face. His pale eyes glittered with tears. 'You're telling me Saul has got off without even a word from his mother?'

'Yes. Well, maybe. I don't know.' Holly's anguished face in her study came back to Jules. Her words. *Saul's not in any state at the moment to have things like this levelled at him.* Jules was pretty certain, too, from Saul's relaxed bearing that morning in the park that Holly hadn't spoken to him about it.

'While Saffie has had her childhood snatched from her? Right. I'm going round there now.'

'Rowan, please.'

'I'll beat the living daylights out of him.'

'Really, that's not the way to deal with it.'

'I'm going to show Holly. All her highfalutin feminist ideals, all that bellyaching about women's rights and she's produced a rapist for a son.' He made a sound that was half laugh, half snort. 'I'm going to punch his lights out. And then I'll deal with Holly.'

'Ro, you need to let yourself simmer down. Remember anger management?'

There was a silence. They rarely referred to the anger management course Rowan had been on several years ago now as a result of punching someone – putting him in hospital – for making a pass at Jules in a pub. Rowan had been cautioned by the police and advised to go on the course. Since then he hadn't had an outburst, though he'd come close a couple of times. Jules remembered the guy who'd said something suggestive about Saffie recently and how angry Rowan had been. She'd been stupid to tell him about Saul, who had done something *so* much worse, and not predict this reaction.

'I need to talk to Saffie.'

'She didn't want you to know. I don't want her to know I've told you . . . Ro!'

'She's my daughter,' he said. 'I'll deal with this as I choose.'

'She's probably still asleep. Please be gentle. She's frightened. She's traumatized. She mustn't be made to feel she's to blame.' *She could be pregnant.* The unspoken words were loud in her ears. Jules had a sense of everything unravelling. She'd promised Saffie she wouldn't tell Rowan and had done precisely that. Saffie would feel betrayed, and as for Rowan – God knows what he might do now he knew.

'Make her feel to blame?' Rowan said. He turned to her. 'It's not the girl who's to blame in these circumstances. As Holly is so quick to point out in the papers. Saffie's been the victim of a sexual assault. I want to tell Saul he's not going near her again. Near any girl if I have my way.'

There was silence for a moment. Then Rowan said he needed a walk to clear his head and that he'd be back later and he went out, slamming the door behind him. The image of the man Rowan had assaulted in the pub for making a lewd comment about her came to Jules's mind again. He'd ended up with a black eye and a broken jaw.

In a panic, Jules picked up the phone and rang Holly.

'Have you spoken to Saul?' she asked. Then, when Holly answered in the negative, 'Please do. Because Rowan knows. She's his daughter, Holly. His thirteen-year-old daughter. Put yourself in his shoes. If you don't do something about Saul, Rowan's threatening to beat the living daylights out of him.'

'That's mature of him.'

It pained Jules to hear her friend's gentle voice expressing sarcasm. It was out of character. But when Holly softened, and pleaded with her to discuss this with her as a friend, Jules replied in the voice she usually reserved for suppliers who were late with deliveries or for customers who hadn't paid her invoices.

'Talk to Saul now. Ask him what happened that night. Say he has to explain himself. Before Rowan honours his word, or calls the police. It's all I can do to stop him. He's not giving up on this. So just do it. And then I suggest you get Saul some psychiatric help. I'm surprised Pete hasn't suggested it already.'

'You're dictating to me how I should deal with my own son?'

Jules paused. She had assumed Holly would, by now, admit she had to confront Saul. Her next words were out of her mouth before she could stop them. 'I wonder if you're refusing to face the fact Saul could be a rapist because of what it'll do to your reputation.'

'What?'

'Your reputation, Holly. At work. As the one who protects women from predatory men.'

After Jules put the phone down, she stood for several minutes, not moving. How had things come to this? She had never, ever spoken to Holly like that. But Rowan's words still rang through her ears. And wasn't Rowan right? Holly was the one who advised on sexual consent at her university. It *was* Holly's job to establish what her son had done. And to deal with it.

*

'How could you do that?'

Saffie had come to the doorway of the home gym in her nightie, her hair mussed up, her eyes pink. She must have overheard her parents arguing, and the slam of the door as Rowan went out. Jules was on her tenth hamstring stretch, trying to calm herself. She had one round of abs and glutes to do, and then planned to get into a hot shower.

'I can't believe you would tell Dad,' Saffie said. The dark rings had deepened under her eyes, and her haunted expression hinted that she hadn't slept well, that she was still suffering the effects of the assault, and the anxiety that she might be pregnant. 'You promised you wouldn't. You went behind my back and you . . . you've let me down. I wish I'd never told you. I can't trust you. I . . .' She was ranting. Her voice reached a hysterical pitch. 'You should *never* have told Dad. I wish I'd never told you now.'

Jules flicked off the soundtrack, wiped her brow and sat down on the sofa next to her daughter.

'Come here, darling. Listen. He's your father. He cares deeply about you. He has a right to know. You must understand that we both want the best for you. We want to protect you.'

'And now he wants to tell the police . . . It's what I was most afraid of. I don't want the police to know . . . I didn't want anyone to know. Except you, and I only told you because my period was late. All I want is to go back to normal.' Saffie was trembling.

'Darling,' Jules said, alarmed by Saffie's level of distress at her father knowing. She seemed even more upset than when she'd first told Jules. 'Calm down. You don't need to get so worked up about this.'

'You promised me.'

Jules sighed. 'I promised I'd do all I could to look after you. Which, after I'd given it some thought, included telling Dad. If you really don't want anyone else involved, then I'll make sure he doesn't take it further. But you have to let us take care of this. You're too young to do so yourself.'

'Dad gets so angry, though,' Saffie muttered.

'Understandably. What's happened is very upsetting.'

They sat quietly for a while until Saffie's breath slowed.

'I wanted *you* to sort it out, Mum,' Saffie said quietly. 'Because you're Holly's friend. I thought you'd tell her you weren't going to invite Saul over anymore. And Holly could teach Saul about the stuff she lectures on, consent and everything. Make him understand when a girl wants sex and when she doesn't. And then you could both be friends again.'

'If only life were so simple,' Jules said.

'Why couldn't you, though, Mum? Why couldn't you and Holly have sorted it out without telling anyone else?'

'Because . . .' Jules didn't know how much she should disclose to Saffie about Holly's reaction. Holly had implied that Saffie was a liar. Holly was someone Saffie was supposed to trust. Her guardian if anything happened to her and Rowan. It would undermine Saffie's faith in the adult friends who had always been there for her. And Saffie wasn't old enough to understand that when a mother's own child was accused, her rationale went out of the window.

'Holly's taking a little time to talk it over with Saul,' was all Jules said. 'It's difficult for her too. To hear what he did. But we'll get there, darling, we will.'

'And Dad won't go to the police?'

'Not if I tell him not to,' Jules said. 'He does as he's told where I'm concerned.' She smiled and hugged her daughter to her.

'You didn't tell Dad my period's late?'

'Of course not. It still hasn't come?'

Saffie gave a small shake of her head.

Jules thought of the pregnancy test upstairs, tucked into her underwear drawer.

'Sweetie, I think it would help if we found out for certain whether you are pregnant. The sooner we know, the better. If it's negative, we can relax about that at least.'

'What if I am, though?' Saffie clutched Jules's hand with her own hot, damp one.

'Donna will know what to do. And she'll find someone you can talk to about what you've gone through.'

At last Saffie nodded and, looking as she did at six, or seven or eight, followed her mother upstairs.

*

In the bathroom, Saffie did as Jules instructed, weeing on the little stick, and Jules put it back in its case to wait for the test to work. Saffie shut her eyes tight. Jules put her arm round her.

'Whatever happens,' she whispered into her ear, 'I'm here to help you. You're not to worry.'

When the stick had stayed in its case for the required two minutes, Jules felt her pulse quicken. She was about to discover whether or not her daughter was pregnant. She tried to repress the other thought that slipped out anyway: if the test was positive, it would prove to Holly once and for all that Saffie was not 'a devious little troublemaker'. That Saul was so obviously the one with serious problems, not Saffie.

How on earth, Jules wondered with a shock of misery, had a potential teenage pregnancy turned into a weapon between friends?

5

HOLLY

I'm still in Saul's room on Saturday morning while he's out on his bike, staring at the words 'Rape Me' on his iTunes, when the blare of the landline interrupts me and I run downstairs to answer it.

It's Jules. She tells me if I don't ask Saul outright, Rowan is threatening to 'beat the living daylights out of him'.

Once, in the days when Jules was trying and failing to get pregnant, she had sat in my kitchen weeping. Saul must have been barely two years old. He came in with the baby doll Archie and I had given him for his second birthday and placed it on Jules's lap. We hadn't told him why she was upset. He knew. He was intuitive and generous-hearted and had – still has – extraordinary empathy. A year or so later when Saffie was born and we went to visit her, a little bundle wrapped in a cellular blanket, Saul, just three, placed his own teddy bear in her Perspex hospital cot for her to keep.

'A boy like Saul is gold dust,' Jules had murmured, picking up her baby and crooning in her ear. 'Saffron, my girl, Saul is perfect husband material. Don't ever forget it.'

Saul was only ten years old when his dad died. And yet through those weeks when I walked around in a mist of grief, he comforted me. He burst into tears once when he saw a man with a terrible speech impairment begging on the street and insisted on giving him all the pocket money he'd saved for Match Attax cards. He was, and still is, one of the gentlest and most compassionate boys I have ever met. He has at last found something in his life to look forward to.

Jules and now Rowan must not be allowed to spoil Saul's future. I won't let them. I make a vow to find out what lies behind Saffie's accusation. Whatever it takes, I decide, I will do it.

*

When Jules met Rowan during our final year at university, she fell so head over heels in love with him I was willing to put any reservations aside. But there was always something in Rowan I felt uneasy about. A kind of brutishness. An intolerance.

Rowan wasn't as smart or perceptive or sensitive as Jules. He would take offence sometimes at benign comments people made and got embroiled in drunken student fights. Then there was the time he actually hit someone – broke his jaw – and was given a caution. But Jules loved him and was attracted to him physically, and would do anything, it seemed, to please him. And as I got to know Rowan better over the years, I began to understand what she saw in him: apart from his obvious good looks, blond hair, naturally golden skin, clear blue eyes and brawny physique, he had some very appealing characteristics. Affability. Warmth. Hospitality. Things that overrode the attitudes I found distasteful. Such as his pejorative remarks about immigrants, which I hoped he meant semi-ironically since Jules's family were from Poland and he himself had a Serbian grandmother. He was successful too, working in the City in some software business where he made, if not millions, a good deal more than Pete or I would ever see in our lifetime. Recently Rowan had been made redundant, but it hadn't dented his pride too much. He'd continued to provide Jules and Saffie with the lifestyle they loved.

He had a great sense of fun, welcoming everyone into his home. And he had been determined to build a beautiful house for his wife and daughter, and to give them the best life he could. He loved Jules, and so I had grown to love him. Besides, I suspected that if I expressed my reservations, Jules would choose Rowan over me. In spite of the violent temper that had occasionally upset her. (He'd never hit her, of course, but had been sent on an anger management course after the incident in the pub. Jules didn't talk about it. So I didn't either. It was a silent agreement between Jules and me that we overlooked Rowan's flaws.)

Rowan was obsessively proud of Saffie. He would gloat over her beauty. The emphasis he put on her looks when she was still barely pubescent seemed at times excessive to me. And he spoiled her, in my opinion, buying her, even as a small child, anything she asked for. I remember Christmases we shared, when Archie and I gave Saul one or two small gifts, something old-fashioned or educational such as a chemistry set once, or a children's encyclopaedia, while Jules and Rowan lavished Saffie with the latest crazes: Barbie dolls and fancy-dress outfits, scooters or roller skates, craft sets and accessories for her bedroom. Her present-opening went on for hours, while Saul's was over in seconds. But I knew that behind Rowan's adoration of Saffie was a sadness. Rowan and Jules had planned a big family. 'We're banging out at least four kids,' Rowan used to crow when they first married. But that hadn't happened. And so Rowan, and Jules to a certain extent, put everything, all their hopes, dreams and ambitions, onto Saff.

After they first moved to the village, when I was still in London, Jules met a microbiologist called Rob, a single parent, and began an affair with him. Only I knew about it. This man sounded like Rowan's opposite, a quiet academic whom Jules found intriguing and gentle. Then Rowan found something, a card from a restaurant Jules had been to with Rob, that raised his suspicions. Jules had come to me in abject terror that Rowan might have found out, and that he might hurt – seriously hurt – Rob. I agreed to cover up for her, to say she was with me the evening she'd spent with this man. She finished the affair, and repaired things with Rowan. We hadn't spoken about it since, and I respected her decision, even while secretly wishing she might have left Rowan for Rob. So when she tells me about Rowan's threat, I don't take it lightly. I know what he's capable of. I know how intense his feelings are towards Jules and his only daughter.

There was no way Rowan's response was ever going to be calm and measured.

His default way of dealing with strong feelings is to lash out.

*

Saul comes in just after midday. I hear his footsteps on the stairs and the slam of the bathroom door and the hiss of water as he starts up the shower. I wait until I've heard him go back to his room and give him time to dress. It isn't because of the things I've found in his room, or that I have begun to believe Saffie's claim. That's not why I am driven up the stairs, my heart racing. It's the fear that if I don't, now Jules has told Rowan, things could get worse, a lot worse, for all of us.

'Saul?'

I stand outside his room. The weather's changed again: the sky has become overcast, and the rain's pattering on the roof. Sometimes this house is like a cave. It's something to do with the fact the Fens were once under water, the houses built on land that is only just above sea level. Whereas in our London house you went up steps to reach the front door, in this house you step down to go inside.

There's a light shining from beneath Saul's door.

I knock again. There's the sound of rustling, of things being moved about or put away. A grunt: 'What?'

I push open the door. He's on his bed, headphones on, iPad resting against his thighs. John Donne is open, face down on his duvet.

'Saul, we need to talk.' He takes his headphones off and closes whatever he's doing on the iPad. I sit on the bed. 'Where did you go? On your bike?'

'Down the river. Bumped into the park runners.'

'The park runners? Did you meet anyone?' I know Jules was probably there.

'Nah. Why?'

'No reason. It's just some of your school chums do the park run.'

'School chums? Mum, I don't have *school chums*.' Then he adds, 'And especially not ones who do the park run. I saw Jules, but I don't think she saw me.'

'Ah.'

He doesn't elaborate.

'Do you want some lunch? A cup of tea?'

'Ate a doughnut from the park cafe,' he mutters.

'Sweetie, you need to eat healthily. You can't revise on carbs alone.'

'I'm not revising.'

My knee-jerk reaction is to say, 'Well, you should be.' Instead, I bite my lip.

'Saul, I don't know how to put this. There's something I

need to talk to you about. I'm bringing this up for your own good – you must believe that. I want to stem any rumours that might be flying about.' I sit down next to him on his bed.

'Now you're freaking me out,' he says, blinking. When he smiles, two little lines like brackets appear at the side of his lips. He's had these since he was tiny. For a few seconds, the little boy I know and adore rises to the surface. He is still fundamentally that child, no matter what anyone says about him. Deep down, he's the sweet-hearted, adorable, loving boy he always has been. No matter what's going on for him at the moment. However difficult he's finding adjusting to life here, or to the changes that are turning him from child to adult.

But I can't ignore Rowan's threat. I have to find out if anything went on between Saul and Saffie that night. Whether it was just a teenage fumble or whether – though I still can't believe it for a moment – some demon got inside my son and possessed him to push her further than he meant to. And so I plough on.

'The night you went round to Jules and Saffie's,' I begin, watching him for a reaction. His expression reveals nothing. He just frowns and looks down at his screen. 'To use the internet . . .'

'What about it?'

'Did you . . . Have you and Saffie been having any kind of a relationship?'

'You're kidding me, aren't you?' he says, looking up at me, disbelief written across his brow. 'She's in year eight.' The corner of his lips twitch as if he wants to laugh, but then his expression changes as he sees mine.

'It's not unheard of,' I say. 'But that's not really the point. What I need to know is if you tried to perhaps kiss Saffie that night.'

I'm making a mess of this. Why would I ask him if he'd tried to kiss a girl, for goodness' sake? It would, in any normal circumstances, be none of my business.

'Mum, I just said, she's in year eight. She's *thirteen*. I can't believe you're asking.'

'It's not me,' I say, floundering now, wishing Pete were here, with his experience in dealing with all kinds of difficult situations through his counselling. 'It's something Saffie told Jules.'

'What *did* Saffie tell Jules?' His voice is not even broken properly. It still occasionally goes up several decibels and he flinches, embarrassed.

'You don't know?'

'Not if you don't tell me. How could I?'

My muscles soften. My shoulders drop. If he doesn't know what I'm referring to, then it can't be true. It didn't happen. So I can say it and clear the air and tell Jules Saffie has fabricated this story to get at Saul for some reason of her own. As I first suspected. That Jules has to find out why. I close my eyes.

'She says ... Saffie says ... Saul, just reassure me, will you? That you didn't try to ... sleep with Saffie that night?'

'I'm not going to answer that.'

'You do know about consent? What it actually means?'

'What do you think of me, Mum? That I'm some kind of monster? That's so insulting.'

'Sometimes the lines can seem fuzzy. Sometimes a girl might look as if she wants it when she really doesn't and it can be ... hard ... or ...' This is not how I'd have put it in the past. I'd have put it straight. Only 'yes' means 'yes'. And as Saul seems to realize, Saffie's too young, legally, to consent anyway. 'It can be easy for boys to misinterpret what a girl wants. By the way she dresses, or by her manner ...'

'Fucking hell. I can't believe you're saying these things.'

'If you just tell me nothing happened between you, we can find out why Saffie said what she did. We can work out where the misunderstanding occurred and—'

He balls his fists. 'If Saffie's been raped, then she was asking for it. She dresses like a slag.'

'Saul, I—'

'Get out of my room. Just go.'

I shut the door and stand with my back to it. His words echo through my mind. The very words Jules reported.

Asking for it.

And he hasn't done what I wanted him to do. He hasn't in so many words denied raping Saffie.

*

It's Saturday evening and Pete is back. I'm angry with him for abandoning me. We're in the kitchen, a roast chicken still in the oven. Saul has refused to come down even though I've called out that supper's ready.

'I could have done with you here to help me talk to Saul,' I say. 'I didn't deal with it very well. He's gutted that I suggested he might be in a relationship with Saffie, let alone have forced her to have sex with him. He was disgusted, actually. I don't know what to do, Pete. He won't speak to me.'

'Where is he now?'

'Upstairs. He's been up there all day. Won't come down.'

'Normal, healthy teenage behaviour, I'd say.'

'How can you say that? He's been accused of rape! That's hardly normal. He's upset. With me. He's offended and hurt.'

'You did the right thing. You had to confront him. You couldn't just hope this would blow over. He's taking time to assimilate what Saffie's said. He'll be processing a whole gamut of emotions.'

Pete goes over to the cupboard, rummages about and draws out a bottle of gin. Then he goes to the fridge and takes the bag of ice cubes to the sink and bangs it on the draining board. He drops the ice into two glasses and sloshes in a large measure.

'We both need a drink,' he says.

'I thought he'd say he hadn't gone near Saffie. That we could tell Jules, and she could find out why Saffie made it all up. Instead of which, he said I was insulting him and Saffie shouldn't go around dressing like a slag.'

'He said *what*?'

Pete bangs the freezer door shut with unnecessary force.

'That Saffie dresses like a slag. I told him that had nothing to do with it.'

'Holly, I know you don't want to believe Saul has it in him, but that's misogynistic language.'

'It's just words, Pete.' I don't tell him he also said she was asking for it.

'You know very well language is not *just words*.'

'He was being a sixteen-year-old. Deliberately provoking me. Us.'

There's a fizz as he pours tonic into the glasses and the ice crackles satisfyingly. He cuts a lime into quarters and drops it in. He hands me a glass and takes a long draught of his. 'I'll have a word with him.'

'To say what?'

'I'll explain we can sort this out but that we need him to be open and honest. That it's not on to call any girl a slag. That using that kind of language is inflammatory. I'll ask what happened that night and tell Saul it'd be better to be absolutely clear in the long run.'

'He's not going to confess to something he hasn't done.'

Pete sighs, as if I'm beginning to frustrate him.

'We have to get the facts straight. For all our sakes. We're his parents, Holl. Of course we don't believe he's capable of rape. But we have to ask him what might have motivated Saffie to make this claim.'

'You're saying what?'

'I'm saying it would be sensible to get Saul's side of the story. And then I really think we should seek some help. For all of us.'

'You're the counsellor, Pete – you must know someone.'

'I don't mean that kind of help.'

'What *do* you mean?'

'I think we should get legal advice,' Pete says. 'Someone to consult if Jules and Rowan press charges.'

'*What?* But they aren't. Jules says Saffie doesn't want to report it. She wants it kept between ourselves.'

'Holly. Be realistic. Does Rowan know yet?'

Jules's voice on the phone earlier comes back to me: *Rowan's threatening to beat the living daylights out of him. Say he has to explain himself. Before Rowan honours his word, or calls the police.*

'Jules rang earlier. She told him. He hasn't responded very . . . calmly.'

I sit down again. Stare into my glass.

'Fuck,' he says. 'That's what I was afraid of. I can't imagine Rowan keeping the law out of this, whatever Saffie wants. And Saffie is obviously going to stick to her story. In which case, Saul needs to be ready with his defence or he could be charged. And if I remember rightly, men convicted of rape face a seven-year prison sentence. At least.'

'You don't seriously think it's going to come to that?' Panic rises in me.

'It would be sensible to be prepared. You must know someone in the legal field?'

'Well, yes. There are people I could think of.' I mentally rifle through Archie's lawyer contacts. 'There's a colleague of Archie's I used to be in touch with. A defence lawyer. Philippa. She works with sex offenders. But surely we don't need to . . .'

I can't believe I've just uttered the words 'sex offender' in relation to my own son.

'It might be a good idea to have a chat with her,' Pete says. 'Just in case.'

*

Pete and I are in bed by the time I hear Saul's door open, his footsteps on the stairs, a clattering in the kitchen.

In the morning, I find the chicken carcass, and am relieved to see Saul has finished it, cleaning all the remaining meat from the bones.

*

On Sunday afternoon, Pete comes in from the supermarket, where he's picked up things for the meal he's promised to cook. He leans across the kitchen table where I'm sitting marking exam papers, trying to take my mind off things, and takes my hand.

'How is he?'

'Still won't speak to me.'

'I . . . Look,' he says. 'You will understand that I had to tell Deepa about all this. And she has, quite reasonably when you think about it, said she doesn't want the girls coming here again until it's sorted.'

I remove my hand from Pete's. '*What?* You told Deepa? Why? Why did you have to do that?'

'Obviously, she has a right to know that her daughters' stepbrother has been accused of rape. She has to put their safety first.'

I stare at Pete. Pete is excellent at his job. I know that because people have told me how highly thought of he is in psychotherapeutic circles. But one of the reasons he's so good at it is that his face can be inscrutable at times. It's a professional stance he has to take, to appear without emotion in certain situations. It's inscrutable now.

He gazes back at me, but I don't have a clue what he's thinking. Which puts him at an unfair advantage.

'None of us knows yet what really happened. And you told Deepa?'

Pete looks down. The tiniest flicker of an expression does pass over his face. Something clicks into place.

'It was your decision to take the girls to Deepa's yesterday morning, wasn't it?' I say. 'It had nothing to do with her father visiting. Did it?'

He draws in a breath through his teeth.

'Pete!'

'I was going to talk it over with you, of course.'

'It was *your* decision to take them away from here? You took them to their mother's because *you* didn't want them in the same house as Saul? You made that decision before Deepa even knew about it? Is that what you're saying?'

'It wasn't quite like that. I knew what Deepa would think. I was pre-empting her. That's all. What difference does it make?'

'It makes a huge difference.' I can barely breathe. 'Because it tells me *you* don't trust Saul. It tells me you don't trust your own stepson with your daughters. I find that . . . I find it so hurtful.'

'Look, Holly. It isn't quite as simple as all that.'

'What do you mean?'

'This isn't just about what Saul did or didn't do to Saffie. After you told me, I lay awake, and I realized I have to think about my clients. My reputation at work. As do you, in fact. We have to be seen to be doing the right things.'

'I can't believe you just said that.'

'I work with vulnerable teenagers, Holl. If my clients hear about it, it will jeopardize my credibility – as it will yours, and the work you're doing with the consent work-shops. We have to be seen, at least, to be taking reasonable precautions.'

'Saul isn't a rapist. So we don't need to take any bloody precautions.'

'Don't you see?' Pete sounds exasperated. And I know his irritation is partly due to guilt that he's not a hundred per cent supporting me and Saul. 'It's not a question of whether or not this thing actually happened. It's whether the rumour gets out of hand. People are very quick to judge.'

'Unless you believe absolutely in his innocence,' I mutter, 'I don't want you here.'

'You keep insisting nothing happened between those two. You have to take on board the possibility that some-thing did.'

'Whoa. Hang on a minute. Whose side *are* you on here? Fucking hell, Pete. How dare you? You're Saul's stepfather. You should support him unconditionally. You're my hus-band, for goodness' sake, or at least I thought you were. I now begin to wonder if it means a thing to you. You dis-appear when I need you. You won't let your girls stay here.' A terrible thought crosses my mind. 'You believe her. You believe Saffie, don't you, Pete?'

He's about to reply when a shadow passes across the

table and I look towards the doorway. There's the familiar creak of the wooden stairs.

'Saul?'

He's there, on his way up. He's been outside the door listening to us. He goes on ahead up to his room and I follow him.

'Saul, I'm so sorry you had to hear that.' I stand in his bedroom doorway.

'Pete believes Saffie,' he says.

I want Saul to deny the rape, in unambiguous language. Once and for all. So I plough on, playing devil's advocate, wanting him to say he didn't do it.

'Well, can't you see why everyone believes her? The smell of her perfume on your jumper . . .'

'What?'

'I smelled Saffie's perfume on your jumper. And you were playing a song called "Rape Me", as if rape is a joke.'

Saul suddenly swipes a pile of books from his desk onto the floor. 'The song's ironic, if you bothered to listen to the words,' he shouts. 'Tell Saffie if I was going to go for someone, it'd be a looker, not her. She's ugly as fuck.'

'We're a little upset, that's all,' I try, taking a step towards him. I want to clasp him to me, to tell him it's all going to be OK. That I know he would never have touched her and that things are spiralling out of control.

But he steps back, holding up his hand. 'Stop. Don't come near me. *I'm* not upset,' he says. '*I'm* fine. Everyone round here's the same. All gagging for gossip to make their boring little lives more exciting. Let them have it. They're all fucking sickos. Saffie. Her school mates. The lot of them.'

6

JULES

Jules listened out for Rowan but could hear nothing. The time was up.

'You ready, Saff?'

'Yup.'

Gingerly she pulled the pregnancy test from its plastic casing and looked.

Emblazoned across the tiny window was the word PREGNANT.

Jules's ears seemed to fill with cotton wool; the world about her retracted. It was like being muffled, protected from the onslaught of emotion that was about to assail her. Them. She gripped the edge of the bath to steady herself, then sat down on it while she took in the implications. Saffie looked at her.

'Mum!' she wailed.

How could it be – her thirteen-year-old, her baby girl, carrying a baby of her own? A baby made in the worst imaginable way.

'It's OK, Saff,' she heard herself say. 'I've already booked you in to see Donna. It will be sorted. All you need to do is rest, stay strong. Oh, honey, I'm sorry.'

Saffie sat on the edge of the loo seat.

'What does it mean? What do I do?'

'You don't have to do anything.' Jules was counting the

127

days since Saul had been here, silently. Saffie would be around two weeks pregnant.

'I can't have a baby! I don't want it.'

'You don't have to even think about that, if that's how you feel. Donna will give you a pill, just a little pill and it will bring on your period, OK?'

'Will Dad know? Does it show?'

'No, darling. It doesn't show. No one is going to know but you and me.'

'You're sure?'

'I'm certain.'

Jules sat on Saffie's bed and let the information sink in. Saffie had climbed back under her duvet, saying she wanted to stay in bed for the rest of the morning. The bear Saul had given Saffie when she was born sat on the pillow. It had lost one eye. In the end, Jules had to lean over, turn it round so it wasn't winking at her anymore.

This was all Jules's fault for letting Saul come and use her internet when her daughter had expressly said she didn't want him to. And when her husband, too, would have refused to have him in the house. Jules closed her eyes and breathed deeply. The feelings that swept over her weren't that different to those Rowan had expressed when he heard his daughter had been raped. All of a sudden Jules wanted to beat the living daylights out of Saul.

*

Sunday was an impossible day to get through. Jules knew to keep this new information to herself at all costs, for Saffie's sake. The only person she would tell would be Donna Browne. And of course, at some point – when she could get her on her own – she would tell Holly. In order to prove that Saffie was not, never had been, 'a devious little troublemaker'.

*

Rowan continued in his irate mood anyway, threatening to go to the police, threatening to punish Saul in whatever way he could for laying his hands on his virgin daughter. Asking Jules what she had done about it, whether she'd confronted Holly again. Saffie stayed in her room. When Jules found a moment, she went up.

'We should take you to a clinic straight away, you know, get the pregnancy sorted.'

'Please, Mum. I don't want some stranger finding out.'

'It would be confidential. They deal with things like this all the time. They are very discreet.'

'Do we have to go to a doctor at all? Can't I just take the pill you said about?'

Jules sighed, gazed over Saffie's shoulder at her children's books and teenie magazines jumbled on her shelf. From her past, a saying came back: *too old for toys, too young for boys*. Whatever had happened to that stage in a young girl's life?

'Even if we could get hold of the pills, it wouldn't be safe,' she said, immediately regretting it. She didn't want to alarm Saffie, or hint that there was any risk involved in the termination. 'Besides which, it's important for you to have someone to talk to, confidentially, about what you've gone through. Donna's not back until Friday. Are you OK to wait until then?'

'I'd prefer to wait if it means I can see her.'

'Will you be up to school, in the meantime?'

'I'm not ill,' Saffie snapped. 'If I'm off school, everyone

will want to know why. As long as it doesn't show ... Are you sure it doesn't?'

'I'm sure.'

'I'll just wait to see Donna, then. Get the pill, get rid of this ... this ... *thing* and go back to normal. I'm fine. Holly will talk to Saul, won't she? He won't dare come near me again.'

'Of course,' Jules said at last. 'Of course she will.'

*

Rowan seemed to have simmered down toward evening, and they all sat and watched some costume drama together, silently, before he said he was having an early night.

The next morning, Monday, Rowan was up when Jules woke, which was unusual since he had been made redundant.

'I'm driving Saffie to school,' he said. 'Since she insists on going. Saul gets the same bus as her and I don't want that boy anywhere near her.'

'Yes, I suppose that's a good idea,' Jules said. 'If she'll agree to it.'

Later, in the kitchen, as Saffie finished her cereal, Rowan said, 'We're going to school in the car, Saffie.'

'What?' Saffie dropped her spoon into her bowl.

'I want to make sure that boy doesn't come near you.'

'Dad, that's *so* embarrassing,' said Saffie, swinging round and giving him one of her most withering thirteen-year-old looks. 'Everyone will want to know why you're driving me when you never have done before. Please, leave me be.'

'Then I'm taking you to the bus stop. And I'm going to stay and watch you get on the bus safely.'

'Saul's not going to get rapey in broad daylight on the way to school. You're making everything worse!'

'I'm protecting you,' Rowan said. 'As your father, I think that's quite understandable, isn't it?'

'Saffie, you must see how concerned we are,' Jules said.

Saffie pushed her uneaten breakfast away and got up from her chair. 'If you start fussing and Saul notices, he's more likely to take it out on me. I'll walk to the bus stop and I'm calling for Gemma on the way.'

'In the car,' Rowan said. His face was red, revealing his frustration at the bind they were in. 'If you won't let us report that boy, we have to deal with this in our own way.'

Jules glowered at him, hoping he would realize that getting angry was not helping Saffie. Not for the first time, she wished she could form a clearer take on the whole business, that she knew what to do for the best. Rowan, meanwhile, refused to pick up on her unspoken message. He pulled on his Timberland boots and she watched from the door as he and a furious Saffie climbed into the Audi and drove up the road across the fen towards the village.

*

Rowan wasn't back by the time Jules had showered and dressed, so she checked her bag for money, make-up and mobile (the three Ms – the mantra she and Holly had created to remind themselves of the essentials they needed for work), and then got into her little Fiat to drive to the station. She would park there and take the train to the shop and immerse herself in the business until as late as she could. There was nothing like work to take your mind off things.

A fair was arriving on the green. Lorries and machinery were pulling up on the grass, and Jules had to stop to let a car with a trailer pass. And then, in an auspicious twist of fate, as she waited, Jules spotted her GP and friend, Donna Browne, coming out of the village shop with a newspaper, dressed in Lycra, trainers and a puffer jacket. Jules drew down the car window and leaned out. She knew it wasn't strictly professional but she had to ask Donna if she could talk to her before Friday.

'I'd see you now but I'm on leave,' Donna said. 'We're off to Paris for a couple of nights on the Eurostar later today. Shall I put you in as an emergency patient with Dr Alwin?'

Jules looked at Donna's healthy, clear-skinned face, framed by her dark cropped hair, her tall, athletic figure, and wondered how anyone could carry on as normal while her life felt like an alien landscape with no pathways or clues as to how to navigate it. She took a deep breath. 'The receptionist already asked me that, but I need to see you, Donna.'

Donna looked over her shoulder and took a step nearer the car window. 'Is there anything you want to get off your chest now?'

Jules looked up at the doctor from the driving seat. 'Would you mind?'

She remembered again Donna's reservations about treating people outside her practice. But Donna's children were similar ages to Saffie. She and Jules had run parents' races at the primary-school sports day together. They'd sloshed back wine at parties. And Prosecco that night in the pub. Saffie had expressed a desire only to talk to Donna about what she'd gone through. And Jules trusted Donna. And she was desperate to know what she should do about Saffie's pregnancy. So she opened the door for Donna, who slid into the passenger seat.

'I'll pull in over there,' Jules said, indicating a parking space. 'I don't know who else to talk to.'

Donna smiled. 'It's a funny old life being a GP. I often end up playing the role of priest, counsellor, pardoner. As well as doling out prescriptions. Go on, Jules, I'm not judging. If there's anything to judge.'

When she'd parked alongside the shop, Jules swallowed. 'It's about Saff.'

'Oh?'

'She's been raped,' Jules said.

Saying the words so bluntly made her afraid she would cry. She wanted to blurt out that she had no idea how to handle this. She blinked hard to push back the tears. Swallowed.

'I'm sorry to hear that. That's very difficult for you both.' Donna was measured, professional, as Jules knew she would be. She was neither over- nor underreacting. 'Do you want to give me details?'

Jules clutched the steering wheel, feeling the sweat pool beneath her fingers. 'It's harder still because the boy who did it is a family friend. He was in our house. It happened at home.'

'Saffie told you this?'

'Yes. Not straight away. She didn't want to tell anyone. Was afraid. Of getting him into trouble. Or of him taking it out on her. But then she missed a period.'

'O . . . K. Have you told the police? Have you reported the assault to anyone?'

'Saffie doesn't want me to. The boy's a friend's son. He's at her school. She's afraid of her friends finding out.'

Donna's face revealed something, Jules wasn't sure what. There was an almost imperceptible movement of the eyebrows. Was Donna guessing she must know the culprit too, if he was local?

'But that's not why I need to talk to you. As I said, she's missed a period . . . and . . . we've done the test. It's positive.

I thought it best to know and ... the truth is, I also wanted proof, which sounds awful, I know ...'

'That can be tricky, of course. Even with a pregnancy. Because of all the possible permutations. Who was it? Was it consensual? Was it done with both parties' full consciousness, et cetera, et cetera? And with a child of Saffie's age, it can be because they often feel guilty for having sex at all. Rape might be an excuse for something they feel they shouldn't be doing.'

Jules looked at the GP. Had she really just said, 'Rape can be an excuse'? What would Holly have said to that before her son was accused? She'd have been incensed. 'Only 0.5 per cent of all rape allegations are false,' Jules remembered Holly quoting to her once. 'Which means 99.5 per cent of reported rapes did indeed happen. And how many rapists are actually convicted? Hardly any. Because of the misogynistic culture we live in even today.'

Look at Holly now, thought Jules. Look at how the mother in her reneged on all her years of campaigning for rape allegations to be believed.

'I didn't want proof because I doubted Saff,' Jules said. 'I believe her. She's clearly been deeply unhappy about something. Traumatized even. Not eating. Exhausted all the time. Completely out of character. And anyway, why would she lie? No. I needed proof because the boy's mother wouldn't accept her son had done it. I had to have proof to make her take some responsibility.'

'Of course, a positive test doesn't prove *who*'s responsible,' Donna said coolly. 'It only proves Saffie's had sex with *someone*.'

Jules gritted her teeth. 'Saffie's never even had a boyfriend,' she hissed. 'Unlike some of the girls in her year.'

Donna put her hand on Jules's. 'I'm sorry,' she said. 'I was just pointing out—'

'There's no one else it could be. I want the mother to do something about her son. To stop Rowan taking it further and going to the police, which Saffie doesn't want. And I have to sort out a termination for Saffie as soon as possible so she doesn't have time to worry and we can focus on what to do about this whole nightmare scenario.'

Jules wondered whether Donna was judging her for the way she was handling it all. But everything she was doing was for Saffie. To protect her. As if Donna could read Jules's mind, the doctor said, 'There are limits to what we can protect our children from. Limits to how much we can control their lives. When did it happen?'

'Just over two weeks ago. Friday night.'

'It's too late for the morning-after pill. In case that's what you were thinking.'

'No, I know that.'

'But if you've got the dates right and her period's only a few days late, she'll be in time for a medical abortion.'

'I did do some research.'

'So you'll know it's in the form of a pill. Three doses, actually, taken a few days apart. Very simple. She can take them and they'll bring on a bleed.'

'How soon can we do it?'

Donna sat up straight. Shifted in the passenger seat. 'In theory, straight away. But even if the pregnancy is a result of rape, you can't simply decide *for* her. She'll need counselling first. She'll need someone to talk to about what is happening to her. She'll have to agree to it.'

'She will agree to it,' Jules said. 'I've already talked to her about it. But I don't want her to worry about it for longer than she has to. Can't you give me the medication now?'

'I can imagine how awful it is to see your own child going through a trauma like this,' Donna said. 'And I think you're right to minimize the time Saffie has to think about it. Even so, it's her body. She has to have a say in it, however obvious it seems to you and me that it's an unwanted, unplanned pregnancy. You have to give her time to assimilate what's happened. To consider the consequences of whatever course of action she decides to take.'

'She's thirteen. She can't have it.'

'And I don't suppose she wants to. But she has to have agency, Jules. You can't take it all into your own hands. You aren't the one to make this decision for her. And you know that we have to get another doctor's consent. In addition to mine. If she does decide to terminate. It's a legal requirement for any abortion. Bring her in the minute I'm back on Friday. There'll still be time to take the medical route. And in the meantime, I'll arrange some counselling for her.'

Without knowing she was going to, Jules burst into tears. Donna let her weep.

'I can see you're trying to prevent her suffering any more than she has to.'

'It's not that,' Jules said, looking up at Donna through her tears. 'It's the thought of the child Saffie's carrying. Saul and Saffie's child.'

'Saul? Saul Seymore?'

'Holly's son.'

Donna Browne blinked. She clearly hadn't expected to be given the identity of the rapist, and Jules hadn't meant to reveal it.

'Holly and I always dreamed of sharing a grandchild,'

Jules said. 'And now we do. And it couldn't be more different to what we imagined.'

*

Work for Jules that morning might have been easier if it hadn't involved unpacking hand-knitted Babygros, booties and pram blankets. When Jules had set up the business, it had been a purely practical venture. Or that's what she told herself. She remembered how Holly had asked her if it was the right area for her to go into, given her history. But Jules had argued that Cambridge was missing a high-end children's clothing outlet. She knew from the demographic that there were plenty of affluent parents who would be hungry for the kind of clothes she planned to sell. Her choice of business had nothing to do with any personal feelings about the children she had or hadn't had herself. And they had all been taken aback by how successful the business had been.

Now, after her conversation with Donna Browne, Jules tried to continue as normal. She checked orders, chased up invoices, did a stock count. The shop was quiet on a Monday morning and Jules had it to herself until lunchtime. Jules liked its view onto the little pedestrianized street outside, the autumn sun just lighting the cobbles and the stone walls of the colleges, a few people idling by heading for the cafes for their morning coffee. When Hetty arrived, Jules was able to get on with all the storeroom jobs while Hetty stayed at the counter.

'I'm planning a seasonal window display,' Jules told her assistant that afternoon. 'I want to exhibit the new range. Look at these.'

There were some hand-knitted dresses that Jules was going to display with opaque tights and tiny leather buckle shoes. 'Thought I'd do a backdrop of pumpkins and some colourful autumn leaves.'

'Adorable!' Hetty said.

But as Jules began on the window, lifting one of the baby vests to put on display, she suddenly felt light-headed and had to sit down. The vest was made of the softest cotton fabric, with poppers that did up underneath, and a tiny embroidered rabbit on its chest. She sat for some time holding the tiny piece of clothing between her hands. In a flash, she could feel the weight of the baby who might wear it, the exquisite flesh, the velvety head with its downy hair and soft, throbbing fontanel. She could picture the bright eyes, the rooting mouth and the button nose. It was years since she'd been assailed with this kind of yearning. She had to put out a hand to steady herself as she stood up again. This was precisely why it was best Saffie had the termination soon, Jules told herself, putting down the vest. If she had time to think of the life inside her as a baby, it would make getting rid of it all the more traumatic. But she wasn't sure whether she meant for Saffie or for herself.

After a while, Jules could bear arranging the little clothes no longer and went into the office at the back. She couldn't concentrate on the invoices. She had hoped, she realized now, that a positive pregnancy-test result would bring her and Holly together. She had even imagined that Holly, faced with the evidence that Saffie had been telling the truth all the time, might apologize, offer to come with her to Donna Browne and to hold Saffie's hand throughout the consultation. The reality was that it was likely to drive an even greater wedge between them. The test, as Donna had pointed out, did not prove categorically that it was Saul who had made Saffie pregnant. It had been easier in a way when there was no proof that Saffie had had sex at all. When there was still a chance that Saffie might confess she'd made the whole horror story up. Though why she would have done that was impossible to imagine. Holly and Jules – and Saul eventually – would have forgiven her, of course they would, and they would all have become friends again.

Now Jules was going to have to tell Holly about the pregnancy. Even if she still refused to believe Saul had raped Saffie, she would have no choice but to get him to tell her what went on that night in Jules's house. Jules knew Holly's world would be turned upside down when Saul confessed at last, as she assumed he'd have to now. Holly would be devastated to know her son was more mixed up than she'd even imagined. That she was going to have to get him some help that would possibly disrupt his schooling for a second time. Might – no, *would* – destroy his future.

And so, instead of vindication at the result, Jules was thrown into greater turmoil. Even if they did as Jules had planned and kick-started the termination the minute Donna was back on Friday, Saffie was still going through something no thirteen-year-old girl should have to. And Saul would have to be dealt with, probably by the police, and then the justice system after all. And then Jules gave rein to feelings that were so confusing she hardly knew how to name them. Fury with Saul for bringing this upon them all clashed head-long with a wish to reverse the last few weeks. Not to have gone out drinking on Tess's birthday. Not to have let Saul come round. Above all, Jules wished she could prevent her bond with Holly being broken by the rape, confirmed for her now by the word 'pregnant' on the little white stick.

7

HOLLY

Early on Monday morning, a fair arrives on the green. Lorries and trailers pull up and people move about unpacking machinery and erecting stalls. A mini rollercoaster arrives. A dodgems rink in pieces. A truck carrying the seats for an ancient-looking waltzer. Signs appear. 'Catch a duck. Prize every time.' 'Two-colour candyfloss.' 'Sugar dummies.'

I watch through the sitting-room window with my coffee as the school kids re-navigate their groups, cowed by the way the fair has laid claim to the space they think of as their own. They move to the edge, pushed out by the rides and machinery.

Saul says very little at breakfast but eats a huge amount, which I take as a good sign.

'Saul, we're going to sort this,' I call as he goes out of the door. And, 'Love you,' as he closes it. As usual, I wish he didn't have to go to school. Especially now there's this accusation hanging over him. I trust that Jules and Rowan have honoured Saffie's request not to report it. Because the last thing I want is for the name-calling and bullying to start up again. And this time, it could get worse. Much, much worse.

I gather up my stuff and take my usual route through the village for the train to London.

On the train, I check my Twitter feed. More tweets have come in from the Stag. The usual, telling me that I want raping but no one would have me and so on. I ignore them and lean my head against the window. At least the Stag can't know my son's been accused of the very thing he objects to me campaigning against.

*

This morning, I don't go straight to the university but walk a different route from King's Cross. Past Coram's Fields, where children's voices float from the playground, down the narrow, tree-lined Lamb's Conduit Street, with its chic, independent shops, across High Holborn and along the north side of Lincoln's Inn Fields. I arrive at the cafe where I've arranged to meet Archie's old lawyer colleague.

Philippa sits down opposite me, placing her purse on the table. 'Are you OK?' she asks with a wry smile. 'How's it going out in the sticks?'

'It's different. Taking a while to get used to.'

'I can imagine,' she says, looking about for a waitress.

Queues of suited lawyers wait at the counter for takeaway paninis and frittatas. There's the hum of conversation and the clatter of crockery, the hiss from the espresso machine.

Philippa is older than me. She has sharply cut steel-grey hair, tortoiseshell designer glasses shielding intelligent brown eyes. She's a lawyer who specializes in sex offences, with chambers in Lincoln's Inn close to where Archie's were. I haven't seen her very often in the years since he died. I have wondered, from time to time, whether she had stronger feelings for him than professional ones. I wouldn't blame her. As well as his good looks and his expertise as a lawyer, Archie had an old-fashioned kind of chivalry. Jules used to laugh at him: he'd stand up when anyone came into a room, hold doors open, take the tab at the end of a meal – things a lot of women, if they'd only admit it, find irresistible. I wonder now whether his sudden death was almost as hard for Philippa to take as it was for me. Whether this is the reason we've hardly seen each other.

Now she looks across at me, lines of concern furrowing her brow. 'So what's up?' she asks.

'I have a problem,' I tell her. 'Pete's urged me to talk to you. To get advice. Just to be on the safe side.'

The waitress puts our coffees in front of us.

'It's to do with Saul.'

Philippa doesn't speak, just stirs a little packet of brown sugar into her flat white.

'He's gone through quite a time of it since we moved. Anxiety, school phobia. He was bullied in year nine. The local kids found him a bit of an oddity when we first moved. They called him "emo". Stuff he hated. He's become quite a loner and I'm worried he's been a touch depressed.' I clear my throat. 'He's started reading Donne, the meditations, and—'

Philippa laughs. 'A writing lecturer who's worried her son's reading John Donne?'

'It seems rather an introverted, depressive thing to do.'

'There's something else, isn't there?' she says.

I push away my espresso and take a sip of water instead. 'He . . . Well, he's into photography, and at last he's found a course he wants to apply to. For sixth form. Things are beginning to look up for him for the first time in years. And then, right in the middle of this – bam! Just like that. Some-one at school has made an allegation against him. It's awful. I'm mortified. I can't understand why they would do such a thing.'

Philippa sighs. Leans across and pats my wrist with cool

fingers. 'Anything you tell me will remain in strict confidence.'

'He was with a friend's thirteen-year-old . . .' Something snags in my throat as I say, 'In her house while her mother and I went out. She accused him . . .'

'Go on.'

'. . . of raping her.'

'Rape?' Now even Philippa's eyes widen.

'It's only an accusation. From a naive thirteen-year-old.'

'Hang on,' she says. 'Were they sleeping together? Were they an item?'

'No. They weren't. Nothing happened between them. At all. I simply can't work out the girl's motivation for making the whole thing up.'

'Hmm.'

'I mean it. It seems like another bit of bullying she's been coerced into or—'

'Slowly, Holly. Tell me the details. What kind of relationship do they have?'

'They're just friends. Well, not even friends these days. Saul and Saffie have known each other since they were kids. Her mum's my friend. You met her once. Jules. Blonde, attractive. She is – was – my best friend. Always round at ours.'

'I remember her. So you say they were in her house and you were out?'

'Saul was at her house to use the internet.' I pause. 'Jules asked Saul to put his head round Saffie's bedroom door. To check she'd gone to bed. According to Saffie, he looked in and caught her . . . semi-naked. She says he walked in. Grabbed her. And when she fought him off, he said she was "asking for it".' I choke over these words.

'How far has she gone with this allegation?'

'Saffie doesn't want her mum to press charges. She asked her not to involve the police, not to tell anyone.'

'OK. That's fairly common. Girls are scared of . . .'

'Not being believed.'

'Yes, that, but also of being interviewed, or even examined. It's humiliating, the procedure they have to go through, and often for nothing. It's so hard to get a conviction for rape.'

'I know that, Philippa. My God, I spend half my time getting women to recognize when they're being silenced by spurious arguments. That they were drunk, or had dressed wrongly, or had asked for it. Urging them to press charges. Trying to make men understand what consent is. Women don't lie about rape. I know! But in this case I simply don't believe her.'

'That wouldn't have anything to do with the accused being your son, would it?' Philippa puts down her cup. For the fraction of a second I feel irritated by her, with her expensive clothes and her composed face. What would she know? She doesn't even have children. She has no idea how it feels to be a mother and to know your own child through and through.

'What reason would the girl have to lie, if nothing happened?' she persists.

'That's what I can't understand.'

'Were they maybe high? Were there drugs involved?'

'No. Nor drink. Well, Saul may have had the odd beer.' I remember now Jules commenting that bottles had gone from her fridge.

'Let's rewind a second,' Philippa says. 'If they're not pressing charges, what *do* the girl's family want to do about it?'

'Jules wanted me to make Saul confess. She thought we could deal with him between us. What's awful is she's implied he's got social problems and that I haven't helped him.' I swallow. 'The reason I've come to you, Philippa, is that I have talked to Saul and he has, understandably, taken offence that I even questioned him.'

'Hmm.'

'And now the girl's dad has threatened us. Says he's going to the police. I'm afraid it's going to escalate and I suppose I felt . . . Pete felt . . . we should be as prepared as we can be to defend Saul if he does.'

'You say Saul denies anything happened at all?' Philippa says.

'He was shocked I could even ask him such a thing. Because she's in year eight. They have very strict codes about these things. And anyway, I brought him up to respect women. Girls. And he's hardly confident around them. It just isn't Saul,' I add, lamely. 'He wouldn't behave like that.'

'If what she says *is* true,' Philippa says, ignoring my last remark, 'Saul has broken the law according to the Criminal Justice Act 2003.' Her voice has taken on a professional briskness. 'He could be given a five-year sentence at the least.'

'That's why I've come to you. If Saffie doesn't retract her allegation and her dad does what he's threatening to do, Saul could end up in prison for an offence he never committed.' My voice quavers dangerously, though I'm trying my best to stay composed.

Philippa looks at me over the rim of her coffee cup.

'They definitely weren't in a relationship?'

'Not according to Saul. No.'

'Is there any evidence? To indicate they had intercourse?'

'Like what?'

'Condoms, underwear, clothing ripped off. Not to put too fine a point on it – stains?'

I think for a second of Saffie's scent on Saul's jumper. Of his pornographic images. Of the song 'Rape Me' that he insists is ironic. Of his even reciting those words to me, 'She was asking for it.'

I shake my head. 'Nothing forensic, as far as I know. Saffie only told Jules two weeks after it happened.'

'Did Jules see any sign of a struggle?'

'Not that I know of.'

Philippa is looking at me steadily. And all of a sudden, I have the oddest sensation that I'm dabbling my fingers in something toxic. Something that will stick and won't wash off. Philippa's asking the kind of questions I know are used to catch out complainants in rape cases. The kind of insidious, intimate questions that are dredged up to humiliate the victim and grind them down. Until they retract their allegations. Should I be here at all? Seeking help to *defend* an alleged rape? Then an even more unpleasant thought occurs. Is Philippa doing this deliberately? To highlight what I'd be putting Saffie through by pursuing this? Is she trying to put me *off* seeking help to defend my son?

She sighs. 'Holly, this is obviously hard for you. You've brought Saul up alone. It's been you and him for so long. You probably still think of him as the little kid he once was. But children change when they hit adolescence. Sometimes catastrophically. The best ... Well, the *only* thing you can do is tell Saul that the girl's father will take legal action if he doesn't explain himself and, if necessary, accept help. Which might mean involving the school and social services. Then perhaps he'll see it's better to settle this between you.'

'But he didn't do it.'

She raises an eyebrow at me. 'Nevertheless, I can't envisage this father believing that. Would you? If it was your daughter?'

'That's why I called you. My question is, Philippa, would you be prepared to defend Saul if they do decide to involve the law?'

She sips her coffee slowly. 'I might know someone who . . .'

'I'd like it to be you, Philippa. I know you. I can trust you. I don't want some stranger who doesn't know Saul. Someone who might humiliate him.' Again, the feeling I'm somehow soiling my hands sweeps over me. 'I don't want someone who might humiliate either of them, Saul or Saffie,' I add. 'To get to the truth.'

Her face has changed imperceptibly. She looks uneasy.

'You know what Saul was like, don't you? You remember what a sweet child he was? Still is.'

She puts down her cup. For the first time since we arrived she looks ruffled.

'It'll be her word against his,' I plead. 'I need someone who has absolute faith in him.'

'I can't represent Saul,' she says. 'It wouldn't be . . . Let's just say you'd be better with someone else.'

'Because you believe Saffie?'

'That's got nothing to do with it.' Her tone is clipped. 'It just wouldn't be appropriate for all kinds of reasons.'

'I don't see why not.'

'I'm a family friend. There's a conflict of interest.'

'Philippa, we've hardly seen each other in the last few years . . . No one's going to associate us.'

Why do I feel a sense of doom? A crushing in my chest, as if all I've been clinging to is about to topple? The version I've always had of my son, my family, my past, it all teeters.

'I'll give you the numbers of a couple of colleagues who I know will be completely professional.'

'I don't want a stranger. I don't want to put Saul through the stress of talking to someone he's never met before. He's had such a tough time.'

'It'll be someone very experienced.'

I glare at her. 'I thought you'd want to help,' I say. 'For Archie's sake, if no one else's. But I can see you don't want to. Let's forget it.'

To my surprise, Philippa pushes her chair back at this, gathers her nice suede gloves to her, prepares to leave. Tears prickle in the corner of my eyes. I don't stand up. I've made a fool of myself. I haven't presented a rational front and now heat rushes to my face. I don't want to tell her that I am this desperate because Pete took his daughters back to their mum's. That I'm afraid he believes Saffie too. That I am alone. That Archie would never have believed her for a second because he knew his son. And that therefore I thought Philippa, as Archie's colleague, would support us as well. I catch her hand as she begins to walk away. 'I'm sorry,' I say. 'It's at times like this I miss Saul's dad so very badly.'

'You're not the only one,' she says, looking down at me. 'Everyone misses him.'

And I feel the scratchy wool of her coat press against my cheek as she pecks the air over my shoulder, before she hurries out across Lincoln's Inn Fields back to work.

Philippa's abrupt departure leaves me shattered. I wish I'd been less emotional. Hadn't upset her. I can't face work, and, since I haven't got tutorials until later, I wander along the north edge of Lincoln's Inn Fields to the Sir John Soane's Museum. This is a mistake. The area is steeped in memory. There's a queue outside the museum already. Saul loved coming to this museum, with its collection of sculptures and artefacts, when he was little. The dim light lent it a mysterious atmosphere, and he was fascinated by the wall panels you could open to discover paintings behind, like mini-theatres. He was always intrigued by secret doors, those low doors under stairs, doors into secret passages. Crawling into small spaces behind doors to hide. He had a phase, too – perhaps it was when they were doing the Egyptians at school – when he was intrigued by the funerary urns in the Soane's Museum. And the gruesome shackles that showed how slaves had once been kept. Saul was horrified by these, couldn't believe humans could have their limbs forced into those tiny metal hoops to be chained up. And yet he would ask me time and again to take him there, to look at them, and ask me to tell him that John Soane helped to free slaves.

I turn and stare for a few minutes back across Lincoln's Inn Fields trying not to imagine the spot where Archie collapsed.

In Saul's early days, we would often walk across the grass from here to Archie's chambers to meet him from work. We would stand beneath the fan vaulted ceiling under Lincoln's Inn Chapel, and I'd read the engravings on the gravestones laid out flat on the ground. Saul was intrigued by the fact you could walk over the graves of dead people. Most of the names were of barristers and benchers, but the oldest stones included servants who'd worked at the Inns of Court. Saul was especially amused by the servant 'William Turner', who was a 'Hatch-keeper and Washpot', and would beg me to read out the words, which always made him collapse into fits of childish giggles.

On other days, Saul and I would go for pizza in the Lincoln's Inn Fields cafe and wait for Archie there. Sometimes, around the time Jules was setting up her first business, I would bring Saffie. Often it would have got late by the time

Archie arrived. I was content to sit with Saul and Saff while they ate ice cream, or went outside to play under the trees. I'd drink a glass of wine and my heart would sing when I spotted Archie coming across the fields from his chambers, tall and handsome in his suit. Once or twice he brought Philippa with him and Saffie or Saul or both would fall asleep on our laps while all three of us adults sat and talked until late.

Why won't she represent him? I leave Lincoln's Inn Fields wishing I'd never gone there, never remembered those more innocent days.

*

Later, on my way home after work, I rest my head against the window on the train as it pulls out of King's Cross. My meeting with Philippa has left me deflated. She was so frosty, so unyielding. The one person I thought would sympathize and jump at the chance to help me and Saul has refused to.

I wake with a lurch at Cambridge Station, realizing I've slept most of the way home. The back four carriages of the train are unhooked, leaving just the front four ploughing onwards into the Fens. It feels symbolic, this unleashing of the city train after Cambridge. A lizard dropping its tail to protect itself from predators. From here on, we enter uncharted territory. *Here be dragons.* A bucolic region where the modern world is left behind. Where Philippa's cool, calm rationale has no reach. The villages out here were isolated, surrounded by swamps, houses built on stilts to protect them from the incoming tides. Before the land was reclaimed by the Dutch, mythology held sway, and rumours spread like the malaria that was endemic here at that time. I wonder how much has really changed.

It's a quarter to seven by the time I'm walking up the road from the station through the drizzle. A car passes, drenching my coat and tights and my soft leather boots with spray from a puddle. My city wear. I swear under my breath at the driver, but the truth is, I'm feeling near to tears again as the cold soaks through to my skin. *The whole world is persecuting my son and me.*

Of course, getting wet is my own fault. Pete's been saying for some time that I should buy clothes suitable for living in the country. A Barbour jacket and wellies. I'm still in denial. Still insisting on clothes better suited to stuffy buses and Tubes and well-heated offices. Clothes that I wore as a PhD student with grand plans for professorships in the inner city. When I saw myself – smugly perhaps – as part of an urbane professional couple. I have to let that image go. *It's over two years since we moved*, I remind myself. Two years. And six since Archie died. High time I moved on.

The walk home refreshes me. The air, though damp, is invigorating after polluted London. There's the scent of woodsmoke mingling with the soil and rain. I remind myself the driver didn't mean to spray me. Getting upset with the world is not the way forward.

The fair's in full swing on the green. Music thumps; generators roar; kids screech as they're twirled about on the waltzer, flung towards the sky, hurled round in circles or dropped from great heights.

A bus passes and stops by the green. The schoolgirl who jumps off and springs along in front of me is Saffie. I remember telling Jules on our way to the pub that Saffie must be on an emotional rollercoaster, and her replying it was more like the dodgems. Joking together in the car on our way out for drinks, unaware we were about to fall out. Now, seeing Saffie walk towards real dodgems, real rollercoasters, I think how crazy it is that we're letting Saffie's story wrench us apart. And I have a sudden thought. I'll talk to Saffie myself. Saffie can explain to me why she said Saul raped her. Once she realizes she can tell the truth without getting into major trouble, the whole issue will be dealt with. We won't have to involve Philippa or her lawyer contacts. I will explain to Saul that it was all a terrible childish mistake on Saffie's part.

Saffie and I always used to be close. I used to regard her as the daughter I never had, and she knows that. It's why she came to me instead of Jules when she stole the cosmetics recently, and I'd reassured her everyone makes mistakes, that it was better to confess what she'd done to her parents, learn not to do it again.

When Jules and I used to meet up for Saturday-morning coffee in the park in London, before they moved up here, Saul would tear around on his bike while Saffie was still small enough to want to sit on our laps. I would hold her, and take her to look at the ducks or the deer. I would often have her overnight, or take her to children's theatre – or, as my earlier meeting reminded me, she'd come with Saul and me for pizza in Lincoln's Inn Fields. I used to pretend for a few hours that she was mine, and to imagine what it might have been like to have a daughter as well as a son. And I loved it. I loved her. My beautiful little odd daughter.

I speed up, but as I get close to Saffie, she stops at the kerb, looks both ways, then crosses to the fair on the green. A shadow detaches itself from behind one of the kiosks and another girl steps out to greet her. They chat for a while, and tiny lights flair up. They're smoking. They stand together in the darkness as I approach the shop and go in. I buy milk, some cereal for Saul for the morning, a couple of packets of horrible bars of chocolate and crisps to placate him after complaining that we never have any food of the type Jules stocks. When I come out, Saffie's coming back across to my side of the road.

'Hi,' I say. 'You're late home from school.'

'Extra maths,' she says, blanching quite clearly at the sight of me.

I search her face for signs of trauma. But how can you *see* trauma on a young girl's face, for goodness' sake? Girls of twelve, thirteen, fourteen, they're changing every second, the expressions that cross their faces mutable. I know that.

'Saffie, please, can we talk?'

'I need to get home,' she says, and I wonder if the wide-eyed look she throws me before she turns on her heel is fear or defiance.

*

The house when I open the door has that chilly quality buildings quickly take on when they are empty of people for more than a few hours. Saul goes to the darkroom after school on a Monday to develop photos from the old film cameras they're being taught to use. He won't be in until later.

I switch on the lights, a stab of resentment hitting me that Pete's stopped the girls from coming over. Even though it's a weeknight, when they are usually at their mum's, they would have come over for the fair. And right now I could do with seeing them more than ever.

Pete comes in at seven thirty. I'm at the stove, stirring the rice, a glass of wine already poured beside me.

'Smells good,' he says, hanging his coat up on the hooks we've screwed onto the back of the kitchen door because the hallway is too narrow to accommodate five people's outdoor wear. 'What is it?'

'Mushroom risotto. I had to cook, to take my mind off things.'

Instead of the relief I was anticipating at seeing Pete, I feel irritation. How can he act as if nothing's happened? We haven't made up since our argument the night before about his taking his girls away from me. From Saul.

'Holly, I'm sorry,' he says. 'I behaved badly. I can see that now. It was a knee-jerk reaction. My first thought was, I have to let Deepa know I am protecting the girls. I didn't give enough thought to what you were going through. Or how my response would look to Saul. Can you forgive me?'

I stir the rice, slosh in a splash of wine, add some stock. My interest in food has evaporated. I'm cooking for Saul, not for Pete or for myself.

'What did you actually *tell* the girls?' I ask him. 'How did you explain they weren't going to be coming here for . . . for how long?'

'It was only this weekend,' he says. 'Unless this whole thing gets drawn out.'

'What's that supposed to mean?'

'If we don't get a confession from Saffie that he didn't do it. So that we can all move on.'

'We're not getting one from Saffie,' I say. 'I just saw her. She wouldn't speak to me. I expect she's afraid of taking it back now.'

Pete doesn't reply to this. I know what he's thinking. That she's not going to take it back if it's true.

'I hope Freya and Thea don't think it was my idea that they went to their mother's this weekend. I've worked so hard on gaining their trust,' I go on, 'as their stepmother, and now it's going to be undone just like that.'

I'm also hoping Pete hasn't told them about the rape

claim. They're young girls. Freya goes to the same school as Saffie. They're not going to keep such a story to themselves.

'I made it very clear it was their mother who wanted them home this weekend. To see their grandfather.'

'Was he actually there?'

'Yes, he was. I wouldn't have lied to them about that.'

I switch off the hob and sit down. Pete's expression is one of anxiety. Or fear. Of me?

'How very convenient for you. What would you have said if he wasn't there? I hope you didn't tell them the real reason.'

'Of course I didn't. I don't want this to spread any more than you do, Holly, please. If Umish hadn't been there, I would have thought of something. Try and see this from my point of view, as their father.' He's stomping across the kitchen now, looking for a drink. 'Where is Saul anyway?' he says.

'Why are you even interested?' I say. 'Do you care where he is? Wouldn't you rather he was in police custody?'

'For goodness' sake. No, I wouldn't rather. What's up with you, Holly?'

I sit down.

'I saw Philippa,' I tell him. 'She refuses to defend him if, God forbid, it ever goes to court. I think she believes Saffie as well.'

'Oh, Holly.' Pete comes across and sits on a chair next to me. 'Look. I've been thinking,' he says. 'Let me talk to Saul. As I suggested yesterday. Let me give him a listening ear, man to man. I'll tell him I can find a counsellor for him if necessary.'

'Because you think he's a rapist . . .'

'No, Holly. To support him. After all the bullying he

went through, if he's being unfairly targeted again, he'll need help.'

'He goes to use the darkroom on Monday after school,' I say, grudgingly. I'm grateful to Pete for appearing, at least, to give Saul the benefit of the doubt. 'I'll text him. Tell him the food's on the table.'

Pete levers the lid off a bottle of beer and I notice for the first time the bald spot that is appearing on the back of his head. It makes me want to pull him to me. Kiss him. It makes me want to cry. The vulnerability of it. He's trying so hard and I wish I hadn't been irritable with him. Then, I think, Archie was never old enough to go bald. A ridiculous thought but it's these small, ridiculous thoughts that can still choke me up.

*

Even after the darkroom, Saul's usually in by eight, so when by eight thirty he hasn't answered my text, I ring, but his phone goes straight to voicemail. This isn't unusual: Saul has a habit of keeping his phone in the bottom of his bag and failing to answer it. Nevertheless, I begin to worry, even as I send him another text instead. 'Where are you? Supper's been ready for ages. Mushroom risotto.'

'Why isn't he answering?'

'He'll come through the door in a moment and laugh if he sees you looking so anxious,' Pete says. 'Come here. Are we friends?'

'I can't concentrate on anything else, Pete. Not until I know where Saul is.'

At nine, I pick up my phone and check again. 'Why hasn't he replied to my text? Where is he?'

'He must be on his way,' Pete says. 'Unless he's gone to the fair with a friend maybe?'

'Please, Pete,' I say. 'Don't you know Saul at all?'

'Do you mind if I go ahead and eat anyway? I'm starving. You should, too. It's late.' Pete piles his plate with risotto.

'I can't eat if I don't know where he is,' I snap.

As the minutes tick by, I try to behave normally, because I think if I behave normally, Saul will come in as usual. After nine thirty, I can no longer contain myself.

'I'm afraid, Pete. I'm afraid something's happened to him.'

'Don't be daft,' Pete says, taking his plate to the sink. 'He'll have gone out with mates and forgotten the time.'

'I know a lot of boys would do that,' I insist, 'but Saul isn't like that, as you know. He hasn't got mates. He's a loner. For him not to come home means there's something wrong.'

Pete comes over and massages my shoulders.

I shake him off. 'This is all to do with what you said. He was devastated to hear that you believed Saffie. It must have felt as if his last ally was turning on him. He loves you, Pete. He looks up to you. He thinks you're so cool, with your interest in rock music and festivals and all that stuff. And now you've let him down.'

'I'll go and see if he's at the fair.'

'I'll go. I can't bear to wait here any longer.'

*

I cross the road to the green, weaving between trucks and trailers, stepping over wires and round generators to the heart of the fair. The faded pinks and greens of the morning's stalls are lurid now in the neon lights. Music blares out, its heavy bass a thump in the stomach. The air resounds with screams of delight from teenagers on the dodgems and the waltzer. Groups of kids I recognize from the bus stop move about in packs, browsing the stalls, having a go at 'Catch a Duck'. They munch on hot dogs or toffee apples and look at me with wary teenage eyes. There's a strong smell of engine oil mixed with fried onions and hot spun sugar. Toys swing from hooks above stalls. A small child elongated out of proportion ripples in the Hall of Mirrors.

'Have you seen my son?' I ask the woman at the hoopla stall. She looks me up and down, her skin cherry-coloured under the bright bulbs. I feel pathetic and pale, begging for her help. 'He hasn't come home. He's tall, long dark hair . . .'

'Fair's full of teenage boys,' she says. She turns to serve a group of girls holding out handfuls of change. 'Is he with them?' She nods at a crowd of kids taking it in turns at the rifle range.

I open my mouth to say Saul isn't a boy to go about in a group, that he would have been on his own, but she's turned away. Another group of teenagers bumps into me as I make for the dodgems. The man operating them barely glances at me as I try to attract his attention. He leaps onto one of his cars and swivels his hips as he's whirled round. A girl, not much older than Saffie, blushes the pink of the candyfloss she's scooping into plastic bags when I ask if she's seen my son. She shakes her head. The group she's serving look at me and move off, leaning towards one another, giggling. I walk on, past the ghost train, with its skulls and ghoulish faces, past a clairvoyant's tent. Behind me, there's shouting, a fight breaking out. I remember Jules telling me this village used to have a three-day 'feast' in the summer, in which tents were erected as temporary brothels and the drinking and ribaldry and opium-taking would lead to drunken brawls and fights. I wonder suddenly if a place absorbs the atmosphere to which it's always been exposed. And whether outsiders, like me and Saul, will ever fit in.

*

'I'm going to have to phone Jules,' I tell Pete, as I get home, shutting the door, kicking off my boots. 'I'm going to find out if Saffie saw him on the bus this morning. I don't know anyone else I can ask. And the school'll be closed now.'

'D'you want me to call her for you?'

'It's OK.'

My fingers tremble as I press in Jules's number.

She picks up quickly.

'Jules, it's me. I need to ask whether Saul was at the bus stop this morning.'

She doesn't reply.

'He hasn't come home,' I say into her silence. 'I wouldn't have rung but I'm beside myself with worry. I tried to talk to him about ... about what Saffie told us, and now he's vanished. There's no one else to ask.'

I curse how dependent I am on Jules. How long it's taking me to establish a network here. If I was back in London, there would have been any number of friends to call on. I realize how completely alone I am here. And then I think, if I was still in London, this whole horrible situation would never have arisen to start with.

'Please,' I hear myself beg. 'I'm afraid, Jules. I'm afraid he's done something stupid. Could you just check with Saffie? Did she see him this morning?'

There's another silence, muffled this time, as she covers the mouthpiece.

'The answer's no,' she says eventually.

'But there's just the one bus to school, from the village?'

'Yup.'

'So he might not even have gone to school?'

'I have no idea, Holly.'

'Why wouldn't he have told me?' I'm almost expecting

159

the old Jules to reassure me, so it takes me aback when she snaps, 'Maybe because he's sixteen? Maybe you need to ask yourself why Saul is looking for ways to shock you.'

I take a deep breath. 'I didn't know who else to call,' I say. 'I don't know his classmates, or their parents . . .'

But she's already put down the phone.

*

I scroll through the contacts on my mobile and remember, suddenly, Samantha giving me her number at the pub, when she'd asked me about degree courses. (I wish I'd remembered that before calling Jules.) Samantha is Saul's form tutor's wife. He'll know whether he was at school today. My hands tremble as I press in her number. She picks up and I explain I need to talk to her husband about Saul.

'Of course. He's right here,' Samantha says. 'I'll hand you over.'

I apologize for calling Harry Bell out of hours on his wife's personal phone.

'Saul wasn't at registration today,' he says. 'But it's quite possible he came in later and signed in at reception. I'll check his timetable and contact his relevant teachers. I'll call you back.'

'That's kind.'

Pete comes in, raises his eyebrows in question. I shake my head. When my phone rings, I snatch it up.

'I've checked with Saul's history and art teachers. He didn't go to either lesson,' Harry Bell says. 'I'm sorry. If he was younger, reception would have called you. In year eleven, we trust them to let us know themselves if they're not going to be in. If they don't, it gets recorded as an un-explained absence to be followed up. Please let me know the minute you hear anything, will you?'

When he's gone, I turn to Pete. 'He didn't go to school. He's done something stupid, I'm sure of it.'

'Don't think like that,' Pete says. 'Saul's been going through a tricky phase. As I said, he needs time alone to work things through. To face up to what Saffie said about him.'

Pete's got a sweet, eager, almost boyish face and he means so well, but all of a sudden, I miss Archie with an overwhelming, crushing ache. Pete is not Saul's dad. He doesn't feel for him or know him the way Archie did. He doesn't share his DNA. He doesn't put Saul before everything, the way his real father did and would still have done. He doesn't understand that for him not to come home is utterly out of character. He would never, ever disappear without telling me where he was going. Not unless he was hurt to the quick by things that had been said about him. Not only that. Saul would never, ever use violence to make someone have sex with him.

I speak without forethought and without caring about the consequences of my words.

'You don't really understand Saul,' I say to Pete. 'You never have done. All you really care about are your daughters. We are on different sides of a great barrier, and we are never going to break it down.'

'That's unfair,' he says quietly. 'I love Saul like my own son.'

'You say you love him, but you took your daughters away because you believed this accusation against him. It makes me question where you really stand towards me and Saul.'

'I've already apologized for that,' he says. 'And Saul doesn't know why I took them over to their mother's. It could have been for any number of reasons.'

'Saul's not fucking stupid. He sees his stepsisters being

whisked off to their mother's the very day he hears he's been accused of rape. Think what that's done to his trust in us as his parents. But that's not my point; my point is you *believed* her. You believed Saffie over Saul. You've shown me where your true loyalties lie and they are not with me and my son.'

He flinches, his hurt palpable.

'Well, I think you underestimate me.' There's a look of indignation in his eyes. 'You're upset. Let's talk about this when you've calmed down and when you begin to see things rationally.'

'I am perfectly rational,' I say. My voice is hoarse after my outburst. 'I am all too rational. What's terrible is, now I'm being rational, I've seen how things really are between us. And I'm not sure we have a future together.'

Just as when Jules came to visit me in my office, once the words are out, there's no taking them back.

8

JULES

Rowan had taken it upon himself to cook the meal when Jules got home, later than usual, on Monday evening. Saffie had just got in too; she'd put an apron over her school uniform and Rowan was using her as his sous-chef. She was peeling potatoes. Saffie often helped with the cooking and was clearly making a valiant attempt to carry on as normal. But the rings round her eyes and her demeanour – a new look of hyper vigilance, twitching every time there was a loud noise, glancing about her – spoke volumes. Jules's heart lurched.

'How are you, Saff?' she asked.

'I'm fine,' Saffie snapped.

Jules and Rowan exchanged a look.

'Why do you have to keep asking how I am? I'm trying to forget what happened.' She plucked at the sleeves of her school jersey. Another new mannerism she had acquired.

'Saffie, you must understand . . .'

'You can see I'm all right. I thought you'd be pleased I was helping with the cooking.'

'I am pleased,' Jules sighed.

'We thought we'd surprise you,' Rowan said. 'Didn't we, Saff? It's a beef Wellington and mashed potatoes.'

'Smells fab. Rather calorific, though.'

'Mum. Don't spoil it for Dad,' Saffie said. 'He thought you'd be tired. He was trying to help.'

Jules did indeed feel exhausted. Tension could cause fatigue, and she had felt tense all day. About Saffie's pregnancy. About the conversation she'd had with Donna Browne that made her realize she couldn't take control over her daughter's body or her life or make decisions for her.

Saffie was slicing the potatoes with more force than was necessary and dropping them with a splash into a pan of water, working hard to divert attention away from what she was going through. Jules tried to spot any visible signs that she was pregnant – things Rowan might have noticed. Apart from the puppy fat she'd gained recently, it was impossible to say. And it was very early days, as Donna Browne had pointed out that morning. Nevertheless, Jules wished Saffie had agreed to go to a clinic, get the thing dealt with immediately.

'Where did you get locally raised organic beef?' Jules picked up the label lying on the work surface.

'Ely Market,' Rowan said.

'Oh?'

'I went up there after dropping Saffie at the bus stop this morning.'

Jules glanced at Rowan, but he had his face turned from her. She was about to ask what had prompted him to go to Ely Market when Saffie said, 'Oh yes. There's a fair on the green. Can I go up there after supper?' She scooped up the heap of potato peelings.

'I'll take those peelings out,' Rowan said. 'You'll get the wrong bin. And no, you can't go to the fair.'

'I was trying to help.' Saffie was almost in tears again. Her emotions were so close to the surface, the tiniest thing tipping her over the edge. 'But you do nothing for me. You want to ruin my life. You interfere all the time. And then, when I ask for one thing, you say no!'

'It's too late to go to the fair,' Rowan said. 'You're not going up to the green with everything that's happened and that's that. The food will be ready in half an hour and you can spend the time until then revising your French.'

Saffie turned and stomped up the stairs, and at the top she slammed her bedroom door as hard as she could.

'This is a nightmare,' Jules said, turning to Rowan. 'She doesn't know how traumatized she really feels.'

'I know,' Rowan said. 'I've told her she's to leave it to us. That we're considering the best course of action to take next.' Rowan sounded uncannily calm after his reaction at the weekend. 'Go and have a bath, Jules, and I'll open some wine for you to have with dinner.'

Upstairs, Jules opened Saffie's door and went into her room. Saffie lay face down on top of her duvet.

'I know how upsetting this is for you,' Jules said.

'You don't.'

'Dad and I are doing everything we can to help.'

'All I want is for things to be normal,' Saffie said into her pillow. 'I want to go to the fair with Gemma and the others. I want things to be back how they were. They would have been back how they were if I'd never told you.'

Jules sighed. 'After what you've gone through, you must understand we're concerned about you being out there.'

'Dad knowing has made everything worse. Everyone's going to notice something's wrong.'

'You did the right thing, Saff. You had to tell us. We're here for you, darling, and things will be better soon, I promise.'

'How can they be better soon? When I'm *pregnant*?'

'I saw Donna Browne and we've got an appointment for Friday. So that's all taken care of.'

'Things will never be how they used to be!' Saffie began

to cry, quietly. 'It feels like this has ruined my life. It's made everything that used to be good horrible.'

'Oh, Saff.'

'I used to like going to school. You used to let me meet up with my friends. Now that's all spoiled.'

Jules lifted Saffie's hand and squeezed it. 'It probably feels like everything's ruined. But you will come through this and we'll move on.'

'What has Holly said to Saul?' Saffie asked at last, sitting up, rubbing her eyes.

'She's talking to him. You don't have to worry. It's going to be fine, Saff. It might not feel like it at the moment, but we'll sort it out between us. He'll get some treatment and he won't come near you again. I promise. But until we've sorted it, we have to keep you safe. Please try to see that we're only doing this to help.'

Saffie put her arms round Jules.

'Everything's going to be all right,' Jules said again.

Saffie said something into Jules's chest that Jules couldn't hear.

'What was that, Saff?'

'I said, I don't think it is. I don't think anything's going to be all right ever again.'

'You're upset. Which is completely to be expected. But this will pass. And things will be good again.'

And at last Saffie gave Jules a small, weak – and slightly unconvincing – smile.

*

Once Saffie had settled down again, Jules went to fill a bath as Rowan had suggested. As she climbed into its blissful warmth, she thought about Rowan's change of heart this evening, how dramatically he had calmed down after his rage at the weekend. No one eavesdropping would imagine he had threatened to beat up Saul only a day ago. Perhaps it was because he'd had time to process the news. Or perhaps he was brushing it all under the carpet. Which was his other way of dealing with things he couldn't handle. And almost certainly meant the issue would rear its ugly head again later, to sink its teeth into them all.

Then, as if on cue, after the beef Wellington and a panna cotta that Rowan had bought from Waitrose, the landline rang. It was Holly. Holly didn't give Jules time to speak but asked straight away if Saffie had seen Saul at the bus stop that morning.

For a few seconds, Jules felt the wind knocked out of her. She was unable to answer, astonished that Holly had the cheek to ask such a question in the circumstances.

'He hasn't come home,' Holly was saying. 'I wouldn't have rung but I'm beside myself with worry. I tried to talk to him about ... about what Saffie told us, and now he's vanished. There's no one else to ask.'

Jules was tempted to slam the phone down. If Saul had gone off because he couldn't face up to what he'd done to Saffie, then he was a coward as well as a predator.

'Please,' Holly said. 'I'm afraid, Jules. I'm afraid he's done something stupid.'

Jules hesitated, then put her hand over the mouthpiece. 'Rowan,' she called.

Rowan came back into the kitchen. 'I know you don't want to hear his name at the moment, but just a "yes" or "no" will do. Did you see Saul when you dropped Saff for the bus this morning?'

'No, I didn't. Luckily for him,' Rowan said.

'The answer's no,' Jules said into the phone.

'But there's just the one bus to school, from the village?' Holly asked.

'Yup.'

'So he might not even have gone to school?' Holly's voice was desperate, but Jules wasn't going to let that affect her. Not after witnessing Saffie's distress just minutes ago.

'I have no idea, Holly.'

'Why wouldn't he have told me?'

'Maybe because he's sixteen? Maybe you need to ask yourself why Saul is looking for ways to shock you.'

'I didn't know who else to call. I don't know his class-mates, or their parents . . .'

Jules couldn't bear to hear any more, and before she could stop herself, she slammed down the phone.

*

Jules didn't tell Holly that Rowan had insisted on driving Saffie to the bus stop and waiting to see her onto the bus, that therefore if anyone had seen Saul, it would have been Rowan. She was sure, anyway, that Holly's concern over Saul's not being home was due to what Pete had called Holly's 'separation anxiety'. What teenage boy, after all, bothered to text his mum when he stayed out with mates for a few hours longer than he'd said? Especially one like Saul, who was obviously rebelling in a way Holly refused to acknowledge.

Jules took Saffie up a mug of hot chocolate, checked she was settled in bed and then went to snuggle up next to Rowan on the corner sofa to watch the ten o'clock news. Jules wanted to feel her husband's large arms around her. She wanted, too, to sense something she could only experience through physical contact with her husband. His warmth. His guiltlessness.

'Rowan. I know you don't want to hear his name, but you definitely didn't see Saul this morning when you dropped Saffie off at the bus stop?'

'Why would I want to see that little prick?'

'I know,' Jules said. 'I don't want to set eyes on him either at the moment. It's just . . . Holly says he hasn't been home.'

Rowan didn't reply. After a while, Jules sighed and said, 'Rowan, I think we need to talk in an adult way about what happened. Without getting upset.' *Without you knowing your daughter's pregnant*, said a voice in her head.

'There isn't an adult way to deal with a monster like Saul,' Rowan said. 'Animal behaviour warrants an animal response.'

'I think if you continue to feel this strongly, my love, it would be better for all of us to seek some outside advice.'

'Where from? Saffie doesn't want the school or the police involved. We've got our hands tied!'

Jules stopped herself from saying that Saffie hadn't wanted Rowan involved either but that didn't mean she was right. 'Where *did* you go this morning, after you dropped Saffie?' she asked instead. 'You weren't back when I left for work at nine thirty.'

'Went to Ely to get stuff for dinner,' he said. 'So I could cook for you. You looked tired and stressed this morning. I wanted to do something to help.' He turned to her. Put his arm about her neck, pulled her face to him and kissed her on the cheek.

'Yes. Thank you, Ro. It was lovely; I do appreciate it when you cook. Look, Rowan, don't get angry, but I was wondering whether the way to deal with this – the rape, I mean – if we're not involving the police, and since you don't want to contact Rape Crisis, might be to get some counselling or family therapy. To allow Saffie to talk through what's happened and what we all feel about it?'

Rowan threw the TV controls down on the sofa and sat up to look at Jules. 'The only people who need family therapy are Holly and Saul and that limp-dick Pete. He obviously doesn't therapize himself or he would have dealt with Saul. Given him a good thrashing at the very least, if Holly hasn't got the guts to do it. Surely as his new step-father he should take some action? But he's too lily-livered. They're the ones who should be seeking therapy. They're the ones who've let their son destroy my daughter.'

'She's *our* daughter, Rowan.'

Jules looked at her big, tall, blond husband. He had put on weight over the years and carried a bit of a paunch these days, but he was still handsome. Still big-boned and muscly and masculine. So it tugged at her heartstrings to see that he had tears in his eyes as he repeated, 'He's destroyed her. I'm trying to find a way to deal with this, but I just can't.'

Jules leaned over and stroked the back of his head where his short hair felt soft and velvety. 'She's not destroyed, though, darling. You underestimate her resilience. Saffie is disturbed, and very upset by what happened. Especially at the moment. While we're coming to terms with it. But she's not destroyed.'

'Saul has ruined her childhood,' he muttered. 'And it's all I can do to stop myself going round and smashing Pete's bloody head in for not keeping a proper eye on that boy. Have they done anything about him yet?'

Jules didn't reply to this. Instead, she said, 'Rowan, what worries me is your level of anger.'

'It warrants bloody anger,' Rowan said.

'And you're sure you didn't see Saul this morning?' Jules

asked again, compelled to reassure herself. Rowan didn't answer this time. Instead, he got up and walked out of the room, taking a swipe at the side of the leather sofa as he did so.

9

HOLLY

Saul still isn't home by half past eleven. I'm beside myself with worry. I've contacted everyone I can think of, including his one old friend Zak in London, but nobody has seen him. The fair's fallen silent. The families who've worked non-stop since dawn are inside their trailers or gone home to wherever they usually live. Pete, having disappeared upstairs after my outburst, comes back down.

'He isn't in yet?' Even he looks worried now.

'Should we phone the police?'

'I think perhaps we should at least register our concern,' he says. 'I'll do it, Holly.'

I sit and listen to his side of the conversation, grateful that he's trying to help.

'Since this morning,' I hear him say. 'The last time she saw him was eight o'clock, when he set off for school . . . No. He didn't go to his lessons. His mother checked . . . Yes . . . He had his school stuff when he left this morning. I think so.' He turns to me. 'Did you see him leave?'

'Pete, give the phone to me.'

I tell the policewoman I saw Saul go out of the door this morning.

'And the bus stop is just over the road from us. There was a fair arriving so I didn't see him get to it. Which is ironic, because I can usually see him from the front room in this house. I often watch him cross the road . . . just because

I can.' I don't say I watch him to see whether anyone will talk to him.

'Has he got family elsewhere? A friend he might be visiting?'

The policewoman has a high-pitched, girlish voice.

'I've checked everyone I know. Please,' I say. 'He's in some kind of danger. I'm sure of it.'

'He's not in a relationship? Been seeing a new crowd of friends? Has he been messaging anyone new on the internet?'

'Not as far as I know. He's never done this before. He always tells me where he is.'

'You're not aware of unwanted attention from anyone? He's not been the victim of bullying or of persecution?'

Saffie's accusation. The bullying he endured when we first moved here, kids calling him an 'emo' and other things that upset him.

'I . . . We had a bit of a disagreement on Sunday night,' is all I say.

'It's early days,' she says. 'It's quite common for kids of his age to go off after a family argument without telling anyone for a few hours. I'll file a report. Get back in touch if he's not back by the morning.'

I turn to Pete.

'She says to get back in touch if he's not here by morning,' I say. 'Morning! Surely that's far too long!'

We wait up. I pace up and down, alert to every sound – the wind rattling the letterbox, the creak of the pipes – longing for the turn of Saul's key in the lock. Pete tries to distract us with the TV, but the inane babble of voices simply irritates me. I text Saul again. He doesn't reply. I try ringing. His phone goes to voicemail. Bloody mobiles. They trick you into thinking you can keep tabs on your kids. By three in the morning, I tell Pete I can't wait any longer, and silently, he dials the police again.

'They're sending someone round,' he says.

*

The police arrive at 5 a.m. A man – it's difficult to tell his age: he's got the swagger of experience, and pockmarked olive skin – and a woman, with pale eyes and fine strawberry-blonde hair and the kind of delicate white complexion that blotches easily. They introduce themselves as Carlos Venesuela, detective inspector, and Detective Constable Maria Shimwell.

'Mind if we sit?' Venesuela asks, waving his hand over the sofa I've been contemplating getting rid of. Now I decide I'll never get rid of it. It's where I breastfed Saul and where Archie and I used to sit, my feet in his lap, to watch TV when Saul was in bed.

The two police officers sit side by side and the woman gives me a quick, nervous smile, a pink circle appearing on her chin. I wonder if she's allergic to things. I remember how Saul as a little boy got rashes when he ate strawberries, little pink weals appearing all up his soft arms and rounded thighs, his lips turning puce and raggedy round the edges.

They ask questions. They ask about timings, what he was wearing, where he was going, what he said as he left. I tell them everything they need to know. Saul's distinguishing marks – a crease in his left earlobe. Double-jointed thumbs, which he used to bend back just to horrify me. A birthmark the shape of Italy inside his right thigh.

Any piercings, tattoos, scars? they ask.

None. Unusual maybe, for a teenager.

I tell them all this. I don't tell them the way, when he was a child, the arches of his hot little feet fit exactly over my

174

thighs as we lay on the sofa. Or that the gulley in the back of his neck used to smell of almonds. Or that when he was little, you could humour him easily, as if the laughter were sitting there waiting to spill over. Before his dad died. Before he lost his joie de vivre. I don't tell them either, not yet, about his school refusal when we first came here, about the persecution of the other kids, the name-calling, about how hard I've worked to settle him in, about how he's still a loner. That he's sensitive and artistic and poetic and the loveliest boy you could hope to have, but how these attributes make life harder for an adolescent than others.

They ask if they can go upstairs to Saul's room and I lead the way.

He's taken his phone and iPad. But I show them his desktop computer.

DI Venesuela sits down and asks for Saul's password.

'I . . . I'm not sure.'

'That's fine,' he says. 'We have ways and means. Just speeds up the process if you know it.'

'I'm sorry. He's changed it.'

'OK. Well, I'll need a bit of time,' he says. 'If you wouldn't mind staying . . .' he says to Pete.

The woman asks me to accompany her back downstairs. She wants to have a more in-depth chat.

'He hasn't been seeing anyone new, you say?'

I explain again that he's a loner, that it's something I've worried about since we moved here.

'When was that?'

'Two years. Just over. It was hard for him, switching secondary schools, moving from London. He hasn't adjusted very well.'

'Does he have friends in London he's in touch with?'

'Well, yes. One. I thought he might have met up with him, but he hasn't.'

'Names? Contacts? We'll check them out again. Is there anything, anything else at all that's changed recently that might have triggered an out-of-character running-away?'

'His father died six years ago,' I tell her. 'And I remarried last year. But he's always got on with Pete.'

Saffie didn't want the rape reported to the police. And a little part of me, the godmother part, wonders if it's fair on Saffie, when she's asked her own mother not to report it. Or am I unconsciously protecting Saul by not telling them? It will certainly paint him in a negative light. However hard I plead that I don't believe it's true. So what do I say now? How's it going to help them find Saul? What relevance does it have? Then Jules's voice comes back to me: *Rowan's threatening to beat the living daylights out of him.* My son has been threatened because of Saffie's allegation. The police should know.

'Recently,' I say, 'my son was falsely accused of rape by a girl at his school.'

'I see,' she says. 'You'd better tell me more about this.'

'Do you . . . ? Can I make you a cup of tea?'

'Thank you.'

She follows me into the kitchen. I feel as if I'm seeing everything for the first time. The Matisse calendar, with Pete's and my work schedules marked on it. Invitations and unanswered letters stuffed into the wooden letter rack that once belonged to my mother. Reminders about when to put the recycling out pinned to the cork noticeboard. Saul's clutter on the surfaces: plastic water bottles, bike lights, a tangle of mobile charger leads. Everything's taken on new significance. *Look at us*, it seems to say. *We belong to a time you took for granted when everything seemed safe and predictable. You never bothered to register us until it was too late.*

'We need to rule out the possible connection between his disappearance and the allegation,' DC Shimwell says. 'Tell us everything you can. Since we're talking about rape, we also, obviously, need to ensure we're doing all we can to protect other women.'

Protect other women? DC Maria Shimwell believes my son is a danger to other women. She needs to know him. She needs to see him. Instead of forming an opinion based on the allegation of a thirteen-year-old.

'He was distraught when I told him what the girl said,' I tell her. 'Distraught that I could think such a thing of him. I work with students, teaching them about consent. He knows I have a low opinion of any kind of misogynistic behaviour.'

'Why would this girl have made it up?'

'I don't know why Saffie would lie,' I say. 'I know victims should be given the benefit of the doubt in rape allegations. I'm passionate about it. I get enough stick for it. I've been trolled on Twitter for speaking out about it. But it's just not Saul. He's not that kind of boy.'

'That's what they all say,' Shimwell says with a wry smile. 'Don't you remember the boy who tweeted, "This is not what a rapist looks like"?'

'He's my son. I'm not talking about what he *looks* like. It's who he is. I *know* him.'

'Why tell him what she said at all if you were so certain the girl was lying?'

'It seemed only fair to hear his side,' I say. 'To see whether they might have been having, I don't know, a teenage fumble . . .'

'Whether he *misunderstood* her when she said to stop?'

Heat rises to my face. I've just told her . . . I've dealt with scenarios like the one she's suggesting hundreds of times.

'That's not what I'm saying. I had to check there was nothing going on between them, something Saffie might be covering up.'

'And why would she cover it up?'

She lifts up her mug. She doesn't sip from it. I wonder if she really wanted tea to start with.

'Saul . . . People avoid him at school. He's not cool in their crowd. Perhaps it was to save face?'

Maria Shimwell appears to brush this theory aside.

'Is it possible he shocked himself by his behaviour, and when he realized you, his mother, whose opinion he clearly values, knew about it, that's what triggered . . .'

'Triggered what?'

'Whatever he's done.'

I stare at her. What does she think he's 'done'?

'As I say, he was shocked when I told him what Saffie had said. Horrified, in fact. And then he overheard Pete say he'd taken his daughters to their mum's because of it. Which would have devastated him. That Pete would think they needed protecting from him.'

She regards me for a moment. Then, 'Why question your son about it at all?' she asks again, 'if you were so certain from the start the girl was lying?'

Haven't we been through this? Is she never going to give up?

'Because,' I burst out, at my wits' end now, 'Jules's husband, the girl's father, threatened Saul. He said he'd sort him out himself if I didn't. I had to be seen to be doing something or I was afraid he'd keep his word.'

Now she puts the mug down.

'He told you this? The girl's father?'

178

'Her mum – Jules – she told me. She warned me if I didn't deal with Saul myself, her husband was going to do it for me.'

'What were her exact words? Can you remember?'

'She said . . .' I scroll back, trying to remember exactly what Jules said. *Rowan's threatening to beat the living daylights out of him.*

I relay the phrase to Shimwell, who looks at me through her pale blue eyes.

'That's why I asked Saul about what Saffie had said. I was trying to protect him. Things were getting out of hand. I wanted to be able to tell Jules and Rowan that he had categorically denied it. I even thought we could get the kids to talk to each other. Through a mediator, if necessary. Anything to get Saffie to confess to us what made her lie about Saul like that, and stop Rowan taking the situation into his own hands.'

'Do you think this . . . Rowan . . . meant it? Or was it the kind of empty threat any father might make after hearing his thirteen-year-old has been raped?'

I think of Jules, her love for Rowan. All the times I thought she ought to leave him but said nothing. If he was a genuine danger to her, I would have urged her to seek help, of course I would. But in spite of everything, he never laid a finger on her. And he made her happy. And I knew that when you love someone, you do not want to be told you're making a terrible mistake. You don't want to be told the man you're with isn't who you think he is. Jules loves Rowan. If I'd expressed my views, I would have lost her. And that was something I couldn't bear. Can I bear it now?

'Rowan's been OK recently,' I say to Shimwell.

'Recently?'

'He had to attend anger management classes. He used to

179

have a temper on him. He had a caution for something – lashing out at someone. But it was years ago.'

'And you were afraid he might assault your son, for what he believed he did to his daughter?'

'He threatened to. Their daughter didn't want you involved. She was adamant. And her mum – my friend – she wanted us to sort it out between ourselves. But once she'd told her husband, I could see the situation was going to escalate. I took his threat seriously. I told Saul myself about the rape claim to stop Rowan from doing so. I wanted to hear him say out loud that he didn't do it. I thought he might have some theory as to why the girl lied. I was going to report it back to the parents. But I never believed for a minute he was guilty.'

'Thank you,' she says. 'All this will help with our enquiries.' She stands up and I'm struck by how thin she is. I admire her pluckiness, taking on a job that must put her in some very risky situations when she appears so frail. 'I'd like to check those tweets you mentioned. I'll make a report and we'll be in touch.'

*

As Maria Shimwell gathers her things, Venesuela comes back downstairs with Pete. 'Has your son ever expressed suicidal thoughts?' Venesuela asks, coming into the kitchen.

My head shoots up. 'Why?'

'There's something I think you should look at on his computer.'

I follow him upstairs and into Saul's room, where Pete is sitting at the computer, staring at the words *I hate myself and want to die* emblazoned across the screen.

'It's the title of a song,' I say. My words feel crumbly, insubstantial, because I know what it means. 'Isn't it?'

Venesuela doesn't reply. He clicks on the mouse pad and opens another window. A Nirvana fan club page. I read the posts on the alternative methods of suicide Kurt Cobain could have used if he hadn't shot himself. Suggested overdoses, how to get the right vein when you slit your wrists, the best knots for a successful hanging. Venesuela won't allow me respite. He clicks on 'history' and up pops Cobain's suicide note, packed full of his angst-ridden self-hatred. The empathy he has for human suffering that means he can't tolerate life anymore. Saul has always had an excess of empathy. He knew when Jules had lost a baby; he knew when I needed comforting after Archie died. Has all this empathy become intolerable to him? On top of the fact he himself has been so completely misunderstood?

'We'll get the crime investigation department involved straight away,' Venesuela says. 'They'll instigate a search.'

He pulls something black and rectangular out of a pocket and says into it, 'Potential suicide, young man, six foot, white, dark hair.'

Those words will ricochet around my head forever.

*

The police leave at 6.30 a.m. They've looked through my Twitter feed, gone through Saul's computer again, and they tell me they'll be in touch the minute they hear anything. My eyes are dry and itchy from lack of sleep. Pete's in the kitchen making me more sweet tea that I don't want.

At eight o'clock, twenty-four hours since Saul left the house, I try to recreate the moment he went off, heading, as I thought, for the bus. Was there anything different about him? Did he reply when I said I loved him? Did he look back?

I didn't watch him go for once. The fair with its trailers

and stalls had stolen Saul's space on the green. I didn't want to see him pushed into the midst of the school crowd against his will. I try to visualize whether he was wearing a coat. He'd always argued he'd be too hot. Even on days when the north wind was blowing straight off the Urals. Was he carrying his school bag? Or something bulkier, fuller? Had he planned to get away? None of the details I need will come back to me.

Outside the window, on the edge of the green, where the fairground has left a little gap near the bus stop, the children are gathering, starling-like, twittering, in their black school uniforms, with their bags and their water bottles. Saffie's there, flaunting her short black skirt, white shirt and tie so that she looks like a model in a magazine. She's surrounded by a crowd of admiring girls, none of them quite as striking as she is. A tall boy I've seen before approaches her, says something to her. She turns from him and begins to walk away, saying something over her shoulder. He chases after her, and in the end she turns and shouts, and he falls about laughing. I remember from my Rape Crisis days how survivors of rape report a violation not just of their bodies but also of their whole person, their agency, of who they are. Saffie, I think, doesn't look cowed, or ground down, or weighted by guilt, or on edge every time some boy moves close to her. The only clue that she's less than happy in her skin is her habit of clawing obsessively at her sleeves – a little tic she's acquired recently. But I rein in these thoughts because I am doing what I know I should not do. Generalizing. Making assumptions about how rape victims look. The way assumptions are often made in court. When the reality is that there is no blueprint for how a victim looks. Everyone is different. Everyone deals with an assault differently. You cannot judge by a person's demeanour.

I phone work and explain to Luma that under the circumstances I can't face going in. She's sympathetic, tells me to take as long as I need. But then the day lies before me, long and empty.

'No, thanks, Pete.' I push the mug of tea away. 'I have to go and look for him.'

'Leave it to the police,' Pete says. 'They know what to do.'

'How can they? They don't know him.'

I've remembered the conversation Saul and I had the night we walked over to Jules's house. When Saul said he loved the Fenland skies, and the swans' nests and the muntjacs. Perhaps Saul didn't get on the bus but took one of the tracks away from the village through farmland to the river. Walked alone into the Fens. If he'd gone into the countryside, it would be why no one had seen him.

He'd said he liked spending time on his own, that it was his choice.

That would be just like him. Wanting to be alone. After overhearing Pete saying he had to protect his girls from him. I remember what he said when I tried to get him to deny the rape once and for all: *Everyone round here's the same. All gagging for gossip to make their boring little lives more exciting. Let them have it. They're all fucking sickos. Saffie. Her school mates. The lot of them.*

No wonder he wanted to get away.

'I'm going out,' I tell Pete. 'It's all I can do. I have to keep moving. Can you stay here in case he comes home?'

I pull on my parka, some trainers. Pete looks anxious but agrees to stay at home, says he has work to do. 'I'll ring the minute there's any news,' he promises.

I walk away from the village, over the level crossing to the cycle path that leads through the young wood of beech saplings, their leaves copper brown now, and then join the river at the old toll bridge. I start to walk north towards Ely. The path is empty. It runs along a raised flood bank from which I can see the Fens laid out flat to either side. A mile or so along the bank, over the river and beyond the railway line, Jules and Rowan's sprawling modern home is visible, with its kitchen extension and its decking and large garden. I wonder what Jules is going through. What she's thinking about now she's had time to reflect on Saffie's allegation. I'd love to go and talk to her, as I would once have done. To ask her for her advice about Saul. I imagine her reassurance. I imagine us talking the way we did in the car that night on the way to the pub. The last time we spoke to each other compassionately, as friends.

You can see for miles across the flat land. Land that was once under water. Swampland where communities sustained themselves among sedge and willow, on reeds, rush and peat. There is so much of it, and so much sky. The clouds part, allowing shards of pale sunlight through. The reeds along the shallows of the river turn white. I walk past the pumping station and the long drain that cuts a brown gash between the fields. Ditches that carry flood water, glittering to the edges of the land. Time carrying Saul further and further from me. Have the drains swallowed up my son? Carried him out to the Norfolk Wash? To the deep North Sea, lying beyond the Fens?

When I first visited Jules here, Saul and I had just come back from a week in Italy, one of the villages of the Cinque Terre. Everything there was vertical, soft pink and terracotta palazzos piled above our heads. Vineyards clambering up terraced cliff sides. Rock faces dropping down to clear blue water. Peaks of mountains soaring into the clouds.

I couldn't believe the contrast. How everything in Jules's new environment was horizontal, as if the landscape we'd seen in Italy had been tipped over on its side and rolled flat. Lines, stripes. Ploughed fields like brown corduroy spread out, the flat satin ribbons of drains, stumpy willows fraying on the banks. Telegraph wires strung across the endless sky. Railway tracks disappearing towards the horizon. I didn't know how Jules could bear the exposure. The knowing there was nothing out there but what was in front of her eyes. Now I know even this wide-open landscape contains secrets. Its open face is deceptive.

I keep on walking. At some point, I find myself in some thin beech woods, light coming between the sparse silvery branches. A swan's nest, a big circle of organized twigs like a basket, is built into a gap in the reeds beside the river. Is this the one Saul referred to? Did he come this way to find it again? I beat my way through the reeds, startling a small bird. The nest is empty, abandoned. There's nothing here, no clue, no sign. A hare leaps out of the undergrowth and away from me. A heron takes flight, its broad wings dragging a shadow across the surface of the water as it sets off along the trajectory of the river.

The wind turns cold; it smells like rain. There's the faintest hint of salt on the wind from the sea, from Hunstanton or Brancaster, from the Norfolk Wash. Dark clouds gather in a bank on the horizon and roll towards me.

I want to walk forever. But I'm walking for my own sanity. This isn't the way to find Saul. I've come so far, I feel light-headed, shaky, in need of a sugar boost. I turn and make my way home, taking the long country road back towards the village that crosses the railway line north of the station, past Jules's house. It's too late to turn back when I realize the woman coming towards me is Jules. We can't avoid each other on this exposed road, raised above the fields to either side. As she gets closer, her eyes meet mine, and I see she too has been crying. My instinct is to reach out, hug her, tell her I love her. That we have to work together. That our friendship is invaluable to me, even now.

'I'm looking for Saul,' I say as she reaches me. 'He hasn't come home. All night. I'm beside myself.'

'I'm sorry to hear that, Holly. I'm sure he'll be back. And I'm glad I've run into you.'

'Me too.'

'Because I have proof. That he did rape Saffie.'

I blink at her harsh tone, when I was expecting reconciliation.

'Saffie's pregnant.'

'*What?*' I hear the words, but they don't make sense.

'Saffie's pregnant. So there's no more doubt about what happened. I'd like you to take back what you said about Saffie being devious. That was hurtful, Holly, and it was untrue.'

Behind her, the earth is purple-black as far as the eye can see, rich alluvial soil that looks like darkest, richest cocoa. Push a sapling into it, they say, and it will spring up in seconds. Poke seedlings into that soil and you have a crop in weeks. Saffie has conceived a child. Just like that. When women twice or three times her age and desperate to conceive, as her mother was, find it so difficult.

The rain I'd seen coming reaches us in a gust, knocking into us both. Jules pulls up the hood on her mac, tightens the cords, leaving just her eyes, nose and mouth on view.

'That doesn't mean it was rape,' I say. 'It doesn't mean it was Saul. I'm sorry she's pregnant. But it could be anyone's.'

Jules looks at me aghast. 'Are you implying Saffie sleeps around?'

I open my mouth to explain that I'm simply saying the fact she's pregnant proves nothing about Saul, but Jules goes on. 'Saffie's thirteen! She hasn't been out with anyone ever. The pregnancy tallies with the date he raped her. It's keeping me awake at night. The enormity of it for her. The responsibility of it. She doesn't want anyone else to know. In fact, you're the only person, apart from Donna, who I've told. You've no idea what a burden that is.'

I pull my parka closer around me. I wonder now if the tears in Jules's eyes are caused by the wind rather than crying.

Jules goes on. 'Your . . . son is putting us through hell and you've let him walk away, scot-free, without suffering any consequences and without taking any responsibility for what he's done.'

We're no longer able to speak to each other without raising our voices over the rain, which is torrential now, drumming on the road, running down my face. The rumble of a train adds to the background cacophony. I turn round to watch it pass, its carriage windows lit up, yellow squares flickering in the gloom. I decide to ignore the gap she left before the word 'son'. What epithet she thought better of applying to him.

'Saul has nothing to do with this pregnancy,' I say with as much dignity as I can muster. 'He's done something terrible to himself. Because of what's been said about him. I wouldn't have even questioned him if it wasn't for Rowan's threat. I wish now I'd had the courage to ignore that. Your husband is a brute.'

'He was defending his daughter.' Jules is shocked, I can tell, by my insulting Rowan.

'Can you imagine what this has done to Saul? The police think he may have killed himself in despair at the way everyone – you, Rowan, Pete – misjudged him.'

I wonder if there's a momentary look of concern on her brow, but if there is, it's short-lived.

'Perhaps he's run off because he doesn't want to face the consequences of raping my daughter,' she says. 'If he'd hung around, he'd know he'd left her pregnant at thirteen with a termination to go through. She says it's ruined her life. Well, I think, don't you, that he should suffer a little too? Saul's life should be a little bit ruined as well, since he did this to her. You've done nothing to sort him out!'

I want to walk away from this conversation. It seems that the more each of us says, the more irreversible our recriminations become. We are sinking into a kind of verbal quicksand.

'Saul isn't a coward,' I tell her. 'He would never have run away from something he knew was wrong. But to know he'd been falsely accused, on top of all the other vindictive things that have been said about him at that school, that was *hell* for him. He couldn't cope with it.' I have another sudden, almost unbearable, pang of longing for Archie. 'It would have been different if his dad were still alive. He'd have stood by Saul, helped him get through it. But Archie's not here and I've never missed him more than I do right now.'

I wish in a way I hadn't uttered this last sentence. I'm beginning to sound self-pitying, and as if I'm trying to divert the subject away from the central one. But I've said it, and it hangs in the air while the rain patters down on the mulch that's formed on the verges. Jules is quiet for a few moments, her mouth open, as if she's debating what to say next. At last she speaks again.

'Actually,' she says quietly, 'I'm not sure Archie would have stood by Saul, because he cared about *justice*.'

'Yes, he cared about justice. He would have known Saul

was innocent. He would have fought to prove it. He knew his son.'

Jules frowns. 'Oh, please, Holly! Stop putting Archie on a pedestal. He had other things on his mind when Saul was a child. Archie wasn't there for Saul all the time any more than Pete is.'

'What do you mean?'

She stops for a second; then, as if she's made a decision, she goes on quietly, almost in a whisper, 'How did Archie get to the hospital so quickly? When he had his heart attack? Who was with him? Did Philippa ever tell you?'

'I don't know what you're saying. What's Philippa got to do with it?'

'You're in denial,' Jules says. 'In denial about Archie, in denial about your son.'

I look at Jules. My friendship with her, which I had taken to be the steadiest in my life, has veered off into a territory I never foresaw. Because friendship does not remain constant, as I had once believed, and Jules's response to her daughter's allegation is revealing a different woman to the one I thought I knew. A woman who has turned on her odd son as if she was waiting for an opportunity to do so. Who has been secretly judging me for the way I've brought him up. Not only that, Jules is a woman who is prepared to insult my dead husband.

I walk away from her towards the village, and Jules moves towards her house across the railway line, as the barriers on the crossing clang down behind her.

*

There was only once in the past when Jules and I almost fell out.

Soon after Archie died, Jules came round to see me. Saul,

just ten, and Saffie, seven, were playing together upstairs and I was showing Jules photos I'd taken the previous month while we were all on holiday in Aldeburgh. We'd rented a house overlooking the broad pebble beach, the scuffed hulls of upturned boats lying against a restless sky. We spent days wandering up and down the High Street stopping for coffees or queuing for fish and chips. Jules and I had browsed in delis and shops selling sea-themed bric-a-brac, second-hand books and antiques while Archie and Rowan went fishing and drank pints in the pub. Saul and Saffie trailed along behind us begging for ice creams, to go to an arcade, for more chips. A classic English seaside holiday. Nothing special, nothing remarkable.

Until I realized I would never have one like it again.

'Look,' I said, poring over the photos on my laptop of a smiling Archie, black hair swept by the wind off his high forehead, eyes shielded behind Ray-Bans, holding up a pint in a pub garden. 'We had no idea as we sat there that in a few weeks Archie would be dead.'

'You mustn't think like that,' Jules had consoled me. 'You must hold on to those good memories. See them as something to cherish.'

I rounded on her. 'How do you know,' I snapped, 'how it feels to have lost someone?'

I banged the laptop shut. I didn't want to look at those happy days, so recent and yet so infinitely far. For a little while, I couldn't speak to Jules, whose lack of understanding made me feel even more bereft than before. I left her and went into the kitchen to fume silently on my own.

When I got back to Jules, half an hour or so later, she looked at me sadly.

The sadness was partly because I was being selfish and abrasive with her while she was trying to help. But it was also, I was about to realize, because she *had* just lost someone. When she told me quietly that she had been pregnant but had had another miscarriage just after that holiday, her third in a row since she'd had Saffie, I couldn't speak for shame.

'I'm so very sorry,' I said eventually. 'I have become horribly volatile and self-centred since Archie died. And I've become so inward-looking I have forgotten other people have tragedies too. What I said was unforgivable.'

'It's OK,' she said. 'You're grieving. I'm not surprised you feel angry when people say stupid things. And it was a stupid thing.'

'It wasn't. It was a wise thing. You were telling me to cherish what I had. It's just so hard to put into practice.'

There was perhaps a small pause then that I didn't register at the time. Jules's beautiful blue eyes gazing into mine with a look I took to be sympathy at my loss.

'I can't see much good in life since losing another baby, either,' she murmured.

'You're grieving too.'

'Yes. For my last chance to have another child.' She tried to smile.

'But it's not your last chance. You mustn't think like that. You can try again. You *must* try again.'

'No, Holly,' she said. 'I decided if I lost this one, I couldn't go through it again. Saffie's perfect anyway. She's healthy, she's beautiful, and I'm grateful to have her.'

'If it's any consolation,' I said, 'Saul's the only child I'm ever going to have too. I wouldn't want another child with anyone else now I've lost Archie.'

We sat for some time at the table and drained the rest of a bottle of white wine, and commiserated, and I knew she forgave me for my outburst. That was the sort of friend Jules was.

Saul and Saffie came hurtling downstairs then, Saffie dressed as a superhero, Saul brandishing a lightsaber at her. I poured them juice, and Saul opened the garden door and ran outside, Saffie in hot pursuit.

'Wouldn't it be nice, and kind of right somehow,' Jules said, 'if Saul and Saffie have a baby when they grow up? Their child would be both of ours.'

There was a crash and a howl and Saul came to the garden door saying Saffie had pushed him off the climbing frame. Saffie, six inches shorter, three years younger, rosy-cheeked, came behind, saying Saul had called her a wimp and he deserved it. Jules and I looked at each other and laughed. I suggested it was time for a DVD, and once they were quiet, I returned to Jules.

'Their baby would be the other child neither of us is going to have,' I said.

She put her hand out and squeezed mine, and I knew then that our friendship, in spite of everything, was intact. Would always be intact.

Now, on the wet fen road, as I make my way home to see if there's any news of Saul, it seems the very thing we dreamed would seal our bond forever – a mutual grandchild – is smashing our friendship apart.

'Grandma Holly and Granny Jules,' Jules had said. 'That's if the kids don't kill each other first.'

*

'The police are rerunning all the CCTV footage they've collected from around the village,' Pete says from the kitchen as I come in the door. I peel my parka off and fling it on a chair. 'They're interviewing the fairground folk. Been down at the train station questioning commuters. They've done house-to-house enquiries. A couple of kids say they saw Saul come out of the house yesterday morning.'

'That hardly helps. I saw him leave the house. It's what happened afterwards that matters.'

Pete barely reacts to my mood. He fails to pick up the fact I'm reeling from another blow.

Saffie pregnant! Archie not being there for Saul? What did Jules mean?

'They say it was hard to see where he went,' Pete goes on, 'because of the fair on the green. No one saw him on the bus. They're running checks on drivers leaving the village yesterday morning.'

'I saw Jules,' I tell Pete. I sit down at the kitchen table, hug myself. Rock back and forth on the chair. 'Saffie's pregnant.'

'She's *pregnant*?'

'It doesn't prove anything except that she's been sleeping with someone.'

'Oh my God. That poor kid.'

'Why do you keep sympathizing with Saffie? Saul's missing and you continue to believe she's the victim.'

'But she's pregnant,' Pete says. 'Perhaps it's time we considered Saffie is telling the truth. Perhaps if we support them, they'll support us, and we can work together to find Saul and—'

Without knowing I'm going to, I pick up a wineglass – the first thing that comes to hand – and hurl it across the kitchen. It shatters on the quarry-tiled floor. In that second, I see Saul lifting his iPad as if to hurl it across my room the night I was getting ready to go out with Jules. Frustration, anguish – we all have our tipping points.

'She might be pregnant, but it wasn't Saul who raped

her,' I say. 'He's done something terrible to himself because he's been wrongly accused.'

I want to add that Archie would never have doubted Saul, but Jules's words are fresh in my mind. *Archie had other things on his mind when Saul was a child.*

Pete catches my arm before I pick up the next thing close to hand – a jar of marmalade – and stops me smashing that on the floor too. I sob, beating my fists against Pete's chest until he enfolds me in his arms. 'Calm down,' he breathes into my ear. 'It's OK. Saul's going to be OK.'

*

By evening, the local news has got wind of the fact Saul's missing. The coverage shows villagers searching through the river, along the ditches, across the muddy fields and through disused farm buildings. I recognize the family who run the village shop. The barman from the White Swan. They're all out there helping. Doing what they can.

'Keeps himself to himself a bit,' says a boy introduced as Noel, the tall, good-looking boy I've seen chasing Saffie on the green in the mornings. 'He's, like, quiet. Takes a good photo.'

The boy's dad, Rob, comes on. I recognize him. His name is familiar. I realize with a jolt that he's the man Jules had the affair with when she first moved up here. The microbiologist.

'We all feel for him,' Rob says. 'All of us with teenage boys ourselves. We want to do everything we can to find him.' He's slender, dark, quietly spoken, with a sensitive face. I can see why Jules was attracted to him. Rowan's opposite.

'He's one of our quieter, more serious students,' Harry Bell, Saul's form tutor, says into the camera. 'A good pupil. One we value highly. We're deeply shocked at school to hear he's missing.'

Saul's head teacher, Joanna Blackwell, comes on, says they're all devastated about the news and are doing everything they can to help find him. I don't want to watch anymore. I reach for the TV controls to switch it off. Pete and I still haven't spoken, the tension of earlier hanging in the air between us. Pete gets up, and goes upstairs without speaking. I'm about to follow him, to apologize for my outburst earlier, to explain it's because I can't handle this any longer, that I'm at my wits' end, when there's a ping on my phone. It's a text. I don't recognize the number. I open it and read. I stare at the text for some time, my head throbbing.

'Gone to be close to Dad. Love you, Mum. Saul xxxx'

'Pete!' I call, at last.

He doesn't answer.

I look again at my phone.

'Gone to be close to Dad. Love you, Mum. Saul xxxx'

My fingers tremble as I text a reply. 'Saul, I'm worried sick. Where are you?'

The minute I've pressed 'send', a window pops up. 'Your text was not delivered.'

I dial the number, but the phone tells me the number is blocked to incoming calls.

I go to the bottom of the stairs, call up to Pete.

'Pete, come here, please. Look at this. Read it.'

'We should tell the police,' Pete says. He holds my phone, gazes down at it.

'I'll ring them. Give them the number.'

'What does he mean, though? "Gone to be close to Dad"?'

Pete frowns.

'Do you think perhaps he's gone to Archie's grave? Isn't it in East Finchley Cemetery?'

I stare at Pete, relief flooding through me, thankful that

he has come up with a plausible explanation. That he's doing what he can to help after all.

'Maybe! Maybe you're right.'

'You're to relax, Holly. I'll bring you a drink. This could be the news we've been waiting for.' He pulls me to him and kisses me. For a few moments, I allow the warmth of his body against mine to squeeze all the tension and fear and anxiety away. Saul's text means he's alive. That we'll find him. That everything will be OK.

Pete brings me a glass of wine, and I stare out of the window while he goes to phone the police. It's dark outside, and the leaves on the trees, lit up by the street lights, look white underneath, blood red on the top. The grass, black in patches, silvery under the lights, is churned up now the fair's departed. If Saul's run away because of what we said, it's obvious he would choose a place he feels he might be close to Archie. Why hadn't I thought of that? Pete comes back in, puts his arms round me.

'She says they'll send some officers to check out the cemetery. They'll do all they can to track the number.'

'Oh, oh God. Thank goodness. Thanks, Pete.' I turn to face him, letting him embrace me.

'This is good news,' he says into my ear. 'They'll find him, Holly. They will.'

*

Later, overwhelmed with exhaustion, I go to lie down in bed. Jules's face looms and fades, the way she looked on the road in the rain, begging me to share the trauma of the termination with her. After a while, I sleep.

Soon after Archie died, I used to have a recurring dream in which they discover Archie is not dead after all, has just passed out for a while. When I woke up, the sense that he was in the bed next to me, his chest rising and falling, was warm and comforting. If I reached out, I would be able to touch his shoulder, his back, to snuggle into him. I experience the same sense of relief as I wake with a start now. Archie is next to me, a mound of warmth. Saul is sitting on the bed. If I stretch out a hand, I can hold his. For a few minutes, before fully waking, I have a sense of completion. I haven't lost my husband after all. Saul has come home. Saffie has dropped her allegation against him. Jules and I are friends again.

Then something disturbs me, the wind rattling the windowpanes, the patter of mice in the roof, and reality slams in.

I look at the alarm clock on Pete's side of the bed. It's three in the morning. I'm not in our London house at all, but out in the Fens. Archie's dead. Saul isn't here.

I shake Pete awake. 'Did the police phone back? Did they look in the cemetery? Have they found him?'

Pete puts his arms round me. 'Not yet,' he says. 'They promise they'll ring the minute they have anything. I've been lying here, half awake, in case the phone goes.'

Saul's text floats into my mind's eye and I pick up my mobile to check it again.

'Gone to be close to Dad.'

I shake Pete again.

'I know what Saul means. He's done it, Pete. I'm sure. "Gone to be close to Dad." His dad's *dead*, Pete. It's as the police first thought. What else can he mean? Except that he's killed himself?'

10

JULES

Bumping into Holly on the country road left Jules feeling desolate. Holly hadn't been at all supportive. On the contrary, she had refused to show any sympathy. Jules understood Holly's anguish at not knowing where Saul was. But Holly had made no attempt to understand *her* distress at discovering Saul had left Saffie pregnant. It was as if they were two different women to the ones who were best friends until a few days ago. Jules needed Holly to take back what she'd said about Saffie. She'd hoped she might even agree to share the emotional burden of putting her through a termination. But to do that, Holly had to first stop denying that Saul must be responsible, which she point-blank refused to do.

Jules hadn't meant, ever, to tell Holly those things about Archie. She had always thought it better that Holly cherish her memories of him as the perfect husband and father she believed him to be. But Holly had driven her to it, with her insistence that if Archie were alive, he would somehow prove Saul's innocence. It was ridiculous of Holly to continue to see Archie through rose-coloured spectacles. (Jules didn't admit to herself, not yet, that her response might also have been to do with Holly's calling Rowan a brute.) And so Jules had cracked, and told Holly the one thing she had sworn she'd keep from her. That Archie wasn't such a golden boy after all. It was time she faced up to reality: her men were no more perfect than Rowan was.

A lot less perfect, in fact.

As she walked home, the only human figure on the wet arable landscape that rolled away to the horizon, she realized that without Holly to share what she was going through, she felt lonelier than she ever had in her life.

*

Later that afternoon, Jules found Rowan slumped in front of the TV. The police and a posse of local volunteers were combing the Fens, dragging the river. Looking for Saul. Familiar faces blown up so large on their home cinema screen they might have been here in the sitting room rather than out there beyond the picture windows, crawling through the wet mud of the Fens. The good, neighbourly people of the village. People Rowan and Jules knew. People they had competed with at the pub quiz, or chatted to in the playground when Saffie was still at primary school.

'We're here to help the lad,' Tina from the village shop said into the camera. 'We're here to help find him.'

'All lines of enquiry are open,' Detective Inspector Venesuela, in charge of the investigation, said. He faced the camera. He was youngish, and looked as if he was enjoying his fifteen minutes of fame. He spoke in a self-important tone, puffing out his chest. 'We are in the process of questioning witnesses. There is some evidence the sixteen-year-old may have intended to harm himself, but this is not conclusive.'

Jules knew very well what the detective meant by 'harm himself' and she objected to this ludicrous euphemism. It shocked and angered her in equal measure. Saul leaving evidence that he was contemplating suicide was harrowing, but at the same time deeply guilt-tripping. How was that going to make Saffie feel? Jules would do her best to keep her daughter away from these news bulletins.

'Holly's honoured Saffie's request that no one else should know Saul raped her, at least,' Jules said, sitting down next to Rowan.

'She's afraid of her son becoming the stuff of gossip,' Rowan said. 'That's all it is.'

'Maybe it's a police strategy. I mean, it's quite possible Saul's disappearance has nothing to do with what he did to Saffie. The main thing is,' Jules said, 'everyone's pulling together to find him.'

She told herself Saul would soon turn up. And when he did, she would make sure he finally admitted what he'd done. And then they would all share the trauma of the termination together. And once that was done with, Saffie could be given counselling, and Saul would be given anger management, or something, just as Rowan had had, and they could move on.

Rowan wasn't about to move on, however.

'Good student, my arse,' he growled as Harry Bell, Saul's form tutor, came onto the screen and spoke about Saul's studiousness, his seriousness, what a treasured pupil he was. 'That boy's a waster. Everyone knows that. And just look at that load of do-gooders.'

Rowan had a can of beer in one hand, and sat and swore at the people whose food he had eaten and drinks he had drunk, at the people who had come to their barbecues and joined in with them at dances in the school hall, cursing the lot of them for trying to save the life of a rapist. 'Why are they wasting their time? That boy deserves whatever's happened to him.'

'Rowan, please,' Jules said.

When the news had finished, Rowan said he was going to the pub 'to calm myself down'.

It wasn't much more than thirty minutes after he left that the doorbell rang.

Two police officers stood at the door, silhouetted against a greenish sunset that lent them an eerie, otherworldly appearance.

'We'd like a word with you about the disappearance of Saul Seymore,' said the man. 'This is my colleague Detective Constable Maria Shimwell. I'm Detective Inspector Carlos Venesuela.'

The same faces Jules had seen on the TV screen only an hour or so earlier come to life in front of her. Venesuela and Shimwell glanced around Jules's large sitting room, the one with the picture window that gave a view over the fen down towards the river. Everything out there, the wet fields, the pollarded willows just losing their leaves, with their stumpy trunks and flailing young branches, was washed in the same bottle-green light.

Jules could see that this beautiful room impressed the detective constable. Her pale face coloured as swiftly as litmus paper as she took in the home cinema and the enlarged photos of Saffie as a baby that they'd had printed on to canvas, the cream corner sofa, and the other one in pigeon-grey buttery leather.

'We hear that your daughter made an allegation of rape against the boy who disappeared on Monday morning,' she said, turning away from the window at last and facing Jules.

Jules stared at the thin policewoman. They had all worked so hard to keep the allegation quiet, and surely – *surely* – as she'd just said to Rowan, Holly wouldn't want to tell the police about something that would cast Saul in a negative light.

'Would you mind if we spoke to her?' Shimwell went on.

'Saffie didn't want to report the rape,' Jules began. 'She

was afraid you wouldn't believe her. That you'd want to examine her for proof. We decided we'd honour her request. It seemed better not to upset her any further.'

'It wouldn't be like that.' The woman smiled reassuringly. 'We have a special suite for investigations involving children and sex offences. But at the moment we only want to talk. This isn't a rape investigation. It's a missing person enquiry. And we'll be careful with her – please don't worry. I'm Detective Constable Maria Shimwell – she can call me Maria.'

'Where did you hear about it? The rape, I mean?'

'The boy – the one who's gone missing – his mother told us an allegation had been made against him. Didn't want it made public either. We're doing our best to keep the media off it.'

Jules stared at the police officers, taking this in. Holly's words just a few hours earlier rang in her ears: 'The police think he may have killed himself in despair at the way everyone misjudged him.' She should have realized Holly had given the police the full picture. It was understandable, she supposed. Her priority was finding Saul and she would have wanted to provide any information that might help. Being accused of rape might well have given Saul motivation to run away to avoid the consequences.

'I'll go and get her,' Jules said to Maria, 'but please be gentle with her. She's been through a lot.'

'Of course.'

Jules went into Saffie's room. She was reading a book and looked up as Jules pushed open the door.

'Saffie, listen. The police are here . . .'

'What?' Saffie leaped up from her bed and backed away from Jules. 'No, Mum . . . no. You promised you wouldn't tell them. You *promised*.'

'I didn't tell them anything Saff. They're not here about

the rape. They're here because Saul hasn't been home. They're trying to find him. They just need some background information.'

'What kind of background information? *I* don't know where he's gone. How am I supposed to help them? Oh, Mum. Please don't make me speak to them.'

Saffie began to shake visibly, her teeth chattering.

'If you prefer, I can ask the woman – she's young; she seems really nice – to speak to you up here? I'll stay with you. She won't ask you anything embarrassing or awkward, I promise. If she does, I'll be here to step in, OK?'

'A woman?'

'Yes. Young. Nice.'

'OK,' Saffie said after a while. 'I'll come down. If you promise to stay with me.'

Saffie followed Jules silently downstairs and sat without speaking on the edge of the corner sofa.

Maria squatted down in front of her. Jules couldn't help thinking that Saffie didn't look much younger than the strawberry-blonde, pale-faced Maria Shimwell. Saffie's thighs, Jules noticed, bulged in the tight leggings she was wearing, and her T-shirt strained over her burgeoning chest. Were these physical symptoms of what was going on inside her, that only she, Donna Browne, and now Holly, knew about? It made her want to cry. For the child she still was. For not protecting her.

'You mustn't be frightened, sweetie,' Maria said. 'You are not in trouble. We just need to ask a few questions because a boy who goes to your school has gone missing. We're asking everyone who knows him, not just you. We're trying to get a picture of everything up to and including the day he didn't come home. Do you mind if I call my colleague in? He's a detective. I can ask him to stay out if you'd rather.'

'Yes, please,' Saffie said. 'I would rather he stayed out.'

'But your mother can stay here, if you'd like her to?'

'Yes.'

'I'm going to ask some questions about a boy called Saul. Saul Seymore. Do you know who I'm talking about?'

'I didn't want to tell anyone what he did to me, in case *this* happened,' Saffie burst out. 'In case you – the police – got called in. But Mum told his mum. And now I'm in trouble for—'

'Right. You are not in any trouble,' Maria said. She was far more assertive than her appearance implied. 'You are *not*. You are not to worry about that. All we want to know is whether you have any idea where the boy might have gone.'

'No.'

'How well do you know him?'

'Quite well. Or at least I did when he was younger.'

'You don't hang out with him at school? Or at weekends?'

'No way. We don't talk. I only know him because he's Mum's godson. Well, not godson, because she and Holly aren't really religious. They say "odd son". But he's three years above me in school. And everyone thinks . . .'

'Everyone thinks what?'

'Everyone thinks he's a creep. Because of how he acts.'

'Acts?'

'He kind of prowls around on his own, and sometimes he . . . stares.'

Jules flinched as she heard Saffie trot out this description of Saul. *He stares.* How could she have got him so wrong?

Maria wrote copious notes on her iPad. 'Anything else?' she asked.

'And 'cos of the way he dresses and his hair. He's an emo and . . . well, no one really likes emos at school.'

'And by "emo" you mean . . . ?'

'He's miserable and moody and silent. He goes about on his own.'

'OK, and can you tell me a little more about your relationship with him?'

'I wasn't in a relationship with him.' Saffie shuddered at the suggestion.

'Was he friends with any of your friends?'

'Nope.'

'Do you think he might have been under the impression he was having a relationship with you?'

'I don't see how. We never talk. We don't hang out together.'

'But he was in your house last . . . two Fridays ago?'

'He came round to use our internet,' Jules interjected. 'I feel so bad now . . . trusting him alone in the house with Saff. But he's my oldest friend's son, and I know him. Thought I knew him. I mean, I regarded him almost as another child of mine when he was younger. To be honest, it didn't occur to me there was any reason not to trust him.'

'OK,' said Maria, turning to Saffie again. 'So, you mentioned earlier you didn't want to say what he did to you. What did you mean?'

Saffie glanced at Jules. Jules gave her a smile of encouragement, communicating that it was fine to tell this police officer what she had told her.

'OK. Well, when I was getting ready for bed, I spotted him looking into my room. I told him to go away. But he didn't. He . . .'

'He what?' Maria urged gently.

'He came right in and grabbed me. Then . . . I don't want to say.'

'If you can, it will be very helpful,' Maria said, glancing up at Jules.

'OK. He made me have sex with him.'

'He forced you to have sex with him?'

'Yes. I told him to stop, to go away, but he . . .' Her voice was so faint, the police officer had to lean forward to hear her. 'He said I was asking for it. Because I'd been undressing – ready for bed. And maybe because I'd forgotten to close my door. He pushed me down on the bed. I couldn't get him off me.'

'Oh, you poor thing,' Maria said. 'It must have been very, very frightening.'

Saffie nodded. She was pulling at the sleeves of her top, that frantic new mannerism she'd developed since the rape.

'OK.' Maria made more notes. 'Not many more questions now. I know this is difficult for you. But do you remember what happened afterwards? Did Saul go home? Did he hang around? Did he seem upset about what he had done to you? Any information is going to help us, Saffron.'

'I . . . I don't remember.' For the first time, Saffie sounded a little uncertain. She looked up at Jules again. 'Mum and Holly came in, I think.'

'Where was he when your mother came in?' Maria glanced at Jules. She didn't want Jules to answer for her daughter.

'I think he was . . . I don't know,' Saffie said. 'I expect he was downstairs in the sitting room, as if he hadn't done anything except watch TV all night.'

'And so what did you do? When your mum came in?'

'I didn't do anything. I didn't want to tell my mum. He warned me not to tell. And his mum was with her. And I didn't think they'd believe me.'

'Did you hear them come in?'

'Of course. I couldn't sleep after what he did to me.'

'Do you remember what time it was?'

'About eleven, I think. I can't remember.'

'OK. Thank you, Saffie. You've been really helpful and I must reiterate you are not to feel guilty in *any* way about what's happened.'

'I just wish nobody else had found out about it,' Saffie said again. 'I didn't want them to. Especially my dad. I knew he'd go crazy.'

Maria looked at Jules. Then back at Saffie. 'What do you mean by your dad going crazy?'

'I knew he'd go all overprotective. That's why he wanted to take me to school in the car the day after he found out. I wouldn't let him. But he still made me go up to the bus stop with him. It was so embarrassing.'

'And did you tell anyone, apart from your mother, what happened? Do any of your friends know?'

Saffie shook her head.

'If they find out I've been with Saul, they'll think I'm desperate.'

'OK, listen, Saffie. You've done all you can to help us with our enquiries. You've been super helpful. You are to let your mum look after you. OK? Now, do you mind if I have a word alone with your mother?'

Saffie got up and went out of the room without looking back.

'Saffie didn't tell you that night about what had happened to her?' Maria asked, looking down at her notes.

'She was asleep when I went up to bed.'

'She says she couldn't sleep.'

'Maybe she couldn't, until we came in. Then I made some tea. Oh, and I've just remembered – Saul had been upstairs.

He was coming down when we came in the door after midnight. He said he'd fallen asleep in one of our spare rooms.'

'I see.'

'But it was a while before I went up to bed and Saffie was asleep by then. She said nothing until two weeks later. And then only because her period was late. She was afraid she might be pregnant.'

Maria raised her eyebrows as if she expected Jules to expand. Jules felt panic rise through her. She hadn't told Rowan about the test, so would it be right to tell this baby-faced police constable?

'The test was positive,' she said, eventually. 'That's how I know Saffie wasn't lying about the rape. Not that I thought for a minute she was. Why would she? But she doesn't want anyone to know she's pregnant. Please don't tell her I told you. We're dealing with it as swiftly and as privately and with as little fuss as we can.'

Maria was gazing at her. 'How terrible for you all,' she said. 'How very hard for a thirteen-year-old to be dealing with such a thing through no fault of her own.'

'Saffie really didn't want us to press charges. She wanted the whole thing kept quiet.'

'They so often do,' Maria said. 'Poor things. They think it's their fault. Girls. They think they brought it upon themselves. Or they are afraid no one will believe them. Or they blame themselves for being drunk, or for allowing a boy into their room, or for accepting a lift, or for dressing a certain way. They are, even in this day and age, too quick to take the blame. However often we tell them they weren't the one to force themselves on someone.'

Jules stared at Maria Shimwell. She was beginning to like her. For a split second, she thought how Holly would like her too.

'But our brief at the moment is finding the boy,' Maria said. 'We're pretty sure the rape has a bearing on his disappearance.'

'How?'

'Guilt? Fear of being found out? Not wanting to be exposed? Fear of humiliation? There are all sorts of possibilities. Whether Saffie wishes to take the rape allegation further will come later – if and when we find him.'

If? Surely there was no 'if' about it. They would find him. When Holly had, only this afternoon, said 'if', Jules had brushed it aside. It was a question of *when*. Wasn't it?

'Look,' Maria said, fishing a card out of somewhere. 'These are the details if your daughter does decide to take the rape further at some point. She might think she's over what this lad did. If it was him. But sometimes an assault comes back to haunt them later.'

'We aren't questioning who it was. There's no one else it could be.'

'Whatever. She would be seen by our Sapphire team at a special unit called the Haven. Nothing to be afraid of – they're very experienced and extremely sensitive. And you can, of course, be there with her too.'

'Thank you,' said Jules. It felt a huge relief that there might be somewhere else to turn to, at last. If only Saffie would agree to it.

'Just one more thing before I go,' Shimwell said, looking at her iPad. 'Saffie said something about knowing your husband would go "crazy" when he heard about the rape.'

'Well, yes. Saffie didn't want me to tell him. He's very protective of her. As any father would be of such a young girl. You do know she's only thirteen?'

'Of course.'

'But I decided he had to know. I felt he would deal with

it better than I could. Saul's mum's my oldest friend. I was there at the boy's birth, for goodness' sake! I couldn't bring myself to accuse him face to face. It felt too brutal, I suppose, to turn on a boy I almost delivered into the world. I'd already spoken to Holly, Saul's mum, but she wouldn't believe that Saul raped my daughter. So neither of us was doing a thing about him. I knew Rowan would know what to do.'

'And did he? Know what to do?'

Jules stared at Maria. So young and slight and yet so sharp. She wasn't going to miss a trick. Jules couldn't possibly tell her Rowan's words when he heard. His *I'll beat the living daylights out of him.*

'I don't think he did know what to do, no,' Jules said. 'He was upset, naturally.'

'He didn't suggest reporting the assault to us?'

'Saffie begged him not to. For the reasons I gave. She was afraid of being examined, of word getting out. Her father doesn't know she's pregnant, by the way. We both – Saffie and I – thought that would be too much information for him.'

'And Rowan didn't take action? He didn't go to anyone, a teacher, for example?'

'Saffie didn't want any fuss made about the whole thing. She was quite adamant about that. And we – perhaps mistakenly – felt we should honour her wish. Rowan wanted to drive her to school, though. To protect her from the boy. Saffie was mortified – she thought people would ask what had gone on. But she let her dad take her up to the bus stop on Monday morning.'

'Yesterday?'

'Yes.'

She made a note.

'Does Saul normally use that bus stop?'

'They all do. It's on the green. Right across from Saul's house, in fact.' Jules felt she was walking into a trap here, but she couldn't turn back.

'And does he, Saul, get the same bus as Saffie too? Usually?'

'Of course.'

'But he didn't yesterday morning,' Shimwell said. 'He left the house and didn't come back. Did you see your husband after he dropped Saffie at the bus stop?'

Jules knew what the young detective constable was getting at. Rowan wasn't back when she expected him to be. He should only have been gone about fifteen minutes, and when he hadn't returned after an hour, Jules had given up on waiting for him and gone to work. She'd met Donna on the way, she remembered. She'd sat in the car asking for her advice. There had been no sign of Rowan.

'Jules?'

'No. I didn't see him. I had to go to work. I'd left by the time my husband got in.'

'Times? What time did he leave? What time did you leave?'

Jules gave the rough time Rowan and Saffie had left. Then, not wanting to implicate Rowan any more than she already had, she said she'd left about fifteen minutes after that.

But Maria wasn't letting anything slip. 'I'd like to have a word with your husband as well. When might he be available to speak to?'

'He'll be back any minute, I think,' Jules said. 'He should be here now. He went out, but he wasn't going to be long.'

'Do you mind if we wait, then? And do you mind if I call Venesuela in? I need to update him on what you and Saffie have told me.'

Jules felt drained. How could her family have got so embroiled with the police when they were not guilty of anything?

'I'll make you some coffee,' she said.

Jules saw Rowan's tall silhouette through the glass panel of the front door, which was visible from the open-plan kitchen. She heard the door open and watched as he came in, levered off his boots, then stopped in the doorway to the sitting room. He'd spotted the car outside, and now he could see the two police officers in his house.

She took the coffee through to the police officers and he mouthed at Jules, asking what they were doing there. They had both agreed not to report the rape to the police at Saffie's request, so he was clearly surprised to see them, standing on his nice sheepskin rug. Drinking his coffee from his big, top-of-the-range machine.

'Do you mind?' Venesuela indicated to Jules that he wanted to talk to Rowan alone.

Maria Shimwell accompanied Jules into the kitchen, so that the two men could talk.

'What's he going to ask him? Rowan doesn't know any more than I do. He wasn't here the night of the rape. He was away.' Jules had begun to tremble, unaccountably. Perhaps it was the stress of having police in her house. Or perhaps it was a result of too much coffee. Maria told Jules not to worry, that they were just eliminating things at this stage.

'Eliminating what?' Jules asked, though she knew. Because it had crossed her own mind when Holly had rung to say Saul was missing. When Rowan had said he'd gone to Ely Market after taking Saffie to the bus stop yesterday morning. Why hadn't he come straight home? He had taken Saffie to the bus at the very time Saul had set off for school. But Saul had never arrived. Jules hadn't let herself think about it. She couldn't bear to fit all the pieces together – Rowan's fury, his shouting, 'I'll beat the living daylights out of him.' His driving Saffie to the bus stop and then, that same morning, Saul going missing on his way to that very bus stop.

It was all too much for Jules to make sense of.

For her to *want* to make sense of.

Venesuela came into the kitchen then and said he'd asked Rowan if he would help with their enquiries at the station.

'You're taking him to the police station?' Jules was shocked.

'Only to help with our enquiries. Since he's willing,' Maria said. 'It's nothing to worry about. The detective inspector wants to rule out a few things, and it's best done down there.'

'But . . .'

'We'll only keep him an hour or so.'

*

Jules went upstairs to check Saffie was OK, telling her Rowan was at the pub with his golfing mates and would be back later. Saffie said she was tired after the questioning and wanted to get a decent night's sleep.

'Mum,' she called out, as Jules began to close her door.

'What, darling?'

'I'm frightened.' She put her hand on her belly.

Jules paused. Then she said, 'Only a couple more days and we'll see Dr Browne. She'll sort everything. Try not to think about it – you've enough on your plate at the moment.'

'Not just about that. About Saul. Where is he? What if something happens to him and it's all because of me? Because I told you. When he warned me not to?'

Jules sighed. 'Sweetheart, you were right to tell us.

None of this is your fault. He's just lying low for a bit because he doesn't want to face up to what he's done. And you're not to blame yourself for that.'

'But ...' Saffie didn't seem convinced, and Jules had a sudden longing for the days when the biggest things she had to deal with were grazed knees and lost teddies.

'Try and sleep.' Jules hoped she sounded authoritative enough to stop Saffie worrying, at least for tonight. She crossed back over the room to kiss her goodnight, squeezed her daughter to her, kissed her again, rested her cheek against her soft hair. How had things come to this? How was it that her husband was down at the police station and her godson was missing and her daughter was pregnant? And she had no one to turn to because her best friend was no longer talking to her.

*

It was dark and Jules was in her bedroom, rubbing in the cream that was supposed to protect her décolletage from going crêpey, when she heard the car pull up outside, the front door slam, and knew that Rowan was back. She heard him go straight into the sitting room, the TV come on, the murmur of voices on some late-night panel show. In the mirror, she saw the tendons in her neck relax and realized how tense she had been, how terrified that the police were going to arrest Rowan. Jules crept downstairs and into the sitting room.

'Cup of tea?' she asked. 'Or something stronger?'

Rowan glanced up at her. 'I could do with a beer now you mention it.'

Jules got him a bottle of iced Becks from the fridge and sat down next to him. He kept staring at the screen, on which a panel was discussing the migration crisis.

'So what did they ask you?' Jules said to the side of his face. His eyes were bloodshot. A network of thread veins had appeared on his cheeks that she was sure hadn't been there before. She worried about his blood pressure.

'Wanted to know where I was on Monday morning,' he said without looking at her.

'And?'

'Where I went after dropping Saffie at the bus stop. Wanted to know how I felt about the rape, about Saul, all that stuff.'

'And?'

'I told them.'

'Ro, it's quite understandable that you are so angry with Saul,' Jules said. 'Any dad would have felt the same. But you didn't . . . ?'

'Didn't what?' he snapped. 'What are you asking, Jules? I've just been put through two hours of interrogation by the police. While the person they should be questioning has done a disappearing act. Don't you start.'

'I want to reassure myself,' Jules said. 'Or rather, I want you to reassure me, that you didn't do anything impulsive.'

'Such as?'

'I don't know. Such as try and punish Saul in some way.' She couldn't say what she was really afraid of, what she was increasingly convinced her husband was capable of. She couldn't say she needed to know if Rowan had taken Saul somewhere. Done something terrible to him. Something he would be regretting.

'I've told the police all that,' Rowan said. 'I've told them I didn't see Saul that morning. I told them to ask the bloody pikeys on the green instead of one of their upstanding citizens.'

Ordinarily, Jules would have taken Rowan to task for

such a derogatory comment, but nothing about their current situation was ordinary. Instead, she said, 'You know I love you. And you know we've always said we'd never have secrets from one another.' The moment the words were out of her mouth, the word 'pregnant' in the window of the test floated into her mind's eye.

Rowan did glance at her briefly now. 'Please, Jules, leave me be. I really need to switch off from all this.'

Jules gave up and went upstairs. On the way to her room, she glanced in again on Saffie. She was asleep. Had she been asleep when they'd come in after the pub that night? Jules had looked in on Saffie when she had gone upstairs and Saffie had looked just as she did now. In a deep slumber. Why had Saffie told DC Shimwell she couldn't sleep? Perhaps Saffie's memory was clouded by the traumatic experience she had gone through. Or perhaps she'd fallen straight to sleep after hearing Jules and Holly come through the door. Or perhaps Jules's own memory was clouded by all the Prosecco she had drunk that night. Whatever, Jules wished Saffie had told her then and there what Saul had done to her. One morning-after pill and Jules wouldn't be dealing with a pregnancy now. She wouldn't be the worst hypocrite in history, telling her husband they kept no secrets. Keeping the secret of his daughter's pregnancy from him. And yet using it against Holly to prove her daughter wasn't a liar. Which hadn't worked anyway. How much more devious could *she* get? And then she thought of the way she'd let what she knew about Archie and Philippa slip out of her mouth, and Holly's shocked face in the rain.

Saul's actions have brought out the worst in everyone, she thought. Including me.

11

HOLLY

In what other circumstances do we count the hours rather than the days? We do it after giving birth, in order to savour every moment of our newborn's development. But this, this measuring an absence, means I want to hold back time for a different reason. It's forty-eight hours since Saul walked out of the door and has been slowly disappearing from my life. I need to stop time, to stop him vanishing. Forty-eight hours sounds less like a lifetime than two days does.

I find my phone, check Saul's text for the millionth time.

Is it from Saul? Or could it have been sent by some prankster – the troll? – someone who knows he's missing and wants to torment me?

'There's no GPS so we can't tell where it was sent from,' Maria Shimwell tells me over the phone. 'Our colleagues in East Finchley have searched the cemetery, but there's no sign. There's a community of homeless people down there, so the guys did a thorough investigation. No one's seen him. They've not found anything. Is there anywhere else he might have meant? By saying he'd gone to be close to his dad?'

Hearing the words spoken out loud convinces me more than ever. He's not gone to any physical place. I feel sick and I can't bring myself to say what I'm actually thinking.

*

Saul's story on the local news has been edited.

'The boy who went missing from his home on Monday was accused of rape by a thirteen-year-old girl a few days before his disappearance. Police are not dismissing the links between the two events. The victim claims the seventeen-year-old, a family friend, assaulted her in her home while her parents were out.'

So. My sixteen-year-old son is now seventeen, according to the news.

And a rapist.

Shimwell rings again later and tells me they've still found nothing. The weather has worsened, relentless rain tipping down from morning till night. The rivers have swelled; the Fens up towards the Great Ouse are flooded. The search parties have given up. Because of the weather? Or because they now believe my son raped a thirteen-year-old?

On my way upstairs, my mobile rings again. I barely dare hope anymore that Saul will get in touch. That he's OK.

'Holly.' My heart plummets. It's not Saul, of course.

'How are things?' It's Luma, from work.

'Pretty bloody awful. I was going to come in tomorrow. Take my mind off the endless waiting, worrying, fretting. It's exhausting, Luma.'

'Actually, Holly, we're wondering if you should take some time off. The tweets are coming in thick and fast. Rumours are spiralling.' Luma's voice is soft, conciliatory.

'What rumours?'

'Haven't you checked your Twitter feed? What they're saying about you is pretty vile. They're calling you a hypocrite. They imply that you call all men potential rapists, then deny it when your son's accused. They're nasty. There's the Stag, as usual, but he's precipitated a stream of other abusers. They're all hashtagging the university.'

'How do they know?' I cry. 'How do they know what Saul was accused of?'

'The story's all over the internet, that he's disappeared, and that there's a rape claim attached.'

'Who *is* the bloody Stag?' I ask, pointlessly.

'We may never know. The fact is, the tweets are undermining all the work you've put into the consent workshops. If your students get wind of the allegation against your son – and they're bound to – they could lose confidence in you as their tutor as well. We all feel it'd be better if you took time out.'

My students' faces float into my mind's eye. Eleanora. How I've helped her with her novel, how close she is to handing it in. Mei Lui. I wanted to help her extract herself from whatever racket she's involved in. I need to be there. I've always been there for my students; it's who I am. It's what I do.

'I'm beside myself, wondering what's happened to Saul,' I say. 'I don't know what to do. I don't know where to be. Work might help. It would be a distraction.'

'I'm sorry, Holly, but it could damage the university's reputation if we're not seen to be taking action. Just as we're recruiting students for next year.'

'Isn't that giving in to them, though? Isn't that letting the Stag get what he wants? To shut us up and stop us making things better for women? I need to be there, Luma. I need to help Hanya with the workshops.'

'That's just it,' Luma says. 'Hanya feels having you involved, after all that's happened, might be ... controversial. Counterproductive even.'

I let her words sink in.

'Are you saying she believes my son's guilty as well?'

'Look. No one's saying that. But the fact he's been

accused of rape ... and that he's run away, it gives these trolls ammunition to say your workshops are hypocritical at best.'

I stare out of the window. The trees are releasing their leaves. The air is full of burnt-orange flakes shimmying on eddies of wind before floating to the ground. I'm beginning to hate my view of the green, of the seasons slowly changing before my eyes.

'What I'm going through ... what this has put Saul through,' I say, 'it's worse than anything I imagined. Having an allegation like this attached to his name' – I try not to break down – 'could have driven him to suicide. That's what the police are thinking. It's what I've begun to think. I don't know how to cope. I don't know what to do.'

'Oh, Holly. This is particularly fucking awful for you, isn't it? As the workshop adviser. Of all people.'

'I'm a mother, Luma. It would be particularly bloody awful for any mother.' I swallow back the urge to cry.

I hear Luma sigh on the other end of the line. She's caught in the middle too, of course.

'There are only a few more weeks until Christmas,' she says at last. 'I can hand your tutorials and lectures over to Ayesha. It would help if you could say you've taken sick leave. Due to stress? It might help you, too. Because I'm sure you're going through hell, and you don't want or need animosity at work.'

'I suppose I have no choice.'

'Just for the rest of this term,' Luma says again, softly. 'I'm sorry, Holly.'

*

'Who was that?' Pete asks, coming into the bedroom. He's working at home this morning on his computer up in the

'We'll need a photo. I hope you're OK with this. You can choose the one you want us to use. It could be his profile photo, anything, as long as it's recent.'

I'm swiping through photos on my phone when there's another knock on the door. DC Maria Shimwell is back, with DI Carlos Venesuela. They stand side by side on the step. Venesuela says he wants to talk to Pete.

'What for?' I ask stupidly.

'Standard procedure,' Venesuela says. 'We just need to ask a few questions. We'll do it down at the station.'

'I was on my way to work,' Pete says, coming down the stairs to see who's there. 'I've got back-to-back appointments this afternoon.'

'Shouldn't take too long,' Venesuela says. 'Though you might have to cancel everything before about three.'

'I managed to deactivate the account,' Pete says over his shoulder as he leaves.

Fatima and I stand in the sitting room when they've gone, watching the police car pull off round the green. I never usually witness how caved out the village is in the daytime. How human beings have been replaced by large plastic five-foot wheelie bins. The village, as Jules told me before I moved here, is empty of life during the day. Everyone's somewhere else. Not quite everyone. Maybe I imagine it, but as I gaze out at the green, I think I see a face at the window in one of the houses opposite. When the police car has gone, the face disappears and the curtain drops again. It's a small village. Nothing else to do. What did I expect?

'The photo?' Fatima asks gently.

'Here.' I hand her my phone.

'Ping it over to this number?'

I do as she says. 'Why have they taken Pete?' I ask,

searching her warm brown eyes. 'He doesn't know any more than I do.'

'They're not leaving a stone unturned.'

Pete's reaction when I first told him of Saffie's allegation comes back to me. The way he'd sat up in shock and said, 'She *what*? That's a very serious allegation.' His first instinct was to take his own daughters away. But that doesn't mean he played a part in Saul's disappearance. Pete wasn't here when Saul left on Monday morning. He'd gone to work for an early appointment with a client. I shudder. I have to trust Pete. Who else do I have?

'They're talking to everyone who has a relationship with Saul in case they've seen or heard anything they might have forgotten the morning he left,' Fatima says, reading my mind. She settles down on the sofa and looks at her phone as it pings and the photo of Saul arrives.

'He's a good-looking boy,' she says. 'A heartbreaker in the making.'

I appreciate this. Her attempt to be kind about a boy she's been told might be a rapist. Her attempt to show she isn't judging. That he's innocent until proven guilty. *Every beetle is a gazelle in the eyes of its mother.* Is that what she's thinking?

'I'll get it over to the station. And I'll arrange for you to go to the TV studios to make an appeal if nothing's changed by tomorrow.'

'A *TV* appeal?'

'It does help,' Fatima says kindly. 'Witnesses often come forward after seeing relatives on the TV.'

'You do realize it's got out there. That he was accused of rape? No one's going to sympathize with me.'

'He's innocent,' she asserts, 'until proven guilty. Remember that. Keep it in mind as you go on air. That's what you're going to communicate subliminally. As long as you believe it.'

'Of course I believe it. I *know* it.'

*

I ask Fatima, later, if she still has a long day ahead of her. She laughs and says yes, today is a long shift but tomorrow she'll be able to pick up her kids from school. 'Which is a treat,' she says. 'I don't often get to do that. Only once a week. And their faces when they see it's their mum! Makes it all worthwhile.'

'Who picks them up when you're working?' I need small talk, the comfort of it.

'Their grandma. She gets them four days a week. If I'm lucky, I get home in time to read them a story before they go to sleep. But not often.'

'Don't you want to go home now?' I ask. 'I'll be OK without you if you want to get back.'

'I'm on duty,' she says. 'Couldn't go home if I wanted to. But I'm fine here with you. Keeping you company. Don't you worry.'

I feel sorry to think Fatima's children have to make do without her four days a week. We all need our mothers. Right now, I could do with my own. But mine has been incarcerated in a care home for the last five years in Glasgow and no longer recognizes me. It's ages since she's been anything like a mother to me. The only way I've been able to deal with the loss of who she was, before the dementia eroded her character, is not to see her too often. It's cowardly, perhaps. But since my sister Suzie and I fell out, after Archie died, my visits to Glasgow have tailed off. Suzie and I haven't spoken since she hinted, at Archie's funeral, that there was someone present who knew Archie better than she should. Her words come back to me now, chiming with what Jules told me yesterday. What did Suzie and Jules know about Archie that I didn't?

All of a sudden, I yearn to be enfolded in my mother's warm embrace, not to have to think about any of this. When did I last feel I could lean completely on anyone? Let someone take the strain? Longer ago than I can remember. Which is why I've always needed Jules. 'Our friends are our families,' Jules had said once, 'now we all live so far from our blood relatives. You, Holly, are my sister. My soul sister.'

The fact is, however, my mother was never the maternal type to start with. Always deeply involved in some social work case or other that took her attention away from me and Suzie when we were children. My notion of a mother's warm embrace is a fantasy. My father was the demonstrative one, the one who spent his leisure time at home helping us make things in the garden. A treehouse, dens, go-karts. Or reading to us at bedtime. He was always warm and affectionate. But he died ten years ago. I am an orphan, I think, indulging in self-pity. An orphan and a widow. Please let me not also have lost my child. There is no word for a mother who has lost a child, I realize. Because it's too painful a concept to encapsulate in a word.

A memory sweeps in, from the days when Saul was little, and he would run across the landing at night in our London house and leap into my bed to lie close to me. I would promise silently to protect him forever from danger. Then, when there was only me, once Archie had gone, the responsibility to keep watch over Saul became all the more pressing.

'Everything's all right,' I would whisper to him as he fell back to sleep. 'I'm here. I will keep you safe, always.' Which I knew was a lie. I hadn't been able to stop his father from dying, had I? One day, Saul would grow up and have to face

the danger of the world on his own. And ⎍
to protect him from it. I've always worked tire⎍
Saul safe, to the point where Pete thinks I have se⎍
anxiety. Checking where he is, making sure he's home w⎍
he says he will be. Asking him if he's OK. If he's happy, it
he's made friends. And it hasn't worked. I have not kept Saul
safe. Either from the world or from his own demons.

'There. That will do very nicely.' Fatima interrupts my
thoughts, holding up Saul's photo on her iPad. 'Now, I think
we should have more tea and you can tell me what kind of
a relationship your son and Pete had with one another.'

*

Pete looks exhausted when he gets in. Fatima leaves when
he arrives, promising she'll be in touch the minute there's
any news.

'That questioning was gruelling,' he says. He's pale,
washed out, his face shiny with sweat. 'Thought they weren't
going to believe me when I said I was at work the morning
Saul went off. They wanted to check my alibi. They phoned
my client, everything.'

'And it was OK? Your alibi was watertight?'

'I can't believe you'd ask me that, Holly.'

'It's just . . . everything seems so precarious. I don't know
what to trust, who to depend on.' I want you to reassure me,
I think.

'It's a small price to pay, really,' Pete says. 'To help them
eliminate me from their enquiries. It's the least I can do.' He
turns and looks at me. Something's written across his face,
a mixture of apology and guilt and resignation.

'I'm sorry, Holly, but Deepa's texted me.' He sighs. 'She
and Tim are going away for a couple of nights – it's a work
thing they can't get out of.'

'*What?*'

'Her father's staying at her sister's and has gone down with the flu, so they've let her down. She's asked me to stay. I'm going to have to go over there, but I'd really like you to come too. I don't want to leave you on your own. In fact, I think it would do you good to come. Have a change of scene. Spend some time with the girls.'

'Now?'

'They're leaving in the small hours – some science conference in Lisbon – and they've got an early flight. So yes, I should go straight away. I can go ahead and you can follow, if you like?'

He goes over to the cupboard under the stairs where we keep bags, boots, old coats, and rummages about inside. He pulls out the weekend bag he takes when he's off to Bristol for his course.

'Can't the girls come here?' I say to his back. 'It's mad you going over there when there are empty beds upstairs. All made up for them.'

'The girls don't want to come here at the moment.' He turns round and looks at me helplessly. 'They're frightened – understandably – about what's happened to Saul. That he walked out of the front door and didn't come back. They . . .'

'They don't know what Saffie said, do they? They don't know about the rape thing?'

He pauses for a beat. 'We've tried our best to keep that from them. But now it's all over the media, it's impossible to say.'

'This is getting worse. By the minute. I don't want you going over there. If Deepa's sister's let her down, that's her problem. She'll have to cancel her trip.'

'I don't think Deepa will do that,' he says.

'It's not up to her! It's up to you, and me, and what the girls want and need too.'

'Where are my jeans?' he asks. 'I put them in the wash the other day.'

'Forget your bloody jeans, Pete!' I shout, incensed now. 'You can't go. You can't go off and leave me. I need you. You have to stay here.'

I follow him across the kitchen to the little utility area by the back door, where he bends down and peers into the tumble dryer, pulling out clothes that have been left in there. He stands up, shakes out some crumpled jeans.

'It's only for a couple of nights, my love. Until Deepa's back. I need to be there, to reassure them. You do understand that, don't you? Please come too?'

'Fucking hell . . .' Pete jerks his head up in shock. 'I can't leave the house. In case Saul comes home. You know that. I can't believe you're even contemplating going. Don't you care? Don't you want to stay here so you can hear every latest bulletin? And Fatima's asked me to do a TV appeal. Tomorrow, if we haven't heard anything. I'd like you to be with me.'

'A TV appeal?'

'She says witnesses often come forward after seeing relatives on the news. I can't do it on my own.'

Pete places his hand gently on my shoulder.

'You can,' he says. 'You can do it, Holly. For Saul. You'll be fine. You're good at that kind of thing.'

'*That kind of thing*? I've never done anything like this before.'

'You teach. You lecture. You're used to talking in public.'

'You have no idea, do you?' My words come out in a low growl. I'm trembling with fury.

'Don't make this difficult for me, please,' Pete pleads.

'You can see that I'm torn. Of course I'd prefer to stay here with you, but I have to fulfil my duties as a father.'

'It looks to me like you're doing this for Deepa. Not for the girls,' I mutter, immediately regretting it.

'Is that what this is about?' Pete asks. I wish I hadn't revealed this sliver of jealousy. It undermines my real argument, which is that I need Pete here, with me. But it's impossible to retract now. 'Tell her you're staying here.' I adopt as assertive a tone as I can muster. Deepa's tone, in fact. 'You're staying here with me because I'm your wife now. Not Deepa.'

Deepa and I regard each other with a kind of cool respect. Pete admits their break-up came about in part because she considered him beneath her. After she and Pete split up, she married Tim, a colleague at the fertility clinic where she works as a scientist, and moved into his beautiful, large old house in the leafy area of Cambridge north of the river. The girls continued going, with Saffie, to the local schools, spending half their time with Pete, and more recently weekends with me and Saul too.

I have a civil, if not entirely relaxed relationship with Deepa. I picture her now; she's an attractive woman of Indian origin with long dark hair and beautiful large green eyes. Her clothes always look glossy – Indian silks and shiny boots and slick trousers with a sheen on them. She can carry this kind of thing off. Designer wear that clings to her svelte figure. She's probably one of the chicest women I've ever seen and I've always been in awe of her intellect, her beauty. And aware of the fact I'm living with the partner she discarded. But I've also been grateful to her for lending us her daughters every other weekend. It's only since all this Saul business that I've felt any animosity towards her at all. I can't help hostility creeping into my voice now she's taken the girls and snapped her fingers to get Pete back when I need him most.

'Tell her she can sort out a babysitter for herself,' I add, weakly.

Pete ignores this.

'If you're sure you won't come,' he says, stuffing clothes into his weekend bag, 'I'll be on the end of my phone at all times.' He won't make eye contact with me. He's angry, because I've made him feel guilty. And because he feels trapped. Caught between his daughters and his new wife. 'Ring me the minute you hear anything.' He walks towards the door. Turns.

'I promised Thea,' he says, his voice softening. 'I am doing this for her and for Freya. If you can't see that, then you don't really know me at all.' He gives me a searching look. I could pull him towards me. Kiss him. Tell him that of course he has to put his girls first. Always, but especially at the moment, while they are afraid because Saul is missing. But I don't. I can't. It's pride, and it's humiliation at having revealed any insecurity about Deepa, and it's hurt that he can leave me in my hour of need.

I speak to his back as he walks away.

'I don't really know you at all, then,' I say.

*

It doesn't matter that I turn the heating up high, pull the curtains over the dark windows, put the oven on, though I'm not going to cook anything – nothing would induce me to put food in my mouth – the kitchen stays cold in the hours after Pete leaves. Trembling with fury at him, and at my own powerlessness to stop him going to his daughters, I'm still shivering when, later, I press Philippa's number into my mobile. It's some form of masochism now things – so

I believe – can't get any worse. Philippa picks up, and asks immediately what the latest is on Saul and the rape claim. She must be feeling contrite after her refusal to help me.

'He's vanished,' I tell her. My voice cracks. 'He's been missing since he heard he's been accused. The police have no leads.'

'That's terrible,' she says. 'That must be dreadful for you. I'm so sorry.'

'You have no idea,' I say, and I don't even care about the bitterness with which my voice is laced. 'You have no idea. Dreadful doesn't come close to what I'm going through. Not knowing. Fearing the worst. But that's not why I'm phoning.' I feel removed, as if I'm not attached to the real world. As if I can say what I like and it will make no difference. 'I'm phoning because I need to know why you wouldn't defend Saul. Because when ... if – no, *when* – he comes back, Jules and Rowan aren't giving up on it. Saffie hasn't retracted her allegation. What was your thinking?'

There's a long silence.

'Philippa,' I say, 'did something happen between you and Archie? Jules said something,' I press on, into the abyss of her silence. 'I guess she was trying to hurt me. To get back at me for not believing Saffie. Or for criticizing her husband. But I have to be sure.'

'Oh, Holly,' Philippa says at last. 'It's six years since Archie died.' My pulse quickens. 'I thought if you never found out, we would never have hurt you. And I assure you neither of us wanted to hurt you. I can say that with my hand on my heart. I'd swear it in court on a Bible. But you were so wrapped up in Saul back then and Archie was lonely and I was there.'

'What are you saying, Philippa?' I reach for the kitchen table to steady myself.

'It was platonic – you have to believe that.'

'*What* was platonic?'

'We never slept together. Jules knows that. It was more a meeting of minds. We were working very closely on a difficult case and we admitted we felt things for one another. It wasn't so much physical as—'

'How did Jules even know this?' Jules is *my* friend, I'm thinking. Not Archie's. Not Philippa's.

'I used to meet up with her sometimes, around that time, to talk, over coffee.'

'You're telling me . . .'

Philippa and Jules used to have coffee together? I'm not sure which hurts more, her clandestine relationship with my husband or the one with my friend.

'Holly,' she goes on in her measured tone, 'perhaps it will help if I tell you what Archie's dying words were.'

'How do you know what his dying words were?' I hiss. 'He was alone. He was alone when I got to the hospital.'

I'm wishing I'd never phoned her now. Ignorance was better. Ignorance was kinder.

'I was there,' she says, oh so gently. 'I went with him in the ambulance. I was with him when he died. And his last words were . . .'

'That's why you wouldn't defend Saul? You were afraid people would think . . . what? That you might be biased because Saul was your lover's child? Or that you were trying to atone for stealing my husband? I don't want to hear what his dying words were.'

'You've got it wrong, Holly. We weren't lovers. I swear.'

I'm crying now. But I'm not going to let her off the hook. 'I don't want you to tell me what his dying words were. Not just so it makes you feel better. I've suffered enough for the last six years. All this time I believed I'd lost someone who really loved me.'

'He did love you. It's possible to love more than one person. Surely you understand that?'

The way she's talking, it's as if she knew Archie better than I did. I begin to hate her. With her composed face, her designer haircut and expensive glasses, and her calm insinuation when we'd sat in the cafe that I didn't know what my own son might be capable of.

'His last words were "Ask Holly to forgive me." But I couldn't tell you. Not without telling you what you had to forgive in the first place. I thought it would be better if you could grieve in peace. I thought it would be better if you never knew.'

'You want me to thank you for that?' I spit, and then jab the 'off' button on my phone so hard my thumb stings.

Saffie's accusation hasn't just changed the present and the future for us all; it's altering the past as I know it, and I'm not sure which is harder to deal with.

12

JULES

'I've got extra maths after school today,' Saffie said. 'Won't be back till six.'

Jules was putting her make-up on in the mirror, pouting as she applied the Rosebud lipstick Holly had given her all those years ago. She observed her daughter in the mirror. Saffie was plucking at the sleeves of her school blazer again in that nervy, frenzied way she'd recently adopted. Saffie's own make-up seemed to be getting thicker each day, but did nothing to hide the shadows under her eyes. There was something in her daughter's expression that had changed since the rape. It wasn't just that imperceptible thing Jules had noticed before, the loss of innocence. It was as if her brows had dropped a fraction, her eyes were more wary, more . . . world-weary.

'I'll give you a lift home,' Jules said.

'I don't need you to. Why do you have to keep going on about lifts?'

'After all that's happened, we don't like you being out there alone after dark.'

'I'm fine, Mum,' Saffie said. 'Gemma will be there. We'll come back together.'

'I can ask Dad to pick you both up.'

'That's crazy,' Saffie snapped. 'I'm going to look like a complete wimp if Dad keeps turning up everywhere to give me lifts. Someone will guess about this . . .' She put her hand on her belly.

'OK.' Jules turned. 'You don't want us drawing attention, I understand that. But please make sure you come back with Gemma and that you have your phone with you all the time. Switched on. Not on silent. And don't be later than six. Oh, and I'm checking with Tess that Gemma's with you.'

Saffie came over to Jules and kissed her, leaving a sticky residue of lip gloss on her cheek.

'Stop worrying, Mummy,' she said. 'You're treating me like a baby. I'm over what Saul did. And I'm perfectly capable of looking after myself.'

There was something about the forced way Saffie said this that betrayed how troubled she really was. Jules tried to remember whether she'd heard Saffie laugh in the last few weeks and failed. What had happened to the girl who used to get the giggles at the slightest thing? Whose laughter you could hear from miles away as she walked home with her friends? Jules knew very well Saffie was not over what Saul did, either physically or emotionally. But perhaps it was better that Saffie was able to put on a brave front if it enabled her to get through today. Tomorrow they would see Donna and the pregnancy would be dealt with.

Then, perhaps, they could start moving on. Or trying to. Jules knew Saffie was shaken up by Saul's disappearance and, as her mother, couldn't help blaming him for that too: he'd hurt her daughter not just once but twice now.

'Do you need to wear perfume to school?' Jules asked, nevertheless, catching a waft as Saffie turned from her.

Saffie frowned. 'You wear perfume to work.'

'Yes, but I'm forty-three; you're thirteen.'

'It's better than smelling like a rancid trout.'

'You could just smell like your lovely natural self,' Jules said. 'But never mind – you're going to be late. Off you go.'

*

That afternoon, Jules got home from work early, to make sure she was there for Saffie. Saul's disappearance was unsettling on two levels, she thought. In addition to the fact it had upset Saffie. It was quite possible he might be out there, lurking, wanting to get at Saffie for revealing what he'd done. On the other hand, who knew what had happened to him? They all assumed his disappearance was linked to his guilt about the rape. But it might have nothing to do with it. There might be someone out there, a serial killer stabbing young solitary teenagers, or ... Jules wasn't usually given to flights of fancy, but everything lately had been turned on its head. The Fens, so open and calm and bright when she had first moved here, now seemed full of menace.

Rowan came downstairs as Jules stood at the counter, texting Tess: 'Is Gemma at extra maths this afternoon? Just checking she and Saffie are coming home together on the bus?'

There were other unread texts – requests for repeat orders on stock for the shop, and invitations from Jenny and Tess – that she had failed to answer. She closed them and looked at her husband. Since being made redundant, Rowan had tried to occupy his time with golf and bird-watching, but it got more difficult when the days were short, and today it had been dark for almost an hour by the time she got in and bird-watching was out of the question, as was golf.

'Where's Saff?' he asked.

'She went to extra maths. She's getting the bus back.'

'In the dark? With that boy out there, roaming about?'

'Yes, Rowan. She doesn't want to be treated like a kid. She's with Gemma. It's all fine.'

'I'll go and pick her up.'

'There's no need. Honestly, she won't like it.'

He sighed, looked at Jules. 'I feel so pent-up since all this,' he said. 'I can't relax.'

'I do understand. But it's important we let her continue as normal.'

Jules put her arms round her husband. She squeezed him to her. It was a relief to know Rowan was worried about Saff being out after dark. Rowan wouldn't be afraid that Saul was still a threat if he had done anything to him. Would he?

'I was going through pictures of Saffie on the laptop,' Rowan said, freeing himself from Jules's embrace. Jules looked at her husband. There was nothing strange about looking at pictures of your own child on the computer. All parents did it.

'There were ones of her in her ballet dress. She was always the prettiest girl wherever we took her,' he said. 'I was always so proud of her.'

'I know you were, darling. I was too. Still am.'

'Yes, but now it's as if her looks are backfiring. It's as if because she's so good-looking, other men think they have the right to touch her.'

This was what Jules sometimes found odd. The fact Rowan thought about men touching Saffie at all. And it wasn't just since the rape. Rowan had always been like this about Saffie. It was as if he thought about her as an object for men to ogle at. He liked his daughter to look pretty, but disliked it when this drew attention. She wondered if his attitude to Saffie was healthy. And yet he adored her, would do anything for her.

'I hate to think of anybody else putting their sweaty hands on her. I hate to think that she's going to have more and more men groping at her as she gets older. And to think ... to think of anyone forcing their filthy flesh inside her perfect body.'

'I do know how you feel,' Jules said. 'But, Rowan, she's all right. We have to put up a united front and show her we're fine too.'

Jules congratulated herself on the rational front she was presenting. Because it wasn't how she felt. The pregnancy nagged at her mind. If only they'd been able to go to Donna sooner. Every day made it more likely Rowan would discover that Saffie was dealing with an unwanted pregnancy on top of the rape. Had she made the right decision? To do as Saffie had begged her to do? Should she have taken Saffie straight to a clinic somewhere?

'The way Saul's gone off,' Rowan went on. 'It's like he's guilt-tripping her. For telling us what he did to her.'

'I hardly think he'd go to those lengths,' Jules said. She swallowed back the urge to tell him she'd had the same thought. 'It's obviously upsetting for Saff that Saul's gone missing, but she mustn't be made to feel the two things are linked any more than she already does. We have to play it down. We have to communicate that the two incidents are not *necessarily* related. And if they are, it isn't her fault. Saul is a troubled boy and it's being played out in all kinds of ways, some very unacceptable.'

'Understatement.'

'OK. But she needs to feel she was right to tell us about the rape. You accusing Saul of guilt-tripping her doesn't help. If anything nasty has happened to him, she'll think she shouldn't have told us.'

'Fact is, he deserves everything that's come to him,' Rowan muttered.

Jules was about to reply when the doorbell rang. It sounded louder than usual, making them both jump. Saffie had her own key. She never rang the bell.

Jules shivered. Rowan's last sentence had unsettled her. But she was more concerned that Saffie was home safely. She glanced at her mobile to see if Tess had replied to her text. There was nothing yet. So her heart plummeted as she saw that it was DC Shimwell back with DI Venesuela outlined through the misted glass of the front door.

'Oh God, please don't say . . .' Jules began, opening the door. 'Is Saffie all right?'

'She's not home?' Maria Shimwell asked, and Jules felt her head spin.

*

The police hadn't come to report that Saffie had had an accident, or been assaulted again, or any of the scenarios that flashed through Jules's head, but to ask Rowan to accompany them to the police station for a second time.

'We'd like another little chat,' they told him. 'About the missing boy. We'd also like our forensics team to examine your car, if you wouldn't mind handing over the keys?'

'Rowan?' Jules turned to him, her eyes questioning.

He gave her a resigned look, grabbed his coat from the cloakroom and followed them, his bulky form, Jules thought, oddly passive as he trod behind the slight figure of Shimwell to the police car. Rowan's shape had changed, Jules noticed. There was less definition between his ribcage and his hips; it was all one line now. He was ageing, she realized. She wanted to chase after him, hold on to him, tell him it was all going to be all right. Because she was there for him and always had been.

Then, as if from nowhere, a truck appeared, and the Audi, Rowan's pride and joy, was lifted onto the back of it. She watched the truck follow the police car up the road. She felt as if her life as she knew it was disappearing along with the red tail lights receding into the darkness.

Jules shut the door at last and went into the kitchen. She looked at her mobile. Still nothing from Tess. It was a quarter to seven. Where *was* Saffie? She texted her daughter, her fingers slippery on the keys. Her heart racing. She should have insisted on picking her up after all.

'You OK? Sure you don't want a lift?'

The reply came quickly, reassuring her. 'On the bus. Home in 20.'

Jules looked around the hall. If Rowan *had* done something to Saul on Monday morning, there must be evidence somewhere. She had to know. She had to be one step ahead of the police and those spooky-looking forensics people in the truck. Police got things wrong sometimes. Often. If they decided Rowan was guilty when he wasn't, she would have to defend him. On the other hand, if he *had* done something, she had to know before the police did, so she could work out what to do about it.

She stood still. She went over in her mind what had happened when she had come in on Monday evening, the day Saul had disappeared. She'd found Rowan cooking, which was unusual but not unheard of. She remembered he had snatched the potato peelings from Saffie, wanting to take them out to the wheelie bins himself. Why? Why hadn't he wanted Saffie to do that for him, since he was so busy cooking? Was Rowan covering something up? Trying to divert her attention from something by playing the good husband?

Although part of her felt it was crazy, Jules was driven to check.

The bin men hadn't been yet. They were due in the morning. She pulled on her wellies, which she kept by the shoe rack in the lobby by the back door. She stopped, looked down. Rowan had worn his Timberland boots on Monday morning, she remembered; she'd noticed because they seemed a bit cumbersome to wear just to drive to the bus stop with Saffie. They were here on the rack, caked in mud. He said he'd gone to Ely. To buy food. A city. No mud there. But he might have gone for a walk at the same time, in the countryside. It was muddy in the Fens at this time of year, especially after all the rain they'd had. There was nothing odd about having mud on his boots. He often had mud on his boots. And yet he hadn't mentioned a walk. Heat swept over Jules, making her head prickle, her palms clammy. Everything seemed significant suddenly.

She flicked the switch that operated the patio light, went outside and pulled the black bin bags from the wheelie bins they kept behind the shed. She tipped out the contents, not knowing what she was looking for. But if Rowan had harmed Saul, there would be evidence. There would be something he might have used. There was definitely some reason he didn't want Saffie going out to the bins that evening.

Jules knew suddenly how Rowan must have felt when he became suspicious that she was having an affair all those years ago. The compulsion to know. She was driven to turn each piece of rubbish over, shine the torch on it, sniff it. Examine every receipt, every ticket. She wouldn't be able to rest until she had reassured herself that there was no clue, no incriminating piece of evidence to show Rowan had harmed Saul. Made him run off. Some piece of evidence that Rowan had wanted to hide on Monday evening.

Then she found it. Torn, screwed up. A scrap of a petrol receipt. She rummaged through the rest of the rubbish until she found more scraps. The receipt was dated that Monday. It was as if she knew. It wasn't even a surprise. Rather than shock, she felt a kind of perverse relief that she no longer had to wonder. Her heartbeat slowed so much she had to hold on to the top of the wheelie bin and put her head between her knees to stop herself fainting. Rowan had filled up the car with petrol at a service station in Downham Market, way north of Ely. On Monday morning. He'd said he'd gone to Ely. He'd never mentioned driving into the remoter part of the Fens.

When the blood had returned to her head, Jules stuffed the scraps of receipt in her pocket to look at again later. To think about later. (To show the police later? Or to hide from them?)

She took one more cursory look in the bin and stopped. The Peacocks bag was odd. Who in their house bought clothes from Peacocks? Peacocks was in Ely. A cut-price clothing shop. Jules felt the bag. There was something soft inside it. A lurid scene flashed up, as if it had been waiting there, in her mind's eye. Rowan using some cheap polyester scarf he'd got hold of from somewhere he never usually shopped, to strangle Saul – his daughter's rapist – to death.

Jules remembered a trip she had taken not too long ago to the Museum of London, to see the crime exhibits. She was struck by the evidence left behind that led to a conviction of murder, how banal it often was. How obvious. How easily overlooked by the murderer. As if a part of them had wanted to be caught. A train ticket that didn't tally with the times the suspect had given. A smudge of lipstick on a sleeve. A woman's patterned silk scarf found in the wrong place.

She was about to put her hand inside the bag when the security light at the front of the house flashed on, there was the crunch of footsteps on the gravel and Jules realized Saffie was home. She would have a look at the contents of the bag and the receipt indoors later on. She stuffed the bag into her coat pocket and went inside to greet her daughter.

'Hi,' she called out to Saffie. 'How was your day?'

'OK.'

Jules could hear Saffie's footsteps bang up the stairs. Her daughter had always had a heavy step; it was surprising to think she had ever done ballet. Jules took the bag with the fabric in it into the kitchen. She needed to hide it somewhere. She put it at the back of the cupboard where they kept used carrier bags since no one but her bothered to take them out when they went shopping. She could hear the shower water running. Saffie never used to have a shower after school unless she'd had netball or football, which she hadn't today. It had been extra maths, as far as Jules remembered. But Saffie had become obsessed lately with her personal hygiene. Another symptom of her newly teenage, self-conscious self? Or a result of having had her body violated? An obsessive need to wash away the contamination of Saul's body in hers?

Jules tried to concentrate on making supper. She'd got a chicken fajita kit, which Saffie usually loved, and was easy to assemble. As she put the chicken in the oven, she tried to concoct a story for Saffie to explain why Rowan was out. In the end, she said he had gone to the pub and Saffie didn't seem very interested anyway. She toyed with her food for a while, then went upstairs saying there were some exercises she had to do for the extra maths class. She was certainly working hard lately. Trying to placate Rowan by showing him she was doing her best? That she hadn't been adversely affected by the rape?

Rowan came in at seven. The police, he said, had asked him again to assist them with their enquiries, and again thanked him and let him come home.

'What are they thinking, Rowan?' Jules asked, her thumb stroking the thin paper of the pieces of receipt in her jacket pocket. She knew he'd be angry at having his evening disrupted for a second time. She put his meal in front of him and he sat down at the table to eat.

'They've examined the CCTV footage from the shops, and they saw the Audi was parked on the other side of the green to the bus stop at the time Saul left that morning,' Rowan said between mouthfuls. 'They've put two and two together and concluded it means I took Saul somewhere. They say the car had gone when the bus left, that it must have been driven out of the village soon after, because they have footage of it going in the direction of the main A-road towards Ely. I said, well, surprise, surprise – that must be because I drove to Ely after dropping Saffie that morning, to go to the market. To get food for the nice meal I made you both that evening.'

He didn't mention going on somewhere else. He didn't mention driving beyond Ely into the Fens. And yet Jules knew he had done.

'Thank you, sweetie, for that dinner,' Jules said, her breath catching. 'It was kind of you to cook. Did they ask anything else?'

'They asked if I had a Twitter account and I said that I don't do social media. Then they asked about the DNA they found in the car. Saul's. Some hair, some skin cells apparently.'

'But, well, of course there's Saul's DNA in the car. You've often given him lifts in the past.'

'Yeah, well, *you* know that.'

'And you told them?'

'Of course.'

Rowan was unwilling to talk much more other than to give Jules a curtailed version of some other questions they had asked him – and then he began to vent his rage at *her*. 'If you hadn't reported what I said to Holly, I wouldn't be their main bloody suspect.'

'What do you mean?'

'You told her I'd threatened Saul.'

'But what did you expect me to do?' Jules cried. 'You *did* threaten to beat up Saul if Holly didn't talk to him. You wanted her to confront him. I had to tell her. I had to give her the opportunity to sort him out herself. It was what you wanted.'

Rowan finished his food and pushed his plate away. 'You didn't have to repeat my exact words. She had a duty to talk to her son. You didn't have to terrorize her into it by telling her I wanted to beat the living daylights out of him.'

Jules gave her husband a hard stare. The fact was, though she didn't tell him, it was actually Saffie who had alerted the police to Rowan's suspect behaviour, when she'd said she knew her dad would 'go crazy' once he knew about the rape. She bit her lip.

'Of course I bloody felt like kicking his head in,' Rowan said now. 'What father wouldn't feel like that? Most fathers would feel the same.'

Jules wanted to say, *Most fathers haven't been sent on anger management courses for punching strangers in the face*, but stopped herself.

'I'm going to bed,' she said. 'We'll talk about this when you're less stressed out.'

On the way up to her room, she looked in on Saffie. She was sleeping soundly. Jules gazed at her daughter in her stripy pyjamas, with a Michael Morpurgo book she used to read when she was little open and face down on top of her duvet. She must have fallen asleep reading it. A surge of something went through Jules's body. A yearning to return to the days when she would have snuggled up with Saffie under her duvet and read to her. Those days weren't even all that long ago. It was only once Saffie started secondary school that she'd objected to her mother reading to her. And now, while she slept, the child in Saffie was very present, in the curve of her cheek, in her slightly upturned mouth. In the way her eyelashes curled where they met the cheekbone. Jules bent down and kissed her gently. It was impossible to think there was a baby developing inside her daughter. How dare Saul have done this to her? To them.

And then that memory swept over Jules again. How she and Holly had joked, years ago, that Saff and Saul might one day have a baby together and how it would make up for those neither she nor Holly had been able to have. Be careful what you wish for, she thought, ruefully.

13

HOLLY

Pete phones me early the next morning on our landline. 'Holly?'

Saul's Nike trainers lie by the front door on their sides, untouched since he left. What was he wearing on his feet that morning? That was something the police failed to ask. Or if they did, I've forgotten. His coat, the one he never wears, hangs limply on its peg. He'll be cold out there now the weather's turned. And that thought upsets me so much, I can barely speak.

'Holl, Thea has lost her maths book. She thinks she might have left it in her room. Could you take a look? If it's there, I'll pop in for it. I take it there's no news?'

'You think I wouldn't have told you if there was?'

'I . . .'

'I'll go and find Thea's maths book,' I say.

Despite my resentment that Pete's gone to them, the girls' space is a comfort to me. The smell of the perfume Freya and Saffie both wear hits me in the face as I lean over Freya's desk. A tropical-fruit aroma. I draw it in. The horrible memory of it on Saul's jumper after he'd been in Saffie's house returns to me. The doubt it raised in my mind. Now I realize he smelled of it not because he'd been close enough to Saff to have picked up her perfume but because his stepsister has been wearing it. Why did I accuse him of having

Saff's scent on his jumper? Why didn't I think of that at the time? Why let Saffie's accusation influence everything?

The girls' spare pyjamas are neatly folded on their pillows – a Deepa-ism that they have always observed. The rest of the room is very much as I last left it, the carpet pretty much bare, the two desks under the Velux windows tidy and uncluttered. Pete works in here sometimes, when it's Deepa's weekend with the girls, but he's always careful to take his laptop and books with him when he leaves. It's a room that looks unlived in, which makes me sad. I'd like the girls to spend more time with us. Larking about, messing things up, giving me things to do – beds to make, pillows to plump, clothes to pick up off the floor, toys to arrange on their shelves. I'd like to spend more time reading to Thea and chatting about girlish things to Freya. I'd even like to have more washing to do, to hang out and iron.

My mobile pings as I bend down to look at the girls' things and a reminder pops up; I'm due at the TV for the appeal on the local news in an hour.

There's not much on Thea's little desk, a pencil case with panda- and mouse-shaped rubbers in it, pencils and pens. There are a couple of books, a Jacqueline Wilson and a Stephenie Meyer, neatly placed one upon the other. I can't find the maths textbook. On Freya's, there's nail polish and remover and a bag of make-up and hair bobbles. Lots of girly *stuff*. There's a pad of heart-shaped Post-its in a drawer in the side of her desk with notes scribbled on them. A struck-through name scrawled inside a love heart, pierced with arrows. ** ****, it says. *I love him*. She's got a teenage crush on someone. No name visible. I hold it up to the light. It's hard to see the name except that it ends on an upward stroke, an 'l', I think. Though it could be a 'b', or a 'd'. Then

I spot a little pink diary with a padlock. I pick it up, try to open it. It's locked.

I rummage about to see whether Freya has left the key anywhere, tucked inside a drawer, under her pillow even, but it's nowhere. She must have taken the key with her, keeping her diary here, away from Thea's prying eyes, but locked up so no one else – me? – can read it. It's against all my principles. But still fizzing with fury and upset at the world, and especially with Pete for leaving me here on my own, I decide I'm entitled to what I do next. Freya is a link between Saul and Saffie. She might know something about what really went on between her friend and her stepbrother the night Saffie claims he raped her. Girls talk to one another. And Saffie and Freya are, or were, best friends. Why didn't Pete think to grill Freya himself before he whisked her to her mother's? He's so afraid of upsetting his girls. But at the expense of Saul! The sense of injustice this arouses in me is what drives me to find a pair of scissors to force the lock. The scissors prove frustratingly useless. I try one angle and then another, bending the blade in the process, and in the end, still in self-righteous fury, go in search of a hammer.

The hammer's in the shed. I fetch it and return to the attic room. Anyone looking in would be perturbed, horrified even, to observe me, senior lecturer in creative writing, MA, middle class, middle-aged, kneeling on the floor bashing at the tiny gold lock of my stepdaughter's diary with a hammer. These are the depths I've been forced to stoop to in order to prove that my son is innocent. At last the lock breaks in two, spitting a piece of brass across the room, and I pull off the rest of it. Now I can turn the pages of Freya's diary.

The contents are at first glance disappointing. She hasn't kept it very religiously. In fact, she has barely written in it at all. The only entry seems to be irrelevant to the day.

I absolutely love him, she has written over several pages.

I turn over a few more blank weeks and then come to a centrefold. Here, she's scrawled over the double-page spread, *I love him!!!!*

But he doesn't love me. He loves Saffie. She loves him too. She says if I tell anyone, I'll be in trouble. We all will. Because it's illegal. It's not fair. I wore the perfume he gave her today. She let me have some. But he still didn't notice me the way he notices her.

I am afraid my heart is going to break. I am going to die of heartbreak!!!!!!

I sit on Freya's smooth duvet and gaze at her writing. It's calming to rest for a bit, letting the sun pour in from the skylight, just being. After a while – I don't know how long – I look at Freya's writing again. I turn it over in my mind. I unravel the last two weeks, going right back to the point at which Jules stood in my study at work and said that Saul had raped Saffie.

Girls don't lie about rape, I'd told myself. And yet, this time I knew it couldn't be true. Because Saul would not do such a thing. Why would Saffie lie, then? Say something so abhorrent about a boy she used to play with as a child? What would be in it for her to say my son raped her? *This* is what I've been searching for. An explanation. In my volatile state, my feelings swerve all over the place. I move from anger to sympathy in a swift arc.

Freya and Saffie are in love with the same boy. His name ends in an 'l'. Saffie has told Freya she'll get in trouble because it's illegal. Saul is Freya's stepbrother. Of course Saffie would think it illegal for Freya to have a relationship with her stepbrother. But she must've thought it was OK for *her*. Even though she's beneath the age of consent. The point is, what this tells me is that Saffie *wanted* to sleep with Saul.

It wasn't rape. She loved him. And Saul loved her, according to Freya's diary. Then when Saffie became afraid she was pregnant she must've panicked. Poor child, I think. Poor children. I want to weep for them. For all of them. For their naivety. For their hopeless, blind innocence.

And so I do. I hold Freya's diary in my hand, put it to my nose, breathe in the scent, cloying, girlish, and I cry.

*

By the time I arrive at the studios, my eyes are swollen, my face puffy and red. Panic threatens to take over my earlier serenity as I sit on a slate-grey sofa in the grey reception area, waiting to be called into the studio. How much greyer could they make this space? They must have used gallons of grey paint on the walls, on the doors. Then I envisage all those shopfronts and interiors painted this same drab colour. I think of Jules's home, painted a fashionable pigeon through-out. If the 1970s were a brown decade, we will see, when we look back on it, that the 2010s were a grey one.

*

'OK . . . If I can drop this wire inside your jumper and clip the mic here, please . . . We'll do a light check and then you speak into this camera.'

The newsreader finishes his bulletin and the producer nods at me. The blazing lights make my face sticky. I put up a finger and wipe a dribble of sweat from under my eye. The studio is tiny, no bigger than a cupboard, and it's too hot. I've been given a grey swivel chair to sit on. My thighs inside the 'velvet touch' tights I'm wearing begin to perspire.

The producer advises me, when I ask, not to muddy my message by referring in any way to the rape, or anything I have found out since.

'Keep to the point,' she says. 'You want your son to come home. That's what you want to put across. If you begin to justify things or cast aspersions or make excuses, Twitter will go berserk and the tabloids will have a field day. And that will be counterproductive. Just a nice, emotional appeal for him to come home, OK? Or for anyone who might have seen him to get in touch. We'll broadcast contact details afterwards. Straight into the camera, lovey. You can start speaking . . . now.'

'Please,' I say into the black eye of the camera, 'Saul, if you're watching this, get in touch. You are not in any trouble.' I pause. '*No* trouble,' I say again, glancing at the producer. She shrugs, nods 'OK.'

I feel a fool. Saul isn't going to watch this. He isn't going to hear.

'All we want is to know you're safe.' I trot the words out, aware of the thousands of locals who will feel sorry for me, thanking their lucky stars this isn't them having to make this appeal. All those families convinced this could never happen to them. All those families who believe I've brought up a rapist. 'I miss you so much, and we all – me, Pete, Freya and Thea – love you. Everyone does. Come home.'

I don't cry. The producer tells me it will add weight to my appeal, but the tears won't come. I want to say something about the love he and Saffie felt for one another. How she must have taken fright, once she realized she thought their affair would get out there, but before I can open my mouth again, the producer says, 'OK, that's a wrap. You can leave now.'

I'm about to get up from the swivel chair when Saul's face appears. Blown out of all proportion, long, straight hair falling over one half of his face, the eye that's visible squinting into the sunlight. The photo Fatima and I found yesterday flashes onto the screens all around the studio. I shut my eyes. I can't look at it. It's too much like the kind of photo you see of the murdered.

Afterwards, I feel soiled by the whole experience. Exposed and degraded. Saul hates being noticed, and now his face has been blasted all over the local news into sitting rooms everywhere. I've stooped to my lowest point since this whole thing began.

I leave the studio and take the train home from Cambridge alone. I walk away from the station towards the village. The air is cool in my throat after the heat of the TV studio. The sun sinks over the Fens. Bare canopies of distant trees make copper-coloured sprays against the last light in the sky. The puddles turn amber, the drains almost black, sucking the lifeblood of the land out to sea. I imagine I can hear it, the water seeping away, the peat drying out, crackling, leaving the silt banks we live on. I hear Saul, before all this happened, quoting a Fenland word to me. *Roddon.* We live on a roddon.

There are lights on in the Baptist Chapel, as if there's a service on. It's a flat-fronted brick building dwarfing the rows of cottages at the edge of the village. The double doors of the chapel are, unusually for a weekday, flung open, light spilling across the road. Posters stuck to the doors advertise the Auction of Promises. The event the women were planning that fateful night in the pub. There's the chatter of voices floating from within. I've never seen the place so throbbing with noise and life. I'm about to cross the road to avoid being spotted when someone steps out in front of me.

'Hey!' It's Samantha. 'Holly, I'm so desperately sorry about what's happened to your son.'

Something about her kind face warms my heart. I remember we'd half arranged to meet, and feeling pleased and flattered; she's at least fifteen years younger than me. I didn't follow it up, but guess she'll understand that given the circumstances, I've been preoccupied. She's holding a cigarette, huddled into her blue coat, standing on the gravel yard to the side of the chapel.

'You must be beside yourself. If Freddie disappeared, I'd be gutted. I couldn't go on. I think you're so brave.'

'It's OK.'

'No, really. It's so unfair on you, all the things people are saying about you and him and . . .'

'What *are* they saying?'

She gulps. 'Just, you know. People can be so judgemental when they're scared. Scared it might happen to them. I've told them, "Look, no one knows the facts. All we know is it must be hell for you, as his mother." I spotted you coming up the road and you looked so dejected. I was just sneaking a cheeky cigarette. That's the only reason I was standing out here in the cold. It's blinking freezing. Let's go in.'

'I'm not going in there, Samantha.'

'Come on, it might cheer you up. Or at least take your mind off things. I got myself a spa day. You could've got all kinds of things – a computer overhaul, a month's personal training, a day of doggie day care.' She pauses, as if waiting for me to smile. 'If you'd been earlier. You've missed the auction itself, but I could get you something to eat. We're raising money for a multi-sensory room at the school.'

'I'm very happy to donate some money. Here . . .' I begin to rummage in my purse. The villagers are great charity-givers, always fundraising and doing marathons and triathlons for some cause or another. I know I should participate more.

'Oh, come on,' Samantha's saying. 'Stick with me – you'll be fine.'

I hesitate for a second, then remember Samantha and her husband on the local news, helping to search for Saul. I feel ashamed at how self-centred I've become. And then I think, Jules will be in here, and I can tell her how I know why Saffie lied, say we can work together, now I have an explanation that makes sense.

'I suppose I could,' I say. 'For a little while.'

'I'm rooting for you, you know,' Samantha says. 'Come on, I'll get you a drink of something and you can leave as soon as you feel like it.'

It's colder inside the chapel than out. The old-prayer-book smell mingles with the fresher scent of tea and freshly baked cakes. Several people turn their backs on me as I follow Samantha through the crowd. They may have had sympathy for me when Saul disappeared, but they have lost it now they believe he raped a girl they've known since childhood.

Samantha leads me to a trestle table laden with home-made quiches and cakes. I've dressed for the TV interview in my best burgundy jacquard coat over a black dress, bought over ten years ago for a formal 'do' I had to attend with Archie, and a silver brooch that belonged to Archie's mother. I'm wearing more make-up than usual too – some now-smudged eyeliner, a slick of cherry lip gloss. I don't think I imagine the eyes on me, people looking over and whispering. I hold my head up. I try not to look like a mother whose son is missing. I try not to look like the mother of a rapist.

Then I see her. Jules. Her blonde hair gleaming, among a group of other women on the far side of the room. Instinctively I raise a hand and automatically start to smile. 'I have something to tell you,' I begin to mouth. But as her eyes meet mine, with deliberation, she moves them disdainfully away. She has not smiled. She has not acknowledged me. The hurt takes my breath away.

It takes some time to track Jules down alone. She's coming out of the kitchen, two large tin teapots in her hands. When she sees me, she turns, places them down on the counter.

'Jules. I need to talk to you. We said some hurtful things to each other last time we met.'

Her blue eyes are sad. 'I know,' she says. 'And I'm sorry for that.'

Encouraged, I plough straight on.

'It wasn't rape,' I say.

'I haven't time for this.'

'No, listen. I'm not saying they didn't sleep together. I'm not saying Saul hasn't left Saffie pregnant. But the point is, Saffie loves Saul. And he loves her. She said it was rape to save face at school, or to protect herself from Rowan, or . . . only she knows why.'

'Please, Holly,' Jules says.

'I found Freya's diary. She's written that they both love Saul. Both she and Saff. But what this means,' I go on, 'is that after all, I'd like to share everything you and Saffie are going through. Can we talk to her? Together? Get her to tell us the truth?'

Jules looks at me peculiarly, as if I've lost my mind, but I push on.

'If she will admit, just to us for the moment, not to anyone else, that she loved Saul, but panicked when she realized she might be pregnant, so said it was rape, I'll forgive her for everything she said.' My voice cracks. 'And then we can work together, to get her through the abortion, if she wants it, and to find Saul.'

We will be friends again, I want to say.

'There are so many ways in which what you are saying is wrong.' Jules gazes at me as if she believes I've lost the plot completely. 'I barely know where to begin. You're deluding yourself.' I look at her mouth as she speaks. She's wearing the lipstick she swears by – Rosebud, it's called. I got it for her one Christmas years ago. It's been her signature colour ever since. It says something, doesn't it, about us?

'Saffie isn't in love with Saul,' Jules says. 'He raped her. He's left her with a termination to go through. However unpalatable it is for you to accept, it's the truth. Please don't make it harder for me.' Her eyes fill with tears.

'Jules. Listen for a minute. I found Freya's diary. She's written that she loves the same person as Saffie does. It's Saul. She thinks it's illegal, because he's her stepbrother. Or because of their age. She's also written that he loves Saffie. I can show you the diary.'

'Saffie doesn't love Saul,' Jules says again. 'She begged me not to let him come round that night. She's frightened of him. She and her friends avoid him – for a reason, I see now.'

Her last utterance leaves me speechless. I'm not sure I've heard her right. Saffie's friends avoided Saul *for a reason*? Saffie was frightened of him?

She goes on: 'And I blame myself for letting him come to our house while we were out. I've been tormenting myself for being such a fool as not to listen to Saffie. Or to Rowan. Even if he thought they were in some kind of a relationship – which is not the case – he still raped her and I would still be taking her for a termination tomorrow. Hasn't it occurred to you how ghastly this is for me? Love, I'm afraid, doesn't come into it. The pregnancy is the result of a violent act that has left my daughter traumatized. I can't put Saffie through any more anguish by questioning what happened to her again. I would have thought you'd understand that, Holly.

With your Rape Crisis work and your consent workshops and your articles in the papers.'

I have to reach deep within to find the resources to reply without shouting. I try one last time.

'If Saffie admits she loved Saul, at least his reputation won't be sullied.'

'Is *that* what you're most worried about?'

'I care that Saul isn't thought of as a rapist! Of course I do! But, Jules, it isn't only that. If they love each other, then . . . Look, this is our grandchild Saffie's carrying. We're in it together. Don't you remember what we used to say? Grandma Holly and Grandma Jules.'

We're in the cramped area to the side of the kitchen, but people are beginning to push through and it's getting hard to talk.

'If I begin to think of the pregnancy in that way, I won't be able to do what I have to do to give Saffie her life back,' she hisses. 'Please stop this, Holly. Now, excuse me. I have an event to help run.'

Jules picks up her teapots and pushes past me. I turn to leave, elbowing my way past the villagers, people I've sat with in the pub, Tess, Jenny, Fiona and her partner. All barely acknowledge me. I spot Saffie, handing out trays of tea and snacks with the other young people. Her eyes rest on me for a second; then, in an uncanny mimicry of her mother's, they swivel downwards in disdain. Or perhaps it's something else. Guilt? She bustles over to some other young people and they all giggle, their heads together.

It doesn't take me much longer to realize I'm not wanted here. I pop to the loo on my way out. As luck would have it, as I come out of the cubicle, Saffie's standing there, leaning in towards the mirror, putting on mascara, eyes downturned as she brushes her lashes.

'Saffie.'

She drops her hand, startled.

I shuffle past her, so my back's to the exit. I don't want her to slip out and avoid me. 'Listen, sweetie,' I begin. 'We need to talk. You realize that, don't you?'

She stares at me, her mouth open, her mascara wand held halfway to her eyes. I see the rings under them, that she's tired, and pale, and has lost the childish bubbliness that used to define her.

'All I'm asking,' I say, 'is that you admit Saul didn't rape you. That you wanted it too.'

I try to smile at her. To show her I understand. 'Freya wrote a note about it, left it in her room. She loves him as well. It's nothing to be ashamed of, though, Saff. I understand you don't want your school friends to know, so we won't tell anyone. Except perhaps the police, because it might help them find Saul. They can let him know you're sorry for what you said. That you still love him.'

Saffie has blanched. She holds on to the washbasin with one hand. For a second I'm afraid she might faint.

'I don't love him,' she says, backing away from me. 'He's ... Ugh, he makes my skin crawl. He made me do things I hated and I never wanted to.'

'Saffie! This is Saul we're talking about. He would never do those things. He's my son. Your godbrother.'

'There's no such thing as a godbrother.'

'Odd brother, then.' I want to make her smile. But she says nothing.

'Please. I understand you don't want anyone to know you love him, but *I* need to know. I have to. Because ...'

I'm breaking down. I don't mean to, but it's rising through me. The terror that I've lost Saul. That this accusation might have driven him to suicide. The way he'll be remembered forever unless Saffie confesses. The whole village, the whole country have labelled him a rapist. A rapist who was such a coward he ran away instead of standing up to his own actions. They have no sympathy for me. I'm the hypocrite feminazi who won't recognize rape when it's right in front of her eyes. My son! A rapist! The word makes me feel sick.

'Confess that you and Freya love Saul. I've *seen* it,' I repeat, 'in her diary.' I move closer to her, wanting to slap her. For being a liar. For putting her reputation with her stupid peer group before the way my son will be judged for eternity. For taking the person I love most on earth from me.

'Why did you lie?' I ask her. 'Why are you afraid of admitting you love Saul? Is it because of what your friends will think? Were you afraid your dad would be angry that you'd had a loving relationship with my son? Because the people around here think he looks a bit different? What does that matter? It would be so much better if you tell the truth and then we can all be friends and perhaps Saul will come back and ... tell me. Or I'll show the diary to your mum and dad. And then they'll know you and Freya have both been fighting over him ... that you lied. That you've continued to lie and that he's disappeared because you lied.'

I've said what I swore I wouldn't say. I wanted to keep Saff on side and now I've told her she's responsible for Saul's disappearance. She backs away from me.

'Stop it,' she wails. 'Stop going on and on at me. It's frightening me. Leave me alone. We don't love Saul. I don't love him and neither does Freya. If she wrote she loved someone, it must have been Justin Bieber. Saul raped me. He did.'

With horror, I see I've made her cry and I move to comfort her, but there's a harsh rapping on the door. Saffie moves aside and the door opens.

'Hey,' says Samantha, looking from me to Saffie and back again. 'Holly, I've been looking for you.'

Saffie ducks away and rushes out to her friends.

Samantha says, 'I want you to talk to my husband. Saul's tutor. He wants to know what's happening with him. Come on.' She drags me by the arm to the man who spoke on the TV about Saul being a good student. Who I met briefly at a parents' evening at the beginning of term. When things were normal. When Saul was simply a withdrawn adolescent boy.

'Harry. Meet Holly.'

I breathe deeply. My hand trembles as he takes it in his. I can't believe the strength of feeling that almost made me hit Saffie in order to get her to confess to something she is going to such lengths to hide. I went too far, I know I did. I think perhaps I'm going – or have gone – mad.

Harry scoops their little girl into his arms. 'I want to offer my condolences. Oh my God, is that the right word? For what you're going through. As a dad myself, I can't imagine how horrible this is for you.'

'Daddy?' A small boy comes up and tugs at Harry's jacket. 'Could I have another cupcake?'

'Just a minute, Freddie. I'm talking.'

'I know it's awkward for people,' I say. 'I do appreciate you mentioning it.'

'Saul's a good lad,' Harry says. 'Quiet in class. But interesting. We're all keeping our fingers firmly crossed that he'll be found safe and well.'

You don't think he's a rapist? You don't think he deserves it? I want to ask.

'Everyone wants to help,' Samantha agrees, putting her hand on her husband's arm. 'Holly's the lecturer I've told you about, Harry. We met again at Tess's drinks do at the Plough.' She looks up at Harry, her eyes shining. She's so obviously deeply in love with her husband. For a second I remember feeling that way with Archie.

Love struck. Those are the words that come to mind. *Blinded* by love. *Smitten*. I envy her that feeling. I want to rewind time, to rediscover the woman I was when I gazed as adoringly at Archie. When I believed I'd struck gold. When I believed everything could only get better and better. When our future seemed to spread before us, brimming with possibility. I loved everything about Archie, his voice, his hands, his smell, his gentle, courteous manners. We were both smitten with Saul, too. Or that's what I thought.

Now everything's changed. My once clear-eyed view of the past has misted over. Everything's turned opaque, unreliable.

'Holly's a creative writing lecturer,' Samantha's saying. 'In London.'

'Yes, I think I knew that. Samantha's interested in doing a degree as a mature student, aren't you, Sam? You two have a lot to talk about,' Harry says, looking from me to Samantha. 'I'll leave you to it. Nice to meet you, Holly. At last. We're praying for you. For Saul too, of course.'

Saffie approaches with her tray of iced cupcakes. Her wide eyes, with their long mascaraed lashes, her erect posture, the way she's able to carry on as if our exchange never happened, tugs at my heartstrings. But when she spots me, she pauses, turns and goes the other way. It's not her fault, of course, not really; she doesn't understand the enormity of what her claim has set in motion. She's too young. I should never have harangued her just now.

Harry and Freddie wander off. Desperate to get away from a grieving woman, I think.

'I have to go. But do text me,' I say to Samantha. 'Please. I'd be happy to talk about degree courses. One of the worst things about what's happened with Saul is the isolation, in fact.'

'Come with me,' Samantha says. 'Let's sit down and I'll check I've got your details.'

She's being so kind to me, and I could use a friend. I sit in the lobby with her while she checks my number on her phone. 'I'll be in touch,' she says. 'Thanks, Holly. And good luck.' She looks at me for a few moments, sadly, and then goes off to find her young family.

When I return to the hall, it's cleared of people. I look around but can't see Jules. More morose and lonely than ever, and guilty about the way I've upset Saffie, I step out into the night. I'm passing the pub a few doors along from the chapel when I hear my name and turn.

'Holly.' It's Rowan. 'Just the woman I was hoping to see.'

'I . . . Rowan, is Jules with you?'

'She's gone,' he says, standing squarely in front of me, blocking the pavement. 'Wanted to get Saffie home and safe.' He glares at me. Saffie's name hangs in the air between us. After a significant pause, he asks, 'Where's Pete? Or are you on your own?'

'He's away.'

'Not escorting you? A bit foolish of him, with you looking so attractive.'

I can hardly speak. I feel exhausted and wish again that I had gone straight home after the television appeal.

'He had to go over to Deepa's. To be with the girls.'

'So you're off home now?'

'Yes. I'm tired.'

'I'll walk you.'

'There's no need. I'm all right on my own.'

'Not saying you're not. But it's on my way and I was going home now too. And you know, a woman on her own on a dark night in a slinky black dress, you can't be too careful. Not with all that's gone on.'

'What about Jules?' I ignore what I assume to be a reference to the phrase 'asking for it', which Saul allegedly used. 'She was presumably on her own?'

'She was driving,' he says, 'and I wanted a drink. They don't allow alcohol in the house of God next door. I've had enough now. I'll walk you.'

I don't want this man near me. He's the one whose threats prompted me to ask Saul if he'd forced Saffie to have sex. The reason my son's disappeared. But I'm too exhausted to argue, and so say nothing. As I stride ahead, I can feel Rowan behind me. His footsteps follow me up the street and along the shortcut to the green, a road of new-builds. Security lights flick on as I pass, illuminating perfectly manicured front lawns, white garage doors and casting Rowan's shadow over me. I turn.

'It's fine,' I say. 'You can go. I'm perfectly capable of walking on my own from here.'

'It's my duty to protect you,' he says sarcastically.

There's nothing I can do to shake him off. He walks alongside me now, over the green towards my house, the great big elephant of Saul and Saffie lumbering along between us. He's waiting for me to bring it up. But I am not going to mention it. I don't want to talk to the man who said he wanted to beat the living daylights out of my son.

At my house, I take out my key and the door swings open. I turn to thank Rowan. My thinking is, by remaining civil, he will be forced to do so as well.

'Goodnight. Thank you for accompanying me.'

He wedges his foot in the gap as I close the door.

'Aren't you going to ask me in?'

'Rowan, I'm tired. I've had to do an appeal for Saul on

local TV and I'm done for, to be honest.' Reminding him that Saul's missing, I imagine, might garner me some sympathy.

'Interesting he disappeared just after being found out. Is it cowardice? Or a clever bit of guilt-tripping?'

'*What?*' I stare at Rowan, aghast at his skewed logic. 'I don't think anything was further from his mind.'

Rowan shoves the door. I lose my balance and stumble backwards. He moves in and steps towards me.

'You're despicable,' he says, slamming the door behind him. 'You and your son. As far as I'm concerned, you and he deserve everything that's come to you. But I'm not allowed to say it. I'm not supposed to say what everyone else is thinking. That you've been bellyaching about all men being potential rapists but refuse to see when your own son's one. That Saul deserves . . .' He swipes a finger across his throat.

'What do you mean?' In spite of myself, I begin to tremble. 'Rowan, can we please be adult about this? Saul's missing. Isn't that satisfaction enough for you? If you still insist on believing it was rape.'

Rowan's eyes are black in the dim hall light. I step back, to get to the kitchen. I don't want this conversation in our narrow hallway. Rowan follows, matching me step for step. For a second it feels as if we're performing some ridiculous kind of foxtrot. I wish Pete were here.

'The police have been grilling me down at the station as if *I'm* the guilty party, as if it's me who's to blame for what your son did to my beautiful child.'

'He didn't do it,' I say. 'Not the way she says he did, anyway.'

I fold my arms, jut out my chin, determined to stand up for Saul, no matter what.

'You refuse to admit your son raped her,' he says. 'You do him a disservice – he's become a sociopath.'

'You do your daughter a disservice by refusing to find out what's really going on with her.' Infuriatingly my voice shakes. 'Why she's so scared of telling you the truth.'

He backs me up against the cooker. I will not be intimidated by him. I've let him intimidate me once, into questioning Saul against my instincts, and the consequences were catastrophic. But my words seem only to have incensed him more. He comes up close to me, so close I can see the pores around his nose, the thread veins in his cheeks. His breath smells of beer and stale onion. There are deep creases along his brow where little pinheads of sweat are breaking out. I wonder how Jules bears him, with his foul temper and his aggressive bearing. Rowan's a big bloke. There is probably about fifteen stone of male flesh looming over me.

'Look, Rowan,' I try. 'We're both upset. But we can talk this through.'

'I want you to understand what you and your son have put my family through.' He's almost weeping, his eyes screwed up, his mouth in a grimace. I look about for something with which to defend myself in case he comes any closer, but the only thing within arm's reach is a wooden spoon.

Then he shoves me and I slip against the cooker. I wonder, as I try to sidestep him, if he meant to push me so forcefully, whether he knows his own strength, but before I can speak again, I lose my balance. My arms flail as I try to break my fall, and then I find myself on my back, my head banging against the quarry tiles.

'I've a good mind to hurt you,' he pants, staring down at me. 'The way Saul hurt Saffie. I'd do to you what your boy did to my girl, but you know what? You just don't do it for me.'

With a final swipe at the wall, he walks out of the kitchen. The whole house reverberates as the front door slams.

I stare up at my kitchen, viewing things I've never seen before. Cobwebs veil the underside of the table. A small spider is working its way across the top of a table leg. There are crumbs in the cracks in the tiles, and dust bunnies have collected under the cupboard doors. The quarry tiles beneath my back – a detail that attracted me to the house in the first place – make the floor an ice block. One of the windows is ajar. The wind is catching a pan on the rack. It's knocking against another, a regular tinny beat.

I move an arm and a leg. Only the back of my head hurts, so I push myself up and try a sitting position. Blinking, trying to get things into focus, I shift onto my knees and use the table leg to pull myself to standing. Water's all I can think of. And it's a relief, splashing into my face as I put my mouth under the tap to drink.

I pull the window shut and move toward the stairs. Then on second thoughts I turn round. I get the key we're supposed to use as extra security for the house insurance but never do, and lock the window. I'm about to bolt and Chubb-lock the front door when I pause. Does Saul have a bunch of keys? Or just the Yale? In the end, I leave it on the Yale. Better that Saul can get in than that I keep Rowan out.

I drag myself up the stairs, holding on to the banister, and fall into bed. I burrow down under the duvet, curl into a foetal position. My whole body's shuddering. I don't sleep for ages. I lie and stare at the ceiling. I wait for morning, twitching at every sound. The creak of the roof tiles, the wind in the trees outside, the intermittent rumble of trains passing on their way from King's Lynn to King's Cross. Or the other way. The urgent, almost frantic wail of the level-crossing siren every time a train approaches.

Eventually I must have fallen asleep because I dream of the unborn baby, Saffie and Saul's child. I dream that Jules and I are holding it between us, and she's trying to pull it away from me and in a re-enactment of the Solomon story, we're tugging at it until it is screaming, and another person – Donna Browne I think it is – says she'll cut it in half if we can't agree to share it. Jules nods. But I let the baby go to save it. I have a terrible sense of loss as I do so, but at least I know the baby will live now. That I've done all I can to keep it alive. 'There,' says Donna. 'We know now who the true grandma is. It's Holly. But she's lost her baby.'

And then I wake up.

It's light outside, though I have no idea of the time. It's a struggle to climb back up to consciousness. What day is it? Where was I last night? Why am I wearing my best dress in bed? Slowly it comes back to me. Rowan leaning over me as I lay on the floor telling me he'd like to do to me what Saul did to Saffie. Is this sense of disorientation induced by concussion? Should I seek medical help?

When I've rolled out of bed, I take off my dress, stagger to the bathroom, wash, pull on some loose clothes, a pair of leggings and knitted jumper over the top, a pair of Pete's socks. Downstairs, I stare out of the front window. The trees on the green have released the last of their leaves overnight. Perfect pools of bright copper lie beneath bare canopies. It's as if the trees were inverted. Their crowns at the base, their roots in the air. The world turned upside down.

After a while, I feel dizzy and take myself back to bed. I check my mobile again, pointlessly. I try to work through some essays emailed to me by students on my laptop, screwing up my eyes to make the words on the screen come into focus, but each time I near the end of a sentence, I've forgotten the beginning. The meaning of the words is slippery as wet soap. I try to compose an email for Samantha instead, with some information on access courses. It's hard to focus on this, but I cobble something together, ping it over to her, and at midday, I put on the local news.

My item comes on last. It seems like longer than eighteen hours since I sat in the studio and begged Saul to come home. The bead of sweat I wipe from under my eye makes it look as though I've been weeping. I watch myself plead into the camera, telling Saul he's not in trouble, telling him we all love him. Embarrassed, experiencing again the same sense of shame and exposure I felt while recording it, I switch it off.

I should phone Fatima, the kind liaison officer, tell her what Rowan did to me. Would his attack be classed as attempted rape? Sexual assault? I try to remember from my Rape Crisis days. We urged women to report any kind of attack. It didn't matter, we told them, if they hadn't been penetrated. What counted, what had to be reported, was the terror induced, the emotional trauma undergone. Right now, however, in spite of my years of persuading women to bring attacks like Rowan's to light, I decide it isn't worth the effort. The collection of forensic evidence required, the questioning I'd have to go through. I make a solemn promise to myself. No one need know what Rowan did to me last night. He has taken his revenge on me for what he believes Saul did to his daughter. And I'll leave it at that. The irony that Saffie didn't want her alleged rape reporting to the police either isn't lost on me.

Pete texts. 'Deepa says her sister can come tonight to be with the girls for the weekend. If you'll have me, I'll come home. I miss you. I want you. I want to support you, Holl.'

From the moment we first slept together, I loved the

warmth Pete's body gave off and his faintly musky smell. I loved the way we had a chemistry between us so that we knew instinctively what each other liked. Sex with Pete was an easy thing and I could do with him now, beside me, the comfort of him. But I'm not sure I've forgiven him yet.

And even were I to let him touch me, I don't want Pete to see the bruise on my thigh. The cut on my head. I don't want him to see how every sound makes me jump. I don't want him to ask questions.

'Stay with the girls,' I text back. 'They need you more than I do.'

Then, on second thoughts, I compose another message.

'If you want to help, ask Freya who she and Saffie are in love with.'

I consider softening my tone, but in the end, I just press 'send'. Then I go to the kitchen. I find a bottle of wine. It's not chilled and tastes a bit rough. But the alcohol hits my empty stomach straight away. I put on Leonard Cohen and wait for Pete's reply. After my second glass, the kitchen begins to look soft around the edges, the world a more approachable place. I'm on my way for a third refill when someone knocks loudly on the door.

I recognize Fatima's comforting figure silhouetted in the glass. She's come with news. I barely let myself think. They must have found Saul! She's going to say that he's OK and is on his way home. He's seen my appeal on TV. He realizes how much I love him and how I never believed the things that were said about him. He'll forgive us all. And I can show Fatima the diary entry. Prove Saffie and he were in love. And Fatima can go to Jules and Rowan and tell them Saffie is forgiven for panicking and telling such a disastrous lie because she's only thirteen. Everything's going to be all right.

I open the door glad to see Fatima, to have another woman for company.

'I was about to ring you,' I say. 'I've got new evidence as to what happened between Saul and Saffie.'

She doesn't answer, the expression on her face sombre.

'Can I come in?' she asks.

When she next speaks, the colour literally drains from my world. No one says these words unless they are going to tell you something truly horrible. I want to rewind the scene, go back and replay it differently so I don't have to experience what I know Fatima's going to say next. Everything goes kind of non-colour, like dead flesh, as she begins to speak.

'I think you need to sit down, Holly.'

14

JULES

Jules felt exhausted. Saffie had been silent and sullen on the way home from the auction event. Jules assumed it was because they were to see Donna about the termination the next day, but Saffie refused to speak to her about it. When they got in, she made sure Saffie got straight to bed. Then she'd gone up to bed herself. Sleep was elusive, however, and her mind began to whir. The auction had taken a lot of organization in the end. Why was it that constructing quiches and delegating ticket sales took up so much more energy than it had once done? It had proved tiring on top of work, which had been quite frantic lately, with orders not arriving on time, profits suffering as a result. Then, of course, there was the mental and emotional strain of worrying about Saffie, whose mood swings had become even more extreme of late. Jules put this down to a combination of pregnancy hormones, the after-effects of her trauma, worry about the termination and possibly anxiety over the fact no one knew what had happened to Saul – but door-slamming and shouting matches were not the half of it. Saffie was refusing food, and snapping each time Jules asked if she was OK. And although she was determined to go to school as normal, and even to attend the revision classes Rowan nagged her about, she came in looking drawn, haunted even, with a look on her face that suggested she might snarl if

Jules asked her how she was. And the sleeve-plucking had become more frantic.

Then, of course, there was Rowan. Jules had tried to quash the nagging fear that he might be to blame for whatever had caused Saul's disappearance, but at times like these – he still wasn't back, two hours after she had left the auction – she found it hard. She fretted about what the police had wanted with him earlier, and suddenly remembered the ripped receipt, the Peacocks bag. She wondered about going downstairs to check them, but her body – and mind – felt bone-tired and she couldn't face it. They'd still be there in the morning.

It was almost midnight when Jules finally heard the door slam. She wanted to talk to Rowan, and she sat up, waiting for him to come into the room. It was clear, however, when he did, that he was drunk. He didn't speak as he slid off his trousers, then collapsed on the bed. She could smell the beer on him. It was best not to broach any kind of sensitive subject when he was in this state. Years of dealing with his temper when drunk had taught her to steer clear.

And anyway, a few minutes later he was snoring.

She was alone.

Funny how you could feel more alone with your husband in the bed next to you than when you were on your own. Alone with the image of that fabric in the bag. And the petrol receipt. Alone with the doubt about where Rowan had been on Monday morning. And just now.

Meeting Holly at the auction had tainted the evening. Jules couldn't help wondering what had made Holly come in when she must have known – *known* – the hostility she would arouse. Jules had tried to give Holly a look to indicate that she should leave, but Holly had refused to pick up on it.

The tide of sympathy for Holly had turned now the rape had been made public. Most of the villagers – those who had helped in the search for Saul – now felt they'd been cheated. If they had known Saul was a rapist, they would not have been so keen to help search for him. They had been duped into helping a boy who had assaulted a young girl, a child, in her own home in *their* village. It had been the main point of conversation in the Baptist Chapel as they prepared the food and drink for the auction. While some people admitted they felt sorry for what Holly was going through – Samantha, in particular, sympathized with her – the general feeling was that she had dealt badly with the allegation and had brought Saul's disappearance on herself.

'I mean, if your son raped someone, you'd want to know, wouldn't you?' Tess had said, standing in a tight little circle by the buffet table, taking cling film off trays of quiche. 'You'd force the truth out of him immediately.'

'It's really hard to imagine, if you haven't got boys,' Samantha argued. 'I mean, if Freddie is ever accused of rape when he's older, I will never, ever believe it.'

'Freddie's only six,' Tess insisted. 'When he's a great big hulking teenager, it will seem more plausible. And you'd have a duty to believe it. To protect other girls.'

'I mean, it clearly indicates Saul's got major problems, as Jules tried to point out to Holly,' Fiona said.

'Exactly,' Jenny agreed. 'If Holly had sought advice immediately, they could have dealt with it and moved on.'

'I told Holly as soon as I knew,' Jules said. 'I thought she and Pete would talk to Saul. Then ... I don't know, we could have got him to confront what he'd done and, if necessary, take him to see someone professional.' She picked up a foil tray of smoked salmon sandwiches and arranged some wedges of lemon between them. 'What's made it so hard for me, and Saff, of course, is Holly's point-blank refusal to admit Saul did it.'

'I think that's awful of her,' Jenny said. 'Holly's son is as likely to be a rapist as any other man. For a mother to be in so much denial says something about the mother, in my opinion.'

'Absolutely. It makes you wonder what kind of mother she is, to have brought up a rapist for a son to start with. Let's not forget that Saff's only thirteen,' Tess said. 'It wasn't just rape; it was sexual assault on a minor.'

'Is that actually classed as paedophilia?' Jenny asked. 'That makes it so much worse somehow.'

'Whether it is or it isn't, that boy's on the loose. It puts other young girls at risk.'

'Isn't Holly also some kind of a women's rights activist?' someone else piped up. 'Hasn't she written about men getting away with rape, even in this day and age?'

'She's got a point there,' Fiona said. 'It incenses me. The way the courts look for any way to blame a woman when she reports a sexual assault . . .'

'But therefore you would have thought Holly would sort out her son. Not only for Saffie's sake but for the sake of womankind.'

'It's pretty damn hypocritical when you think about it,' Tess pronounced. 'To call yourself a feminist, lecture about consent and then to point-blank deny rape when your son's accused.'

Even though her friends were saying nothing Jules hadn't thought, she felt sick rather than vindicated, and every time she closed her eyes, she saw Saffie's pinched face begging her not to tell anyone. In fact, the whole evening had been marred for Jules by this emerging sense that her story, her daughter's suffering, had become the stuff of gossip and conjecture and judgement. And to top it all, there was that awful conversation with Holly, just as Jules was trying to serve the tea. Holly begging Jules to believe that Saffie loved Saul. Of course it was a wonderful fantasy, but it was absurd. Saffie was so obviously repelled by Saul, and had said as much that fateful evening, before he'd even come round. It had made Jules feel sicker still to see Holly's desperation, and had left her upset and in conflict. As a result, she'd gone home early, unable to stand being in such close proximity to Holly as she grasped at straws in order to save Saul's reputation.

Now Jules was able to give it more thought, she could see why Holly believed it was a plausible theory. In Holly's eyes, it was perfectly understandable that a young girl might fall for Saul. And, Jules supposed, Saffie's protestations that she didn't like him could, feasibly, be a cover. Saul was considered odd by the local kids and Saffie wouldn't want them to know if she had feelings for him. But just as Holly was adamant Saul was innocent because she knew her son, Jules knew her daughter – Saffie hadn't been lying about her feelings for Saul. Or what he'd done to her.

Jules couldn't bear to think about what else lay beneath her rejection of Holly's new theory that their children were in love. She knew if she gave it a second's credence, she would uncover something so dark, so awful and haunting it didn't bear thinking about. Not yet anyway. Not unless she had to.

As she lay in bed with these thoughts racing round her head, Rowan continued to snore quietly beside her. Why had he come home so late? And where had he been, instead of coming straight back from the pub? She knew he'd gone for a drink. To drown his sorrows after being interviewed by the police again the previous afternoon. And yet he had an air about him when he'd come into the bedroom. Removed. She'd seen him like this before, after he'd had a meltdown. It made her recoil from him. She couldn't confront him when he was like this. She knew from experience he would either clam up or become defensive and angry.

But she needed to talk to him. She wanted to hear more about what the police had asked him yesterday. She couldn't believe they kept carting him off to the police station 'to help with their enquiries' as if he was their main suspect in Saul's disappearance. And yet she *could* believe it. She didn't want to give shape to her own doubts about him. It would make living with him impossible. She had to keep her faith in him. If necessary, she thought, she could help cover for him.

Jules didn't sleep. She stayed awake all night, images and thoughts trooping relentlessly through her mind. The fabric she'd found the day before in the Peacocks bag. The petrol receipt from Downham Market. The mud on the Timberland boots ... Rowan didn't know his own strength. He might have meant to teach Saul a lesson and gone too far.

And then her thoughts did take the darker turn she'd tried to avoid. It would be easy to hide a body up in the remote parts of the Fens, where there were no houses or villages or people for miles. Rowan knew the roads out there, the long strips of tarmac that swept across miles of empty arable farmland between banks and ditches. There were secluded droves and wide expanses of water, the Ouse Washes, the Hundred Foot Drain and the Old Bedford River. People thought of London, of the city, as the hotbed of crime, but the Fens had an effect on people's minds. The flatness, the openness that brought you face to face with yourself – it drove people crazy.

Jules had wanted Holly to suffer for what Saul had put

them through, it was true. She had wanted her to share Saffie's pain. Had wanted Holly to admit her son's culpability, thereby taking on some of the burden of Saffie's trauma. But Jules hadn't wanted her to pay as dearly as this. She didn't want things to have gone this far. Didn't want Rowan to have done to Saul what she was increasingly afraid he had done.

And if after all Saul was innocent . . .

Please, Jules thought.

Please don't let Rowan have done what I'm afraid to think he's done.

Please don't let Saul be dead.

279

15

HOLLY

Fatima stands in front of me, in the kitchen doorway. I walk backwards, and rest on one of the kitchen stools.

'They've found remains,' she says without bothering to sit down.

Remains. The stupid images that flash through my mind are of Roman things, broken pots and fragments of mosaics from ancient times.

'Somewhere out near the Ouse Washes in the Fens. The media have got wind of it, so we had to inform you before you heard anything. The forensics team are doing all they can. When they have more information, they will be in touch.'

'You don't know any more?' The words come from far away, as if someone else has spoken them. As though they came from somebody with a mouth full of heavy alluvium mud. As though they came from a person who was already dead. 'You don't know anything else?' I try again.

'Initial investigations suggest they belong to a young adult male and have been there for several days.' I can barely breathe. 'I'm sorry, Holly. I'm so sorry, but I have to tell you that, due to the condition of what they've found, it's going to be a bit tricky to extract them.'

'I can't see him?'

'Not yet. There's still some work to do before they can remove what they've found intact.'

Fatima begins to recede. A rush of heat sweeps through me and stars begin to swirl about my head.

'I need to take some more DNA, so if you could find something of Saul's, a hairbrush, toothbrush, anything really . . . I'm afraid that's all we can tell you at the moment.' Her words are thick, muffled. She's echoing, then fading into the distance. The last thing I hear before I pass out is her kindly voice saying, 'Now, I'm going to stay with you. Remind me where you keep your tea . . .'

*

Pete's sitting next to me. I'm lying on the sofa in the sitting room. I don't know when he came in or how he knew.

There's a mist outside the window behind him. I cannot even see as far as the green. I stare at him. At his rounded face with its plump, cheerful cheeks and his kind, sad eyes.

I don't want to wake up. I don't remember why, yet. I just know I want to stay asleep because something has happened.

He puts his hand on my arm. 'You're to stay where you are,' he says. 'I'll get you some tea, or would you prefer something stronger?'

I don't want anything; I don't want Pete to touch me or to speak. This feeling is familiar. The world has taken on a new and distorted shape. The last time I was here was when I heard that Archie had had a heart attack and hadn't survived. That was how they put it, when they rang me from the hospital and told me he'd collapsed, halfway across Lincoln's Inn Fields in the early evening, near the tennis courts. Taken to the hospital with a cardiac arrest. But that he 'hadn't survived'.

They phoned my mobile to tell me. I left Saul with Jules and made my way to University College Hospital. I blocked out the words 'hadn't survived'. Completely erased them from what I'd heard. Told myself people usually recovered from heart attacks.

It was only when I saw him I knew.

He was thirty-five years old.

Saul was just ten.

'They haven't made a definitive identification,' Pete says now.

He's trying to help, I know, but it's pointless. Saul went missing on Monday; the body has been there for a few days. They know it's a young adult male. He's been out in the Fens for four days.

I can work out the odds.

I shut my eyes.

I try not to be here anymore.

*

The mist has gone and a weak sun is playing through the bare branches of the trees around the green, oddly giving them a rose-gold glow. I throw back the covers. I can't sit here all day like an invalid. As I lift myself, a searing pain shoots through my lower back and I see Rowan shoving me against the cooker, then my stumbling and falling in the kitchen.

'I need some air,' I tell Pete. 'I'm going for a walk.'

He asks if I'd like him to come, but I say I need to be alone.

I walk in a daze, ignoring the pain. Past the Baptist Chapel, the church and the Salvation Army hall. The Fens are known as England's holy land for a reason. If there's one thing this land isn't short of, it's places to worship. Places to seek forgiveness from the opium-taking and the drinking and the rape and the deviance.

I walk down the road towards the station. The poly-tunnels in the fields are empty, their frames blackened like the giant, burnt-out carcasses of animals. The polythene that provides protective covering for soft fruits in the summer is now rolled up into lumpen bundles that sag like body bags.

Leaving the buildings behind, I take the straight road towards the river, envisaging, out there in the remote farm buildings, migrant workers doing gruelling hours peeling vegetables for below the minimum wage. Hidden enclaves of modern-day slavery.

Across the level crossing, the woodland path is sludgy with leaves that have turned into thick blackened mulch since I last walked this way. The path emerges in the same exposed Fenland landscape I walked through the day after Saul went missing. Now winter is moving in. White horizon, steel-grey clouds, white light spilling through. Black crows scattered across dark soil. I take the raised path along the river. I walk north-west, heading into the path of the sinking sun. No trees. Flat all the way to Ely, all the way to the Ouse Washes. Far away, vast acres of black solar panels gleam darkly up at the sky.

I keep on walking towards my boy. The words echo in my ears: *Remains . . . several days . . . tricky to extract them . . .*

How long?

How can a body become that unrecognizable in under a week? Has he been devoured by eels? Rats? Has his body rotted away in the water? Or is it worse than that? Was he cut up? Mutilated? Burned? I wish I could stop the thoughts.

I don't know what I'm doing, but I have to keep walking. I have to move. I try not to think about Rowan bearing down on me. I don't want to give his violence headroom. But I cannot help thinking how Saffie's allegation has unleashed some previously dormant dark energy: blame and counter-blame, hatred and contempt. It has bubbled up and washed over all of us in a dirty, sullying tide. And buried my beautiful boy.

After I've been walking for an hour or so, I come upon a traveller settlement. A few women move about pulling washing off lines. Fairground travellers? The ones who were on the green the morning Saul went off? Children sit on the steps of trailers; a couple of men fiddle with a waltzer car. One of them sits on the steps to a trailer, smoking.

That's when I see him.

He's facing away from me, leaning over a water butt, doing something, his shirt ridden up, a few centimetres of bright white spine showing. It's his skinny frame, the way his trousers won't stay round his waist but slip right down, revealing the tops of his boxers. I begin to run. He's alive. He's there. I run along the bank, and then down over tussocks of grass, almost losing my balance, falling over myself to reach him.

As I run, the clouds part and the landscape takes on colour. The black soil turns purple; the pewter grasses turn green. Copper light steals across the countryside and creeps towards the settlement.

He has to know I want him back, that I never believed he raped Saffie. That he belongs to me. That Saffie simply panicked, and that's why she lied. Tears spring to my eyes as I run. I love him. I never doubted him. I reach a ditch dividing this side of the fen from the settlement and jump over. I ignore the searing pain in my lower back and run towards him. A woman steps into my path.

'Yes? What can I do for you?' She bars my way, making it clear she doesn't want me here. I recognize her. She's the woman at the hoopla stall, the one I asked about Saul the first night he didn't come home.

'My son,' I gasp, pointing beyond her.

'Your son?'

She blocks my view. She's wearing a yellow fleece and lilac tracksuit bottoms. I can smell smoke on her breath.

'There . . .' I gesture over towards the boy and she turns her head, then looks back at me.

'Your son?' the woman repeats again.

'That's him, there. Look.'

I go to move past her, but another woman draws up alongside her, blocking my path, and I dive to the side.

'*Saul!*'

The boy stands up straight. He's stockily built. Shorter than Saul.

He turns.

'Oh . . .'

It's not him.

Of course it's not him.

'What about your son?' the second woman says. She's thinner, with an irregular face, one eye set a little higher than the other above a narrow nose, a kinder expression than the hoopla woman.

'He's gone missing,' I half sob. 'I thought that was him.'

'He's the one the cops were asking us about the other day?' the thin woman says. 'They came asking if we'd seen him. We hadn't. So he's still missing. How old is he again?'

'Sixteen.'

'Grown up, then,' the first woman says.

'Yes. No. I suppose you could say that. He's still a child to me. He went off and didn't come home. I thought he might have decided to walk up the river. Come into the Fens. Likes to be alone. He's tall, six foot, thin . . . I thought . . . I thought that was him. But his hair is, well, it's . . . longer, darker.'

She goes to speak to a group of women on the far side of the encampment. I see them looking over towards me, talking to each other and then calling a man over to them, a big, muscular man in a white T-shirt with his tattooed arms bare despite the cold.

'We haven't seen him,' she says, coming towards me again. 'We'll keep an eye out. Won't we, Sandy? Long hair, you say? Thin? Taller than Charlie. If we see him, we'll let you know. Give us your number. We'll call you if he comes by.'

'Thank you. Thank you so much.'

'He's your child,' she says. 'Nothing worse than something happening to your own child.'

I look at her for a few minutes, grateful for her sympathy. Should I tell her that I'm clutching at straws? That the police have a body? I can't say the words. I can't bear to see the anguish she, too, would feel on my behalf if she knew.

When I've left the travellers, I turn back. I'm not really going to walk as far as the Ouse Washes. I climb a stile, jump down on the other side. You can see the pumping station from here, a tall, imposing, windowless building silhouetted against the sky. And beyond it lies the lock. When I get back to the river, I'll take the metal footbridge over the lock and head home along the road that cuts between the black fields of silty soil and passes Jules's house and the railway line. I have to know now. I have to hear what they have discovered. I would rather confront it sooner than later. I have to get home.

Through the swing gate, my feet clanking on the metal steps, I reach the bridge over the lock, the railing icy against my palm. Then up onto the second bridge, over the sluice.

Here I stop, suddenly exhausted, and gaze down into the water. Perhaps I can't face going home after all. The water falls in white sheets from the upper level into amber river water below. It smells very rich in the evening air, of mud and grass and fish, with a rotten, sludgy undertone. I don't know how long I stay there, unable to move, but I shut my eyes and let the last of the sun's rays fall against my eyelids, and when I open them again, it's almost dark.

I change my mind once more. I have to get home now. I want to be unconscious. Under the covers. To black everything out. Why did I think I'd feel better out here? There's nowhere I will feel better. This feeling will accompany me wherever I go. Forever.

It's only a few metres to the other side of the bridge, but the distance seems insurmountable to me.

I'm still there, leaning on the railings, when there's the bang of iron and I feel vibrations under my feet and realize someone is coming up the steps of the bridge on the other side. A head appears in a purple bobble hat, and then I see that it's Saffie, stomping towards me.

Something bursts, a small explosion inside me. She looks so *normal*, in her tight, high-waisted jeans, bomber jacket and trainers. So *alive*, with her dark eye make-up and her pretty blonde hair poking out from under her jaunty woollen hat. So unaffected by what's happened to Saul. She comes closer. This is the girl who is responsible, through her allegation, for the terrible thing that has happened to my son. She's coming towards me, and the river is tumbling deeply and hungrily and lethally beneath me. And there is no one else for miles around.

16

JULES

Jules got up early. The appointment with Donna Browne was later that day. At least that was something to be thankful for. Nevertheless, she felt unrested and nervy.

'Saff, make sure you come straight back from school. We're seeing Donna at five fifteen.'

Saffie nodded silently as she stuffed her school bag with books, water bottle, mobile. The things that made her look as if she was going for a three-day hike rather than a few hours' lessons.

Jules watched her daughter walk down the drive. It tore at her heart and she felt dread in the pit of her stomach at all Saffie was going to have to go through that afternoon. Repeating her ordeal to Donna. And the other doctor Donna said she'd have to call in. Then the pill-taking. Then the bleeding it would bring on.

*

Tess rang to say they had raised more than they expected for the school at the auction. 'Over two thousand quid,' she said.

'Great.'

'It *is* great, isn't it?'

It should be a good feeling. But Jules didn't feel good. Not with the abortion looming. Not after seeing Holly at the Auction of Promises. Not after Rowan coming in so late with that air about him as if he'd done something he regretted.

To stave off her rising anxiety, Jules drove to the country park for a run before work. The fear about what Rowan had done came and went as she pounded along the tracks between trees whose few remaining leaves had turned yellow, and trembled, ready to fall and join others in a mulch on the paths. Rowan, Jules thought, could not possibly have bundled Saul into his car without being spotted by one of the school kids who were waiting for the bus on the green. Then anxiety sliced in again. There were ways and means. There had been the fair that morning, blocking the edges of the green from view. The police had analysed CCTV footage and had seen the car leaving the village and heading towards Ely. Rowan had corroborated this, saying he had gone to Ely to buy the things for the meal that evening. But why had he done that, when he'd never done it before? And why had he not mentioned going to Downham Market? The thought made her feel nauseous. Rowan might have got Saul to talk to him, got him into the car somehow. Trusted that the fairground machinery and lorries would obscure them from view.

As Jules ran, she told herself this idea was absurd. Rowan was her loving husband. He had occasionally got into brawls when drunk, but he would never do the kind of thing she was imagining. And yet her thoughts refused to be silenced. The landscape around her took on a new aspect of menace. The natural world wasn't natural out here at all; it was a man-made construct. The corrugated sides of the windowless storage units that backed onto the country park. The lake that was really just a great big, water-filled gravel pit. The motorway just a few metres away, with its relentless roar of traffic, cars shooting past, oblivious to what went on beyond. And the Fens, flat lands that should be under water, drained, over-cultivated, ploughed and furrowed to bits. The natural order had been interfered with. Now everywhere seemed like a place where a murderer might hide a body.

The images flashed through Jules's head as she pounded past the lake: Rowan climbing into the car with Saffie, to drive her to the bus stop, his face set. Rowan playing the perfect husband that night, cooking the meal for her. The mud on his boots. The receipt from the garage at Downham Market when he only said he'd gone to Ely. Had he driven out into the Fens first, deposited Saul somewhere and then coolly gone shopping in Ely Waitrose as if nothing had happened? It was the kind of thing you heard on the news. Murderers who carried on as normal after chopping up a body and hiding it and cleaning away the evidence. Popping to get the weekly shop after depositing a bleeding corpse in a river or a drain or a shallow grave.

By the time Jules finished her run, in record time, as it turned out, she was more convinced than ever that her husband had done something to her odd son. And if he had, and if Holly's new theory that the kids loved one another was right, then . . . But she must not go down this line of thought. Holly was wrong. Saul had raped Saffie. And Rowan's irate reaction was understandable. But he would not have gone that far.

Would he?

*

When Jules got home, the house was quiet. Rowan had left a note saying he'd gone to meet the lads for a game of golf and wouldn't be in until that afternoon. He spent most of his time out with his mates these days; Jules didn't care. She felt tense when he was in the house. Was almost relieved each time the police came back and took him away again to help with their enquiries. Almost disappointed each time he came home, though it was hard to admit that, even to herself.

As she did her post-run workout to a Motown compilation in the home gym, she wished she had honoured Saffie's wish and never, ever told Rowan about the rape. She wished Holly had never told the police about it.

They could, and should, have kept it between themselves.

She and Saffie. Holly and Saul. Between them, they could have dealt with it without any of the repercussions telling others had caused.

*

At least the shop was busy today, the bell on the door ringing constantly as wealthy parents came in to buy their children's winter wardrobes. Hand-knitted pullovers flew off the shelves, and the new line of baby parkas was selling out fast.

'We'll have to put another order in for those,' Jules told Hetty.

At lunchtime, Hetty went out to get them their usual bagels and coffees from Indigo. There was a lull at about half past one and they sat at the back of the shop. Jules couldn't eat.

'I may have to leave a bit early today,' she said, folding the paper bag back over her bagel. 'Will you be OK on your own?'

'I'll be fine,' Hetty said.

'I knew so. It's so great having you, you know, Hetty. You're a real find.'

'You OK, Jules? You've been looking preoccupied recently.'

Jules's head shot up. 'I'm just having a few issues at home,' she said, giving Hetty a weak smile.

'To do with Saffie?'

'How did you guess?'

'You have that mother's frown on your forehead!'

Jules wished she could blurt out what was really on her mind. 'There's always something to worry about,' she said instead, 'once you have a child.'

'You're only ever as happy as your unhappiest child – that's what my mum used to say,' said Hetty.

'Tell me about it,' said Jules.

*

When Jules got home that afternoon, she went straight to find the bag she had pulled out of the bin and stuffed in the back of the kitchen cupboard. She took it up to her room, sat on her bed and, shutting her eyes as she did so, pulled out the fabric.

She didn't find what she feared – and half expected – she might. It wasn't, after all, a scarf or any kind of garment that might have been used to strangle a person to death. The pieces of fabric were barely long enough to go round a small child's neck. Instead, Jules saw, they were sexy undergarments – a few triangles of silk and a couple of ribbons, barely anything to either piece. They'd been worn, and were Saffie's size. The sight set Jules's heart thudding anyway, gave her a hot and uncomfortable feeling in her gut. Why had Saffie bought sexy lingerie like this, worn it, then thrown it into the bin?

Jules went into Saffie's room and glanced around. She had done this several times in the last week, seeking evidence for the rape. She never really knew what she was looking for, and had found nothing. Now she spotted the Michael Morpurgo book, with a page marked with a little business card. She pulled out the card. It was for a beautician in Cambridge Jules had used herself. She picked it up. A date was scrawled on it, for a wax. The appointment was for next Wednesday at five o'clock. Jules shuddered. Saffie didn't need to start waxing her legs: her hair was still soft and golden and invisible. When she checked again, however, she saw it wasn't for a leg wax at all but a bikini wax. A Brazilian. Saffie had only just begun to develop hair there. What was she waxing it off for? Jules resolved to talk to her daughter about that once things were back to normal. If they were ever back to normal.

Jules then opened up her daughter's laptop. Saffie used a MacBook, one Jules had passed down from the shop. It seemed intrusive looking at it, but since the rape, and everything else – the waxing, the underwear – Jules felt she had a right to look. All Saffie's emails were innocuous and mostly to friends about the various arrangements they had at the weekends. She had hundreds of WhatsApp and Instagram followers, but none stood out particularly. There were photos of models posing in skimpy underwear, people whose names Jules had heard Saffie mention, girls with what looked like fake eyelashes and enhanced figures, the Instagrammers and YouTubers they all liked to emulate these days. But no photos of Saffie wearing that slinky underwear that Jules could find. Thank God.

Nothing else seemed different to usual. The soft toys Saffie still slept with were piled on the pillow, including the teddy bear Saul had given her when she was born. Thank goodness they were going to sort it all out this afternoon, Jules thought, so that Saffie could reclaim her childhood.

*

At three thirty, Jules listened out for Saffie. She was keen to get the visit to Donna over and done with, the pregnancy terminated once and for all.

Saffie, however, still hadn't come in by four. The early school bus usually dropped them off at around three forty-five, and Saffie had promised to get it today, in order to be in time for her appointment. When by four thirty she still wasn't home, Jules began to feel anxious. She reassured herself – if Saffie had missed the first bus, she would be back at five. Or sometimes Saffie stayed to chat to the others at the bus stop before ambling home, forgetting the time. But it seemed highly unlikely she would do so when she had the appointment hanging over her.

Jules became more uneasy as the clock turned past five. If Saffie wasn't back soon, they would be late.

Jules texted her.

'Where are you? Have you forgotten the doctor?'

It was getting dark. Jules began to really fret. Saffie was usually good at texting straight back, but the minutes went by and no text came. Should she get in the car and look for her? But then if Saffie took the shortcut through the housing estate from the bus stop on the green, Jules would miss her.

She would wait.

*

It was five thirty when Saffie finally came in. Fifteen minutes late for the doctor.

Jules stood in front of her, arms folded.

'Where have you been?'

294

'Nowhere.' Saffie pushed past her mother and headed for the stairs.

'Do you realize you've missed the appointment? I'm going to have to phone and make another one and—'

'I don't need to go to the doctor.'

'Saffie. We've waited all week for this. Come on. I know it's scary for you. But you'll feel much better once we've spoken to Donna. You knew about the appointment. Why were you so late home?'

'My maths teacher wanted to talk about my assignment.'

'If I were to ring your maths teacher, would he confirm that for me?'

'Why do you want to ring him?' Saffie snapped, swinging round. 'He'll think you're insane.'

'Because something's going on with you, Saffie . . . You're not telling me everything. I think you're finding ways to avoid dealing with this whole thing! Why didn't you tell him you had an appointment?'

'How could I tell him? What did you expect me to say?'

'There's no shame in saying you had a doctor's appointment.'

'Why won't you leave me alone?' Saffie wailed. 'You go on and on and on at me and I can't take any more!' She was backing away from Jules, her face screwed up – furious, or terrified; probably both.

Jules was angry with herself; this wasn't the time to start chastising her daughter. Not when they needed to get to Donna's. Not when she was clearly so distressed about the looming abortion.

'OK. Listen, Saffie. I understand this is very difficult for you, but right now we need to get you to Donna. I want you to get in the car.'

'I'm not going.' She stomped up the stairs.

'I'll phone the surgery and explain we've been held up,' Jules called after her. 'I'll say we'll be there in ten minutes.'

Jules was dialling the surgery when Saffie's footsteps came banging fast down the stairs again. She'd changed out of her uniform into jeans and a bomber jacket.

'I'm not going to the doctor,' Saffie said, walking backwards towards the front door. 'I don't need to see her because I'm not pregnant.'

And then she hurled the door open and slammed it hard as she went out into the darkness.

'Saffie, wait!' Jules cried. But Saffie had gone.

Jules grabbed a coat as the receptionist answered.

'Yes?'

'I had an appointment with Donna Browne.' Jules was panting, pulling on her Barbour jacket as she spoke. 'We're late, but it's really urgent. Can I make it later? Say six?'

'I'll have a look for you.'

'I can't wait,' Jules said. 'Please could Dr Browne phone me back?'

Jules tugged on her wellies. As she flung back the door in pursuit of Saffie, her mobile rang and she snatched it up, expecting to hear Donna Browne's measured voice.

'Jules? It's Pete. Holly isn't there, is she?'

'Now's not a good time, Pete.'

'I'm worried about her,' he said. 'She's very distressed. She's gone out without telling me where she's going and I'm concerned for her. She's in a terrible state. I'm worried she might do something foolish.'

Jules felt sick.

'Has something happened?' she asked.

'They found a body,' Pete said. 'The remains of. Up near the Ouse Washes. The state of it is consistent with the time Saul went missing.'

'The Ouse Washes?'

Jules stared at the phone. It was where Rowan had gone that morning! To Downham Market. Past the Ouse Washes. The day Saul had gone off to school and never arrived.

The Ouse Washes was a broad stretch of flat, marshy land that acted as a floodplain in weather like this. It lay between the major drains of the Fens, the Old Bedford River and the Hundred Foot Drain. When those channels flooded, they spilt onto the plains, along with whatever waste they were carrying. Jules had been up there with Rowan and Saffie soon after they moved to the area, to watch from a bird hide as swans glided in to feed. She had seen how the water deepened and widened as winter approached. It was a remote, underpopulated area, where the wide stretches of flat water reflected the vast, empty Fenland sky, so the world seemed turned upside down. Where you could walk for hours and not see another living soul. Where there were long, secluded ditches behind high banks.

Where you could do what you wanted and never be seen.

'They're trying to identify the body, but it's in quite a bad state, apparently. They didn't want Holly to know. It wasn't all in one piece, let's say. And they can't move it until they've done various forensic tests, in case . . . I don't want to tell you the details.'

Stars began to appear in the air above Jules, and she gagged. She clutched the table and put her head between her knees. When the sense she was about to pass out subsided, she sat down.

'Holly's not here, though,' she said when she could speak. Her voice was dry. All she could think of was Saffie out there in the dark. It was irrational, in a way, to link this with what Pete had just told her, but something was out there.

Something or someone capable of rendering a body unidentifiable in a matter of days. 'I have to go.'

She slammed down the phone. Grabbed her keys. She had to protect Saffie from whatever evil was lurking out there in the Fens.

Or maybe even within her own walls.

*

There were only two routes Saffie could possibly take from their house in the dark. One was along the road over the railway line towards the village. Saffie had been told not to cross the railway in the dark. Only six months ago, a man had been minced up by the wheels of the King's Lynn–King's Cross service. The other was down to the river, a place she often met her friends on a fine summer's evening. Jules was happy for her to go there when it was daylight because she could actually see the lock from the house. But not this evening. Not when body parts had been found up near the Ouse Washes. And when Saffie was so obviously not herself. Jules wanted her home and safe. Not out there as it grew darker and the wind got up.

As she reached the track that ran from their house down to the river, she could see her daughter, a small figure silhouetted against the first light of a large moon, leaning into the wind, moving along the flood bank. From where Jules stood, she appeared to be the only living thing on the landscape, heading towards the lock. Poor Saffie. Jules should have realized the enormity of the impending abortion for her daughter. She should have dealt with it differently. Sooner. Taken Saff straight to a specialist clinic even if Saffie hadn't wanted her to. Saffie had said she wasn't pregnant as she'd slammed out of the door, which was obviously her last-gasp attempt to avoid the truth. She was clearly more terrified of having the termination than Jules had fully realized.

It was hard for Jules to run along the track in her wellies. The ground underfoot was thick with wet mud, which sucked at her feet. She should have put on trainers and taken the road, but she hadn't thought about that in her rush. The sun sank behind the horizon and Jules stumbled on as best she could in the dark. She would reassure Saffie that the appointment would be over very quickly, and that she would be fine. She would not let her know what Pete had told her on the phone; she didn't know how exactly she would keep this news from Saffie, but she knew she had to, because otherwise Saffie would think she was to blame, and who knew where that would lead them? They were already in about as bad a place as possible. All of them. Saffie. Jules. Holly. Saul.

Saul most of all, from what Pete had said, because there was no hope for him. Jules swallowed the feelings that threatened to engulf her at this thought, and tried to focus instead on catching up with her daughter.

17

HOLLY

Saffie stops a few feet from me and stares. I can see she wants to turn and run away, but we can't avoid each other here on the bridge. I have a compulsion to take her by the shoulders and shake her. Slap her, even. Beat the truth out of her. But the look on her face – sheer horror that she's bumped into me, and something else, her childishness perhaps, or helplessness – stops me.

'What are you doing here?' I ask, amazed at how calm and normal, even, I sound.

'I had a row with Mum,' Saffie says, and I see now that she's terrified, her skin pale beneath the make-up, her voice tight. 'She keeps on nagging me about where I've been.'

I look at Saffie, my odd daughter. At her heart-shaped face under her bobble hat. At her carefully shaped eyebrows and the thick mascara and the veil of foundation that doesn't properly cover her. I want to shout that she doesn't need to do this. To plaster her lovely face with make-up. To act older than her age. To stick to the story that Saul raped her.

When I do speak again, my voice is faint. 'Do you want to talk to me about it?'

It's almost completely dark, but a large moon has risen and the wind has dropped and it's become mild, almost warm. We lean on the damp railing and Saffie takes a packet of cigarettes out of her pocket, cups her hand and lights one.

'Don't tell Mum,' she says, inhaling. Her hand holding the cigarette is trembling and I wonder what's made her so palpably distressed. She can't have heard about Saul. Only Pete and I and the police know.

'I'll have one, too, if you don't mind,' I say. 'I've had a nasty a shock. It's been one hell of a shit day.'

'Do you want to talk to me about it?' Saffie says.

I glance at her.

Yes. She's making an attempt at a joke.

She hands me a cigarette and flicks her Bic lighter for me. The flame flares up, and I put my cigarette end to it and inhale, watching it glow amber in the darkness. It's years since I've smoked. The effect is swift. My head swims. My lungs instantly reject the sensation. I cough, then gasp for breath. Saffie's far more experienced at this than I am. She's inhaling without a flicker of discomfort. But I need it. So I puff again, and inhale. It occurs to me briefly to tell Saffie she shouldn't be smoking since she's only thirteen, let alone the fact she's pregnant. Instead, I say, 'I need to sit down,' and walk towards the bank. She follows me, and we sit, not caring about the wet mud or the damp that seeps up through our coats.

'Has something horrible happened?' Saffie asks at last, her voice tiny. A child's. 'It has. Something's happened to Saul, hasn't it?'

I look down at my cigarette. I don't want to tell her. But she persists.

'Has it? Holly, tell me . . .'

'They've found a body,' I hear myself say. 'Near the Ouse Washes. Up there.' I wave the cigarette in the direction the river snakes, north through the Fens. I probably shouldn't, but I keep talking. I can't stop myself. All the usual boundaries have collapsed. None of the usual rules apply. 'They think it might be Saul, though they haven't identified it yet. It's too ... Well, let's just say it's difficult to tell from the remains who it is.'

The cigarette held in front of me, I watch the smoke rise into the damp night air and wait.

Saffie hasn't made a sound since my last utterance.

At last I turn to look at her. One arm hugs her knees; the other hand holds the cigarette between her fingers. She's sobbing quietly, her head bent, her back heaving, large, round tears falling onto the grass. A wave of shame washes over me. What was I thinking? I've just told Saffie, a terrified thirteen-year-old, that the boy I believe she loves, if she will only admit it, the boy who got her pregnant, might be dead.

I put my arm round her, feel her tense, and then her whole body convulses as she begins to cry openly.

'It's OK,' I say pointlessly.

'It's not OK,' Saffie says when she can draw breath. 'It's awful. It's terrible. It's all because of me.'

Yes, I want to say. *It is all because of you. You are a troublemaker and a coward. You cared more about your stupid friends and what they think of Saul than about your true feelings.* Instead, I squeeze my eyes tight shut.

'It's not all because of you. It's a combination of all sorts of things, and none of us could have predicted it. It might be because of me.'

'How could it be because of you?'

I can't explain to Saffie. The inadequacy I feel as Saul's mother. Jules's words echo in my ears: *You yourself called him a misfit. Well, you were right.* Why hadn't I done more to help Saul fit in? When Jules suggested, soon after we moved out of London, that I should encourage Saul to join some of the more wholesome activities the popular boys participated in, I'd dismissed the idea. But perhaps he'd wanted to – the vision of the dumb-bells and protein powder I found in his room comes back to me. He was ashamed of telling me he wanted to belong, because he knew I loved his creative, individual side. I recall Pete's words: *You have separation anxiety . . . You need to let him be.* Saul was so unhappy. I should have taken Jules's and Pete's advice and then he wouldn't have been singled out and bullied by the Fenland youths. And accused of rape, and run off, and done something terrible to himself so that he has ended up in the swamps north of here. Where he never wanted to live in the first place.

'I don't think I handled things very well,' is all I say.

Saffie doesn't answer. She's still crying, quietly now.

'I'm sorry, Saffie. It was wrong of me to dump this information on you just because I needed a shoulder to cry on. You're too young.'

At last she sighs. Calms down a little.

'I'm not that young.'

'Too young to deal with whatever has happened to Saul. I'm sorry.'

'*You* didn't tell horrible lies about Saul that made him kill himself.'

I look at her. Her words hang in the air, and I have to repeat them to myself silently, to see if I heard them right.

'What did you say?'

'That I lied.' She can't bring herself to meet my gaze. 'Saul never raped me.'

There's a commotion in the reeds then and a swan glides into the water and starts to paddle upstream.

Saffie speaks again before I can respond.

'He's killed himself because I lied,' she wails. 'I said he raped me. I lied. And now he's dead!'

She begins to weep copiously again, a low moaning, keening sound.

I put my arm round her. She's telling me what I always knew. It's a bit fucking late, but the truth is coming out at last. I let her weep for a while longer. When she's quietened, I say, 'You could have told your mum you loved each other. She wouldn't have been angry. Even if you did have unprotected sex. Which was, of course, Saul's responsibility too.'

Silence.

'Didn't you realize how serious it was to say that he raped you?'

She shakes her head.

'Come here.' I pull her to me.

'Saff,' I say. 'You being in love with Saul, it was nothing to be ashamed of. You are too young, it's true, and Saul should have known that. But you'll soon learn not to care what other people think about your choice in boys.'

She tugs away from me and sits up.

'I don't love Saul, Holly. Not in that way. Nothing happened. Don't you see? Saul never touched me. He never came near me. And now he's killed himself because everyone believed that he raped me, and it's all my fault.'

'You didn't have sex with him that night?'

She's looking down, her head bowed, wisps of fair hair sticking to her wet cheeks, and she shakes her head so the bobble on her hat wobbles.

'He's never even touched me. We've never touched each other. Not like that. I made it up to . . . to . . .'

The water roars over the sluice. I try not to think of what the police have found. Of the remains that lie out there in the Fens. I try not to think how this very water has swallowed Saul. Instead, I breathe deeply, beginning to loathe the taste of the cigarette, needing clean air in my lungs in order to assimilate everything Saffie's saying. In order to stay calm. I let some time go by, taking in her confession.

I need to make Saffie trust me. I need her to tell me what's really been going on for her. If Saul didn't go into her room, if he didn't touch her, not even as her boyfriend, then she must have some other reason for blaming her pregnancy – a lie that's turned out to have fatal consequences – on Saul.

'I won't ever forgive myself,' Saffie says. 'For saying those things.'

'Why did you?' I ask quietly. 'Why say Saul raped you if he didn't? You could have told us the truth. Before all this . . .' I have to stop myself going further. I have to play Saffie so very carefully at this point. She's gone to such extreme lengths to stick to her story. I have to dig carefully, an archaeologist with some delicate find, brushing gently to uncover a truth that has been buried for so long. 'Saff, if you tell me why you blamed Saul for what's been happening with you, it will help everyone. Something happened to make you say he raped you. Didn't it?'

She's silent.

'If you explain, it will help me deal with all this.' I wave my arm in the direction of the Ouse Washes and the Old Bedford River and the Hundred Foot Drain. 'With what the police have found. It will help me if I at least know people will remember Saul as the person he was.'

But she turns her face to me and the anguish on it is apparent, like a small child who is so terrified of being in trouble, so frightened, they can't speak.

At last she draws in a breath and says, 'It's . . . Holly, I've been . . . I can't tell you. I can't tell anyone. And especially not Mum. I said Saul raped me when I was afraid I was pregnant. And Mum made me do the test and it was positive, but it was wrong. Because I'm not. I've made everyone hate me. I've been horrible to Mum too. Because I get in such a mood when I'm on my period and it makes me go mental and that's why I was late in from school today, and why I rowed with Mum.'

'You're on your period?'

'Yes. It was late. And it's really heavy and painful, and I always get in such a bad mood when I'm on my period. But this time it's worse than it's ever been. And she wanted to take me to the doctor, but I didn't need the doctor anymore.'

She stops, gulps, the way a child does who's been sobbing so long they cannot get their breath. 'If I'd known my period was going to come, I would never have said that stuff about Saul and I could have kept everyone safe.'

I let her words sink in. She's losing the baby and she doesn't even realize it, not fully. She's so very young. I close my eyes. Behind my eyelids, I see floods, red floods, blood swirling and curdling in eddies. When I open my eyes, I'm aware again of the river water gushing beneath us into the Fens. And for a moment it seems everything and everyone I've ever loved is being sucked away. The way the dykes and drains have sucked away the water that once covered this land and provided a living for its inhabitants, leaving it flat and exposed. And I remember how when I first came here, I thought of the Fens as a land with the life drained out of it, and now it is draining everything I know and care about from me.

'What do you mean, you could have kept everyone safe? What are you frightened of, Saff?'

'I can't say. And Mum keeps asking and asking me where I've been and what I'm doing and checking up on me, and she won't realize that I just can't tell her, because . . . I can't tell anyone . . .'

'*Saffie!*'

We both look up. Jules is hurrying along the bank towards us, her face contorted with worry.

This is where Jules finds me and her daughter, sitting on the damp ridge staring out across the river towards the flat lands, our arms round each other. I'm too tired, too beaten emotionally to talk anymore. Except to say, as I stand up and walk away, 'Jules. Saffie has something to tell you.'

18

JULES

Holly walked away into the darkness, leaving Jules alone with her daughter on the riverbank.

'Come here, Saff.' Jules reached out to hug her, caught the smell of cigarette smoke, felt Saffie flinch away. 'Sweetie,' Jules said. 'I need you to speak to me. We've missed the doctor's appointment. I should have realized how frightened you were.'

'I don't need the doctor.'

'Saff . . .'

'I'm on my period.'

'Ah.' Saffie wasn't on her period, because the pregnancy test had been positive. If she was bleeding, if she was really bleeding and not simply avoiding the doctor, then she was losing the baby. Jules felt swamped by Saffie's words. By everything. She could barely breathe. It was as if she were floundering under the Fenland water that gushed past beneath them. She'd felt out of her depth ever since her daughter first told her about the rape. Now she knew she should explain to Saffie that she was miscarrying, get her to Donna so that she could be checked out, but the words seemed to lodge in her throat.

Before Jules could find her breath and speak, Saffie went on: 'And Saul's dead . . .'

Jules felt herself sink further, but heard herself: 'Hang on a second, Saffie. We don't know that.'

'He is. Holly told me. And it's because of me. Because I lied about him raping me. And I might as well not have bothered because I'm not even pregnant anyway.' Saffie's voice cracked.

Jules began to shiver. The sense that she was drowning subsided a little and now she just felt cold, freezing. She turned over in her mind what Saffie had just said, her teeth chattering. Did Holly know more than Pete? Had they identified the body after all? Then Holly's words came back to her, in her office: *She's turning into a devious little troublemaker.* Words that still cut Jules to the quick. What lengths would Holly go to, to prove her point?

Even now?

What had she just said to Saffie to make her retract her allegation? Had she told Saffie Saul was dead, and by implication blamed her?

When at last her shivering subsided a little, Jules said, 'Saff, we don't know Saul's dead.' She didn't let herself think about the remains that were in too bad a state to be easily identified.

'They've found a body, though. Holly told me.'

Jules swore under her breath. 'They don't know it's Saul's. Holly should never have mentioned it to you.'

'But it must be. And it's my fault. Because I lied.'

'Did Holly *make* you say this? That you lied?'

'No. *I* said it. I told her I lied.'

'You're saying what? That Saul didn't do those things to you that night? The night Holly and I were out?'

Saffie hung her head.

A train went by on the line a few hundred metres behind them, blasting its horn, two notes, in a falling cadence, almost jaunty. Jules wanted to go home. She wanted to be indoors, cooking in the kitchen, pouring Rowan a beer, laughing with him at some picture of Saffie in one of her dance performances on the computer, their arms round one another, that closeness she used to feel that they'd produced this extrovert, confident, pretty child between them. The plans they made for her. The fantasies they shared about Saffie's glittering future. She wanted to be leaning against Rowan's side the way she used to, at parties, with that sense of inner triumph that the man she'd met was prepared to do anything for her. Move to the country, build her a house, tell her she was the most beautiful woman he'd ever set eyes on. Or, better still, she would like to be in bed next to Saffie, the Michael Morpurgo book on her knees, a glass of wine on the bedside table, Saffie's warm head smelling of baby shampoo against her shoulder. She did not want to be out here, in the dark, with her teenager smelling of smoke, telling her she was bleeding, the dank-smelling river water roaring over the sluice, and with a miserable sense that she no longer knew the people she loved most.

Holly's face, desperate to persuade Jules that Saffie and Saul loved each other, came into view. Begging her, in the midst of the Auction of Promises, to believe it.

'Saffie, if you and Saul were having a relationship, and you had sex, it would be better to tell me. Whatever you believe Dad might say. Whatever you believe your friends might think. Let's get it out in the open. Now, before we go home. You can tell me, and you'll feel better for it.'

'We weren't.'

'However embarrassing you find it. I won't tell anyone if you don't want me to. Except perhaps Holly. Because it might just help her. She needs to know,' Jules said, in spite of herself. 'Because it will take away a little bit of the pain of losing Saul, if that's what's happened, if she can reassure herself he loved you and would never have hurt you.'

'I've told her,' Saffie said. 'Saul never came near me. We've never even touched each other. Not in that way.'

Jules closed her eyes. Rowan came into her vision, saying he would beat the daylights out of Saul.

'Then there is someone. Who is it?'

'I'm not saying.'

Jules could nag Saffie until she got the truth out, but Saffie had lied to everyone – to her, to Rowan, to the police even – to protect whoever had made her pregnant. And the damp was seeping up through her coat, and Saffie must be exhausted and starving by now.

'Saffie, let's go home. I won't ask you any more. You need some rest.'

'I don't. I need to stay here. Saul's out there, in the Fens somewhere, and it's all my fault. Because I lied about him raping me. So I should stay here and be cold and get wet, and probably I should just die myself.'

'Don't say that, Saff. Please never say that.'

Saffie's hand was plucking at her sleeve. Jules gently lifted it and tucked it under her arm.

'You are very young,' Jules said after a while. 'Too young to be dealing with any of this.' She reiterated her words from earlier. 'And you are not to blame for whatever has happened. Even if Saul has done something to harm himself.'

'*Kill* himself.'

'You are not to blame. Saul had troubles already.' Jules thought of Holly, in the taxi on the way to the pub for Tess's birthday drinks, bewailing her worry that Saul didn't fit in, that there was something else going on with him. That he might be depressed.

'One false accusation would not be enough to push him to suicide. OK?' Jules said to Saffie. 'Saying he raped you if he didn't was foolish. But you didn't know that, and you did not force him to run away. You're not responsible for whatever's happened to him.'

Jules was still trying to make sense of what Saffie had told her. Saffie, Jules remembered, had been convinced that Jules and Holly, as such old, close friends, would deal with her rape allegation quickly and with little fuss, between them. She had, in her naivety, believed that it would all be swept under the carpet after they'd confronted Saul. He would, of course, have denied it. But no one, Saffie must have thought, would question *her*. And once the pregnancy was terminated, they would, in Saffie's innocent vision, have carried on as they were before. She'd had no idea how her allegation would reveal the fault lines that lay beneath every one of their relationships. Hers and Rowan's. Hers and Holly's. Holly's and Pete's. It was as if Saffie's allegation had precipitated a tsunami that had ripped the surface from each of their lives to reveal the mess that lay beneath.

Saffie didn't reply but continued to weep over what had happened to Saul, repeating that it was her fault, and in the end Jules decided to back off until she was less distressed. She would sit here and wait until Saffie was ready to move. Donna – and everything else – would have to wait. Apart from anything, the poor child was having an early miscarriage and didn't even realize it. Jules reached out again, pulling her daughter to her and squeezing her tight.

There would be time enough to get Saffie checked out, medically, later. And the mystery of who had got her pregnant, and why she'd lied, could be solved when she and Jules and all of them had had time to take on board this terrible news about Saul.

And so Jules sat next to her daughter in the dark, listening to the sounds of the Fenland night. The roar of the water on the sluice. The occasional flap of wings overhead and the intermittent sigh of the wind in the reeds. The clouds had covered the moon now and it was dark, but this darkness was a comfort. Jules thought of Holly, sitting here when she had arrived. Now she knew Saul was innocent, she began to appreciate how hellish this whole thing must have been for her friend. She didn't know how Holly could bear it. Knowing the police had a body but hadn't identified it. It was so cruel of them to have told her.

She sat and waited until at last Saffie pulled her head away from her and said, 'Mum, can we go home now? I want to go home.'

And they stood up and walked, their arms round each other, back towards their house.

*

When Saffie and Jules got in, Jules took Saffie, at her request, straight up to have a bath, gave her two spoonfuls of Calpol and tucked a hot-water bottle under her duvet, as if she were six again. It felt right to treat her as a small child, in need of mothering; she even stayed with her until she was sure she was asleep. Then she sat for a little longer, recalling the anguish on Holly's face when she had found her there with Saffie on the riverbank, and thinking how in a different life she would have wept with her friend over Saul.

She didn't know how long she stayed, trying to take in the news that the police had found a body, but she must have been there at least an hour, watching over Saffie as she relaxed, and her cheeks turned pink, and her breathing became regular. She wondered whether she should call Donna Browne, tell her that Saffie was miscarrying and didn't even realize it. Ask whether there was anything she should do.

But she decided that could wait. For the moment, it was clear Saffie needed to sleep more than anything.

Finally, Jules heard the door slam downstairs and knew Rowan had come in. She left Saffie and went down. She was going to tell Rowan that they had found a body. She was going to tell him Saffie had admitted to lying about the rape. And she was going to examine, in minute detail, his reaction.

*

Rowan stared at Jules with a stony expression for some minutes after she'd told him, before he said, 'I need to get out.'

'Rowan, please. Don't run away. We need to talk. I'm upset, for God's sake. If Saul's dead, this is a nightmare. I need you here.'

'I'm going out. I'll see you later.'

And Rowan had gone into the porch, pulled on his boots and headed out of the door.

He didn't come back until gone midnight. Jules was in bed by then, lying in the dark, trying to shut out the horrific events of the day. She felt the mattress tilt as he got into bed. She felt his arms go around her. She was facing away from him, and he pulled her towards him. She resisted, instinctively. She didn't want Rowan to touch her. Not until she knew he was innocent.

In the end, though, she felt his face against her back and realized that the warm, wet feeling soaking through her nightdress onto her skin came from Rowan's tears. She turned, kissed him dryly on the top of his head. Asked him to speak to her.

'I can't,' he said. 'Not yet. I can't take it in. That he's probably dead. But he never raped Saffie.'

314

And she did then put her arms round him, but more as a mother puts their arms round a child to soothe them when they know they've done something wrong and are filled with remorse. Much as she'd done with Saffie earlier.

19

HOLLY

Pete comes over to me as I get back. I hang my coat up and take off my boots. He puts his chunky arms around me and I let them envelop me. It doesn't matter to me at this moment whose arms they are. I need someone – anyone – to hold me.

'I was so worried about you,' he says. 'Going off like that. Knowing how distraught you were.'

'I needed space,' I say. 'I needed air, and to be alone.'

'I understand,' Pete says.

'I met Saffie,' I say into his chest. 'When I told her they'd found a body, she broke down and confessed. Saul didn't rape her. He didn't touch her. He had nothing to do with her pregnancy, nothing.'

'Oh, Holly.' Pete releases me and walks over to the mantelpiece and leans against it, his head on his arms.

'I know. It's too late. Not that it makes any difference. The damage was already done the day Saul overheard us.'

Pete doesn't reply to my barbed remark, loaded with the resentment I feel again for his doubting Saul. But it isn't fair of me. Because the damage was done before that, when I asked Saul if he'd made Saffie have sex with him and he'd told me to get out of his room.

Pete doesn't tell me either – not yet, anyway – that the police have been for Saul's dental records. Which is as well, because I couldn't take any more just now. After a while, he straightens up. He goes to the kitchen, comes back, puts a glass of whisky in front of me.

I sip the whisky. I can't bear sitting in silence with Pete, so I go upstairs. But then I can't stand being alone in our bedroom and go to the bathroom. I rummage in the medicine box for the Xanax I used after Archie died. I have no idea whether it's still in date, but I need something to take away the pain of being awake. The light's too bright, even when I try switching off the bedside lamp. It isn't the light that's too bright, of course; it's being here at all, knowing about Saul. His remains. What did they mean? Why couldn't they remove them? I sit on my bed, wondering whether, if I crawl under the covers, I will sleep. After I don't know how long, I'm still sitting there. Someone is ringing the front doorbell and I hear Pete open it, his lowered tones. 'I think she's asleep. I'll go and look.'

*

Fatima sits on the sofa in the sitting room. Something about her makes me want to crawl into her arms like a baby. Pete's drawn the curtains, switched on the lamp; he's even lit a fire in the wood burner. The room feels rather womb-like. I prefer being here, with people, I think, than upstairs, alone in the bedroom. Or perhaps it's the drugs beginning to work. Or perhaps anywhere is better than the last place. Until it too becomes unbearable.

'Pete's explained to me that the girl admitted she lied. About the rape,' Fatima says. 'I've informed my colleagues and they're following it up, in case it has a bearing on their investigations. But more importantly, how are you, Holly?'

'Bad.'

'Of course. But it won't be long now.'

'How long?'

'They've had a bit of trouble with the identification,' she says briskly. This briskness, I understand, is because what she has to say is unpalatable. She wants to get it over with. With as little apology or sentiment as possible. 'The dentist contact Pete gave us – they have no records for Saul.'

The room sways. I have to steady my voice.

'I haven't registered him with a dentist since we moved here.' I feel muzzy. Unable to make sense of what she's saying. It might be an effect of the sleeping pills on top of the whisky. It might be the slow after-effects of shock. It would be better to be sharper, not to have everything blurred by these numbing drugs. I need to think straight. 'It was lax of me,' I go on. 'His last dentist was in London, and she retired, and . . .'

'The details I gave Fatima were for the girls' dentist,' Pete says. 'I wasn't thinking. I assumed Saul had been to the same one, but of course why would he have been?'

'Is there anyone from his previous dental surgery, the one in London, we can contact for the records?' Fatima is looking at me.

The muzzy feeling is slowly clearing, like an early morning mist lifting from the Fens. And I become brutally aware of what I couldn't quite work out before. It's that I don't like this conversation. I don't like it at all. Don't they usually, by this time, ask the next of kin to go to the morgue to identify the body? Can't they identify it with the DNA samples I've given them? Why do they need dental records? The remains must be so horribly mutilated there is nothing recognizable left of them. I don't want to think about this, but my mind pursues the thought – it hasn't been long enough, surely, for a body to have decayed so much. Apart from its teeth?

'I don't understand why you can't identify him with the DNA.'

'Holly,' Fatima says slowly, 'the body parts were found in a burnt-out bird hide. There was very little left. It seems ... he tried to get rid of his own remains. Unless ...'

The next words I hear are muffled, something to do with their investigations looking into the possibility of it being murder, not suicide. But the room goes dark, Pete recedes, the stars swirl about my head, and Pete puts a bowl in front of me just in time for me to throw up.

*

I don't know how much later it is that I come back to consciousness. I'm leaning up against the sofa, a rug round my shoulders, and Pete is holding my hand. Fatima is still there.

'Take your time,' Fatima says, gazing at me steadily through her large brown eyes. 'I know this is hard for you, Holly. But we have to ask you ... about the dentist.'

When I can speak again, I say, 'The practice closed down after his dentist retired. It was hers. She sold up and moved away.'

'His records have to be somewhere,' Fatima says. 'Dentists can't just destroy them because they're retiring. They'll be on a system.'

'I'm such a terrible mother!' I say, my thoughts sliding about all over the place. 'I never registered him here. But Saul's always had good teeth. I didn't think it was necessary to continue with six-monthly check-ups.'

'Good teeth?'

'Filling-free. I fed him a strict low-sugar diet from the beginning.'

Through the mists, I think what very minimum-fun parents Archie and I were. Insisting on breadsticks rather than biscuits, nuts where other children had sweets. A vignette slips into my mind, me and Jules next to each other at one of the London lidos in the summer. Saul and Saffie wrapped in towels, dripping with swimming-pool water, Jules producing from her voluminous tote a packet of supermarket chocolate brownies, while I drew some mini rice cakes out of my backpack. Saul's expression of disgust at my offering. He'd sidled up to Jules, looked at her with his big eyes and said, 'Those look good, Jules.'

I remember fleeting resentment – I was neither as much fun as Jules nor as successful as I'd like to be in my quest to be a wholesome mum. But how trivial those minor parental rivalries seem now – and sitting here with Pete and Fatima and their talk of dental records and the horrible image of the burnt-out bird hide, I wish I had been more like Jules as a mother. I wish I'd given Saul everything he ever wanted! Chocolate brownies and reality TV and extra pocket money. Every second of joy and instant gratification possible. For what difference had it all made in the end?

'Well, that might help,' Fatima is saying, and I slide on the back of the Xanax and the whisky into the horrible present. 'I'll let them know. And we'll follow up the contacts. Thank you. I'll be back as soon as we hear anything else.'

*

'I'm so sorry,' Pete says when she's gone. 'To make that mistake about the dentist. It's delayed things . . .'

I don't answer. Right now, I think I would like Pete to leave me alone, go back to his girls. Then I am overwhelmed by fear of being alone, of staring my grief in the face, and I want him to stay.

'Is there anything, anything I can do to make this more bearable for you?'

He's standing, now, his arms by his sides, looking so forlorn and helpless I begin to feel sorry for him. For both of us. For all of us.

'I don't think there is, no,' I say at last, and that's when I begin to sob.

There's no point in going to bed. I know, even after my pill-popping, that sleep is out of the question. I sit on the sofa and Pete comes and sits by me. He puts his hand up to the back of my head to stroke my hair, but I take it away. I don't want Pete to feel the bruise, because it would mean explaining what Rowan did to me and dealing with his response. What would Pete say if I told him how Rowan attacked me? He'd realize, of course, that it wouldn't have happened if he'd stayed here with me as I'd asked him to do the other night, and that would presumably make him feel even worse about everything that's happened. But nothing is worse than the news we've had, and I don't want to divert attention away from it.

Pete stays next to me anyway, and after a while I let him put his arm about my shoulders. We sit side by side like those bereaved couples you see on TV, so poleaxed by grief they can barely move. What you don't see in those shots are the simmering feelings between couples apparently united in their suffering. You don't see how their loss has sent aftershocks jolting the foundation stones of their relationship. No one looking at Pete and me would know that my fear for Saul is matched only by my upset at Pete for the way he doubted him. That I'm only letting him sit with me for his bodily warmth and because if I am left alone, I am afraid of what might become of me.

At three, Pete dozes off for a while, his head lolling uncomfortably. I wedge a cushion under his cheek and slip to the kitchen. I wish I smoked: I'd kill for a cigarette. I think of Saffie, us smoking together on the bank of the river. I could go round, ask her if she'll give me a fag. She, of all people, I imagine, would understand my need.

Instead, I get down an old bottle of some kind of liqueur we've had in the cupboard since Pete moved in, and pour a glass. It tastes of oranges cut through with the bitter tang of alcohol, but does nothing to dull the pain, to help me sleep. I go back to the sofa, sit cross-legged against the arm, pulling the wool throw over myself. The wood burner is still alight, just, the red embers giving off the semblance of warmth. I think about Saffie, breaking down on the riverbank, telling me she lied. Who made her pregnant? Who was she so desperate to protect from the wrath of her parents she sacrificed Saul for him?

In the end, I also nod off, and when I open my eyes, it's because the front door has slammed shut, jolting me out of a dreamless sleep. I'm still sitting up against the arm of the sofa and my neck is stiff. My head throbs and I have to peel my tongue off the roof of my mouth. It's light outside, quite bright. I must have slept for longer than I thought. I feel strangely numb, a peculiar relief.

Pete has been out. He comes and sits on the edge of the sofa, his face moist with mist, his fleece still on, the backs of his hands pink and raw from the Fenland winds.

'I've just been over to Deepa's. I had a talk with Freya.'

I sit up. I feel detached. From my emotions, from Pete's words, from everything. As if reality is just out of arm's reach. Or as if it's happening to someone else.

'What?' I ask.

'I had to do something. I wanted to try and find out why Saffie lied.'

'It's a bit late for that.'

'Look, you may not believe it, but I love Saul too, Holly.

You seem to forget that I took him on as my son when I married you. Believe me, everything that's happened is as painful for me as it is for you.'

'It's not.' The words come from far away, as if someone else is speaking them. 'It could never be as painful for you as it is for me.'

He closes his eyes, endlessly patient. 'Perhaps not quite as painful. But nonetheless. I am grieving for him too.'

'You have no idea, Pete, how it feels.'

Pete's response jolts me back to reality.

'Christ, Holly,' he all but shouts. 'You seem to think you're the only person in the world to feel pain. Can't you *see* how terrible I feel, especially now we know Saul was innocent? About snatching the girls away last weekend?'

I don't reply. There's nothing to say. Nothing expresses how awful this is for both of us. But now, for the first time since I met him, Pete grows properly angry.

'You actually seem to enjoy wallowing in your misery alone, determined to cut everyone else off.' His voice is hard and cold.

I've never heard him like this before. It's unfair of him, I want to object, to speak to me like this now of all times. 'That's not true,' is all I can say.

'You think you're the only person in the world ever to have lost anyone, to have suffered. And when people try to reach out to you, you blank them out.'

This time, I do object. 'No, that's not fair, Pete.'

'Look at the way you cut your sister out of your life . . .' His voice rises, louder than I've heard it before. 'You don't speak to her. You don't visit your mother. You turn your back on people the minute things get tricky. You'd rather cut them off than work at things.'

'It's too painful to visit my mother,' I mutter. 'She's not who she was. I've lost her.'

'Some people make an effort with their elderly demented parents! However painful it is. But not you. You simply turn away.'

I feel the truth of this, and am filled with a kind of shame. Even so, shame is easier to bear than the death of my son.

'It's a pattern with you. It's OK for you to have weaknesses, to have flaws, but when any of the rest of us make bad decisions, you reject us. I wish to God I'd thought before I took the girls away that morning, but I didn't. Yes, it was hasty; yes, it was even perhaps a mistake, but you make mistakes too. The difference is, the rest of the world doesn't give up on you when you cock up, the way you give up on them.'

'I haven't given up on you, Pete,' I say quietly. 'I'm sorry if it seems that way.'

After a silence, he continues more gently. 'When I woke up this morning, I found the text you sent. When I was at Deepa's. Just before we heard the police had found him. The text asking me to find out who Freya was in love with.'

I look up at him, and he goes on, 'I thought, Freya knows something. Even if it's very little. Even if it's not relevant. She knows Saffie as well as anyone. There's nothing else I can do to bring Saul back, but I can at least do my bit to find out what really went on, now we know Saffie lied. Please don't tell me again it's too late. I'm as aware of that as anyone. And if I could rewind time, I would. I would give my right arm to do so. But I can't. So I am doing what I can to work out the truth for your sake and so we can at least honour Saul's true character. And I hope you believe me.'

I look at him at last. 'Go on, then,' I say.

'So I did ask Freya if she was in love with anyone,

and whether it was the same person as Saffie. I explained I needed to know due to everything that's happened to Saul.

'She said it wasn't Saul they were both in love with – it was someone else, but she'd made a pact never to tell.' I glance up at Pete. 'Because she knew it was illegal to love him.'

'That's what she wrote in her diary,' I say. 'Illegal, because of their age and Saul being Freya's stepbrother. They meant Saul, I'm sure. But Saffie still denies that it was him.'

Pete sighs. 'Not her stepbrother, Holly. Their teacher.'

'*What?*'

'Their maths teacher. Saul's tutor. Harry Bell.'

20

JULES

Jules turned over and looked at the alarm clock. It was gone nine. After a terrible night, she had slept late for the first time in days. Her body had shut down after the traumatic news about Saul, then Saffie's revelation on the riverbank, and Rowan's reaction to it. Now she pushed back the duvet and went to the bedroom window. The sky was a translucent grey, weak sunlight filtering through. The fens were black now, the rich soil ploughed into perfectly even stripes that ran all the way to the horizon. She moved her gaze and looked at the bridge over the sluice, beside which she'd found Saffie and Holly the evening before. She shuddered.

There was no sound from Saffie's room.

Rowan was already in the garden, directly below, measuring out the dimensions of the pool he had been planning for months now. Striding up and down, counting his paces. There was something very tight, very tense in his movements. Jules stood at the window watching him. She tried to spot whether there was anything telling in his stance. It was interesting when someone you knew intimately didn't know you could see them. Jules knew every centimetre of Rowan. She imagined his body now, under the grey tracksuit. She thought of his arms, his strong biceps, which she had always loved, with the unlikely girlish freckles that faded towards his shoulders, where the skin became pale and smooth. She thought of the line of silky fair hair down his spine. She knew his smell, an almost biscuity smell that she had always found impossibly alluring, sometimes – when she had been angry, or let down by him – in spite of herself. She knew what his feet looked like. The way his big toes were wide and chunky, but the others tapered in a perfect gradation like a flight of stairs to the smallest one. She knew how he was as ticklish as a child and would giggle if she were to drag her fingers over the soles of his feet. She knew his hands with their muscular fingers, the golden hairs that sprouted from his knuckles and the small, fish-shaped scar on his palm that he had got cutting himself when sawing wood for the decking. She knew the parts of his body that were always warm to the touch. His inner thighs, for example, and his hands. She knew the areas that were cool, such as the front of his thighs and his upper arms. And yet, watching him from the window, she realized she didn't know him the way she thought she did when she was close to him in bed, or moving about the house. Or standing next to him at a party, with friends, proud that he had chosen to spend his life with her.

Now she stood apart and observed him, she saw what other people must see. He had developed bulk, and when he stood still, he held his arms in a way that made it look as if he was either about to embrace or punch someone. His legs were shorter than she always thought, his body longer, and his neck was thicker. But it wasn't just his build, she realized. He was also nervier than she would have described him, jerking his head up and looking around every time there was a sound – a train rumbling by, or a plane passing overhead, or the sudden, distant bark of a dog from the village. He had an intense expression, his forehead creased into several folds, as he concentrated on the job at hand, as if he was working hard to force out other, more pressing, thoughts.

He was less relaxed and laidback and amiable than he used to be. Yes, he was still a warm, affable, sociable man at times. And Jules knew, from experience, how that same side could flip, and become angry and aggressive. But she hadn't ever known before the highly wired man she watched out there now. The man who, she suddenly realized, she hadn't seen smile for days. Ever since she'd told him that his daughter had been raped.

Did she still love him? Did people stop loving their partners when they knew they'd committed a heinous crime? Such as rape? Or murder? Holly had continued to love Saul. But then she'd never doubted his innocence. And the mother-child relationship was different, anyway, from the kind of relationship you had with a partner. If Rowan had been accused of rape, would Jules have been as convinced of his innocence? Would she have stood by him?

She wasn't sure. Or what about murder? The body found in the Fens still hadn't been identified, as far as Jules knew, but it was almost certainly Saul's. She shivered at the thought, pushed down the feelings that threatened to overwhelm her. Had Saul killed himself, or had he been murdered? Was it Rowan who'd killed him? And would she still love him if she discovered the answer was yes?

There were women who visited their husbands in prison for years, standing by their sides long after they knew they were guilty of the most shocking crimes. But would Jules be able to stay with Rowan if she knew he had killed her oldest friend's child? Even if it was in retaliation for believing he'd raped their daughter?

She thought again of Holly and Saul. Would Holly have stopped loving her son if he *had* raped Saffie? But again, it was different with a son. With a child. Because Jules knew that no, Holly would never stop loving Saul whatever he had done, or might do. She would have found some explanation, some chink in her mothering, perhaps, to explain why he had transgressed. A husband, though, that was another matter altogether.

Watching him, as he bent and measured and stood, and rubbed his back, Jules felt confused. She didn't really want a self-cleaning swimming pool anymore. Not that it had ever been her idea. She didn't even care that much about the patio and the deck and hot tub, or the shower with the Jacuzzi function. She didn't want those expansive summer parties Rowan liked to throw. Yes, she had always enjoyed this extravagant side of her husband. But what she wanted, she realized, was a man who cared. And until now, all this material extravagance had seemed to represent that care. Was Rowan's generosity any kind of substitute for a man she could trust? She wished she had a husband she could believe in, as Holly had. Someone like Pete who might not make much money but who was genuine and earnest and kind. For a few moments, she let her mind wander back to the affair she'd had with Rob. How different he had been to Rowan, and how for a short time it had felt good to be with someone mild-mannered and gentle and completely uninterested in material goods.

But in the end, Rowan's passion for her, and her physical attraction to him, had won her back. Love wasn't rational, after all.

And then the truth about Saul hit her again. And the role she believed Rowan had played in it. The reality was too much to bear.

Jules hadn't managed to get Saffie to say who had made her pregnant. What had this person and her daughter and her husband, between them, done to Holly's family? And she remembered again telling Holly about Archie, on the road in the rain that day. She had even destroyed Holly's memory of her first husband. What kind of depths had she and Rowan stooped to because of all this?

At last she heard Rowan come in the front door, drop his boots on the mat and go into the cloakroom to wash his hands. She went down to meet him.

'You made me jump,' he said, as he came out of the cloakroom. 'I didn't know you were up. I've been busy measuring out the space for the pool for us. We're going to need to make it deeper than I thought, to allow for the filter. And to—'

'Rowan, you don't have to keep avoiding the subject of Saul.'

Rowan turned and walked into the kitchen. His neck was pink.

'Ro?'

'I don't want to talk about it.'

'But perhaps we need to.' She followed him. 'To be honest, I don't know why *you* feel so bad about it. Saffie's the one who feels bad. For lying about him. We need to reassure her she made a mistake but what Saul did to himself had nothing to do with her.'

'Did to himself?'

'Yes.'

'But we don't know that, do we?' Rowan turned and snapped. 'The police don't know Saul killed himself?'

Jules swallowed. 'Not yet, no. What do you think, though, Rowan? What do you think has happened to him?'

Jules followed Rowan across the kitchen towards the extension. When he turned to face her, his face was bright red.

'Why are you asking me? All I've heard is they found a body. And that Saffie has told us Saul never did it. I don't know any more than that. But that's bad enough, isn't it?'

'Bad enough?'

'For Holly. On top of everything else she's gone through.'

Jules stared at her husband. This was the first time he had shown an iota of sympathy for Holly since Saffie's accusation. Now his words were laced with guilt, with contrition.

'Rowan,' she said, and her voice was faint. 'It's as if you feel guilty about something. Do you?'

He didn't reply, but turned his back on her again. He walked to the picture window. Stared out. He said, facing away from her, 'I thought that boy had raped my daughter. And Holly was doing nothing about it. I couldn't just stand by and let it happen without doing something. They needed bringing to justice . . .'

Jules's heart rate sped up.

'Rowan, you didn't have a meltdown, did you? You have to tell me.'

Rowan didn't turn round, so Jules ploughed on: 'You did. You forgot everything you learned in anger management. You've done something, haven't you?'

You couldn't change a person after all, Jules thought. It was true what people said.

Rowan would always have the side that flipped and turned violent, however many anger management courses he went on. And this time, the violent side had gone much, much too far.

When Rowan next spoke, it was so quietly Jules had to strain to hear him.

'I was defending my daughter. I believed Saul had raped her. What did you expect me to do? Stand back and let the boy and his mother get away with it?'

'Of course not. I expected you to support Saffie and me, and I don't know . . . I suggested we got help.'

'*You* wanted to drag in *Rape* fucking *Crisis*.' He was getting that look on his face, the irate one, the irrational one.

'It didn't have to be them . . .'

'Look, Jules.' Rowan swung round. 'No one was doing a thing about it. So I had to.'

'Rowan, what did you do to Saul?'

'Mum?' Saffie had come silently into the room and was standing there in her pyjamas. 'What are you two arguing about?'

'Nothing, darling,' Jules said. 'How are you, sweetie? I was about to bring you a drink. Go back to bed and I'll come in a minute.'

Saffie gave a weak smile and turned and climbed up the stairs.

'Perhaps you could leave me alone now,' Rowan said. 'I need to get on with the pool.'

Jules followed Rowan outside.

'You're not walking away from this, Rowan. We need to talk. You have to tell me—'

Jules was about to grab Rowan, turn him to face her, when the doorbell rang. She turned to see the now familiar outlines of DC Maria Shimwell and DI Venesuela in the glass.

She opened the door, steeling herself in case they had come to take Rowan away again for further questioning or even to arrest him at last. So it took some time for her to absorb Shimwell's words.

'We have some information about an alleged case of sexual exploitation. Involving Saffie. We need to have a chat to her. We will be as gentle as possible. May we come in?'

21

HOLLY

'*Harry Bell?*' I repeat. 'Saul's form tutor?' The shock of this revelation momentarily overshadows everything else. It sends my anxiety about Saul a little way away, so the pain is dulled for a while. However, it still feels as if it's another woman, not me, whose voice is able, so rationally, to reply, 'No, they love Saul. Or . . . some other boy whose name ends in "l" – someone who they were protecting.'

'Bell,' says Pete. 'Harry Bell. The name that ended in an "l" in the diary.'

This other me, the calm me, sits for a minute, trying to take this in. Trying to rearrange the facts so that this makes some kind of sense. Because nothing else does. It's quite understandable that a couple of naive thirteen-year-olds would develop a crush on Harry Bell. I remember thinking how handsome he was, as Samantha gazed adoringly at him in the Baptist Chapel, the night of the auction. How I'd envied her that, because it was how I'd once felt towards Archie.

'So they have a schoolgirl crush on their teacher. So what? Harry Bell's married,' I hear myself say. 'With young kids. I've met him. He's Saul's tutor. He wanted to help find him. He's a devoted father. And he's got that lovely wife, Samantha, so that doesn't explain Saffie's pregnancy.'

'Holly. The girls knew having a relationship with him

was illegal. Not *just* because of their age but because he's a teacher. The minute Freya said his name, alarm bells rang.'

I think for a minute. 'Freya wrote that he didn't love *her*. He loved Saffie.'

'There you go. I told Freya if Saffie was involved with a teacher, we had to know. She said she thought Mr Bell, as she calls him, did love Saffie. Because he looked at her all the time and asked her to attend his "revision sessions". He's the one who gave her that ghastly perfume Freya's been borrowing.'

I smell it, even as Pete says it. The nauseating, tropical aroma Saffie wore as she came downstairs the night of Tess's drinks, with that sullen look on her face. The face of a girl who was out of her depth and terrified of telling anyone. The face Jules interpreted as her daughter in a teenage strop. The perfume she wore was the same as the one Freya had worn the night she came in with Pete. But Deepa hadn't given it to her, as she'd claimed. Freya had borrowed it from Saffie to try and attract Harry Bell's attention. As I absorb all these details, I have the sense of an impending storm rolling mercilessly towards me. Saul is innocent. As I always knew. But he's also a victim of someone he trusted . . .

'Freya was heartbroken initially, that he didn't choose her,' Pete is saying. 'Poor deluded kid. But it looks as though things between him and Saffie didn't stop there. I've told the police. They're questioning him now.'

'Harry Bell *slept* with Saffie? *He* made her pregnant?'

Pete grimaces. 'He's the one they were "in love" with. And we know from what Freya told us he crossed boundaries – enough to suggest he was prepared to cross others. We'll find out if there was more to it once the police have interviewed him. I reassured Freya that the police would make sure she and Saff were both safe, whatever she told us. Freya was frightened she'd get Saffie into trouble. It took quite a lot to get anything out of her.' Pete pauses. 'Holl, is this too much for you now?' he asks. He has his arm round me, leaning back against the sofa cushions.

'No, I need to know. I need to know anything else that proves Saul is, and always was, innocent. Not a rapist ... but ...' The storm rolls closer. I shut my eyes.

Pete draws a deep breath.

'I should have taken more time,' he murmurs. 'I should have thought. Before taking the girls back to Deepa's. I should have asked Freya whether there was anything that might motivate Saffie to lie. They were such close friends. But ... my only defence is, Freya wouldn't have told me anything. She was sworn to silence. And petrified, by then. Plus I didn't want her or Thea to know about the rape allegation if I could avoid it. To protect Saul.'

'How? How was it to protect Saul?'

'I didn't want the rumour to spread. Girls talk. You didn't want them to know either, if you remember, Holly? You were adamant they shouldn't know! You begged me not to tell them.'

Pete's doing his utmost to atone. Surely, I think indignantly, as a psychotherapist, he should have been able to see better than the rest of us that his own daughter was hiding something she clearly felt uncomfortable about.

'I believed, when I first met you,' I say at last, 'that you had the skills to understand human behaviour. And therefore you would know what was really going on inside people's minds. It was what made me fall in love with you in the first place.'

'You thought I had some kind of superhuman insight?'

'You're a psychotherapist. You're supposed to.'

'I'm just a bloke, Holly. A fallible bloke. Just skin and bones. And a bit too much flesh.'

What Pete *is* good at, of course, is listening. He's just as prone as all of us to putting his children before everything. Which is why, rather than pausing, and thinking, he hurried his daughters away from my son the minute he thought they might be at the tiniest risk. Does that make him a disloyal stepfather? Or a protective and loyal father? Pete may not be the man I thought he was. But through the mists of whisky and Xanax and liqueur and a poor night's sleep, the thought comes to me that perhaps the man he is is *better* than I realized. Fallible? Yes. A little too much flesh? Yes. But working overtime to do his best by everyone. And, after all, he is the only family I have left.

'I should never have left you alone during any of this,' Pete says, as if he can indeed see inside my mind. 'When you didn't want me to come home the other night, I was beside myself. I thought by being torn between my girls and you, I'd destroyed us. I thought we were over. Because I knew what a hard line you take on people who let you down.'

'Maybe I'm learning,' I murmur. 'Maybe I'll try to change. I do need you, Pete.'

After a while, Pete says, 'Well, I had already decided that I would come home to you and I'd stay and look after you whether you liked it or not. I decided if you wanted to cut me off, I'd make it extremely hard for you.'

He leans towards me, just as someone knocks loudly on the front door.

'I'll get it,' he says.

When he comes back, he has Fatima with him.

'We've identified the body,' she says.

And then the storm breaks and my ears fill with a deafening roar.

22

JULES

Jules and Maria Shimwell sat in Saffie's bedroom. Maria spent some time explaining to the girl that Harry Bell had been questioned about his relationship with her and was being held at the police station. She had also warned Jules that it might be hard for her to hear some of what Saffie had to say but that she should let Maria do her job.

'He won't be allowed anywhere near you again,' Maria said. 'So you can rest assured that you're safe to talk. He's the one in trouble. You can tell us anything.'

Saffie looked from her mother to the young, strawberry-blonde police officer and said, 'It's so embarrassing. It's so terrible.'

'It's important you try to explain what happened between you,' Maria said. 'Take as much time as you need. Perhaps try and start at the beginning. How you first became ... friends with him?'

Saffie appeared to address her words to the teddy bear she was twisting about on her lap, the one Saul had given her as a baby.

'Everyone fancied Mr Bell,' she said. 'It wasn't just me.'

'No one's blaming you, remember,' Maria said. 'You're not to worry about that. But it will help us a lot if you can tell us as much as you're able to.'

'We kind of joked about it at first,' Saffie said. 'Me and Gemma and Freya. We all said we loved him. We wrote notes about it. I don't know if he knew. But then I found out he loved me. More than them. He asked me to stay behind after extra maths. He said I was beautiful. He said he had feelings for me.'

Jules felt winded. Hearing this was like a blow to the chest. How could she not have known? Weren't mothers supposed to have a sixth sense when their child was in danger? She wanted to pull Saffie to her, but Maria glanced at her, and Jules took a deep breath. As with so many things that had happened since Saffie had accused Saul of rape, Jules felt out of her depth. How was it even possible that she was sitting there listening to her daughter describing how her teacher had told her he had *feelings* for her? Her *teacher*, for God's sake.

'Go on,' said Maria.

'He bought me perfume.'

Saffie looked up at Maria, saw that she wasn't judging and continued.

'I told Freya. She was really jealous. Then he said we could have an extra maths lesson at his house, but I mustn't tell anyone. I was so excited. That he'd chosen me. And . . . so when he wanted to . . . you know, I thought, well, he's given me perfume, and the others are jealous. I'm really lucky he likes me, so I can't really say no.'

'Oh God.' Jules tried to stop the pictures that came into her mind unbidden. Pictures of her child, in the clutches of a grown man. She had to fight back the urge to get up, seek out Harry Bell and pummel him until he was crying out in pain – she and Rowan weren't so different after all. But then she thought of Saul and wondered why she'd not felt that same anger towards him when Saffie had said he'd forced himself on her. Had she, even then, had some doubt? She remembered spotting him on his bike at the park run and the bewilderment she'd felt as she tried to match the boy she'd always known with the one Saffie had described that night. But no, a teacher – the gift; a premeditated act; her daughter's insecurity about saying no – was so much more shocking even than what Saffie had said about Saul. The truth – that Saffie felt she couldn't say no to her teacher because she'd liked the attention, the perfume, was *afraid* of saying no – was much harder to swallow even than the thought of a messed-up adolescent forcing himself on her unwilling daughter to prove his sexual prowess. *Was* it worse?

'Go on, Saffie,' Maria said. 'You're doing so well.'

'He started asking me to go to his house for a "lesson" every week. He bought me nice things . . .'

'Oh?'

'Underwear and stuff.'

The slinky lingerie Jules had found in the Peacocks bag. Ridiculously, Jules was incensed that Harry Bell hadn't even bought *nice* things for Saffie, that he'd spent a few pounds on some cheap rubbish, and her poor, beautiful daughter had been so grateful, so misguided that she'd felt she *had* to sleep with him.

She was swamped with guilt, too. What mistakes had she made as a mother that Saffie thought this was OK? That Saffie hadn't felt able to confide in her? And how had she not noticed what was going on? Her mind ran back over the past weeks. With the clarity of hindsight, she could put together the disparate things she'd noticed: Saffie's cowed face, her nervous mannerisms, her loss of appetite, her mood swings and her fury each time Jules or Rowan offered to pick her up from her extra lessons in the car. Why hadn't she added all these symptoms together and realized what Saffie was going through – before the night with Saul even? How could she have been so blind to what her own daughter was enduring? What kind of a mother did that make her?

But Saffie was speaking again.

'He said we were seeing each other now. He said, don't tell anyone because people don't understand love between an older man and a younger woman.' Saffie's lip began to tremble and Jules felt bile rise into her throat and was afraid she might actually throw up.

'But then when my period was late, I got frightened I was pregnant. So I told him. And he changed. He said he was having nothing to do with it. But that if I told anyone else, I'd be in big trouble. He got angry with me. He made me swear not to say it was him who got me pregnant or someone would . . .'

'Would what, Saffie?' Maria asked gently.

'. . . get hurt.'

'He threatened you!' Now Jules did stand up, moved over to her daughter, but Maria put a hand out to her, told her to sit down again.

'You poor thing,' Maria said, her voice soothing. 'You must have been very frightened indeed.'

Saffie looked at the policewoman. It was clear she trusted her, and Jules could see why: it was something to do with her calm, unruffled manner combined with the fact that she so obviously *cared*.

Saffie continued. 'I didn't know what to do. I was so scared. I had to tell you, Mum.'

'Of course you did. I just wish you'd told me *who* had done this to you.' And that you'd told me earlier. But Jules could never say that to her daughter, of course; could never make her feel it was her fault for not speaking up.

'But don't you see? I couldn't say it was Harry.' Saffie began to cry. 'I knew what we'd done was against the law.

340

And he'd said he'd hurt someone if I told. And you kept asking and asking who it was and I remembered Saul had been round here ... Well, I thought it would sound true that he'd come into my room. I didn't really want to get him into trouble ... but you knew I hadn't wanted him here. So it would sound weird if I said we were in a relationship. So I said he forced me. I didn't mean to say it, but you kept asking me and it just came out.'

Jules should have questioned Saffie more, the day she told her. She could see that now. She realized that her inclination to believe Saffie was entangled with so many other things going on between her and Holly at the time. She'd ignored that sense of bewilderment that the boy she knew so well could possibly have raped her daughter and told her to keep quiet. She closed her eyes. If only she'd listened to her instinct. But then, if onlys were pointless. If only she'd been more observant. If only she'd asked Gemma's mum about the extra maths. If only she hadn't taken such offence when Holly accused Saffie of troublemaking ...

'I wish I'd never said it.' Saffie gulped. 'I never meant it to get him into this much trouble. But once I'd said it, I couldn't unsay it.'

Jules opened her mouth to speak, but Maria silenced her again, with a small shake of the head. Jules wondered if Maria was judging *her* – thinking what a bad mother she was, not to have spotted what was going on – but the expression on Maria's face was kind. Sympathetic.

Saffie stroked the teddy bear on her lap. 'And then I thought, well, you and Holly are friends. You'll just talk about it and tell Saul off, and even if he denies it, you'll believe me, not him. Because Holly's always been telling us girls must be believed. And then it would be done with. I thought at least no one would get hurt. By Harry. And

341

if we didn't tell anyone else, we could all just go back to normal.'

'How could things have gone back to normal?' Jules burst out. 'With that man still at school?'

'Is there any more, Saffie?' Maria asked, gently, almost as if Jules hadn't spoken, and Jules swallowed back tears.

'Just . . . yesterday, not long before I was supposed to go to Donna Browne, I started my period. So after school I went to tell Harry. That's why I was late home yesterday, Mum. I told him I wasn't pregnant and so I was taking back the lie about Saul. I was so worried about what had happened to him, and I wanted to make things better. But Harry said, "Don't you dare take it back, or people will start to ask questions about why you said it in the first place. And if they find out what we've been doing, we'll end up in prison." And I didn't want to go to the doctor, in case she asked questions too and found out, and then Harry would know that I'd told and . . .'

Jules thought of Saffie coming in and stomping upstairs saying she didn't need to see the doctor. Her poor, terrified daughter. And even then Jules had just put it down to Saffie's reluctance to face up to what was happening to her. Again, Jules wished she could go back and do things differently.

'You were very confused and frightened,' Maria prompted.

'And then,' Saffie sobbed, 'it was too late anyway, because I met Holly on the river and she told me they'd found a body. And it was probably Saul. And it was all my fault for lying . . .'

'No. What this is, Saffie, is a serious case of sexual exploitation,' Maria said. 'You've been so very brave telling us about it.'

Sexual exploitation, thought Jules. The words were like

something from a crime programme. And Jules hadn't noticed. Hadn't asked the right questions. All this time!

No wonder Saffie had been so volatile. She was terrified of what she'd got herself into, too, terrified of being found out. And there was she, Jules, so incensed that Holly had called Saffie 'a devious little troublemaker' that she had been more concerned with proving Saul guilty than finding out what was really going on. Had she missed other signs? Had she ignored other glaringly obvious hints that Harry was exploiting her daughter? He had been at the Auction of Promises, she remembered. He'd eaten Saffie's cupcakes in front of her, Jules. The phrase *hiding in plain sight* came to her. Or was it that she had been completely, stupidly blind-sided by her argument with Holly?

'Saffie,' Maria said, leaning towards the girl and picking up her hand. 'I want to tell you how helpful you have been. And how we are going to get you lots of help now so you can talk about everything you've been through. It won't make it go away, but it will make it feel better, I promise. In time. And now I'm going to leave you with your mum, who I expect wants to give you a big cuddle, but first I want to thank you. For being so brave.'

Maria smiled at Jules. 'I can see myself out,' she said. 'I think your daughter probably needs you.'

Jules smiled weakly in return. As soon as Maria had gone, she put her arms round Saffie. As she held her tight, she realized that Saffie had been changed irrevocably by everything Harry had put her through. Her body had been violated. Her innocence snatched from her. Her trust in the people who were supposed to look after her smashed to pieces. And Jules couldn't help feeling as if she was, in a large part, to blame.

She thought of Holly, and wondered whether, if Holly

had a daughter, she would have been so blind, and so proud, and so unable to pick up on the warning signs. And decided no, she wouldn't. And she wished she was more like Holly, more attentive, more conscientious. More clear-sighted. She wished she was as good a mother as Holly.

As Holly had been.

*

On Monday morning, Jules got up early to go round to Holly's house. She had to catch her, and then she had to get in to work. Because things at the shop were slipping. Hetty was about to leave. Jules needed to get the business back on track, get stocked up for Christmas.

She left Saffie at home. She had slept in her bed the other night, after Maria Shimwell had gone. She and Saffie hadn't spoken, not really, but being close to her daughter had felt important. The funny thing was, they'd both slept too, even though Saffie's bed was tiny and Jules had been convinced she wouldn't sleep a wink. And yesterday, Saffie had seemed quiet and withdrawn, but less anxious, somehow, as though she'd realized that the worst was over. The doctor had given her a sick note and said she would need time to process everything. They were providing a counsellor. The school had been informed that Harry Bell had been questioned, arrested and remanded in custody. They at least had that to be thankful for. He'd been charged with rape, and with sexual exploitation. There would be a court case, but that wouldn't be for a while, thank goodness.

Jules wanted to summon the strength to apologize to Holly, although how she would be able to convey her remorse, she had no idea.

She got into the Fiat and drove up to the green. She parked outside Holly's and knocked on the door before she had time to give it too much thought. She waited, her breath catching, afraid she wouldn't be able to speak when Holly came to the door. Because how would she begin?

I'm sorry Saffie lied and Saul is probably dead.

I want to apologize for not seeing that my child was being sexually exploited.

I'm sorry I didn't believe that Saul was innocent.

It would sound too trite, however she tried to put it. The reality, the enormity of what it meant for Holly, would be impossible to address.

When the door did open at last, Pete stood there in his pyjamas. He looked terrible. His hair had greyed, even since last time she'd seen him. He was puffy-eyed without his glasses, and he still had that paunch, more apparent in his jersey pyjama top. Behind him, the house looked unkempt, shoes piled on the floor, coats heaped on pegs on the back of the kitchen door. There was the familiar smell of Holly, patchouli oil, a smell that had accompanied her through life since university and that had a powerful effect on Jules, whisking her back to happier times with her friend. Beyond the cluttered hallway, the kitchen door was ajar, and she could just spot Holly's old cafetière on the counter, and the cork noticeboard she'd always had, plastered with photos of Saul at different stages of his childhood. In some of them, Saffie was there too; the two kids had been such good friends, once. All of this made Jules yearn to rewind time, to do things differently. To be able to come round and sit at the scratched pine table in the kitchen drinking wine and talking the hours away. Then she spotted Saul's trainers, lying on the floor just behind the door, and the reality of the situation hit her like a punch in the chest. That Saul's shoes could exist while Saul no longer did.

Pete was reluctant to talk.

'Holly's not in,' he said.

'Poor woman. I don't know how she can continue, knowing the police have a body. Not knowing whether or not it's ... How is she, Pete? Is there any news?'

'You didn't hear?' He paused, and Jules waited.

'They identified it. The body, I mean,' he said. 'It took some time.'

'Oh God ...' Jules put a hand on the door frame to steady herself.

'It isn't Saul.'

'It isn't Saul?' she repeated stupidly.

Pete lifted his hands in a 'that's what I said' gesture.

'But that's good news ...' Jules said. 'Isn't it? That's such a relief for you both.'

'Saul's still missing,' Pete said. 'We still don't know what's happened to him. We still don't know whether he's alive or dead.'

Jules hung her head. Pete was angry, and rightly so.

They stood in the doorway, silent. Pete didn't ask Jules in, and Jules wasn't surprised.

She pulled her coat closer around herself, because she realized she felt chilled, chilled to the bone. It was taking her some time to process what Pete had told her, and the implications. Because if the body wasn't Saul's, then Rowan having gone that morning to the area of the Fens where it was found was no longer significant. Was it? She stood, unable to work out whether to leave or stay.

'I came to talk to Holly. To try to apologize for the terrible misunderstanding ...'

When Pete spoke again, his voice was a little softer.

'Holly's gone to work to collect some books. Can't stand waiting any longer without knowing if or when the wait will end.'

'Pete, look, I know this is a terrible mess, but now things are becoming clear – I mean with Saffie – I want to try and make amends. I was hoping there was something to salvage from our friendship.'

'You might catch her. She was walking to the station to get the eight thirty-five to King's Cross.'

Jules stood for a few seconds longer, before realizing Pete was actually asking her to leave.

*

A few minutes later, Jules had parked. She stood on the freezing station platform. She couldn't see Holly. Perhaps she'd missed her. Winter had moved in over the Fens. On the village side of the station, ponies grazed in a field, and the reeds blew pale and feather-like in the ditch, lending a soft focus to the church spire a little way away. The sound of the church bell floated over the fields, its 'dong' faint, then growing louder when the wind rose. Jules turned the other way to look at the wide, constantly changing sky. She thought of this landscape as darkly beautiful. And it had, until recently, served her well. Enabled her to live the lifestyle she and Rowan had always dreamed of. They had been able to buy a piece of this mostly undeveloped reclaimed land at a reasonable price, renovate a bigger house than they would have been able to afford anywhere else in the South-East.

Was she about to lose it all? When she finally found out what her husband had done? She might have had a momentary doubt that she wanted the house with its fancy features, but losing it now was unthinkable. It was her home. Their home. The hard knot of anxiety in her belly was a permanent feeling now. She thought again about the fact the body that had been found wasn't Saul's. Should she allow this to reassure her about Rowan's part in the whole nightmare? It didn't make anything definite. There was still the guilty way Rowan was behaving, and his admission that he was justified in avenging his daughter.

An icy east wind was blowing up the platform, carrying with it a fine, sharp rain that whipped Jules's face. The fields on the other side of the tracks were black and sodden. Bare black mud and bare shrubs. Bits of ragged bin bag flapped in stark branches. There was nothing beautiful about this landscape today. Suddenly, Jules yearned for the city. Busy stations with warm waiting rooms and coffee outlets and shops.

There weren't many people waiting for the train. A few sixth-formers on their way to college in Cambridge, and a couple of elderly people she didn't recognize. She would give anything to be in a warm cafe with a flat white and the paper to distract her from the nagging fear about what had happened to Saul as a result of her blindness. Then she saw her.

'Holly.'

Holly, who was approaching with her head down, hadn't seen Jules. She hadn't time to pretend not to, and so she had no choice but to acknowledge her, even if her response couldn't be described as a greeting. She nodded at Jules silently. They stood and stared at one another for a few seconds before Jules took a deep breath and let the words pour out. 'Holly, I'm so sorry for what you're going through.'

'Are you?'

Jules's heart plummeted. Holly's brown eyes were unforgiving.

'I just saw Pete.'

'Oh?'

'He said the body they found, it wasn't Saul. I know it

probably makes it no easier, because you're left in the dark still. But please, Holly. We have to talk. There are things I need to say. Things I can explain.'

Holly gave a short, sharp laugh. 'What's the point?' she said. 'What will it change?'

'I do understand . . .'

'I wish to God you had never persuaded me to move here.'

Holly's words stung. She'd persuaded Holly to move here for the best of motives. She'd wanted to get Holly over Archie. It would mean they'd be by each other's sides forever. But there was no point in defending herself now.

They fell silent, the only sound the whistle of the wind in the overhead wires, and Holly went on: 'First the bullying. Then Saul's school phobia. His isolation. Then the accusation. And now this. Saul has been missing for a week. I don't know if he's alive or dead. If he's out there, I have no idea where.'

Jules remembered the way Holly was able to shut people out of her life when they wronged her. And yet the more she doubted Rowan, the more she wanted – and needed – Holly back. Their friendship felt like a shattered thing, and it would require intricate skills she wasn't sure she had to put it back together again.

'I am sorry the truth emerged too late,' Jules tried.

Holly gazed out over the wet fields and blinked tears from her eyes. 'You're right it's too late.'

This was not the Holly Jules knew and loved. This was a different Holly, bitter, broken.

'It's not too late to try and sort things out between *us*, is it?' Jules said.

Holly turned to look across the barren fields towards the church. She had lost weight. Not that she had much to lose.

Now Jules looked closely, she could see there was a gash in the back of her head, the hair matted slightly around it. Holly put her hand up to it unconsciously.

'You've hurt yourself, Holly.'

Holly looked at Jules, her lower lip trembling.

'Did you fall? It looks quite bad.'

'It's nothing,' she said. 'I don't want to talk about it.'

'Look, I wish I could go back,' Jules said, 'and do things differently. I had to believe Saffie, even if in my gut it didn't seem like Saul—' She stopped. This was not the right thing to say. She changed tack. 'I would like to do what I can to make amends.'

Holly shivered. Stepped back so she was sheltered from the wind by the little Perspex excuse for a shelter on the platform.

'I want to make amends,' Jules repeated. 'For the damage my family has done to yours.'

'What's the point, Jules? Now we know what was going on for her, I don't hold her lie against Saffie. She was terrified of telling the truth. She could have chosen someone other than Saul to blame things on, and something less damning than rape, but I can see her logic.'

'You hold it against me?'

Jules's question hung in the air as the level-crossing siren started up, with its rising and falling wail. The train could be seen approaching from across the flat landscape, and the barriers came down, shutting off access across the road to motorists.

'The fact is, I've missed you,' Jules said to Holly's profile, no longer hoping for a response. She went on talking anyway. 'It's been awful. Not being able to talk to you. I can't tell you how terrible things have got at home.'

'I am sorry Saffie has gone through what she has,' Holly

said. 'I really am. No thirteen-year-old should be put in that situation ... but you haven't lost your child. And you haven't been vilified by a whole village.'

'I need to talk to you. There's no one else I can confide in. There never was.'

The train was pulling into the station, the doors sliding open.

'If you have time now?' Jules decided to have one more try.

Jules followed Holly onto the train.

'I was going in to work to collect some books,' Holly said, as the doors slid shut. 'I haven't been in since ... since Saul disappeared. There's only so much time you can sit at home going over and over where your child has gone. What might have happened to them. What he might have done to himself. I was going to get to London early so I can be back before Pete goes out. We try to be at home. One of us, in case ...'

'Have you time to stop in Cambridge, get a later train?' Jules put a hand on Holly's shoulder. 'I'd appreciate it,' she said. 'I could buy you a coffee?'

And at last Holly gave the tiniest inclination of her head.

*

Jules and Holly sat opposite one another, not speaking, as the train pulled away from the bleak little village platform and trundled across the Fens. Outside, the pale grey sky was huge above the dark fields. They passed the river as they approached Cambridge, rowers scudding along the glittering water beneath the yellow stone bridges. The willows on the banks had lost their leaves, and drooped sadly over the water.

They got off in Cambridge and Jules led the way over the

concourse to a cafe, relieved beyond measure to reach its warmth, its soft sofas, to smell coffee, to hear the hiss of the espresso machines. To be out of the wind and the Fens, which reminded her of the fact Saul was still missing, his body possibly still out there somewhere.

They found a corner where they were out of earshot of the young customers who seemed to have commandeered every other table with their laptops and headphones. Jules went to get coffees.

'It's not a Unique Drinking Point, I'm afraid,' she said, searching Holly's face for a softening. 'It's a chain. But it's a reasonable one, and the coffee ticks our box.'

Holly didn't respond.

Jules sat down next to her anyway and began to speak. 'When I heard the police had found a body, it was as devastating to me as it was for anyone, I want you to know that. I didn't know how you could bear it. I couldn't bear it either.'

Holly frowned, and stirred her coffee. 'It took them some time to identify the body parts,' she said. 'Longer than it should have done. Because of the state of them and the fact not many people go missing in the Fens. They knew it was a young adult male, so Saul was top of their list of possibilities.'

'How terrible for you.'

'Turns out the remains belong to a young man who'd been missing from Wisbech. He'd been in care. Then homeless. Had no parents. No one missed him. I was relieved when they told me, for about a second, until I realized what hell the boy must have gone through to want to set fire to himself like that. Anyway, it doesn't bring Saul back. I still don't know whether he's alive. Knowing the body isn't Saul throws me back into the uncertainty about what *has* happened to him. I'm plagued by what he must have felt when he'd been accused of rape. And the not knowing, the lack of closure is a different kind of hell.'

'You know it was Harry Bell, do you, Holly? Who was actually behind Saffie's pregnancy?'

'They told me. It was Pete, in fact, who extracted the truth – or enough of the truth – from Freya. To give the police a lead. Pete's way of trying to redeem himself.'

'For what?'

'For taking the girls to Deepa's to "protect" them from Saul. Which was another betrayal. Of me, and of Saul. Pete didn't want his daughters under the same roof anymore. After he heard about Saffie's allegation.'

Holly stopped, swallowed, and Jules wondered whether she should reply or stay silent. Then Holly spoke again. 'I lost everyone. Saul. The girls. Pete. My memory of Archie. Even' – Holly looked at Jules – 'you.'

Jules looked back. She wondered if this meant Holly wanted them to repair their friendship. That there was a ray of hope.

'The way Bell manipulated Saffie was mindboggling,' Jules said after a while. 'I don't know how much the police told you . . .'

Holly looked down, stirred her coffee.

'They told me enough. To assure me Saul was completely, utterly innocent. A victim himself.'

She suddenly looked up at Jules. 'What I don't understand is why Saffie chose Saul. And why she said he *raped* her. If she wanted to cover up for that low-life scum Harry, she could just have said she was sleeping with someone else.'

'Saul was the only boy she'd had contact with,' Jules said. 'The only boy who'd been in our house and who she could feasibly have slept with.' Jules couldn't think how to relay everything Saffie had said – about not fancying Saul, and him being considered a creep – without hurting Holly further. So she left out this detail.

'Apparently, when Saffie told Harry she'd blamed the pregnancy on Saul, he said it would serve you right for trying to "emasculate" men with your articles in the paper. Saffie told me that last night.'

'He read my article?'

Jules shrugged. 'It *was* all over the internet. And he'd have found it interesting as it was by the mother of one of his pupils.'

Holly was silent, frowning for a few minutes before speaking.

'Well. I'm used to that kind of bigoted opinion. I've had it for months on my Twitter feed. You put your head above the parapet for women's rights and you get shot to pieces by insecure men who go on the defensive. I wish I'd never written the bloody article. I had no idea how it would backfire.'

'You can't let people like Harry shut you up,' Jules said quietly. 'If you do that, then he's won!'

Holly glanced at Jules and did at last give her a small smile.

'These things have to be spoken about more, not less,' Jules went on. 'But let's face it, Harry Bell wouldn't have liked you arguing for better education on consent. He wouldn't have liked that one bit. He relied on girls not understanding the meaning of consent. The police are following up allegations from ex-pupils of his. He has incredible power over teenage girls. They were all in love with him, Saffie said. Freya, and Gemma, Tess's daughter, and all of them. It's Saffie he targeted this time, but there were others before her and there would have been more after. And of course Samantha was only fourteen when she fell for him, and had only just turned sixteen when she fell pregnant and married him. He'd done the same to her at the time. The really scary thing for me is how manipulative he must have been, and how Saffie went along with it.'

Jules wasn't a hundred per cent certain Holly was listening anymore. She still had her head bowed, and her straight hair had fallen over her face.

'I mean, what's haunting me now is how I brought up a daughter who believed she was safe to go back to a teacher's house after school. Because he'd told her she was beautiful, or hot or whatever, the kind of compliment she craved. When Bell first tried to have sex with her, she thought she couldn't refuse. Because her friends were jealous, and he'd given her preferential treatment. Where had she got that idea from?'

'There's a lot more work to be done on all this,' Holly said, sounding a tiny bit more like her old self.

'There certainly is. The police are charging Bell for rape as well as sexual exploitation. Because of course Saffie didn't consent to sleeping with him. She thought she had no choice.'

'She couldn't have consented anyway,' Holly said, 'because of her age.'

And then Jules broke down. 'Thirteen! Barely more than a child. She'd only just stopped playing with her cash register and still sleeps with that teddy bear Saul gave her. How can I have let her get so mixed up with a grown man? But Rowan was packing her off to extra "classes" – so he thought – and that's where Bell groomed her.'

After a while, Holly leaned over, put a tissue on the table

23

HOLLY

We've been in the cafe for nearly an hour. I shift in my seat. I'd prefer to get up, get on a train to London, but Jules has more to say.

'Holly, when I came to tell you about Saffie's rape claim in your study, I wanted us to talk. I hoped, then, that we might talk to the kids. I thought we would get to the bottom of it by ourselves.' She glances up at me. 'Without all the repercussions it caused.'

Jules takes a sip of her now-cold coffee, then pushes it away. I realize she's changed over the last few days. She looks older. Her face is thinner, and she has shadows round her eyes.

'I feel quite shaky. Low blood sugar. Or upset. Or talking to you at last.'

'It's emotional,' I say quietly. 'For me too.'

'Why didn't we?' she says, looking up at me. 'Why didn't we manage to unravel the truth between us? What went wrong?'

There seems no point in holding back, so I take a deep breath and just say it. Everything that's been on my mind since that fateful meeting in my office. 'It was like you'd decided to use the rape claim to vent other opinions about my parenting of Saul,' I say.

Jules frowns. Shakes her head.

'You did. How I'd failed to notice he had social problems.

How I'd done nothing to help him "fit in". You even accused him of being a "misfit" – my worst fear, until then. Things you'd reassured me about before.' I look at Jules and see she remembers, has gone pink. 'I realized you must've thought those things, secretly, all along. The support you gave me over the years, the reassurance, all of a sudden I realized was a sham. You'd been thinking all along I'd done a shit job bringing him up without Archie.'

'That's not true . . .'

'I was determined to prove you wrong. About Saul, of course, but also about my mothering. I thought . . . I thought suddenly, I don't really know Jules at all. I never did. It was such a shock.'

Jules gazes at me for a minute. 'I just wanted you to agree we needed to share it. But then *you* called Saffie "devious" and said she was making trouble. The implication being I'd brought up a child who would be so manipulative or plain cruel as to make a rape allegation about Saul for no good reason. You were supposed to be Saffie's champion. You always had been . . .'

There's something deeply unsettling about this heart-to-heart with Jules when Saul is still missing. I'm not ready for it. I really want to go now. I need to be alone with my thoughts. With my ambiguous grief. I want to take the next train to London, get to work, pick up my books, come home, to keep moving, keep running away from the pain that threatens to swamp me if I sit still for a moment longer. I reach for my bag.

'It's been good to air our grievances,' Jules says. 'The fact is, Holly, now I know the truth, I realize you're a far better mother than I am. I wish I'd been as attentive with Saff as you always were with Saul.'

'Nonsense,' I say. 'In fact, the other day I was thinking

exactly the same about you. That I wished I'd been a more fun mother with Saul. But we all do our best. There's no map, Jules. We're all groping our way through the dark, bringing up our kids. Trying to find the right route. Sometimes we take the wrong turning, that's all.'

I can't bring myself to hug her as I would once have done without thinking. I leave the cafe, knowing Jules is watching me, and that she will be feeling terrible that I am the one who, through everything that's happened, has lost the most.

*

When I get home that evening, I pause. The lights are on, and the car is parked in our little driveway, so I know Pete must be home. As I put my key in the lock and open the door, I realize that Freya and Thea must be here too. Their coats are on the hook on the back of the door and new trainers have joined Saul's – the ones I haven't moved since he disappeared – by the door. Pete comes out into the hallway, pulling the sitting-room door shut behind him.

'Pete, are Freya and Thea here?' I feel my spirits lift, a tiny spark of joy in my dark heart at the thought of seeing them.

'They wanted to come over,' he says. 'We thought we'd surprise you.'

'That's so sweet of you. Of them.'

'I bought a couple of pizzas and some stuff to make a salad. And wine for you. Holly . . .'

'What?'

'Before you say hello, I should warn you. Freya's been really upset about her part in all this; she's blaming herself for not saying something sooner. I told her you didn't hold it against her, but she's desperate to make amends and has got it into her head that the only way to do that is to somehow try to mend the rift between you and Saffie and Jules. She's become quite obsessed about it.'

'Right . . .'

Pete sighs. 'And she's invited Saffie over this evening.'

'Ah.' I drop my bag on the hall floor. Take off my coat.

'I know. I'm sorry, honey – I knew it would be difficult for you. But the way Freya was, it was a question of not having her or Thea at all or having all of them – and, weighing it up, I decided you'd prefer to have all of them.' He waits. 'Than none?' he says nervously.

'I don't know that I'm ready to see Saffie,' I tell him. 'It's not just what she's done to us. It's . . . I was so cruel, telling her they'd found a body when I met her on the riverbank. I feel ashamed.'

'Holly. We've all said and done things we regret over the last few days. But we're the adults, remember?' Pete takes hold of my shoulders gently. 'If Saffie's happy to come here, then we should welcome her. We should show we're willing to forgive. To help heal the trauma she's been through. And to help Freya at the same time.'

I pull back from him, look into his face, which is so full of concern, of love. 'You're right, Pete. I know you're right.'

'So I'll ring Jules? Say Freya's invited Saffie round and you're OK with it?'

'Yes,' I say. 'Yes, OK. But I need that wine.'

I push open the sitting-room door. The girls flood over to me, let me hug them, kiss their hair. It's like having a little part of me that's been dormant brought back to life. Feeling their thin arms round me, hearing their excitable voices, telling me about the latest episode of something they've been watching. I haven't realized just how much I've missed them. They follow me into the kitchen, where Pete's lit a candle and stuck it in a wine bottle. He hands me a big glass of red wine. He's made a huge bowl of salad and decorated it with edible flowers.

'You're such a whiz in the kitchen,' I say.

'It was our idea,' says Freya.

'Mine, actually,' corrects Thea. 'I picked the violas from Mum's window box before we came.'

'It's lovely,' I say. 'Such a beautiful sight to come home to.'

'I'm putting it on Instagram,' says Freya.

Some part of me is able to remember what contentment felt like. This domestic scene, the wine, the voices, the smell of dough warming in the oven. Another part feels like it's carrying a weight, so heavy I can barely stand. None of us will ever feel completely at home here without Saul, is the truth.

*

There's a knock on the door then, interrupting the gloomy direction my thoughts have threatened to take.

'I'm grateful for this.' Jules stands in the doorway.

Saffie pushes past and greets Freya and Thea.

'Come in, Jules,' I say, half-heartedly.

'Thanks, Holl, but I have stuff to sort.' She starts to walk away, then turns back, hesitates a moment. 'I assume there's still no news?'

I shake my head.

'I'm so sorry, Holly.'

We look at each other, unable to speak for a few moments.

Then she says, 'I do recognize what a big gesture this is. You inviting Saffie round under the circumstances. But it'll be good for Saffie to spend time here with Freya, and Thea. For her to get back to normal. Thank you.'

'It's OK,' I say at last. 'It's good for me to have the house full. To have young people around again.'

'There was one other thing I wanted to talk to you about this morning,' she says.

'Oh?'

'About Rowan's part in everything that's happened.'

I don't want to talk about Rowan. But Jules's face is full of something – anguish, pleading. I step outside, into a fractious wind, pulling the front door to behind me. We stand on my little paved path. I hug my cardigan around myself.

'If Rowan hadn't pushed Saffie so hard to stay for extra "revision" classes,' Jules says, 'the meetings with Harry might not have happened. In a way, everything can be traced back to Rowan having unrealistic expectations of our daughter. D'you remember? I told you he watched that ridiculous show *Child Genius* and had Saffie in mind for it. But I can forgive Ro for that. He was doing that in good faith. He didn't know he was pushing her into the clutches of a paedophile, poor man. If he'd only known, he would have been the first to have gone to the police, as you can imagine ... But ... look, I love Rowan. You know that, Holly, better than anyone. In spite of everything. In fact, only you ever understood that when he used to flare up, he couldn't help it; it was the flip side of his sunny one. You always accepted that about him. Which I appreciate.'

I can't bring myself to reply to this. His figure looming over me in the kitchen comes back to me. The smell of his breath. The terror that he was going to rape me. Even as I think about him, the bruise on the back of my head starts to throb.

'But his behaviour around this whole thing,' Jules says, 'his threat that he'd beat up Saul, which I wish I'd never relayed to you. His reaction frightened me. If Rowan had killed Saul – and I was convinced, when I heard they had found a body up in the Fens, that he had – I would have left him in an instant.'

'You believe Rowan might have *killed* Saul?' I don't know if it's the way the street lamp casts a weird tangerine colour on Jules's face or what she's just told me, but the world seems to tilt and I have to clutch the door frame. Rowan might have threatened to 'beat the living daylights' out of my son, but I never took it quite that literally. Jules clearly did, though. And although she says she'd have left Rowan in an instant, there's something in her voice that belies the certainty of her words, something that suggests she's trying to persuade herself as much as me.

'There were clues that he'd been to that area,' Jules goes on. 'But now I know the body wasn't Saul's, I don't know what to think anymore. What I do know is his reaction to Saffie's allegation was extremely violent. I don't know whether I can stay with him. What would you do in my shoes?' Jules persists. 'You know me better than anyone.'

Jules is asking me whether she should leave Rowan. I want to say, 'Of course you should leave him. Get out now! You actually believe he killed my son? Run, Jules!'

A hard, cold rain has begun. I'm freezing and I want to go inside. I can't speak. I can't put my thoughts into a coherent pattern that will form a sentence. Instead, I lift Jules's hand and place it on the wound on the back of my head.

'Feel that.'

Jules places her hand on the swelling and the rough scab that has covered the large gash. I wince at her touch, the bruise still tender.

'That happened right here,' I say, gesturing towards my door. 'After the Auction of Promises at the Baptist Chapel. After you'd gone.'

I don't need to say any more.

Jules looks at me in the way she used to, when she knew exactly what I meant. And she understands. Because even after everything, there's a part of both me and Jules that knows each other inside out.

*

Back indoors, the girls – Freya, Thea and Saffie – are sitting on the sofa, leaning against each other, watching some inane sitcom. Again I have that sense, like a distant memory, that things can feel all right. The rain on the roof, the wood burner alight, the wind swishing through the trees outside, rattling the slates on the roof. Pete is in the kitchen, getting the meal ready. His clattering about makes a reassuring background noise. Then the rain turns to hail, smattering against the windows as if someone were chucking handfuls of gravel at them. I squeeze onto the sofa between Freya and Thea, and Thea rests her head on my shoulder. I put my arms round them. For a little while, I try to imagine this is my family, to ignore the great aching gap in it left by Saul.

The sitcom the girls are watching involves lawyers making a mess of their caseload. And suddenly a scene takes me out of myself.

'Oh my goodness,' I cry, as the camera pans over the very building where Archie used to work. 'There! See that – that's where Archie's chambers were. Lincoln's Inn.'

'You never told us,' Freya says, looking up at me, 'what Saul's dad was like. I want to know.'

'He was a defence lawyer.' The old pride I always felt saying these words edges into my voice in spite of myself. I haven't examined how I feel since Philippa revealed her relationship with Archie. It's been pushed to the back of my mind by everything else. And now's not the time. 'He had chambers in Lincoln's Inn – there, look. They're showing it again. Stone Buildings, it was called.'

The girls want to know all about Saul's birth father. Although Saul's absence nags and tears, a physical pain in my chest, I *want* to talk about him, about his dad. Besides, the conversation is soothing, a distraction of sorts. There's something about the presence of young people that softens the harsh lines of the adult world. Their noise, their chatter is a comfort. We forget the sitcom, let it burble on in the background as we talk.

'Lincoln's Inn Fields looks so nice,' says Freya. 'So pretty. Much prettier than the country around here.'

'It's not countryside anymore. It's right in the middle of London. But you're right. Lincoln's Inn itself is beautiful. Those buildings they're showing, and those gardens and little alleyways all lead off the busy streets outside. It's where lawyers have their offices; they call them chambers. It's tucked away from the traffic and all the hustle and bustle of the surrounding streets. You can stand on Holborn, or in Covent Garden even, and never know that those gardens, cloisters and the chapel are just a few metres away. It's like a secret world within the city. I'll take you there one day.'

Saffie has been completely silent since she came in, but now she speaks. 'Did you just say there's a chapel? In the middle of Lincoln's Inn?'

'There is,' I say. 'It's beautiful. You can walk underneath, because it's built over an arched undercroft. I used to take Saul – and you, actually, Saffie – when you were little. Saul used to like the names on the gravestones in the floor. The barristers and the benchers with the "s"s like "f"s. "Barrifter," he would say. And he used to laugh at the "Hatch-keeper and Washpot".'

Freya and Thea giggle.

'Is it the chapel Saul's dad haunts?' Saffie says.

I stare at her.

'Archie's buried in East Finchley Cemetery. Not in Lincoln's Inn. There are no burials there anymore.'

'I know,' Saffie says. 'But Saul told me his dad haunts Lincoln's Inn Chapel. There was one night, when we were young, he told me his dad wanted to be among the other lawyers who were buried there, so his ghost had gone to haunt it. He scared me! But he said it wasn't scary. He said his dad was there and he liked it.'

I look at this girl with her childish face, no longer thick with make-up, her wide eyes, her round cheeks. Suddenly – momentarily – she doesn't look any different to when she was tiny. I think of the days in London when she would stay over with us, how I liked it that since Saul didn't have a sister, he had her. And I remember the pair of them staying up sometimes, talking, how sweet I found it that they had things in common, in spite of the age difference.

One day, I know I'll be thankful I still have Saffie. And I wonder, after all, whether I should perhaps have persuaded Jules to come in this evening, too. Whether forgiving is less arduous than carrying the weight of a grudge around with you day after day.

Saffie continues, 'I was only about eight, and Saul was eleven. It was when you were still in your London house, Holly. We were talking, me and Saul, about where we'd like to be buried. I asked if he'd like it to be the same place as his dad. He said no. He said he didn't know why his dad was buried in East Finchley Cemetery. He said it was really big and unfriendly with all those thousands of gravestones.'

'I know,' I say. 'But there wasn't really a choice.'

I don't explain to her how I was in no state at the time to argue with the advice I was given. That neither Archie nor

I had made plans for what to do if either of us died. That I was doing what I was told. And that East Finchley Cemetery was the default burial ground for anyone in that part of London.

'He said he wished his dad was in Lincoln's Inn Chapel. Protected from the rain, under the arches. And he thought his dad's ghost would have gone there to talk to the other dead lawyers. He said he wished he could go there, to be close to him, but he didn't want to upset you, Holly. So he never told you . . . and . . .'

'Go on,' I say.

'The other thing Saul said he loved' – Saffie looks at me – 'is that the pews in the chapel above had little doors. He said they were like little rooms that you can lock and hide in.'

'Ha! Saul always loved little hideaways,' I say.

'After dark, he said you could lie down in those pews on the prayer cushions and lock the little door and no one would know you were there.'

'He said that?'

'Yes,' says Saffie. 'He always wanted to go there. Where he could be close to his dad's ghost.'

24

JULES

The storm was right overhead as Jules drove home after dropping Saffie at Holly's, the windscreen almost opaque. She had to lean forward, peer through the glass to see the road, her headlights only making the white sheets of rain in front of her more dazzling.

The rough wound on Holly's scalp had impressed itself onto the tips of Jules's fingers. She couldn't shake off the imprint it had left, couldn't bear to imagine what Rowan had done to Holly that night after the Auction of Promises, before he had come in, drunk, and with that air about him that he'd had one of his red mists.

She drove back across the fen, pulled up in her driveway and hurried through the wind that was now blowing almost horizontally, and let herself in to the house. Rowan wasn't there, and she wasn't sure whether she was relieved or disappointed. Because she knew now she was going to confront him.

She tried to distract herself in the kitchen. She rummaged in the fridge to see if there was anything to eat, then gave up. She wasn't hungry, anyway. Instead, she poured herself a gin and tonic, and sat watching some sitcom about lawyers without taking any of it in. The rain battered against the windows, the skylights in the kitchen rattling under its impact. She didn't know what time it was when Rowan did finally appear, slamming the front door, taking off his boots,

368

brushing rain off his coat. She didn't think. She stood up, went into the hallway and stood in front of her husband.

'What is it?' he asked. 'Is Saff OK?'

His hair glistened with raindrops; his face was chafed and red from the cold.

The words came out before she had time to pause, or to plan them.

'Saff is as OK as she'll ever be,' she said. 'After everything that man has done to her. But you, you total bastard! You did that to Holly! You assaulted her in her own home.' She hit Rowan on the chest. He gripped her wrists, but she wriggled out of his clutches and beat him again harder, pummelling his shoulders, his arms.

'I don't know you anymore, Rowan,' she screamed. 'You are not the man I thought you were. You are violent. You can't control your feelings. After everything I've gone through with you.'

'Whoa! Hang on.'

'I will not hang on. I can't live with a man who attacks a woman for no reason. I can't live with a man who attacks a woman full stop.'

'Jules, come on. You're stressed after everything that's happened.'

'Holly showed me,' Jules said. 'Holly showed me what you did to her.'

She was trembling. Then she quietened, steadied her voice and said, 'And where *did* you go? That morning? The morning Saul vanished? Did you do something to him too? Did you kill Saul?'

Jules was crying suddenly, but she didn't care. The gash on Holly's head continued to haunt her. The thought of Rowan attacking her friend, pushing her over, knocking her down or hitting her head so hard she was left with that gash. What else was he capable of?

'I know you went beyond Ely into the Fens. I know you got petrol out near Downham Market. I know you lied about where you were that morning. Did you kill Saul? Did you? You may as well tell me now because you've already gone too far, Rowan. Then we'll tell the police.'

Rowan left the room. For a second, Jules was aware of how very isolated this house was, out on the Fens, away from the village. And in this weather, no one came down here. Another gust of wind hit the side of the house, blowing over one of the wheelie bins outside, which went crashing over the decking. If Rowan was to turn violent with her, no one would hear. No one would know. She had never been afraid of him before. Even when he'd flipped, she knew she could calm him, that he was always gentle with her. But witnessing the wound he'd inflicted on Holly put him in another category.

Rowan was gone for several minutes and Jules slumped down on the sofa. She had done it. Confronted him with her worst fear.

Rowan, when he came back into the room, did so slowly, and placed a business card on the coffee table in front of her. On it was written, *Hypnotherapist, works with all conditions, including alcoholism, smoking, anger management. Applecroft, Downham Market.*

Jules stared at it for some time.

'What is this, Rowan? Why are you showing me this?'

'When I heard about the rape,' he said, 'I did feel murderous. And it scared me how much I wanted to beat up Saul. I had to deal with my feelings, so I booked an appointment with this hypnotherapist I'd seen on the internet. In Downham Market. The appointment was that Monday morning.

I didn't want to tell you. It would've meant telling you I felt out of control. So I thought if I drove Saffie to school – which I'd decided to do anyway – I could go on there after dropping her and you wouldn't know.'

'So?'

'I'm telling you so you understand. I'm not as bad as you think I am.'

'You attacked Holly, Rowan. If you went to anger management in Downham Market that morning, it obviously didn't work.'

There was a sudden shattering sound overhead. Jules looked up and saw white hailstones were clattering down and bouncing off the skylights.

'As it happens, when I got there and found the house, Applecroft, I couldn't bring myself to go in. I sat outside for some time. And I figured things out. I decided I was *right* to feel as angry as I did. Saul had destroyed our daughter's childhood and he deserved to be punished for it. By the time I'd got that straight in my head, I didn't go in to the appointment. I realized I needed my bloody anger. I was justified in seeking vengeance for what he did to our daughter. I went for a walk on the Fens to think about it. I decided I'd give him a talking to myself since Holly and Pete were doing nothing. But by the time I'd got home, he'd done a runner.'

'And what made you attack Holly, Rowan?' Jules seethed.

After a pause, Rowan said, 'I didn't mean to hurt her. I just wanted her to take some responsibility. Holly did nothing to get the truth out of Saul. There she was, a bloody feminist, bellyaching about women's rights, and yet she did nothing to support our girl when she was raped.'

'But she wasn't raped, not by her son.'

'When we all *thought* Saul had raped her, Holly did

371

nothing to deal with it. You know that. I thought you were with me on that?'

Jules walked across the room and gazed out at the storm. The hail was abating, replaced by white veils of rain.

'I didn't want anyone to get hurt,' she said. 'I wanted to stop anyone getting hurt. I wanted us to sort it out between ourselves so that the kids would be left unscathed and we would all be able to move on.'

'You're an idealist too, half the time,' Rowan said. 'Sometimes you sound as woolly as Holly.'

It took some time for Jules to gather herself. Then she turned and looked at Rowan.

'I don't want you here anymore. Get out.'

'Are you telling me to leave?'

'I'm not sure this marriage is working anymore.'

Rowan stood, his arms hanging helplessly by his side. 'Jules,' he said. 'Please. Don't say that. Don't tell me it's over. I love you. You're the only woman for me, you know that. I need you.'

'I'm not sure I can do this, Rowan. Not now I know you did that to my best friend.'

Rowans eyes grew wide, full of panic. 'Think of Saffie,' he cried. 'How will she feel if she hears we're breaking up?'

'In the long run,' Jules said quietly, 'it could be a good thing for her as well.'

Jules's phone pinged. She turned her back on Rowan and went to pick it up.

There was a text from Holly.

'Get out,' she said to Rowan. 'I want to read this by myself.'

25

HOLLY

Hailstones bounce off my windscreen as I drive to the station. I manage to get straight on a train and it takes sixty minutes to get to London, but this evening it feels like a lifetime.

At King's Cross I take a taxi and we sail down Gray's Inn Road and along Theobalds Road. In the backstreets, little blue lights are strung out in the trees, and it occurs to me with a gasp that Christmas will soon be on its way. The world has continued to happen, while for me, everything has been on hold. We get to Chancery Lane just before the gates to Lincoln's Inn close at seven. I pay the taxi driver and clamber out.

'Please,' I say to the porter in his lobby. 'I need to go to the chapel.'

He gives me a small smile, an eyebrow raised. What must he think I need the chapel for at this time of night?

'You're just in time,' he says. 'We lock up in half an hour.'

I thank him and pass beneath the carriage lamps spilling yellow pools of soft light onto the cobblestones around the entrance. It's a fine, cold night here. Inside the gates, the city falls silent. It could be two hundred years ago, longer. I go past Old Square, and Stone Buildings, the names familiar, evoking the keen pain I always feel at revisiting the place Archie worked. To reach the chapel entrance, I have to pass beneath the low undercroft, my footsteps ringing out on the cold gravestones laid flat to make up the floor. Most of them are the graves of barristers and benchers. It's only the much older stones that were also used for servants. As I step over the words 'Hatch-keeper and Washpot', etched into an ancient slab, I can almost hear Saul laugh, his childish giggles echoing off the ceiling. His ghost? I shudder. Saul believed Archie's ghost haunted this place. I think again of his text – 'Gone to be close to Dad' – and refuse to let myself think the worst.

On either side of the chapel entrance, a carved head gazes down, Queen Victoria and some bishop or other, as if watching me, curious as to what I'm doing here when everyone else has retreated to their homes or to restaurants for the evening. I push open the door. Staircases curve up to either side. I hesitate. Both lead to the chapel, but I can't make a decision, afraid of what I'll find at the top. Or what I won't find.

In the end, I choose the right-hand stairs. I arrive in a little vestibule. I remember with a shock there's a portrait of John Donne here; he was a preacher to the inn in the seventeenth century. Glancing up at the portrait, it hits me all of a sudden that he looks like Saul! Is it a good omen? That Saul quoted him to me that fateful day on our walk to Jules's house?

The handle is icy under my palm as I push open the door onto a dimly lit interior smelling of polished wood. The chapel is silent. And it's empty. As I should have guessed. It was a crazy thing to do, to leave Freya and Thea and Saffie and Pete, say I had to go, to get the train to London, in the middle of our conversation.

But now I'm here, I know this is where I need to be.

I walk over the black-and-white chequered floor, between

the carved benches towards the far end of the chapel. Where the pews are older, they have doors, just as Saul told Saffie. Little lockable doors. But I can see nothing behind them, only shadow. I walk all around the chapel, down one side and up the other. There's no one here. I'll have to leave, get the train back to the Fens, accept at last my loss. Because I realize that what I've been doing is refusing to accept what I always knew ever since I received Saul's text. I've been in denial. It's time to let him go.

Before I leave, I sit down on a pew, just to catch my breath and to be silent for a while. Bowl-shaped lamps on stands along the ends of the pews give off a gentle glow. The large stained-glass windows at either end of the room gleam: sapphire, ruby and gold, gently illuminated. Saul believed his dad haunted this building, and a little part of me half believes if I sit for long enough, perhaps Archie will indeed speak to me, tell me he did love me after all. And that Saul is with him and that everything is all right. There is a deep sense of tranquillity in this space, something I haven't felt for as long as I can remember. After a while, I realize my eyelids are drooping and I'm close to falling asleep. Then something jerks me awake, a dull thud at the far end of the chapel. I open my eyes. And am suddenly aware that there is someone else here. Behind one of the doors to the pews.

He's sleeping on the floorboards when I find him, so deep in shadow it's impossible to see him without looking intently. Behind one of the locked doors to the pews. Head resting on a red hassock.

'Saul,' I whisper. 'Saul. Are you real? Are you really here?'

I put my hand to his face and feel him, his skin, his hair. I need to prove to myself my son is here and he's alive. I shake him gently, and eventually he opens his eyes and he looks up at me.

'Mum,' he says.

And I know then it's going to be all right.

＊

Saul sits on the pew next to me. His hair is stiffened into dreadlocks. His clothes are worn, dirty, and he's wearing a hooded anorak I've never seen before. And he looks older. His stubble has grown and looks coarser than it was before he left. He tells me it's where he always thought he would live if he was homeless. On the streets of Clerkenwell by day ('Good Italian leftovers in the bins,' he says), but hiding away in the chapel to sleep.

'It's easy,' he says. 'I come in while Lincoln's Inn is still open, close the little door to the pew, and no one checks. In the morning, I leave and head for the streets. Beg for a couple of quid for breakfast. Or scavenge a pizza from behind one of the cafes. The best pickings come from Andy's Cafe in Gray's Inn Road.'

At night, he says, he looks up from his locked pew at the stained-glass windows, with their depictions of biblical figures ('All men,' I almost comment, but refrain), disciples and saints, and he communes with his father. It's his secret place. A place where he feels very close to his dad.

How did I not think of it?

We sit side by side, alone in the empty chapel.

'Unmarried women used to leave their babies here,' he says. 'I was in good company.'

He looks at me. I put out my hand and touch his.

'I never abandoned you, Saul.'

'When you didn't believe me, it was like you didn't know me anymore,' he says.

I don't speak for a minute.

'I needed you to say that you didn't do it. Didn't rape Saffie.'

'I shouldn't have had to.'

'No. You shouldn't. But I needed you to. Because I was frightened. Of what might happen if you didn't say loud and clear that you hadn't done it. And I'm sorry.' My words are so inadequate. I wish there was a better, stronger word than 'sorry' in our lexicon.

'I didn't think you'd believe her.'

'I never believed her. I knew you'd never do a thing like that. But I couldn't think why she would lie. And I'd spent so many years urging people to believe rape allegations . . .'

'Because girls rarely lie about being raped. You drove that home to me, Mum, over the years.'

'Did I?'

'Of course. All those conversations you have with Pete about what consent means.'

I feel a shot of vindication hearing this – I'd worried I hadn't got the message across to Saul.

'So it's like I know better than any other guy in the land that only "yes" means "yes". That's why it felt so unfair that anyone could believe I'd do it. But then I thought, it's OK, because Mum knows me.

'When I heard Pete saying he'd taken Freya and Thea away because of me, what else could I do but get away? Pete believed Saffie. I thought you believed Saffie. I didn't see how I could change your minds. I packed that night, and the next morning, instead of getting on the school bus, I went down to the river and started walking to London.'

I hold his hand tight, tight, feel how rough, how calloused his skin has become. They have become a man's hands, no longer a boy's.

'You walked?'

'Across country. You'd be amazed how easy it is to keep out of sight once you put your mind to it. How many places there are to sleep between the Fens and London.'

Suddenly the bells of the chapel begin to peal and we wait before speaking again.

'"Never send to know for whom the bell tolls; it tolls for thee,"' Saul quotes. 'John Donne got the inspiration for that right here. I didn't know until I got here and saw the memorial to him. It's hard to spot – it's in the low right-hand corner of the stained-glass window over there.'

'It's strange that it's the same meditation that you quoted to me on the way to Jules's: "No Man Is an Island."'

'I've often thought, while I was lying here, about what that means. It's like, if one person dies, we all die a little bit. I did think of ending it all. How I would do it. Jump in the river, maybe. Or lie on the train track. I thought I could do it on the railway line that goes from London to our village. King's Cross to King's Lynn. Ironic, eh?'

'Saul, please. That was my worst fear!'

'But then I thought, if I do that, it'll be like killing you too. It may sound whacky, but I imagined Dad speaking to me. He told me to live, for his sake, and for yours. But I still wanted Saffie, especially, to be fucking sorry for what she'd said. I wasn't going to come home until I knew she'd taken it back.'

'She was desperate, Saul. Terrified of what might happen if she told the truth. Harry Bell threatened her. He's been charged now, of sexual exploitation and rape.'

'Fuck. That's crap. Saffie *was* raped?'

'Yes. She was raped. She didn't understand she had a choice. So that's rape. She thought by saying it was you, it wouldn't get her into as much trouble as the truth would. She thought Jules and I would keep it between ourselves.

She didn't want to get you into trouble, but she was trapped. It seems terribly unfair, and she was naive to think blaming you wouldn't be harmful.'

'Hmm.'

'I actually have Saffie to thank. It was she who remembered how you thought Dad's ghost was here. And how you loved these pews with the doors.'

'She remembered that?'

'She did. Some conversation you had when you were children. I came straight away.'

I can't stop looking at my son. I want to smother him, press my nose into his hair, smell him. 'Saul, I can't tell you how much I've missed you. How terrified I was I'd lost you.'

In fact, I want to eat him up so he can never go away from me again, as rodents eat their young when they're in danger. I sit on my hands, force myself to treat him like the adult he is.

'You got my text, though, didn't you?' he says suddenly. 'I chucked my phone away when I left home. To stop anyone following me. But then I thought you'd, like ... fret. So I borrowed a phone. With a withheld number. I texted that I'd come to be close to dad. I didn't want you to think I was ... like ... dead.'

I don't tell him, because it would sound as if I'm chastising him, that I interpreted his message differently.

'Yes,' I say. 'I got your text. Thank you for that, Saul. I just wish I'd known where to find you. Now I think, if you don't mind, *I'm* going to text the others at home, including Jules, because everyone who loves you will want to know you're here, and safe.'

And alive, I think. Saul is alive.

Epilogue

HOLLY

Saul and I walk together down the fen road to the river. It's the kind of winter weather that renders the land paler than the sky. Dark clouds heavy with rain hang over bright fields; white sedge bends in the wind. We take the long country road to the lock and climb the metal steps onto the sluice bridge. I think of the other dreadful afternoon I stood there staring into the water, when I had been told they had found human remains and I believed they belonged to my son. He's here with me. I can feel him, warm, tall and breathing next to me. We stand side by side and watch the water tumble over the ledge. We don't speak. And it's fine. It feels comfortable to stand next to my son and share our silence.

We're about to carry on, to continue our walk upriver, when I spot two figures coming towards us along the road. It's Jules with Saffie. I go to move away – I want this time alone with Saul – but they're upon us before I can get through the swing gate at the bottom of the steps.

'Saul,' Jules says. 'I can't express ... *Words* will not express what I feel. How sorry I am. How happy you're home and safe.'

Saul nods at her but doesn't say anything. Does she see, the way I do, how he's changed in the time he's been gone? He's a man now. He's looking down at us, our inability to see the truth. He wants neither our apologies nor our approval. He walks away, his camera round his neck, towards the far side of the river. The water is still and clear as glass, the bare trees and the slate sky reflected perfectly. I watch Saul move along the flood bank, lift his camera, angle it towards two swans that have landed. I say goodbye to Jules and start after him.

'Holly?'

I stop.

'I need to talk to you.'

I turn round. Take a few steps towards Jules.

'Now I know Saul is alive and safe,' Jules says, 'the decision about Rowan is back in my hands again. I knew he had anger issues, but I never thought he'd do that to a woman. It's as though I never really knew him.'

I put my hand instinctively to my head. It still hurts, a persistent reminder of her husband's attack.

'What I've learned over the last few weeks,' I say, 'is that you don't know anyone. Not completely. Put them in a new set of circumstances and they reveal sides you never knew they had.'

I think of Jules criticizing my mothering. Pete prioritizing his girls over Saul. Saul yearning still for the ghost of his father. Archie needing an intimacy I wasn't giving him and finding it with Philippa. Why didn't I see it? I thought I knew them. I thought I knew all of them. But I didn't. I didn't even know myself. Not really. The way, as Pete pointed out, I shut down on people when they become problematic instead of working with them.

Saffie has walked on, is approaching Saul on the riverbank on the far side. I wonder now, as I look at Jules, with the rings under her eyes betraying what she's gone through herself recently, which of us has had it harder. Jules, the mother of a daughter who was raped, or me, the mother of the boy who was accused?

'Turns out no one's perfect,' I say. 'Not Archie, not Pete. Not me, even.'

Jules laughs.

'Pete and I might have split up over this, but instead, he's embraced my faults and I've done the same with him. We're regarding each other and each other's kids as a kind of reclaimed family.' I smile. 'A reclaimed family from this reclaimed land. We're moving into Cambridge for a fresh start. Between us, we should be able to get somewhere big enough for all five of us when the girls want to come. Saul has found a place in town where he can do his photography course for sixth form. We're leaving the village. It has too many . . . associations. I want you to know. In case you see the "for sale" sign outside our house. Feel hurt that I hadn't told you.'

Jules stares at me for a few minutes, the upset on her face so tangible I want to reach out and stroke it away.

'Well, that's good. For you. But I'll miss having you so close. I understand, though. I said some terrible things, not just about Saul but also about Archie. It was cruel of me. I realize that now.'

'Ha! In an odd way, now I've had time to think about it, to reimagine my own past, it's helped me. Archie has finally come off his pedestal. What I learned has taught me something a little uncomfortable about myself, too. How I chose to see what I wanted to see and refused to see what I didn't where he was concerned. Suzie tried to tell me that, too! At his funeral, probably a bad place and time, but she was trying to help. I'm going to get in touch with her. Arrange to go and see my mum.' I turn and look at the river, at the miles of reclaimed land. 'I need to get back to work. They found my troll, the Stag; he was one of my students, a lad called Jerome. He's been disciplined and they want me back at the consent workshops. I said I'd talk about the reasons women don't always report the assaults they undergo. And why they should.'

Jules gulps. 'That's brave of you, Holly.'

'It's not brave. As you said to me in the cafe the other day, it's necessary. Look what happened to Saff because she was too afraid to report Bell.'

'Look what happened to you,' says Jules.

'I'm OK,' I say.

'You should have reported what Rowan did.'

I can't reply to this. I try to find the words to explain why I didn't. The knowing it would take resources away from those needed to find Saul. But also – and this is what I'm ashamed of and what I'm going to talk to my students about – the ambiguity of what he did, which made me uncertain I could call it an assault. And the humiliation the police would have put me through, the questioning, the doubts, the asking why I'd let him into my house dressed as I was . . . all that put me off pursuing it. It shouldn't have done, but it did. I need to tell them that if rape victims can be aware of their underlying reasons for staying silent, they can defeat those reasons. They must not be made to shut up. And once one of us speaks up, it opens the way for others to.

'I'm pleased, though, Holly,' Jules is saying. 'I really am. I'm pleased you and Pete are giving it another go. I would have felt responsible if you hadn't.'

She's quiet for a while. Then without looking at me, she says, 'I'm giving Rowan another chance too. I was on the verge of leaving him. After what he did to you. But after everything Saffie's been through . . . it would be too much for her to deal with. It's going to take her a long time to get over what Harry put her through. If she ever does. And she needs her dad. He's good for her. Now. He's changed in the way he is towards her. Less pushy, less besotted too – in a good way, I mean. He's giving her space. And he's agreed to go on another anger management course. You're right when you say we all revealed sides we didn't know we had. I – he and I – felt he should have another chance to redeem himself. He's learned stuff through this and he's going to be a better man.'

The sky turns bright and the land goes dark. It does this out here. The world flips over without warning. You can hate this place, but you can love it too. A triad of swans appears, flying towards us, necks outstretched, bright white against the light, and they come so low and so close we can hear the rasp of their wings.

'Maybe we should come and live in Cambridge as well. What do you think?' Jules says.

'It'd be good to have you near, Jules. It really would.'

And for a few seconds, I allow myself to enjoy the thought. After all, we've always lived near each other, apart from the short period when she moved up here, before Saul and I joined her. I always thought of her and Saffie as my family. It could be like the old days: in and out of each other's houses, cooking together, drinking wine. Talking about anything and everything. Nothing makes up for that kind of friendship. Nothing comes close.

'I'm not sure how Saul would feel. He needs a fresh start. It never worked for him here. And we can't get away from the fact Saffie picked him as a scapegoat. He was an easy target, because of the way he's been seen since we moved here. I need to give him some space . . .'

I can see my words have hurt Jules and I wish I hadn't had to say them.

'It would be for Saffie as much as for me,' she says. 'She

needs to feel there's support around her. You're important to her, Holly.'

Beyond Jules, I can see Saul reflected in the still river water. As I watch, Saffie's reflection joins his.

'Jules, look.'

I gesture towards the reflections of Jules's daughter and my son, perfectly depicted, upside down in the still water. But as we look, the reflected Saul makes a move towards Saffie. He towers over her, his arms outstretched as if he's about to grab her neck. Or as if he's about to shove her so hard she will tumble backwards into the deep. The river is freezing. They're close to the sluice. If she falls, it could be lethal.

I take a step forward, opening my mouth to shout at Saul to stop, and Jules turns too. She steps to one side. Reveals them both. Saffie and Saul, as they really are, the right way up, not their reflections. They teeter on the riverbank. Saffie wobbles, arms splayed. She's about to tumble backwards into her mirror image. Jules lifts an arm, waves, shouts. Saul takes a final step towards Saffie, gives her a shove. She begins to fall.

At the last moment, Saul grabs her again, pulling her from the edge. Her indignant scream and his laughter carry in the still air across the flat land as they stagger backwards and fall in a heap among the reeds.

Then a heron swoops in and down and lands on the water, creating a wash as it glides through the still surface, legs outstretched. The huge sky, and the bare willows, and the whole of the upside-down world the broad river throws back at us shatters into a million fragmented pieces, before it stills again.

Acknowledgements

Thank you Jane Gregory, Stephanie Glencross and Mary Jones at Gregory & Company for believing there was a story here to start with.

I feel so fortunate to have found such an insightful and perceptive editor in Sam Humphreys at Mantle. Thank you Sam for showing me this could be a different kind of book to the one I first thought it was. I am much happier with the way it has turned out as a result of your vision. Thanks, too, to all the team at Mantle who have contributed to the making of this book.

Thanks to Jenny Urquart who bid for a 'walk on' character name and to Katie Small from the charity CLIC Sargent.

My thanks also go to:

Anna D'Andrea and John Davy, always my first and most exacting readers.

Sarah Flint for help with police procedural.

Helen Tabor, Kate Rhodes, Judy Foreshaw, Rick Harvey and Guinevere Glasford for reading and contributions, and Susan Elliot Wright for support and referring me to the book *Carnal Knowledge: Rape on Trial* by Sue Lees. Suzanne Dominian for accompanying me on London research walks and drawing attention to the pews in Lincoln's Inn Chapel.

Andy Taylor for all the usual.

Above all, thank you Polly and Emma Hancock-Taylor for your detailed feedback, and Jem Hancock-Taylor for your ideas (including pointing me to 'Rape Me' by Kurt Cobain) and unfailing patience every time I ran a storyline, plot conundrum, or question about current social media practice past you. Your help is more important than you probably realize.

Anyone else I might have forgotten, know how much I appreciate the conversation, debate and input that helped me write this book.

Reading Group Questions

1. *I Thought I Knew You* is told from two women's points of view. What effect did this have? Did you feel closer to one woman than the other? How does the fact that Holly's story is told in the first person and Jules's in the third affect your reading?

2. Holly campaigns for victims of alleged sex offences to speak out. How does she justify not believing Saffie? Do you sympathize with her?

3. Do you sympathize with Jules when she goes over Saffie's head to buy the pregnancy test?

4. The novel is as much about female friendship as it is about the rape allegation. Describe the friendship between Holly and Jules. What bonds them, and what breaks this bond? Can their friendship ever recover? Discuss the nature of different female friendships.

5. Holly breaks open her stepdaughter Freya's diary and searches Saul's room for 'evidence' about him. Jules looks through Saffie's laptop to see what she's been doing. Do parents have a right to pry into their children's lives like this?

6. Do you sympathize with Pete's reaction to Saffie's allegation?

7. Can you still love someone whom you suspect of doing something terrible?

8. How do you think the story would have played out if Saul and Saffie's characters were reversed – i.e. if Saul were outgoing and popular, and Saffie shy and awkward?

9. '*Saffie's accusation hasn't just changed the present and the future for us all; it's altering the past as I know it, and I'm not sure which is harder to deal with.*' What does Holly mean by this?

10. '*Which of us has had it harder? Jules, the mother of a daughter who was raped, or me, the mother of the boy who was accused?*' Who do you think has it harder – Jules or Holly?

11. Since the #MeToo campaign there has been more discussion than ever in the media about sexual harassment and assault. What do you think this has changed for women? What do you think it has changed for men? Discuss what other impact the movement has had.